I0721661

CONTENTS

INTRODUCTION
by Alex Wright

(Contains plot spoilers)

Ten years on, it is time to reappraise a trilogy that offered a transmogrified glimpse of the cultural upheavals of the decade since Brexit and Trump.

The saga began with *The Hungry Wolves of Van Diemen's Land* (2014), a tale narrated by two teens who could no longer bear the illogic and hypocrisies of the Left/ Corporate *haut monde* around them, and rebelled against it in unforgettable fashion.

Sean, the son of a psychiatrist whose specialty is 'repatriating patients *back* into mental institutions', differs from his conservative father in that he thinks the danger posed by wandering crazies is necessary ('you must have a spark of chaos within you to give birth to a dancing star,' as Nietzsche put it). This means he is actually equipped to *fight* the culture-destroying forces, unlike conservatives, who can only drag their heels.

Sean moves from the city to a small town high school, with its attendant drug and mental health problems, and a clique of teachers pushing globalist propaganda, which he later discovers originates from one 'Sheldon Albright, the well-known currency speculator and vulture capitalist.'

He befriends Aloysius Coot, a flawed character with a weakness for substance abuse, yet obsessed with ninjutsu and survivalism. Coot has an idealist streak that waxes and wanes throughout the book; it is clear he needs leadership to thrive, and Sean can't always provide that leadership. The subtext here is Sean's frustration that Coot can't motivate *himself*, or drive under his own steam. Sean's inability to understand 'normies', or those less motivated than himself, is perhaps his biggest flaw.

Sean gradually realises the extent of the town's corruption, with the main cop being a drug dealer on the side. The problem of substance abuse is dealt with skilfully in the book, without descending into puritanism. All over the dying West we see the ruined lives of opioid victims, and hear the clinking glasses of pharma CEOs profiting from their misery.

After confronting these problems, Sean is expelled from school and skips town, headed back to the city. Here he meets Maddy, who has been kicked out of home by her druggie mother after an incident involving a deranged transexual, who had been attempting to sexually assault her (the mother takes the transexual's side).

In a homeless shelter she is raped for real by a member of the criminal underclass, and her life hits a rock bottom of misery – until she meets Sean. They immediately fall for one another, each sensing in the other someone who is out of step with the dumbed-down and increasingly insane society they perceive around them.

Together with their sometime sidekick Coot, they infiltrate a conference aimed at planning the future of Tasmania (without any consultation of the people, of course). The conference doesn't involve high level WEF globalists, but rather their rank and file enablers: academics and journalists. Sean and Maddy quickly dub these self-professed cosmopolites as 'Nowhere Men', as to be a citizen of 'everywhere' means to be a citizen of nowhere.

And so they begin a campaign of pranks against the dreary cosmopolites. This eventually causes them to run up against Antifa, the corporate establishment's shock troops (lest we forget, German Antifa were literally boarding trains to check people's vaccination status in 2021).

It also brings them up against the media, who quickly brand them 'neo-Nazis', distorting an interview they give so it looks like they threatened the life of a six-month-old baby, when in fact it was the Antifa who had threatened it. A few people realise the media are lying, but what can they do?

The normie middlebrow conservatives of *Parabola* magazine (think *Quadrant* or *New Criterion*) throw them under the bus...then the Antifa commit a genuine atrocity, but the police aren't interested in this, only in charging the Hungry Wolves, as they call themselves, with some kind of hate crime. There is no going back.

The book was published a year or two before the terms 'Lügenpresse' and 'fake news' became common. Yet the Wolves realise that that is exactly what the corporate media are. So they undertake an armed siege of the local newspaper, the Hobart *Messenger*, which is the source of many of the lies about them. They direct the staff to publish the truth for once – but even at gunpoint the journalists and editors prove patronisingly arrogant.

The description of the journalists as 'boomers' (which many no doubt still were in 2014) is increasingly out of date in 2024, but everything else about the section rings true, especially the pompous lecture about 'community standards' (meaning the standards of the bourgeois cosmopolitan class). In any case, the afterword, by a boomer psychiatrist, elevates this above some simplistic anti-boomer rant, making it something more sagacious.

The siege ends, but only very late in the trilogy do we find out what ultimately happens to Sean and Maddy. In the meantime, a movement called the Wolves of Joy starts up around the world, inspired by the actions of the Hungry Wolves. It is against the background of this rising movement that the second novel, *The Heretic Emperor* (2015), takes place.

Although the atmosphere here is darker and more complex than that of the *Hungry Wolves*, flashes of love still penetrate the sea of massing gloom. More poetic than the first book, it is full of cryptic allusions, and has an extremely well crafted plot, with the course of the main character's life reflecting that of an actual historical figure (the medieval 'heretic emperor' Frederick II).

Maximillian Scarlotti is a pupil at a finishing school for the kosherised global elite (referred to in this book as the 'Unicursal Curia'), located in an obscure part of Africa. Scarlotti has dreams that set him apart from his fellow students, and secretly comes to embrace a doctrine he calls 'esoteric ethnopluralism', which means he thinks that different cultures should retain their uniqueness and not be mixed into a global corporate melting pot. Needless to say, he keeps this belief well hidden, and his teachers are unaware they are raising a cuckoo in the nest.

It is when he leaves the school, destined for elite jobs in the EU and USA, that he gradually unveils his true power levels, always one step ahead in a 5D chess game with his Curia opponents. Scarlotti quickly becomes immensely popular in America, and the Curia now realise for the first time they have created a Frankenstein's monster who has gotten out of hand.

He establishes a private army, and announces that he is taking over the Curia itself, steering it in the direction of ethnopluralism. This, of course, is news to the Curia, but with the US military now on his side, Scarlotti has become a dangerous force, and a 'global civil war' erupts.

Entertainingly, these events are seen through the eyes of eleven vastly different narrators, ranging from fanatical idealists to cynical opportunists who will work with whichever side appears to be winning. We are treated to the stories of a misogynist Arab poet who secretly worships the gods of ancient Egypt; a deranged military sniper, who embodies the schizoid attitude of the working classes towards the political correctness the media have steeped them in; and a timid pothead in Kurt Cobain's hometown of Aberdeen, who witnesses the creation of a white separatist republic in the Pacific Northwest.

Yet the dramas of these disparate characters serve to relate obliquely the greater drama that is the tragedy of Maximilian Scarlotti, the heretic emperor. Without giving too much away, he abdicates in a spectacular way, having bought a little time for opponents of the Unicursal Curia.

The third book, *Reveries of the Dreamking* (2016), takes place in the aftermath of a plague called the Grey Death (a real plague, unlike Covid-19). The remnants of the old Curia have gone underground, and are now referred to, oddly, as 'Patagonians' (perhaps a reference to secret bases the globalists are said to be building in the south of the world to escape an impending apocalypse).

The book takes place on an imaginary Pacific island called Mantuaroa, which rises 'like a fortress from the deep, shuddering waters of a dream', and another island called Cavendish, which appears to be the last spiritual holdout of the old British empire.

The story, consistent with the title, has a more dreamlike atmosphere than the previous two, but also a more straightforward narrative, which races along almost like a detective story. In some ways it *is* a detective story, as the narrator, an ex-soldier, comes to learn that the technology used in his prosthetic leg is more sinister than it first appears.

The book is filled with bird symbolism. Perhaps this signifies a longing for freedom from the ruined society the narrator finds himself wandering through, for on Mantuaroa everything is a simulacrum: artists whose work literally consists of vomit; mountebank gurus; reality shows called 'slave soaps' where viewers vote on certain outcomes, giving them an illusion of 'choice'.

The narrator teams up with an actress from such a show, who has escaped her gangster manager, as well as a retro-heavy metal musician and an inept secret agent whose life story appears to be a playful nod to the 'Alex Jones is Bill Hicks' conspiracy theory.

They are aided in their quest by an esoteric religious order who believe the world is a dream. Opposed to these is a cult called 'Dead Shadows' who believe that all organic life in the universe must be destroyed (possibly a parody of Thomas Ligotti and other anti-natalist writers), but the real enemy are the globo-totalitarians, and to defeat them involves tracking down the 'last poet', Maddem, 'in an impenetrable thicket of thorns, in the unreachable depths of a chasm that howls.'

The message of the book appears to be: eternal vigilance. There is a malevolent, uniformising spiritual force, always beneath the surface, which can and will try to influence others in the future, even if the current batch of corporate globalists are defeated. Christensen's unspoken worldview seems to be that the universe is a place of endless spiritual warfare and questing.

In the meantime, the enemies we have are still very much with us.

The Hungry Wolves of Van Diemen's Land

For my wife

"Whisper fairy stories till they're real"
-Vashti Bunyan

and

"...hope till hope creates
From its own wreck the thing it contemplates..."
-Shelley

FOREWORD

The following recollections, by two members of convicted terrorist outfit 'The Hungry Wolves of Van Diemen's Land', have been spliced together to form a coherent narrative. Aside from typographical corrections and formatting, the words presented here are entirely their own.

I publish them in the hope of offering insight into a case which, quite understandably, made global headlines, and on which I shall have more to say at the narrative's conclusion.

Dr. Michael Halvorsen
Tas. Department of Corrections

1

SEAN

I'm not sure how far to take the story back. Lapsing too far could only lead to tedium, so skipping to the meat of it – it was at the start of grade ten that my parents moved to East Lynwood, an industrial town of some ten thousand souls in a quiet river valley in southern Tasmania.

Before that I had attended a private school in Hobart, where, being outwardly tepid in everything, and neither outgoing nor especially introverted, I was consequently neither popular nor unpopular. Old 'friends' arched their eyebrows when told I was leaving, but didn't mention anything about staying in touch.

Inwardly, however, I was seething.

Nothing I could see in the world around me made any real sense – it was all a random spray of vegetation and people, trucks and appliances. I grew increasingly agitated at this seeming randomness, which didn't mesh with the patterns I had discerned in fantasy novels, or Tintin comics; those of warriors, explorers and bards. I didn't know the word 'transcendence' back then, not its meaning at any rate, but instinctively felt that something was lacking in the kingdom of my habitation.

My parents did nothing to alleviate this confusion, being above all too sane and well-heeled (or so I thought at the time) to enter intangible areas. My father was a practicing psychiatrist, and perhaps I worried that if I let anything slip he might probe too hard into territory I had claimed for my own future exploration – the deep abyss of the mind. It should also be mentioned that he was a *soi-disant* conservative, an unusual trait for a head-shrinker perhaps, as conservatives have a reputation for not looking overly hard into the essence of things. But then, in my view, neither do scientists – psychiatrists included.

In any case, my father was a smooth-faced anomaly of sorts in an age when the upper middle-class was moving overwhelmingly (though, again, not in essence) to the political 'left'. I knew little of these matters at the time, but sensed instinctively that my parents were ever-so-faintly out of sync with the jabbering matrons around them. That in itself wasn't enough to make me trust them, however – for my own inner syncopation, weak as it was, failed to unite me with *either* rhythm. I was essentially alone in the world, a fact that neither thrilled nor disturbed me – for one's inner nature has little power to do anything of the kind.

My father was convinced, for whatever reason, that I would follow him into psychiatry, or some other branch of the medical profession, and as my grades were consistently high, tended to lose interest in me in other regards. Later events probably led him to regret this, but the regret was foundless, for I believe these things were foreordained. Even a coal biter can't be prevented *indefinitely* from realising his persona.

My mother, too, had started out in the psychiatric field, as a research assistant (where she met my father), but since her marriage had worked only at generic part-time clerical jobs. She, too, called herself 'conservative', although she was essentially apolitical. She was but a faint presence in my life overall – although my most important memory from the pre-East Lynwood period stems specifically from an offhand remark she once made. Perhaps that's the only thing I owe to her (other than my nascence), as the comment, or rather my response to it, still resonates to this day. A documentary about a world war was playing on the television (I don't remember if it was the First or Second), and my mother was tutting and clucking at the destruction on the screen. As she got up to go to the kitchen, she said: "We don't have to suffer like that anymore, thank God..."

An answer welled up within me and escaped before I knew what was happening, although too late for my mother to hear. "But *why not?*" was my rasping reply, and I shuddered intensely. I had a burning sensation for hours afterwards, and indeed, the abyss which opened at the pit of my stomach didn't entirely close for months. Perhaps it is still open...yes, I believe it is, even after all that has happened since. It may even be what *allowed* those things to happen.

We moved to Fincher St., a quiet thoroughfare in the leafier part of East Lynwood (there was no West Lynwood), just a fortnight before school began. The house was both spacious and shadowy, filled with dark and quiet rooms, boxes within boxes, which my mother furnished as her taste and money allowed. The initial period of excitement that every youngster feels on moving wore off surprisingly quickly and, despite all the soft shadows, the collection of rooms soon felt intensely empty. In hindsight, this may have been a premonition that childhood was about to end. Another sign was the gibbering wreck I encountered one afternoon on the corner of Fincher St. when returning from a walk to pick up groceries for my mother.

I say 'wreck', but he was more like a channel or conduit for some blind idiot god of Lovecraft (whose works I had recently devoured like many another teenager). The conduit's words rose and fell in strange yaws and pitches, and at seemingly random intervals, just as his gaze would now and again light on me, but randomly. He seemed to be unmeaning incarnate, his 'words' a string of syllables outside the structure of human grammar. I looked at his greasy, pitted head and formless face, and hurried the few doors back to our house, no longer certain that home was the place of safety I had hitherto imagined it to be. I began to suspect that perhaps there was no hiding from the blackbird – but the thought was one I was afraid to take too far. I therefore did something I very rarely did, and asked my father about it at the dinner table.

"These leftist nincompoops," my father growled, grinding his teeth. "Muddle-headed fools. In their quest for complete equality they have overstepped the mark by several furlongs. Letting these unfortunates into the community benefits *no one*. Neither the patients themselves, nor the community, who have to pay the price. And it's up to me to pick up the pieces, of course," he grumbled, clearly off on one of his favourite topics. His answers were disappointingly predictable. Repatriating patients *back* into mental institutions had been an obsession of his long before he landed his current job of doing just that.

As for myself, I wasn't sure if I agreed with shutting them up. If they existed at all, then shouldn't others be given knowledge of their condition, and not just at hearsay? Wasn't their chaos-danger something we ought all be aware of, that gap between the threads of the cosmic warp and weft, namely entropy? I said nothing of these thoughts, however, and excused myself from the blackwood table, suddenly eager to savour the empty shadows of my room.

School began shortly afterwards, and in the first hour there I had already encountered someone else I thought was mad.

I was assigned a home group, after which the first block was art class. I walked in and sat next to someone who was sketching on a piece of paper, even before the teacher had arrived. He was thin, wearing black jeans and lanky hair that flopped in his eyes when he wasn't brushing it back with his unengaged hand, while snide girls gossiped around him (eyeing me warily at the same time).

I said 'sketching', but to my young eyes it was a masterpiece of the order of Bruegel or Bosch...and I mean that in all sincerity, especially given the circumstances and the lightning-quick time in which he must have knocked it up. Over the coming months I saw his sketches grow into a series of seven paintings, as intricate as they were original.

They remain seared into my memory to this day. Here is a brief description of the seven paintings:

1. A tribe of people in a vast bleaky forest (Siberia?) whose headman has decreed they make an epic journey, to a new homeland seen in a dream vision. They commence to wander through strange lands filled with serpent priestesses before finally reaching the homeland, a lush country of meadows, lakes and forests. There they hold festival. Athletic contests greet with joy the cold sunshine of the new-found Motherland. A foray by a

neighbouring tribe is successfully fought off, and a hymn of praise given to the gods for land and victory. Arm in arm around a mighty bonfire, under the star-swept naked sky, a religious feeling, joy tinged with sadness...

2. Forward generations, perhaps centuries. The tribe is now a Nation, secure in its customs. Elaborate festivals, with roots from before their (now almost forgotten) time of Wandering. A new shadow of danger binds the community tight. Tall hills serve as watchtowers, with youths running up them to scan for approaching armies. War comes with the first frost; glint of rime on bronze helmets; fields of slaughter near ancient lakes, enemies' blood giving crops new life. The Nation triumphant. Chaos conquered, marauders expelled. A time of love, but also an ending. Surfeit in joy.

3. The sun is shining, the warrior at peace. Beams of mote-drenched light call him to the warm woods to contemplate. Ascending a hill he sees, as if for the first time, the vast spread of lakes and forests extending into the remote distance. *How far does it go?* he wonders, knowing he can never rest content without learning for himself. No rest, then, for this veteran of the wars in painting two. He is fated to follow a will-o'-the-wisp onwards; heightening of all faculties.

4. Into the nightside forest, thicket and bramble. A living labyrinth of cold fern and fungus, strange birds in the gloaming. All roads lead inwards, but dark, too dark for any kind of detail.

5. Then emerging through the darkness into a lone tundra landscape. Unintelligible grandeur, frost-bleak beauty. Civilisation to be transplanted here? Not without massive, back-breaking effort. Not for the weak, then, this country. Few come here, and those who do make something of it. Our hero contributes, then moves on.

6. On the edge, edge of everything. White polar distance, and beyond that – nothing? So it feels, standing on the arctic shore, looking out on the ice-covered northernmost darkening sea. Sadness, soft sadness, and everything resolves into a frozen ring around the horizon. All that once occurred turns to melancholia, pure and brittle like ice. You can never return to the

point of origin. Homesickness, a longing for what never was.

7. Without our watcher being aware of it, something is looming out of the sea. A black rock, wet and glistening. Pyramidal certitude, obsidian finality. Shimmering, the return to pure form.

Well, I hope I have given you some idea of this kid's artistic genius. On our first meeting, of course, I knew nothing of how the work would develop, but I did know I was looking at someone possessed of immense talent, and a unique way of looking at the world. This impression was heightened moments later when the teacher, Ms. Bannock, walked in and started haranguing him about sketching before the class had officially begun.

"There's a time and place, Japhrey, to exercise your...imaginative talents," she said, with a palpable hint of frost in her voice at the last word. For some reason, she clearly didn't approve of his work.

So now you know who the *second* mad person was: Ms. Bannock, the art teacher. (Why, who did you think I was talking about?)

During class, I found the time to complement Japhrey on his work. "Thanks," he said with diffidence, and tentatively invited me to his place to listen to music, and maybe eat some magic mushrooms. I declined on the latter, but agreed to stop round sometime to check out his music collection.

That same day I recall another incident just a block from the schoolyard as I was walking home. Three girls from my grade were ribbing a pale, bespectacled student of the male sex with a crimped duck-flap at the back of his sallow head. I don't recall their exact malicious words, only a shoving back and forth as turns were taken to spit on his school windcheater. And while the sight of a male letting himself be bullied by girls filled me with contempt, there was yet a sympathy with the (perceived) underdog that simmered underneath it. "Perhaps he's deficient, or has a physical handicap," I told myself. (That he *did* have a deficiency was afterward apparent, but it wasn't one of the kind I then envisaged).

"What's the problem?" I said, sauntering forward. The girls eyed me uncertainly, something in my look and voice perhaps riling them a bit. But their *victim* didn't look scared at all. He appraised me with a strange, cold look. His eyes reminded me of dark painted marble that had decayed inside, many millions of years ago, leaving a black outer shell. They were, or seemed, how shall I put it...to be inorganic.

"And what's *your* fucking problem?" muttered the surliest girl, as the stump of hurrying heavy footsteps welled behind me.

"What's going on here?"

"This blue-veined cheese is starting trouble!"

"You starting on me girlfriend, mate?" The newcomer skipped forward smoothly and shouldered me, at which I very naturally shouldered him back, without thinking too much about it. This led to a shoving contest, which resulted in a standoff. He pondered my tensile strength warily.

"Bit of a tough cunt, eh? Nah, you're right mate. We'll be friends, what do you reckon?" I somewhat reluctantly shook his hand, which led to a semi-friendly "what's yer name," "where yer from," and so forth. The pale one, the cause of our argument, had already left at some point.

So that was how I won the acquaintance of a few of my new schoolmates. The one who had shouldered me was called Trent, and his girlfriend Belinda – a tough, shoving cunt, and his square-jawed squaw. Perhaps they would be useful to know.

I encountered the paleface, whose name was Thomas, again next afternoon when I had my first social studies block. It was whispered of the teacher (one girl in front of me to another) that "no one likes her much," which in itself wouldn't have disposed me against her...but when she entered, fashionably late, I found in fact that she reminded me of the art teacher; only meaner, slyer, and more intelligent. Something of the fox in her mouth and muzzle, even to the underlying sure-felt sense that she could be brutal, stentorian if she needed to. Accustomed to being obeyed, despite all attempted informalities. Ms. Lindley was the name that she gave us.

She handed some photocopied diagrams around and the class began. The diagrams, headed *It Takes A Village*, appeared to show a societal structure leading pyramid-like to a large circle at the top, emblazoned with the words: "Executive? Some day..."

Then, hooking up her laptop to a slide projector, she showed an image of a newborn baby.

"So...I'm sure your brains are nice and relaxed from holidays. Let's get them back into gear with an easy question. Or *is* it easy? The question is this. Who is ultimately *responsible* for the upbringing of this wrinkled *tabula rasa* you see before you? Deanna...would you care to answer?" She turned her cold stare to the girl in front of me, the one who had disparaged her before class.

"What's a...tabyoola rahsa?" asked Deanna. I heard a snicker, and it was the palefaced one.

"She means the baby," someone nearby muttered.

"Who's responsible for the *baby?* Well...its parents, I suppose."

"Its parents," repeated the teacher, with evident restraint. "Okay. Would anyone care to elaborate on this...*interesting* premise?" Paleface turned round in his chair, and actually guffawed. I had never heard anyone guffaw before, but that's really the only way I can describe it.

"Oh Deanna is right, absolutely, it's the parents," he smirked. "Those lovely rednecks, they'll bring it up so well, it could even turn out like Deanna herself, a fine upstanding global citizen..." The sarcasm was so thick in his voice that for a moment I thought it was put on, but his eyes said otherwise. Then it came to me in a flash of sour mirth that this was how things worked: outside the classroom he was the victim of their scorn, but in class *he* was king, spitting and stomping on them in spirit. A perfect symbiosis, or rather necrosis. And the teacher was the other half of his vaudeville act. He was her poisoned fist, she his velvet glove. And here she was now making a gesture for peace, playing dove to his hawk, good copper to his doughnut-eating thug, although her snide and hollow laugh was not unlike his own. I pondered these matters deeply, so that I failed to take in the rest of the lesson. That I had stuck up for those soulless eyes the day before was more than a bit disturbing.

But something even more disturbing happened during the *next* social studies lesson. A girl who had been absent due to illness now made her appearance. Suddenly I was smitten by a golden apparition with hair like carded sunshine and green eyes like a sea creature. Having always half-disbelieved the stories of love at first sight, I was now a convert – and had to learn to chew my own knuckles to keep from staring at her. She never looked at *me* of course, but that would be in keeping with her persona – shy, trapped in a coarse and fallen world that could never match her golden promise.

She was all I could think about. I became withdrawn and inattentive. I forgot about Japhrey's invitation, which he never pursued.

When the teacher addressed her I found that her name was Olivia...but what did I care for a false syllabic spell that distracted from her true essence, a thousandfold worse (in *her* case) than names are wont to do? My love for her seemed so pure and knightly that I couldn't bring myself to speak of it, nor to ask about her of anyone else.

She didn't seem to mix with the other girls, and it was a mystery what she did of lunchtimes. I did learn her parentage, however, and in an unexpected way. Inspector Tippett, the top local cop, came in to give us all a rousing talk on drugs. Grade ten in its entirety filed into the gymnasium and sat patiently on the floor as Tippett's booming voice assailed us on the evils of marijuana, opiates, psilocybin, amphetamines, and many another proscribed substance.

"Now then, what about datura," he barked. "Is *that* illegal? Who hasn't answered yet? Olivia!" My green-eyed angel stammered shyly that she didn't know. "Cripes, if me own *daughter* don't know, what hope have the rest of yer got, eh?" He swivelled his iron gaze around the room, coaxing a gust of nervous laughter from the assembled pupilage. So, I thought, the chief cop's daughter! That might explain why she wasn't popular with the other kids. (I had already pegged more than a few of my fellow students as substance abusers, and not just of marijuana like at my previous school, but a far wider range of intoxicants. I had strongly resolved to avoid such temptations myself, purely for fear they might soften and blur my experience of what I then generously thought of as 'reality', even if that reality didn't make much sense to me).

One of those very druggies, I noticed, was now acting a bit funny – snickering every time Inspector Tippett mentioned a new drug by name. Those around him were trying to silence him with deadly stares, and I guessed (wrongly) that it was for fear he would give their habits away – but he still continued to snicker.

Next morning at home group I couldn't help noticing that he sported a black eye. A not uncommon sight in East Lynwood, but in conjunction with yesterday's pep talk it gave me cause to ponder – even with my head still spinning at the revelation that Olivia was a copper's offspring.

Next day, however, a new and interesting event distracted me briefly from my malaise. In short, I made a kind of friend. At home group, a late addition to our grade was announced as one Aloysius Coot, late of northern Hobart, who in response to gruff questioning by Lynwoodian females revealed that he had been expelled from his last school after just three days, for testing out a petrol bomb on the hockey field. The 'test' had gone horribly wrong, flames had spread, and he had narrowly avoided criminal charges.

As a matter of fact, Coot had been expelled from *every single government-owned high school in the Hobart metropolitan area* (all ten of them) in the past three years, and now had been turned over to new foster parents in the 'country' town of East Lynwood in the vague hope that he would see out the year there.

Coot's stubborn, monosyllabic replies dampened his interlocutors' ardour, and it was only I who broke through his wall of grimness by noticing he had tucked under his arm a magazine about ninjas. He nodded vigorously, nostrils flaring, when asked if he had any experience in that ancient and deadly art. He then discoursed on his solo adventures in the woods and swamps outside Hobart, punching ferns and throwing twisted bits of metal which he had spent hours sharpening. I suggested a bush walk some time, perhaps with some kind of stealth training involved, and he readily acquiesced.

That same afternoon, though, I was beaten up on the way home from school.

They approached me in a group. Tall, nut-headed Colin I already knew — strong, wiry and unpredictable, he didn't care about much besides drugs. Another one I knew by sight — the one who had snickered at the cop, and would later know by name as nervous Riley; desperate for status, pug-faced, sarcastically insecure. A third would be Kim, a sharp-talking, freckle-faced sneerer. And rounding out the group was Troy, also affectionately known as 'Johnny Boong', allegedly part-aboriginal, and the one who started the violence by shoving a plastic gun in my face. As for my previous shoving partner Trent, he was nowhere to be seen.

I smacked the 'gun' out of Johnny Boong's hand, triggering (no pun intended) a curious mixture of 'racist' and 'anti-racist' bluster. They affected to be outraged that I should so 'criticise' their little 'coloured' friend. In point of fact, and despite his mildly flared nostrils, his skin was as light as mine — maybe even a smidgeon lighter. Yet: "don't bag the *Abo* ya fucken racist cunt" became the war cry as they proceeded to pound me into the pavement. I took the beating — not much I could have done at that point in my life, as it was four against one, and two of them were bigger than me.

It was only grazing, I was told at the doctor's...nothing broken and no internal bleeding, amazingly. I wouldn't answer any of my parents' questions. That really offended them — they reacted more negatively to my silence than to the fact that I was injured.

There were snickers in class next day, but the *jock druggie cult* (as I now thought of them) left me alone for the time being. I wasn't taking any chances, however. I began to work out frequently and vigorously — shadow boxing, chin-ups, push-ups and squats. The only martial arts club in town was a karate dojo of the crassly commercial variety, one where you had to literally kowtow to a picture of a foreigner on the wall before the session began. So I decided to develop my own fighting style, based on controlled bursts of passion. I noticed the gruelling workouts helped me *think* clearer, too.

By now I had also noticed there was something of a clique between three of the teachers – Ms. Lindley, Ms. Bannock, and Ms. Green (the latter being one of the school's two vice-principals). Despite great outward differences in their voices and appearances, there was something eerily similar in the *way* they spoke, and their mannerisms. Something like calcified treacle, or congealed grease – at least that was how it seemed to me. A light was beginning to flicker – at last I had an enemy. Perhaps that was what I had been missing in my life! Yet they seemed such *rotten* enemies...

I'm sure that, whatever you may suspect to the contrary, these enemy-thoughts had occurred to me *before* I noticed that Ms. Lindley was starting to pick on my astral beloved. Olivia must have heard about my beating, because her pure face turned (what I thought was) a radiant look of sympathy upon me as I entered the room. A rejuvenating ray of light – yet what darkness emanated from *me* when I found the trowel-faced snoot Lindley directing sarcastic comments at Pure, not once but *several* lessons running, in a manner I could only assume betokened an unuttered grudge of some kind. Of *what* kind I believed I could guess – it was jealousy that Snoot could never attain to the natural light of Pure. And so now I had a fixed plan and a focus! Not the insolent jock-druggies who had beaten me up (animal savages, yes, but honest ones). No, it was the sly, slithering, smooth-faced slippery snob squad who were to be *my* targets.

Meanwhile, I had a weekend walk ahead of me. Meeting Aloysius in the prearranged place (near the entrance to Pennecott State Reserve), I was morose, and said little during the walk. If this ninja had heard about my recent initiation into violence (and perhaps he hadn't, being in his own world mostly), he said nothing about it. We lapsed into the starry world of bushwalking, where the bright noontide was as still as the night, and where our strides were as those of giants upon the earth.

We reached our goal, the top of a large crumbling hill, just around lunchtime, and after our repast I rose to begin the return trek. But the ninja would have none of it, pointing to something in the distance.

"There," he whispered. "That twisted tree looks *grim*."

There was no mistaking his tone...he meant that we should walk across to it, and despite the swampy appearance of the intervening ground (not to mention the well-known dangers of straying from the track in the tangled Tasmanian bush), I assented – more in recognition of the divine madness of his bulging eyes than of any inherent good in the idea itself.

An hour later, covered in swamp mud, we made it back to the hilltop. Neither of us had said a word along the way, but I had *sensed* things in the thorny branches – inhuman things. Aloysius looked spooked as well. In a sense, we were fellow initiates. So I told him of my plan to spy on the haughty clique of teachers. And while he had little interest in the Snoots themselves, he was only too eager to indulge in espionage of any sort, and so agreed to help me.

The three of them often gathered in Ms. Green's office for a chat, or to carry out their witchy business, so Coot and I went in there when the coast was clear to poke around. The only unusual thing I found was a stack of magazines and pamphlets, each with the same logo at the top. It was something called GLC – Global Learning Centre. There was a pile of written correspondence in one of the desk drawers, which I pocketed. I was just looking around for anything else of interest, when there were footsteps round the corner. I exited quickly and quietly, making a signal to Aloysius to retreat, but he hadn't seen it – and now Ms. Green was passing me in the hall on the way to her office. He was trapped inside!

No sign emerged that she had seen the visiting ninja. I strolled casually back past and glanced in.

Imagine my surprise to see him finely balanced on top of the room's tall, narrow cupboard, clinging white-knuckled to the wall. I could barely suppress a laugh. He saw me, and couldn't suppress one at all – the result being that the cupboard collapsed, falling across the desk and computer, dumping him on top of the vice-principal and pinning her to the floor. I looked on helplessly as she moaned in shock, clutching her injured body.

*   *   *

Coot could give no coherent explanation as to why he'd been on top of the cupboard. The principal, Mr. Davies, believed it was nothing less than an act of attempted murder, but he was talked out of expulsion by Ms. Green herself. Perhaps she wanted to keep her enemies in easy reach – despite that fact that her arm was now in a plaster cast. But Aloysius was ordered to visit a psychiatrist (my father!) and suspended for a week.

I don't know if Ms. Green ever missed the pile of correspondence, but some of it was certainly interesting. The GLC-group, it seemed, were her true masters, and she was pushing to have them send more teachers of her kind ('enlightened' was the word she used) to East Lynwood. In addition, she was much engaged in subtly changing the curriculum via materials given to the regular staff– materials supplied and paid for by the GLC. I set out to research the shadowy group on the internet, but could find nothing save an address (a PO box).

When Aloysius returned to school he was nodding like a madman, wide-eyed with forced earnestness. His conversation was of a similar tone – and when I mentioned future plans for self-overcoming, he nodded rapaciously in agreement – but a sixth sense told me something was not *quite* right. I arranged another walk for the next weekend, but he didn't show up at the appointed time. I spent that day listening to Brahms (metal thunder through crystalline bells), then on Monday when he didn't show at school I heard the following conversation.

"Fucken ninja was off his *face*, man."

"Ha ha, were you there then he sleazed onto Melita, right while she was spewing into the gutter? Classic!"

"So fucking funny. Then he spewed all over *himself...*"

You get the idea. I felt somewhat betrayed that he had gone over to the jock druggie cult, but I was strong enough and cold enough to deal with it. The song of the comrade had wavered. I could rely on no one other than myself. But it suddenly seemed that *any* manifestation of nobility could be corrupted, and I noted to be alert it were not corrupted in myself first and foremost – was even the love I believed I felt for Olivia completely pure, for instance? I agonised over this...

The sheepish reticence (visible even under glazed eyes) that Aloysius displayed on his return has long stuck in my memory. A shadow had passed between us, the flame of an alliance between two warrior souls diminished beyond vision. Nevertheless, we were far from awkwardness, and in the lunch hour would often talk of books and ancient mysteries...without me bothering to ask him on another mission or bushwalk.

As a matter of fact, the next interesting event (or rather revelation) in my life was also courtesy of Coot, when he let slip with a nudge and a wink that he knew something about my parents – and from his tone expected that *I* did, too. When by my frowns it was clear that I didn't, he grew silent, looking embarrassed. He refused to answer my queries, but I guessed it must have something to do with his head-shrinking sessions with my father. We said nothing for a while, then he introduced a seemingly unrelated topic – a plump blonde Hausfrau in her thirties he was banging behind her husband's back. But it seemed that when she was *with* said spouse, this Frau would often participate in something called a 'swinger's club', a kind of tame orgy for married couples held on a monthly basis at a private house in the town. That this fest of communal rutting was barred to Aloysius (due to his single and underage status) clearly caused him some irritation.

"I know who *does* go, though," he grinned, and even as he said it I had a strange cold feeling in my chest.

That's funny, I thought...in hindsight I seem to have known all along that their respectability is a sham. Or *is* it? Maybe rutters' clubs *are* the new respectability.

Anyway, after Aloysius imparted details of all he had learned from the plumper, he seemed to regret his indiscretion (perhaps benevolently intended), and my strange tight silence caught him off guard. He made his excuses, leaving me with my lunar thoughts. I had always been a latent idealist, but this vile uncalled-for knowledge now drove the ideal *deeper* into my heart, severing it from the world outside and gathering its focus inwards. This grim planting left a scar in me that would later prove a valuable hieroglyph: *never trust a fucking conservative*. Not, at any rate, in an age when there's nothing *worth* conserving. But we'll come to that later...

After this revelation, I felt my only course was to move beyond the mundane humanity I saw around me, and into the world of myth. For this, I needed my queen, my consort in the stars, and I would raise her (and through her myself) to the heights.

So I walked up to her quietly (godlike, I thought) one lunchtime and said, simply, "I love you." She stared at me, shy (trembling, I thought) and seeing me seemingly for the first time.

"Will you be my girlfriend?" I asked, certain as to the preordained and immaculate answer.

"Fuck off," she said coldly, and walked away across the courtyard.

*   *   *

The year settled in, passing slowly yet quickly, just as ordinary, hostile time demands, and now I was the wounded king.

My parents continued to treat me with a kind of unnerved ignorance, or so it seemed to me, showing less and less interest in my character or destiny. I felt part of a knighthood cult, true bloodline elsewhere, and now that I knew their secret they held no mystery or terror for me.

The jock druggies mostly ignored me, too, viewing me at best with indifferent contempt.

Ninja, while increasingly distant, would still talk to me, and I felt he was trying vainly somehow to self-overcome, but I was unsure how to help him. Maybe I wasn't *meant* to help him.

Olivia, of course, never spoke another word to me, nor cast the merest unseen purple glimmer of a glance in my direction.

And the weird sisters were up to their usual tricks, those well-funded 'teachers of the people' who continued to despise the people in actuality, if not in abstract. And Thomas, their pet, continued his duplicity too, his bloodless flabby lips perfectly at ease in that slender, sneering face.

And so the year passed...

*   *   *

In October I had another disturbing encounter with a mental patient on the way home from school. He must have been seeking my father, but the door was locked and no one was home, so he accosted me at the head of the street, gargling and cackling in his throat, the stingy grey tufts of hair on his head waving oddly in the breeze.

"I know *you*," he rasped, although I had never seen him before. "I know you."

"Yeah?"

"Yep, yep. You're the *fighter*."

"Really? Who am I fighting?

"You fight nothing. You fight *nothing*," he cackled, lowering his voice to a whisper. "But just be thankful you don't have to fight the *white worm*."

"The white worm?" But even as I said it his hand was unzipping his trousers, attempting to pull his cock out.

"Oh, for fuck's sake," I said angrily, pushing past him. "Get out of our street you filthy old pervert."

"I'm *nothing*, mate. Fight nothing, fight nothing, fight nothing!"

I hurried into the house, slamming the door, but his continuing cackle floated in from the street and chilled me to the bone.

Next morning I awoke with every joint aching, eyes running, shaking and feverish. I was too sick to leave the house, and after the doctor's visit I remember almost nothing from the next couple of weeks. I was told later I was delirious with some kind of virus the doctor couldn't diagnose. The brief dream fragments I do remember were characterised by flight – airports at night, and haunted desolation. Nothing concrete, though, nothing definite.

When I had recovered enough to attend school again, it was a changed world that I returned to. The gate of the horizon was now sealed so finely that I wondered whether it had even been pregnable at all.

Social studies was my first class back, and the teacher whom I had once stalked for bullying Olivia was now, it seemed, her best friend. Ms. Lindley beamed over the class like a ferret-faced Buddha, as I sat unacknowledged by all after my absence, witnessing the scene as if from a great distance.

"Now, how would we respond to this from a social justice point of view? Let's see...Olivia?"

"Well, first you would..." She had virtually learnt the script by rote.

Not only that, she was now fully involved with the 'normals' – which in that school meant the stoner jocks, whose town this spiritually was. It seemed she had even administered salaciously to one of them...Kim, that freckle-faced sneerer. Very hush hush. The whole schoolyard knew...but if her father found out, Kim could be maimed or worse. I was numb, cold. I retreated to a dark, hateful place inside myself for a while, to survey the blasted landscape.

Not long after, on a Saturday afternoon, there was a knock at my bedroom window. Seeing no one outside, I went to the front door, where a strange head emerged from the bushes. It turned out to be Aloysius, dressed all in black, complete with balaclava. The baggy black op-shop track suit was perhaps the closest thing to ninja garb one could buy in East Lynwood. He glanced round nervously, before dropping to the ground and crawling into the house seal-fashion. I followed speechlessly as he flip-flopped his way down the hallway like a wounded sea lion.

"Well?" I put the question as we reached my room.

"You have to hide me," he exclaimed. "I'm on the lam."

"From what?" He stammered out the name of the town's top cop.

"Inspector Tippett? What have you *done?*"

"Tried to root his daughter."

"*Olivia?*" I exclaimed in disbelief.

"Yeah. You know her?"

You know her...so casual. But I feigned indifference with the utmost difficulty, heart pounding.

"Uh, yeah. Just slightly."

"Not a bad looking sheila. And I swear she was giving me the eye, like she wanted to root me. So I asked her address. Second window on the left, she said. So I went round last night, about midnight. Knocked, and it was her fucking *dad's* window."

I chortled inwardly, then unable to control myself I laughed uproariously as he told me how he had jemmied open the window and squeezed into the room, only to find a hairy overweight cop with headphones on, jerking off to internet porn while his wife snored in bed beside him.

"It's not *funny,*" Aloysius spluttered. "That bitch set me up. Have *you* ever been chased down the driveway by a naked cop with a gun and an erection?" I assured him gleefully that I hadn't. "And now he's *after* me. Olivia told him who I was, where I live, everything. Melita said she even told him that I tried to molest her, that I was crawling through the window with intent to rape!"

"Alright," I said, howling with laughter. Olivia's perfidy and Coot's sullen debauchery should have filled me with disgust, but a valve had been released, the pressure was gone, and it felt like a part of my life was over. So it came only as a small surprise, a *very* small surprise in fact, when Coot told me that Inspector Tippett was in fact East Lynwood's chief drug dealer, had been for a long time, and in fact controlled both the crime and law enforcement rackets in the town with an iron fist.

"You can hide out here for a bit," I said, biting my tongue to keep from laughing more.

I went to the shop for supplies, leaving him reading my dog-eared copy of the *Silmarillion*, and on returning found my mother ashen-faced on the doorstep. My stomach turned.

"The *police* were here," she said, with a strange look in her eye.

"What happened?"

"The officer in question...threatened your friend with a gun. He told him to leave town."

"You let him in my *room?*"

"It was the police, I already told you."

"You don't have to let them in without a *warrant*, for fuck's sake. It's not like he was enforcing the law, it was a private vendetta. Does that *sound* like the way a cop is supposed to behave, threatening an unarmed kid with a gun?" She trembled slightly.

My father emerged from his study. "What's done is done," he said. "Aloysius, as you no doubt know, was one of my patients. It's probably better for everyone concerned that he has left town. That boy was a real piece of work, let me tell you. It's best if you stay away from people like that."

I turned and walked away in disgust, ignoring my father's hypocritical words, but even *he* sounded uncertain...as if Tippett's action had shaken, however slightly, his faith in the order of society. I didn't bother filling him in on the inspector's moonlight role as the town drug dealer. Even after seeing him threaten Coot they wouldn't have believed *that*. And I had to be careful what I said...

A week later a letter arrived from Aloysius. He had hot-footed it to Hobart, where he was staying in some dank, oily homeless shelter. He didn't blame my parents for the raid, as he had learned that one of his drug 'buddies' had told Tippett his whereabouts in exchange for some free 'gear'. Tippett had implied as much himself, between threats and grunts. I should come to Hobart myself, Whittington-like, to seek my fortune, Aloysius said. I wrote back that I couldn't possibly make it down until the start of next year (when I would have to attend a matriculation college there, as East Lynwood

High, like all Tasmanian state schools, only went up to year ten).

But I could have saved a stamp. Next day at lunchtime I was standing in the schoolyard pondering something, when a finger prodded me in the back. It was Kim, and his eyes were narrowed in delighted disgust.

"Olivia told me you were *sexually harassing* her."

"*What?*"

"Don't even bother denying it, you dirty little faggot."

The illogicality of his insult mattered not, nor did the revelation that Olivia was a lying whore...what mattered was Kim's fist, sailing merrily toward my head.

I sidestepped it, and palmheeled him in the chin. He staggered back greenly, eyes alight with fury, then laid into me in earnest, raining blows left and right, a cold sneer driving him all the while. My best option was to take him down. I closed in, hooking my leg behind his calves, simultaneously shoving hard at his chest. He went flying, but before I could jump on top of him and beat him to a pulp, two teachers came running up – and one of them was Mr. Bennett, the burly PE teacher. We were frogmarched to the office, where Bennett filled the vice-principal in on what had happened, having apparently seen the scuffle from the beginning. I thought a PE teacher would appreciate my deft use of fighting skills, but apparently there was a proper time and place.

Ms. Green interviewed Kim in private, then turned him out, summoning me in his stead. Her look was bilious and stony, grey like an acid that sought to staunch all organic life in the universe. Her lower lip quivered slightly as she said: "I won't tolerate your kind of thuggery in this school, got it? I have *zero tolerance* for intolerance."

"Huh?"

"It's lucky we're so close to the end of the year, or I would certainly suspend you for this grotesque act of violence."

"He *attacked* me! I was defending myself. Ask Mr. Bennett, he saw the whole thing."

"*Check your privilege* right now, you insolent little lout. Kim Sanders comes from a lower socio-economic background than you." Here her voice fell to a whisper.

"*Your* father is a middle-class professional, your mother...a..."

"Yes? What is my mother?"

"Housewife," she finished, face tightening as if the word was mildly indecent. "In any case, even if he started the fight, *you* shoved him back, or punched him, or something. And that's *not* self-defence." I tried explaining to her the age-old concept of attack=best defence, but she merely stared at me dumbly.

"Liar," she said finally. She had no combat experience, but was unprepared to let anyone who *had* tell her how it should be carried out.

"I'm not a liar, and if someone attacks me then I defend myself. That's how it works, and I don't give a toss what 'background' he's from." I crossed my arms and stared at her defiantly.

Her eyes nearly popped out of her head.

"Don't take that kyriarchical tone with me, you little *thug*." She prodded me in the chest with a pudgy, grain-fed finger. "You're expelled from this school *immediately*, as of now."

"What? You're not even the principal, you stupid pig! Only Mr. Davies has the authority to expel someone."

"I...HAVE...THE...AUTHORITY," she bellowed, and it was pretty clear who wore the pants in *that* school.

So I was expelled, without obtaining my results, just a few weeks before the end of term. To complete grade ten (a prerequisite for further education, and even most menial jobs), I would have to repeat the entire *year* at a different school. My father phoned Mr. Davies and ranted and raged, but there was nothing he could do. That bitch had him by the balls.

So I determined to trash my formal 'education' – if you could call it that – and move to the city to seek some sort of work. My father railed and raved at me, but really, he was a thing of cardboard...I could see through his phoney 'conservatism'.

"What sort of job do you think you'll get without a university degree? Without even year eleven or twelve?"

"What sort of job do you think I'll get *with* those things?" I countered. That enraged him. He forbade me to leave, but I laughed. Packing my bag that night, foregoing sleep, I left with the bright-cold dawn to hitchhike to Hobart. First, however, I climbed Myrtle Hill, the town's highest point, reaching the top just as the sun rose over the horizon.

I meditated on the illusions that permeated East Lynwood like a miasma. Of the cop who was the town's chief criminal, destroying the young minds he should be helping thrive. Of the authoritarian 'anti-authoritarian' GLC-clique and their snivelling pet lamb Thomas. Of my parents and their sham conservatism. Of Olivia, the beautiful but rotten slut. Of Aloysius, who couldn't last the distance – but at least had a heart. And of my own constant dissembling and refusal to engage clearly with the world. The only ones who *weren't* dissembling, ironically, were the town's mental cases...and perhaps the artist Japhrey.

"Virtually nothing is real in East Lynwood, this vale of illusion. But I can't count on things being real in Hobart, either. So I must *make* them real myself. With my heart, with my fists, with whatever pain the future will bring. I will make something *real*. I vow it..."

2

MADDY

My mother was a druggie, and my father was in the air force, that's all she would ever tell me about him. A black look crossed her face whenever his name was mentioned. As a child I would have liked to know more, but now I no longer think of the past, only the glorious bright-shining future. For the purpose of this memoir, though, it seems I must temporarily immerse myself in the mire...so here goes:

We moved to Hobbiton, the capital city of Tasmania, when I was four. I don't remember anything before that, but apparently we once lived in Sydney. From occasional hints dropped, I think my mother was a prostitute at the time. I don't hold that against her, but I do hold other things against her – or would, if I thought about them for long enough.

There, this memoir is grating on my nerves already. It has to be told, though, for the sake of the future – so people *then* will know what weeds most 'people' were back now.

But she never was a prostitute in Hobbiton. She had a retail job in a clothing shop for a while, and she used to get discounts, so I played dress-ups a lot as a kid. Then her behaviour got more and more erratic and she lost the job. After that she listened to the Beatles a lot, really loudly, and got stoned in the kitchen. Then she took to growing marijuana hydroponically and selling it. She refused to sell harder drugs (though she used them herself), and I give her full credit for that. She applied for, and got, a housing commission flat in the Primrose Heights development (they always give the shittiest areas flowery names), and picked up a tough boyfriend called Juan, from El Salvador, who took care of the dealing side so there was little danger to her. I remember Juan almost with fondness. He took care of us in a harsh neighbourhood, and was a strong silent type, who never interfered in my upbringing – and he wasn't a hypocritical leftie, like my bitch-of-a-mother. He wasn't too bad for druggie scum. But by the time I reached high school she grew too erratic for him, so he left, to be followed by a string of sleazebags, wimps and pasty-faced politicos, all of whom I hated. I don't even know where she picked those losers up!

One of them had the audacity to fill our bathtub up with cowshit, because he decided it would grow better marijuana than mum's hydroponic system. We never found out if he was right, because he ripped up the shoots and smoked them before they were even fully grown. Then he stole *mum's* plants and fucked off. At least I could have a bath again – after some hours with a shovel and bleach. Mum had to go to the Salvos for food for a bit after that, until her next batch grew.

She was increasingly unhinged and paranoid, and at the same time more involved in politics, thanks to some of her newfound 'friends' like the weedy bug-eyed ghost called (ironically!) Caspar she was screwing for a while. She and Caspar then both decided they were actually gay, but they kept screwing each other for months afterwards regardless.

Caspar was a 'male feminist', and I once heard him through the wall asking for permission before he made an advance on her. "Is it okay if I put my arm around your shoulder, then, maybe, touch your breast?" Bleargh! It was so clinical, and he was revolting to look at, like a pale stick insect. I'm no Aphrodite myself, but all mum's 'friends' seemed to have something *wrong* with them, mentally and often physically as well. Maybe that was why they expressed (loudly) such concern at the plight of poor people on the other side of the world, yet fouled their own surroundings with total abandon. It seemed like a symptom of mental illness to me.

Anyway, the flat grew increasingly dilapidated and unhygienic, and despite all my cleaning efforts, there was little I could do to stem the tide. I often took mum's *Sgt. Pepper's* CD out and played the song 'Fixing A Hole' really loud...but she never took the hint. It seemed she preferred 'I'm Only Sleeping' from *Revolver*.

It was only when I was expelled from school that she finally showed an interest in her daughter – mainly because it gave her the chance to harangue the principal. I barely attended school anyway, and when I did got called 'ho' and 'slut' (I was still a virgin then, incidentally) by a certain clique of students who shall remain nameless (I hope you're reading this, Untermenschen!), who almost certainly *weren't* virgins, nor were they particularly hygienic. Now I'm starting to sound like Sean, with his long and winding sentences. I like them, for sure, but they're not for me!

So where was I? Oh yes, the English teacher called me a "slovenly, lazy excuse for a student," and I lost it. *You* try doing homework with a bunch of try-hard commies singing 'Glass Onion' full bore in the kitchen all evening...

So I lost control, and smacked the bitch full in the face. There was a fair amount of blood, though it later emerged that the damage was only superficial, sadly. I guess my boxing skills aren't up to much.

I sat sullen and trembling in the principal's office for what seemed like five hours, while they tracked down my mother. She rocked up drunk and stoned, and proceeded to give the principal a loud, shrieking lecture on hegemony, kyriarchy, and things like that. The principal was a dick, but I sympathised with him in the face of such a tirade. It was so embarrassing that I actually snuck out, and have never enrolled in an educational institution since. Maybe that's why I now feel more educated than the average person!

The walk home gave me time to collect my thoughts, but they were already scattered again by the time I opened the door of my room, and scattered further by what I then saw. Sprawled on my bed, smoking a cigarette, was a tall, pudgy walrus-like person, who (despite a carefully cultivated moustache) I immediately knew to be a biological woman, posing as a man. A transexual, in other words, but *what* a transexual. She had made every effort. Not quite enough to earn use of the male pronoun from me (not being a journalist), but it was a good attempt regardless. I was in no mood to appreciate her method acting skills, however.

"Who are you, and what are you doing in my room?" was my predictable enough question.

"Waiting for *you*, Madeleine. Your mother told me all about you, and more. I know you from the photos." Her sideburns bristled as she spoke, and her tongue lolled slightly. She even salivated a bit.

"Get out of my room, please. This is *my* place."

"Not without a kiss." She was clearly intoxicated, and must have been drinking with my mother before she left. I had no idea how to handle this. Then she levered herself off the bed and lumbered towards me. I felt a sudden chill of fear. "Please tell me you're not a *transphobic*, darling. That would be *very* disappointing."

"I'm not a transphobic. Now *fuck off.*"

"You contradict yourself, darling. If you weren't a transphobic, you wouldn't tell me to f-f-fuck off." Her lips wobbled across her yellow teeth as she lurched onwards. I backed into the lounge room, but she bounced forward with sudden blinding speed, and pinned me against the wall. She was slobbering all over my mouth (you could almost taste the testosterone from her hormone treatments) and groping under my clothes as I tried to push her off me. Her moustache scratched my nose as she licked my face. I retched...whether from the alcoholic fumes, or the grotesque realisation that this was actually *happening*, I don't know. Then my focus cleared, and I did the only thing I could, being pinned against the wall. I *bit her nose*. She shrieked and put her hands to her face, and I twisted out of her suffocating embrace and ran to the front door...but she overtook me and grabbed me by the shoulders, turning me round to face her, and shaking me roughly.

"Don't you *dare* tell anyone about this," she hissed. She was stronger than me, but panic was welling up and giving me wings. I fought back. "My life is *hell*," she rasped. Then she screamed violently, spitting in my face: "You fucking little cis-privileged *bitch.*"

Privileged. Yeah, sure...I was so *privileged*. My mind immediately took in the irony and unfairness of this charge...and I exploded. Not noticing the front door opening, I hooked my right leg behind her left calf, and shoved as hard as I could. She flew backwards, sprawling on the wine-stained carpet. The shock in her eyes swiftly gave way to a murderous hatred, and she began to get back up, so I reacted quickly. Taking a two-step run-up, I *kicked her in the cunt*. Hard.

She screamed once, then writhed in agony, clutching herself between her legs. I turned to leave, intending to go to the phone box on the corner and call the cops (I didn't want to stick around to use the house phone), then ran straight into my drunken mother, who was standing there with her mouth spread open in horror.

"I'm calling the cops," I yelled. "And I don't care about your drug paraphernalia. This piece of shit tried to rape me, and I want her *gone*."

"Tried to *rape* you! You dirty little *liar*."

"What?"

"I saw the whole *thing*, Madeleine. I heard Rex from outside the door. He was calling you cis-privileged, and rightly so it seems. I opened the door and saw *everything*. I saw you push him over, and *kick* him. I might be a bit tipsy, but I'm not *blind*. What were you *thinking?* You don't know what this man has suffered! He has the whole of society, the government, and the corporations all against him. Have you gone *mad?*"

Perhaps I had! I was standing there speechless, face contorted, trying to take it all in. Rex groaned, and my mother knelt down to tend her. "It's an ambulance we need, not the police," she pronounced.

I stammered out my side of the story, sure that my mother would see sense once she heard me out. But as soon as I began to describe the sexual assault, she shut her ears.

"Okay, so you're a liar as well as a bigot. Oh Christ, what did I do wrong? Why didn't I get that fucking abortion?" Then she muttered something which sounded like a Hail Mary.

Something went cold inside me. Who *was* this grotesque person, and how could I be related to her? Why couldn't *I* have had an abortion...a reverse one? Why couldn't I have a *good* mother, or at least a mediocre one, and not this foul witch and her repulsive friends?

I will be my *own* mother, I vowed, as I headed out the door, never to return. I knew as soon as I thought it, though, that part of my soul would have to be incised and removed...and I couldn't do it, I couldn't do it. Tears flowed down my face...but in fact this secret place of anguish would fuel me in days to come. As would the sound of my mother's squalid voice floating down the street after me:

"Oh, Rex...did that little bitch *hurt* you?"

*　　*　　*

I slept in a Vinnie's bin that night. It was half full, and the second hand clothes made a very comfy bed...but unfortunately some drunken teenagers decided to dump their rubbish in there around midnight, and I was splashed with leftover milkshake. I kept very quiet – I don't know what they would have done if they had realised I was in there. Flung worse things in, probably.

In the morning I clambered out, but not before making an important find in the pile of soiled clothes – a sleeping bag. It was thin and worn, but a real treasure nonetheless.

A businessman saw me climbing out, and shook his head. I stuck my tongue out at him and moved on, heading for the Centrelink office, sleeping bag slung over my shoulder in its nylon tuff-sack. At Centrelink I waited for nearly two hours, then was told that to receive any kind of benefits I would need some kind of parental permission. I grudgingly called my mother on the proffered phone, to see if she would sign a form for me. Her voice came booming down the line, slurred as usual.

"There's no way I'm signing *anything* for you, not after what you did to Rex. I'm ashamed to even be *related* to you." "It's just one signature, then you'll *never* hear from me again, I promise."

"No way. Rex had to go to the hospital. Do you know what he's been through, and..."

I hung up, before she could hang up on me. My only minuscule weapon, and that was it. I had cut all ties.

"No luck, eh?" said the bored Centrelink man. I shook my head, fighting back tears. "Then sorry, but there's nothing I can do." He gave me a slip of paper, with the number of an emergency homeless shelter, and waved through the next customer in line.

I left, thinking that I would try the housing commission office instead, but after waiting an hour there was told I would have to go on a waiting list, and it could take up to twelve months, even though I was in the highest category. In a way that was okay, because I didn't have any income to pay the rent with!

I let them put my name on the list just in case, and spent another hour filling in forms, giving mainly false answers to some *very* prying questions.

I still couldn't bring myself to try the homeless shelter, so I had to find somewhere better than a Vinnie's bin to sleep rough. First I had to eat, though, as I was weak from hunger and my stomach was growling maliciously, so I went to the City Mission. Lunch was over, but the lady gave me a bag of bread rolls and told me to come back tomorrow, and they would sort me out with some proper food. They did, and I went there every day that week, and on the weekend to a similar place nearby. The other homeless people ignored me, so I ignored them back.

Meanwhile, I had ensconced myself of nights in a children's playground on the Demesne, which is a huge, hilly, tree-covered reserve near the centre of Hobbiton, and it was in this playground that I had my sixteenth birthday. I celebrated by going down the slide. Wheeee...

On Monday, I found it was a public holiday, and the City Mission was shut. I walked away, wondering what to do, then noticed that the Salvation Army just down the block was open, so I went there instead. A young lady with a face I didn't much care for told me they would give me food, and if I would please wait, then someone would see me shortly. Then a middle-aged lady with a face I didn't much care for ushered me into an office, where my examination began. So many questions, but I answered them because I was hungry.

"And where are you staying, dear?"

"In a playground, top of the Demesne."

"Ah, I see. Well, that should cover it." And she gave me a supermarket voucher for fifty bucks, redeemable for food products only, and sent me on my way.

Late that night I had a visit from the police. It was an out-of-the-way place, and they seemed to be expecting to find me there...so I had no doubt who had told them.

"What's going on here?" said the biggest of the two.

"Not much, mate."

"What's this *mate* stuff? You'll address me as 'officer', is that clear?" I could see we were really going to hit it off. They proceeded to grill me (very rudely) on what I was doing there, then instructed me, even more rudely, to pack my stuff and get out.

"But I'm not hurting anyone. And I leave every morning at daybreak."

"You'll do what I bloody well say. And if I catch you here again, I'll kick your arse until your nose bleeds. All right?" What a charmer! The other one, playing 'good cop', said:

"Don't you know that Packo sometimes uses this as a drinking spot? And if *he* finds you he'll bash you, or rape you. So you'd better clear out..."

I did so – but not because of the mysterious Packo. I was actually unsure whether these cops themselves might not attempt to rape me. As I said, it was an out-of-the-way place.

So I hurried down the hill, weaving into the secret shelter of the trees before the cops could follow. I wandered around the Demesne all night, too afraid to sleep in case they came back. In the morning I resolved to try the homeless shelter.

*　　*　　*

So tired, my head full of sand, static behind my eyes. Knocking on the heavy front door, the buzz of breakfast from a large frosted-glass window to the left. Footsteps, door creaks, middle-aged lady standing there, short hair and stature, gnome-like face means business. Lets me into office, long confusing interview, intimidating, pats my head as I sign paperwork. Patronising, don't care, want somewhere to sleep! Leads me to tiny room in female wing, tall wardrobe, sink and a single bed with creaky springs take up nearly all space. Hands me key, breakfast still there if needed, hands me paper with list of rules, shuts door. Flop down on bed. Don't want breakfast, just sleep...

Wake some hours later, starving and disoriented. Padding down hallway, no one around. Descend raggedly carpeted stairs to the black and white checked vinyl floor in the main hall. A soft-drink machine grins from behind its grille as I enter the kitchen. No one here, either. The clock says three, lunch must be over, but scraps? I find a loaf of white bread and start wolfing it, then pour myself water from a stiff tap, sit to read the newspaper. Can't help noticing the 'adult services' column of the classifieds has been ripped out.

Then a voice behind me says: "What on earth do you think *you're* doing? No one is allowed in the kitchen at this hour!"

I hadn't read the rules yet. "Ignorance is no excuse, and blah blah blah..."

So I shuffle into the hallway with the cook's voice still grumbling at me, walking smack into a grinning woman of thirty, with matty blond hair and curved teeth.

"Don't let old Vicky get to ya. Her bark's worse than her bite. Just moved in, eh? My name's Helen..."

I took her proffered nicotine-stained hand, shaking it limply, and stammered my name in reply.

"Some of us are having a bit of a drink later, in Ade's room. You're welcome to join in. Help us get to know you. It's the door at the end of the first floor, in the male wing. Around seven o'clock."

"I don't have any money to buy alcohol."

"First time around, my shout. You don't mind goon?"

"No, it's fine." In fact it was the only kind of wine I had ever tasted. I wasn't much of a drinker.

"See you later, then." She smiled conspiratorially as she walked out the front door. What kind of people was I getting involved with, I wondered distantly. They couldn't be worse than my mother, anyway...

I went there as agreed, for drinks. Someone I didn't recognise opened the door, grinned and ushered me in.

"Here she is, the *new* girl."

"Hey new girl, how's it going?" Drunken laughter, but not unfriendly. Helen was sitting on the bed, next to a boy with a Slayer t-shirt. Others were on chairs or the floor (the room was a fair bit larger than mine, though more shabby), and one man she introduced as Ade, the room's regular occupant, was having a ciggie out the window (so as not to set off the smoke alarm in the ceiling), and turned to nod and stare at me. Bit sleazy, the way he looked at me, but not threatening, and there were two other females present – Helen and someone she introduced as Vanessa, so I felt safe. Vanessa was around twenty, and had just come out of an abusive relationship. They all told me their stories, how they had got there, with neither pride nor shame, but a fair amount of humour, then they asked for mine. And when I had finished they roared with laughter.

"That tops the lot," said Ade. "A psycho tranny. Bloody ripper!" Helen poured me a glass from her five-litre cask of Fruity Lexia, and the evening went quite well, marred only by a few crude sexual remarks directed at me by Ade...but from Helen's feigned outrage I gathered he treated all the ladies like that.

Whatever. It *almost* felt like we were friends, and I would have stayed drinking longer with them if someone hadn't knocked on the door and yelled "Curfew!" at exactly ten o'clock. There was some grumbling, but it seemed we had no choice, and Helen, Vanessa and I made our way back to the women's quarters. Despite being up just a few hours, as soon as I put my head on the pillow I went straight to sleep.

The next couple of days I spent trying to get some sort of job. None of the employment agencies would put me on their books because I wasn't enrolled with Centrelink, so I tried typing up a resume at the library. Then I realised I didn't even have the money to print it out – but seeing as how it was almost blank anyway, that may have been a good thing. So I decided to try the good old-fashioned door-to-door method, and must have asked at least twenty places that first day before becoming discouraged.

"Nah, sorry love. Don't need anyone at the moment."

"Well, can I give you my details in case you need someone later down the track?"

"Got a resume?"

"No…"

"Hmmm, we'll give it a miss, eh?"

It was the same next day. *Everyone* wanted a resume, and most expected you would at least have a uni degree or some kind of diploma – even for retail or kitchenhand jobs. I got 'home' that night feeling dejected and depressed, and it showed. Ade came up to me in the dining room and said: "Whasamatter? Life getting you down?"

"Something like that."

"Come and have a smoke in me room later, then. Make you feel *much* better. Just me and a friend. Well, dealer actually. Packo. He's coming round with some skunk. Real juicy buds, I tellya." I dimly recalled this name as the one the cops had mentioned three nights earlier, but for some reason it failed to trigger alarm bells. Besides, I now hated cops, and would never have dreamt of taking their advice. So I agreed to go up around eight o'clock, even though Ade was something of a sleazebag. What was going through my head I don't rightly remember. I may have just wanted to smoke my mind to another place, somewhere far removed from this modern world and its employment meat market.

In any case, I trod those carpeted stairs at ten minutes to eight with no idea what was in store for me at the top.

I knocked, and the door was opened by a red-eyed, silently grinning Ade, while a hairier, bulkier figure stood at the window with its back to me, pulling at a bong. The figure exhaled, then slowly turned to face me. To say Packo looked like an ape would be a crude understatement, so let's not go there. Placing the bong on the window sill, he walked towards me with slow arrogance, while a smile crinkled the scar (which looked like a knife scar) that played across his features. Even now I find it hard to recall his face without wanting to puke, and to lash out at nearby objects, stabbing and slashing straight through them. In hindsight, I see that it was the face of chaos, of the Frost Giants...but at the time I could only think how fucking ugly it was. Those warning bells were very muted.

He waved a stick of pungent marijuana under my nose, and growled softly: "A cone for the lady?"

"This is Packo, Maddy," cackled Ade. "A hard bastard, but he's funny. Have a cone, have a cone." I allowed Packo (and now I saw where his nickname came from) to pack me a cone, then stepped across to the window, which overlooked a disused alley with a rusty red gate at the end. By the time I finished the first one I was already very stoned, and looking at the texture of the gate with a kind of heavy wonder. This stuff was far more potent than the leafier marijuana my mother had encouraged me to smoke in the past. It was pure resinous bud, and hurt my lungs and throat. But I accepted another cone, stupid little twat that I was. That white bite in my lungs, then sinking down through many layers, funny little tableaux, and down into the carpet. The blood had drained from my head, you see.

"She's chucking a whitey, man. What the fuck do we do?" Their voices echoed from leagues above. I vainly tried to roll over, then a hairy voice growled in my ear: "Good gear, ain't it?" I moaned in pained affirmation. "*She's* alright. Still conscious. Pity." I wondered what he meant by that, then he growled in my ear again. "Ya chucking in, then? Bit low on cash, ya see." He wanted to know if I could contribute fiscally to the drug fund, in other words. My head was spinning and I wanted to vomit, but I stammered out: "No money." I dimly saw the hairy ape elbow Ade in the ribs, and could have sworn that he grinned.

"No money for what you've smoked? I'll have to take it out of your cunt, then." He landed heavily on my thigh, and I yelled in pain, but he laughed, and I felt something cold against my throat. I soon realised it was a knife. "Any more noise and I'll slice you open," he whispered, pawing at my clothes with his free hand.

"Hey, c'mon Packo," stammered Ade. "I don't think she's in the mood for any hanky panky, mate."

"Shut up, you fucking pussy," Packo growled. "She's in the mood if I say she is. Besides, I like 'em dry-cunted. Gives it more traction. And if ya don't want to watch, then fuck off and get an ice-cream or something."

I heard the door shut softly, just as my mind was shutting down in disbelief that this was actually happening.

I will draw a curtain on the scene now. I'll spare you the details of how the subhuman shit raped me, because even though he's dead now, I still feel a cold anger that blocks out my other thoughts and emotions, leaving nothing but the hate.

And if I could dig up his corpse and kill it again, I would.

*　　*　　*

I must have passed out at some point, because I awoke in my own room, in the killing light of dawn, and vomited as the remembrance of what had happened slowly punched me in the gut. *They must have carried me back here, unlocked the door and bundled me in.* I looked around for a weapon in case Packo returned, then vomited again. It was wrong, all *wrong*. I wasn't exactly sure how my life was meant to turn out, but I knew it wasn't *this*. Being raped by a grotesque caricature of a criminal thug, in a homeless shelter, while my mother laughed it up at home with her slimy degenerate friends – one of whom had also sexually assaulted me, just days earlier.

My vagina was filled with a scorching red pain, and for a brief moment I wondered if I would be infertile. My mother would be happy then...the year before she

52

had attended something called World Vasectomy Day, an event aimed at discouraging people from 'breeding'...especially white people, my mother said, although that bit wasn't mentioned in the official brochure.

Then a deeper fear hit me...what if I was *pregnant?* With the offspring of a monster?

In the event, it turned out that I wasn't...and I won't bore you any further with the agony of body and soul that I went through over the next few days. I just pray to the shining gods of Europe that *you*, dear reader, haven't, or won't have to lose your virginity in the horrific way *I* did. Although what's done is done, and (after taking revenge) all we can do is to wisely use the time that remains to us, to paraphrase one of Sean's favourite books, *The Lord of the Rings*.

Anyway, at the time, I had another threat to deal with – the danger of reprisals from Packo. I dimly remembered him saying he would shut me up permanently, by slitting my throat from ear to ear, if I ever so much as breathed a word of what had happened to anyone. There was no one I could tell, in any case...certainly not the cops, who for all I knew might secretly be in league with Packo.

But the threat alone might not satisfy him – what if he tried to shut me up permanently anyway? I crept round in a cold sweat of terror for days, barely sleeping a wink, before I finally heard the news at the dinner table from Vern, a borderline-retarded resident of the shelter. Packo had been arrested for stabbing an elderly man (with the weapon he'd reserved for *me* no doubt), and sentenced to eighteen months in Risdon Prison. It was a light sentence, true, but it gave me some breathing space...enough time to start a new life. I would never let that slimebag defeat me...

I must have smiled faintly at the news, because Vern said, with genuine surprise: "Why are *you* so happy? Thought you was his missus!" My face registered my incredulity. "Well, not exactly *missus*. I think slut was the word he used. You *are* his slut aren't ya? So why aren't you more upset he's in gaol?"

I stood, and stared him to ice. On leaving the room I heard one of the others remonstrating with him for his tactlessness.

"Fair go, what did I say? She *is* his slut isn't she? Everyone knows it, and Packo don't let his sluts go." So Packo had not only stolen my virginity, but also my reputation, faint as it was! And while a *knife*, a small piece of metal, had allowed him to commit the first of these thefts (he would pay for that, I vowed, no matter how long it took), it was the loose, lazy tongues of humans which had enabled him to commit the second, and I wasn't sure who should be punished for that – he or they.

Somehow I soldiered on. I knew there was nothing I could do to change what had happened. My main goal was to get a job. Money would open new avenues and possibilities, and not just of revenge but of fulfilment. I could travel, for instance...something I had always wanted to do.

But the job front was as impossible as ever. My only serious option seemed to be prostitution, but that reminded me of my hated stinking mother, and I would never do it, despite the fact that sex itself now meant nothing to me (Packo having taking all the specialness away from it). I did inquire about work as a life drawing model at the Art School (this involved standing round in the nude for two hours while a roomful of students sketched you), but it was near the end of the year and they didn't need any new models.

I was broke as could be, living purely off the charity of the shelter. At least the food was filling...unhealthy, yes, but filling. The main problem was the other residents. I was now known as a 'slut', and the female tenants showed me their cold side, even Helen. As for the men, some of them positively leered at me, and mealtimes were a real ordeal. There were knocks at my door at all sorts of hours. I ignored these, while I sat reading a mystery novel from the shelter's meagre library (a single bookshelf at the top of the TV) on my sad bed. I lived in fear that someone else would rape me. The one who scared me the most was Ade...about the only male who *didn't* look at me like a dish to be devoured. He was furtive, and avoided my gaze. It may have been shame, but I couldn't be sure that he wasn't plotting something.

And then, just when I thought things couldn't be any worse, I received a summons in the mail. It seemed that the courts had gotten my address from some kind of charities database. The contents of the notice made my jaw drop in disbelief. 'Rex' Fairlea, the cross-dresser I had kicked in defence, was now pressing charges against me for assault! And the only thing resembling a witness was my mother, who was on Rex's side completely.

Well, maybe prison was what I needed. A holiday from all my woes. That night I stayed awake for hours...thinking not of prison, however, but suicide. I was seriously weighing it as an option, and was surprised to find how little the idea of death frightened me.

Yes, it was an option all right. I was alone, and life had become torment. My stomach began to crawl at the very idea of continued existence.

Then something happened that took my mind away from these dark roads for a time. Someone new moved into the shelter. He went by the memorable name of Aloysius Coot. You don't forget a name like that in a hurry, and he was certainly *different* from the other residents. For one thing, he was polite to me (I did catch him eyeing me pruriently a few times, but he *was* a male). For another, he was adamantly opposed to drugs of any kind, and said so in no uncertain terms at the dinner table. I believe someone had offered him a smoke of something, which he loudly denounced as a habit fitting of "subhuman mongoloid degenerates and other AIDS-ridden scum."

But there was a funny look in his eyes as he said it...it may just be hindsight, but it seemed like he was trying to convince himself through his own bluster.

Such talk did not endear him to the other residents, of course, but it didn't bother *me*. I asked how he had ended up homeless, and he said that a girl had done it to him...that's all he would say, keeping largely silent about his background. He did reveal that he had attended the same high school as me (for just two days), but I couldn't remember him, and was no doubt absent myself during his lightning-quick stint there. His main interests, it seemed, were ninjutsu, special forces military groups, and survival tactics. I almost felt that here was someone I could be friends with...but then, a few days later, I saw him coming downstairs from the corridor to Ade's room, his eyes as glazed as spun sugar. My heart sank to rock bottom again. Another fly caught in the web. He was just as weak as me.

I think he may have felt guilty, because next time I saw him at the breakfast table he had trouble making eye contact with me. He was a lot quieter about 'subhumans', but still keen to engage in conversation, like a puppy who knows he has done wrong, and desperate for favour. Perhaps by now he had heard gossip that I was the resident slut, and wanted to get in my pants...I don't know. Anyway, he mentioned that his "best mate" would be coming down soon from East Lynwood, and would probably be staying at the shelter. He had a letter from him yesterday.

I knew East Lynwood's reputation well enough – a crappy decaying industrial town in the Thora Valley, best known for its spooky abandoned lunatic asylum and violent crime rate – so I didn't hold out very high hopes regarding Coot's friend.

Imagine my surprise twelve hours later then, when I found myself falling violently in love, for the first time in my life, and at the most unexpected moment...

I'm not going to go into detail here about what Sean and I talked about that night, because it's none of your business. It's private, for us only...much more private than the rape, which only touched my body, not the pit of my soul.

Just suffice to say I fell in love. And with someone the same age as me, strangely, because I always pictured myself falling for an older man. Well, Sean may have been young, but his sense of self-assurance made me feel weak at the knees. And he was a gentleman, at least to me. Something I had never experienced in my life.

Again, I'm not going to tell you what we talked about, or whether we made love that night, but within an hour we were staunch friends and allies. And the next morning we went job hunting together, and he got us a job almost at once! Admittedly it was a crappy job strapping pallets in a warehouse, but it meant money! We vowed to travel together, and hitchhike all around the world. We would begin saving for it at once...

Sometimes I wish we had actually done so, but at the same time I can't regret much of what has happened since.

Anyway, poor Aloysius didn't get to talk to his friend much that night, because I monopolised him, and when Coot went for a walk to the shop, Sean came back to my room, and we talked and talked. For two introverts, our throats were nearly worn out.

The following day I could repress it no more, and had to tell him about Packo and what he had done to me. He went deadly quiet when he had heard me out. After a pause that seemed to last for hours (I had a terrible fear he would turn against me now he had learned the truth), he at last said: "So, he's in gaol?" I nodded. "But Ade is still here..."

"Yeah. Ade didn't touch me, though."

"He was *complicit*." He pronounced it as a final judgement, and I said nothing. He nodded to himself, then left the room. Sensing trouble, I followed, but he had already disappeared downstairs. I headed for the men's wing, guessing correctly that he was seeking a confrontation with Ade. On reaching the open door I could see he had Ade slammed up against the wall. Although shorter and more slender than Ade, unlike the latter he actually had muscle fibre in his arms. Also, willpower. His eyes flashed fiercely.

"I didn't fucking *touch* her," Ade hissed. Then, as he spotted me, he pleaded: "*I* didn't do anything, did I?"

"Not directly," I said, with tight lips. Now that I had might on my side, I was loathe to use it to take revenge. It seemed like cheating. But at the same time, I didn't really want to stop (nor know if I *could* stop) Sean from fulfilling his natural imperative, so I just resolved to let things take their course.

That didn't turn out so good for Ade.

After his head had been slammed repeatedly into the wall he did a funny little dance, while Sean lectured him grimly on his cowardice and complicity. Then he simply instructed him to leave. To pack his stuff and vacate the hostel...because if not on his own legs then he would be leaving in a coffin.

"Fair go, mate, you've got to be bloody *joking!*" A punch in the stomach assured him it was *not* a joke. When he got his breath back, he spat angrily: "You'll fucking regret this when Packo gets out. He'll grind you into the *dust*."

"Wrong. When he gets out I'll be dealing with him, too." He said it in the soft tone of a gentleman or scholar, looking all of his sixteen years. He was magnificent. I was in love all right!

Ade left the shelter next day, without giving a reason (probably because Sean had threatened to track him down and cut his balls off if he talked). Strangely, Aloysius Coot disappeared the same day, and we didn't see him again for some time.

That evening we took a walk through Hobbiton's tunnels and storm drains, climbing over the old wall near the hospital and entering another world. Sean marched ahead like a pagan hero, while I walked shyly behind. It was dangerous down here, a haunt of junkies and delinquents, but with Sean I felt completely safe.

The light of our torch played on the 'cutting edge' American-style graffiti that already looked so old, part of a broken, dying culture. A large parasitical worm floated dead in the sluice where the water ran, but even the sight of that disgusting creature couldn't bring me down. It felt like we had entered the Hellenic underworld, although there didn't seem to be another living soul down here.

Then Sean kissed me, and gazed so alive into my eyes that it made me swoon and melt. We sat with our backs to the blackened brickwork, and spoke for hours of our innermost dreams and visions. It was then that I had to tell him about Rex and my mother, of how I had come to leave home, and the pending case against me. He looked long into my eyes, as if to ascertain the truth.

Then he told me how, at dawn, on the day he had left East Lynwood, he had become possessed by Ancient Gods on a hill outside the town. And there was no going back, not for him.

After walking me back to the shelter for dinner, he disappeared and I didn't see him at all that evening. In the morning, however, I chanced to gaze at the breakfast newspaper, the Hobbiton *Messenger*, and saw to my astonishment that the front page screamed of a "transphobic hate crime," as a transexual had been found stripped naked, gagged and tied to a drainpipe outside Balmoral Close, a notorious public housing block with a large population of Somalian immigrants. Sure enough, it was Rex.

When I saw Sean later that day I admonished him (between kisses).

"Taking risks for me! I couldn't bear it if you went to gaol..." But I knew, of course, that if he went to gaol I would still be loyal to him until the day he got out, even if I were old or dead by then.

And his approach had worked, because next day I received a letter advising that the charges against me had been dropped, and therefore to disregard the previous summons.

It was *very* strange, but the story of Rex's experience outside the housing block somehow disappeared from the newspaper. Yesterday it had taken up the entire front page, today not a single mention...not even in the 'Crimestoppers' section. Very odd indeed. (I was later to find out that Rex had been raped multiple times that night, and obviously not by Sean...but for the moment I knew little of how the media worked, nor of its hierarchy of 'narratives').

The day after that we started work. As I said, this involved strapping up pallets, but Sean was soon moved onto the production line, lifting heavy boxes, so we didn't see each other except in the lunch breaks. It was money, though, and we were paid in cash at the end of each week! It was the beginning of our dream to travel the world...

We worked a six day week, so Sunday was our day for romantic walks and things like that. I can't tell you how much I admired Sean, and still do. He was a man of action, and furthermore not an *evil* man of action like Packo. He had a sense of justice, and also of romance –
because when he beat people up it was for his girl (me!),

or for an ideal, not for petty egotistical reasons. In fact, he barely even *had* an ego.

The only thing I didn't like was his constant fretting over some blonde slut he had known in East Lynwood. "I could have saved her," he moaned to me on several occasions.

"You can't save someone from shallowness," I would reply, but he insisted: "I *could* have, I *could* have." It was annoying, and the only thing that brought a little bit of darkness between us. Other than that, things were brighter than a diamond in the sky.

*　　*　　*

A few weeks later, however, we had a setback. Brett, our boss, called me into the office for a 'chat', or so he said. Once in there he actually stood behind me and started fondling my breasts! I wrenched myself away and turned to face him with death-defying rage in my eyes, for Sean's presence in my life had given me strength.

(As an aside, I'm not particularly good looking, so why do I seem to be such a magnet for sexual harassment by losers? This was the *third* time...did they think they were giving me something I couldn't get elsewhere?)

I glared at Brett and told him in no uncertain terms that I already had a boyfriend, and that even if I was single I wouldn't be interested in him, not in aeons.

"Boyfriend," he laughed. "You mean that anti-social little dork on the packing line? You need a *man's* love, honey." I assured him that Sean was infinitely more of a man that he, and furthermore that the anti-social little dork would be *very* interested to know that I had just been groped by a primate.

"Violently interested, in fact."

"Don't threaten me, you stuck-up little slag. Since you take that tone, you're *both* fired. You're not on the books anyway, and you can forget about this week's wages." He added as an afterthought: "And if the dork makes trouble, I'll kick his arse purple. Now fuck off."

I went into the packing room to tell Sean what had taken place. At first he couldn't believe it. Then his eyes narrowed.

He strode into the office, myself following close behind. As the door shut Brett looked up, unimpressed.

"Don't bother," he said, with an insolent yawn. But he should have looked deeper into Sean's eyes, or mine.

Not long afterwards he was on his knees literally squealing for mercy. Such a pity that no one could hear him over the loud machinery...

Shortly after that, he was handing over all the cash in his wallet (actually *more* than our wages for the week, but there was harassment and unfair dismissal to take into consideration), and assuring us that he would never *ever* tell the cops...and he knew what would happen to him if he did (vaguely hinted at tortures, followed by his mutilated corpse being found in a public park). Not that Sean would have carried through on this (I think?), but we had to impress our utter seriousness on our opponent. Money was unimportant in itself, but it was part of our travel plan, and so was staying away from the notice of the police. So we left Brett shaking with fear and departed the warehouse, never to return.

Now we were at a loss what to do. We needed work, but it was unclear if we would find it. The warehouse job had been a lucky hit. Unemployment was extremely high, partly due to foreign outsourcing and partly to the tendency of baby boomers to work well past retirement. But then Sean hit on an idea. A naughty idea, true...but whatever it took to get overseas, we would do it.

The idea was simplicity itself. It was suggested to him firstly by the sight of Brett emptying his wallet for us, and secondly by a remark I had made earlier in the week.

The remark concerned the increasing discrepancy of wealth in Tasmania. Middle class kids would leave for the mainland to find work, while at the same time rich people moved down to escape the rat race of big cities like Melbourne and Sydney. This was creating a curious demographic mixture: treacle-tongued snobs on the one hand, and the local underclass (referred to disparagingly by the former as 'bogans') on the other, with increasingly little in between. Although I wasn't too fond of 'bogans' (not Packo and Ade, at any rate), at least the latter *belonged* here...the snobs seemed to come from another place entirely, a land of molasses and smug faces.

So it all seemed to fall into place.

To finance our dreams, which were deeper than the dreams of the bourgeoisie, we would rob rich mainlanders. Only the most revoltingly obnoxious ones, of course, and even then we felt faintly apologetic...but our cause (and our very survival) took precedence. *Our* dreams were the dreams of the future, of a world beyond materialism...and the boomers and yuppies could kiss our arses.

I will never forget the first time we did it. It was so easy, far easier than I expected. We simply followed a pair of fifty-somethings as they left an expensive restaurant – a restaurant that no local could afford. We shadowed them softly through the quiet streets, haunting their footsteps as they yammered unwittingly about food and wine, and so-and-so's brother, who was a something-or-other in the New South Wales Labor Party, or something like that. And when we reached an empty street in Battery Point, with no audible traffic, we sauntered forward and stuck our fingers in the crooks of their backs.

"Wallets out of your pockets and on the ground, do it slowly."

"Oh *no*...this is a joke, right?"

"No joke. Just do it, and don't turn around." Sean put on a gruff voice, unrecognisable as his own gentle tone. They did as he instructed. I suppose a finger *could* be mistaken for a gun, as the back has very few nerve endings. Anyway, I took the cash, touching the wallet only with my sleeve, and told them to stand without moving and count to fifty, then we were round a corner and away before they could blink. Nearly a thousand bucks in total...these boomers really were loaded! And having left them their wallets with cards, addresses and whatnot, we didn't feel *too* bad.

So from that point onwards, we resolved (taking all due precaution) to rob at least two boomers a week. Besides daily survival, the money would be used to finance a pilgrimage around the world, visiting ancient historical sites from what Sean called the *real times*...the times before the creeping sickness blanketed everything. Ours was a sacred journey, a journey to the East like the one Hermann Hesse once wrote about. The 'east' was a symbol, meaning light (*mehr Licht*). In reality, of course, we would be travelling West.

And then some good news came...the housing commission flat I had applied for was now available. We could finally move out of that depressing homeless shelter! The flat was in a medium-density block in South Hobbiton, and fortunately not the Primrose Heights block in North Hobbiton where my mother lived.

It was an unfurnished flat with three rooms – a bedroom, bathroom, and lounge/kitchen – as well as a small balcony. To us it felt like a palace, and it was *ours*, at least for a time. We bought some well-used furniture from an op-shop, then proceeded to stock up on second-hand books – Greek and Roman classics, Norse sagas, philosophy, and German novels. We would devote our time to studying when we weren't robbing the occasional New Class degenerate to satisfy our needs. As a matter of fact, we robbed one that very night – a particularly obnoxious specimen with a 'One Planet, One People' sticker on the back of his late model Mercedes. He only had a few hundred on him, but it was better than nothing. We gave some of it to charity (to the homeless shelter, actually).

Our flat was fairly private for public housing, and it felt like something of a sanctuary from the vulgarity of the modern world. I look back on it with fondness. We celebrated the ancient Yuletide there – our riposte to the materialistic Shit-mas festival taking place around us.

The only sour note came one afternoon, shortly after New Year's, when Sean was reading Egil's Saga on the balcony, and a weaselly little drunk with a loud voice (our neighbour) started harassing him, calling him a 'faggot' because he was reading a book. Apparently this drunken sot thought that it was unmanly to learn about the ways of our ancestors (except through the crooked medium of Hollywood and television).

Sean ignored him, but he repeated his tirade next day, and the day after that. I could tell Sean was annoyed

– it was a violation of our sanctuary. He couldn't beat the wretch up, as we would be identified. And even if the police took our side (very unlikely), we wanted as little to do with officialdom as possible. So we tried a different tack. Next morning we bought a cheap bottle of whisky from the liquor shop on the corner (the attendant there wasn't too particular about asking for ID). We then bought a rope from the hardware shop, attached it to the bottle, flung the bottle through the loudmouth's broken skylight and lowered it down into the flat (the street being steep, his residence was on a lower level than ours). And sure enough, it seemed to work...we saw neither hide nor hair of him that day. So every day we bought a fresh bottle of whisky and lowered it through the skylight. It was costly (and embarrassing – the attendant probably thought that *we* were the alcoholics), but an unfortunate necessity. Anything to peacefully study the classics...

Not long after that, however, our peace was disturbed again, and this time by a tap at the evening window. Sean opened the curtain, and we saw a familiar face peering in at us.

It was Aloysius Coot.

"I'm off the drugs, Maddy," he announced. It was the first thing he said when I opened the door to him.

"How on earth did you find out where we lived?"

He looked a bit shifty. "Saw you in town a few days ago, and followed you back here. Thought I'd drop in when the time was right." So he *did* have some ninja skills, after all. Perhaps he might come in useful for something. I could tell Sean was thinking the same, but with misgivings, seemingly. He paced peripatetically up and down the room, in what I called his 'lecturing' mode.

"Look, Coot. I don't care what private demons you've had to face, or are still to. The important thing is, we only want comrades who are *free of addiction*. We're declaring war on the Tasmanian establishment, and there's no room for hangers on in the ranks. I mean that mangy, tattered monkey you had on your back, and possibly still riding your coattails." This war on the establishment was news to me...it sent a thrill down my neck as he said it.

"I *swear* to you, Sean, I'm off that shite for good. Speed, smack, all of it. The way of the warrior, that's my path.

There's a dim road ahead of me, and I need a leader. I want you to lead me into war."

Sean looked him sternly in the eye, testing for intent. Coot looked shaky, but managed to hold his gaze. Finally Sean said: "Alright...but please don't let me down."

"No way, man."

"As it happens, I do have a mission for you. Something I was going to do myself sometime soon...but it will serve as a little test of your resolve."

"Anything...what is it?" Sean went into the bedroom, and returned with his wallet, from which he took a little scrap of paper.

"This is the PO box of something called the GLC – the Global Learning Centre. I want you to stake them out, find out who they are, or at least the identity of their local representative."

"Fuck yeah. I'll do *that* for you. No worries, man. This is war..." Coot rubbed his hands together and let out a cackle of glee. Although I didn't quite trust him myself, if Sean was willing to give him a chance then I would do likewise.

We bought a bottle of wine, and toasted our enterprise, telling tales of heroes and kings, and of cunning serving wenches who gave great warriors the secrets of killing dragons. Coot crashed on our floor (we didn't have a guest mattress as yet), and in the stabbing light of dawn he rose and set out on his mission. We didn't see him for a week.

When he returned it was with results – of a sort. He had been through travails. On the second day of his staking out the PO box (which was set in a wall at the front of the post office), an employee had noticed a strange young man lurking outside the building, and promptly phoned the police. An officer arrived, and grilled Coot as to what he was doing there, to which he was able to give no satisfactory answer. He was given a stern warning about loitering, and told to move on. ('Loitering' is cop-talk for when they can't find anything else to charge you with.)

The next day, undeterred, he resumed his stakeout, but in a cunningly wrought disguise. The balaclava and black velvet cape were sure to help him escape further notice.

But the employee was too sharp for him, apparently...even the cop could scarcely restrain a snicker as he took Coot's name (prompting further mirth from the flock of onlookers who had gathered), and said: "Don't let me see you round here again, or I'll take you down the station and book you."

After that, Coot wisely invested in a cheap pair of binoculars from an op shop. From then on, his stakeout was conducted from behind a spiky shrub across the road, out of sight of the employees of the post office...out of sight of everyone in fact, and in plain clothes this time.

The first few days of watching proved fruitless, but then he hit the jackpot. A middle-aged woman he described as "like a snooty-looking fox," and "a bit like Ms. So-and-So from East Lynwood," came and unlocked the box in question – there was no mistaking it, he said, as it was the only oversized box on the right-hand side. She took out a parcel and some letters, then closed the box and walked on – followed by our intrepid Coot.

Here things got a little bit uncomfortable for poor Aloysius, as the quarry spent the next hour or so browsing in shops. The first two shops – homeware and books – were fine, as he could tail her through the aisles while pretending to browse.

But the third was a lingerie shop, marked by a pink love heart on the door, which, just to make it perfectly clear, said "For Ladies Only." Normally he could have waited outside the door, but this shop had *two* entrances, and one of them opened onto the crowded, snakelike passages of Hobbiton's biggest shopping arcade, the Fiddle and Dish. If she got in there, he would lose her for certain. So he held his nose, figuratively speaking, and entered. What he found in there was a strange, alien world, lit by the glow of pink neon.

The foxy-whiskered snoot was looking at some underwear, so he dived down the next aisle and ran straight into a curvaceous forty-something with horned glasses and a steely glare. "Not bad for a plumper," was how he later described her, but at the time he was rendered speechless.

"Looking for something for your *girlfriend*, young man?" was how she accosted him. "You'll excuse my abruptness. It's just that we don't get many *males* in here. You know, the sign and all. It's a pretty rare occurrence." Coot muttered something incomprehensible and ran, head bowed, to a nook in the corner. This turned out to be a changing cubicle, and he pulled the curtain, blacking the scene gracefully away before his head split. Inside the cubicle was a chair, where someone had left a pile of peephole bras and crotchless panties, and with these he mopped his sweating brow as he sat down to gather his addled thoughts.

Then, he remembered the quarry! He jumped up and opened the curtain...and the snoot, now waiting to use the changing cubicle, was greeted by the sight of a male head with bulging eyes, pressing several pairs of panties to its temple. And she wasn't the only one who saw it...

"Coot!" boomed a voice from the front of the shop. Sure enough it was his old friend, the cop from the post office, who had been walking past on his regular beat when the store worker had called him in to deal with a potential pervert.

"I've got you now, Coot...sniffing women's underwear, you sick bastard..."

Coot didn't wait to be lectured or booked. He bolted, straight past the quarry, out the other exit and into the Fiddle and Dish, where he managed to shake the cop in the maze of understreet passages.

Then he did something cunning...he doubled back and headed to the last place the cop would think to look for him – the lingerie shop. He was proud of himself as he related his return just as the quarry was leaving, and how he had stealthily shadowed her to an unmarked building in Battery Point. The building didn't look residential, so he figured it must be her workplace.

A few evenings later we embarked on a voyage to that very building.

*　　*　　*

"My enemies will be unmasked tonight," Sean swore.

"*Our* enemies," I reminded him. From what he had told me of the female teachers at East Lynwood associated with this GLC group, I knew automatically that I would hate them. They sounded like more educated versions of my mother. Sean wanted to gather as much incriminating material as he could in their lair, and then somehow find a way to use it against them.

We were going through the middle of town at night, so we took weapons. They were only little hobbit knives – there had been a spate of gun violence in the northern suburbs of late (due to Australia having some of the strictest gun laws in the world, only criminals now had them), but it hadn't reached the inner city yet.

Besides wearing gloves as a fingerprint precaution, we thought we would dress as atavistically as possible, so we all wore cloaks, just like hobbits. The ninja wore his black velvet cape with pride, while Sean and I sported grey numbers hacked from an old curtain we had found at an op shop.

The sandstone buildings of old Hobbiton glowed at us as we headed down Macquarie St., much brighter than the obscene bellowings of service stations, burger chains and video shops that were splayed in between them – the same ones you can find in any city on earth.

It was Friday night, and the drunks were vomiting heavily in the gutters, while the booming yells of young men seeking petty fights echoed through the shallow canyons of the streets from blocks away, and party girls tottered in their heels, shrieking obscenities at taxis.

It wasn't long before we noticed that we were getting some 'looks'. Turning right onto Harrington, some drunk 'wiggers' began walking alongside us, and one of them prodded Coot with his elbow.

"What are *you* supposed to be? Buncha fucken weirdos!" Sean spun round on his heel and began delivering a lecture, with a splendid gleam in his eye, on how, if anything, *they* were the 'weirdos' with their aped Afro-American fashions and mannerisms, false to their blood! "Unlike my friend the ninja here, who sees into the *genuine* depths of an admittedly alien culture...*you* merely grasp at the surface, making you far shallower than the originals themselves." After this harangue they looked a bit crestfallen.

"You use a lot of big words, mate," one of them said. "You must have swallowed a dictionary. It sounds like you're a bit of a racist, though, and I fucking hate racists."

"Yeah, racists *suck*," said his girlfriend, a glare in her puffy eyes as she swigged from a can of rum and cola. "You all *suck*," she reiterated, burping.

That made Sean mad, and me too, as we were highly respectful of other cultures and traditions – just not of phoneys who chose to ape those traditions at the expense of their own. Sean was really on fire now, and lectured them at length on how *they* were the racists (imperialists, in fact) for stealing, in the such a crass and shallow way, the cultural accoutrements of another tribe. But the wiggers grew bored of his lofty words and sauntered off. One yelled insolently as they went: "We're all *human*, mate. Black, white, it don't matter..." It sounded like the cliched refrain of an eighties pop song, but at the time I was unsure how to reply to it.

There was a sour taste in our mouths as we walked across St. David's Park – the old convict-era burial ground, whose headstones had been removed (except for the very wealthy ones) to make a public playspace. And then we disappeared into the quiet backstreets of Battery Point, Hobbiton's old quarter, where there were more Mercedes Benz's parked in the narrow streets than you could shake a stick at. The clouds traced triangular shapes in the sky across the pregnant moon. It was the witching hour when all good children were in their beds, and we arrived at Coot's nondescript building with a sick feeling of anticipation. What dark sorcery was about to be unleashed here in this monied part of Hobbiton? We were about to burgle the hole of a Lobelia Sackville-Baggins, and who knew what 'treasures' we would find there...

It turned out to be easier than expected to get in. We put on our gloves and headed round the back, where there was a Chubb alarm, but our ninja disabled it expertly, using skills he had learnt on the internet. The door was an old one, and a simple trick with two knives was enough to get it open. We walked straight through, into the most boring building ever.

There were three main rooms – a library (full of sterile tomes of globalist propaganda), a dreary office and a small kitchen. We began our search in the office, and it didn't take long to find what we were looking for – a circular, addressed to all GLC subbranches around the world. In itself it was an unimportant missive, dealing with minor administrative details. What *was* interesting was that it was signed (or at least a copy of his signature) by Sheldon Albright, the well-known American currency speculator and vulture capitalist...you know, the same multi-billionaire who has been in the news so much lately for his involvement in the Luxembourg banking scandal. So now we knew who was financing the GLC – and his wallet was virtually bottomless.

But that wasn't the most interesting find...there was something more pressing, in the form of a programme for an upcoming conference called Future Tasmania. To our amazement, it was both financed and organised by the GLC. So these people were trying to mould the very future of our island!

The list of speakers was interesting, with quite a few names we recognised (artists, media, business, politicians etc.), and there were dozens of copies of the programme so we pocketed one and left, but not before Sean had memorised the number of the GLC's landline phone – for his own purposes, no doubt. I tried to be a good girlfriend and not to pry too much, but I have to admit I was curious as to what he had in mind.

We headed once more through the hallowed stillness of Battery Point, before crossing the busy Sandy Bay Road *en route* for South Hobbiton. But as we were crossing – irony of ironies – we were booked for jaywalking. It must have been the unusual costumery that caught the officer's attention. He laughed at us, then called to his partner: "Hey Graham! This the one you were telling us about?" The other cop walked up...and sure enough, it was Coot's nemesis.

"I don't believe it," he roared. "A whole tribe of them!"

We were taken to the Central Hobbiton police station for questioning. I remember the cops standing around, fingering our hobbit cloaks and laughing. They confiscated our knives, and told us we would all be summonsed for "possession of an offensive weapon" or something like that. Then one of them found the brochure, and they laughed even harder. "So the future of Tasmania is in *your* hands?" etc. etc.

You get the drift. But we weren't offended. We had secret smiles. For we had unmasked the enemy, you see...

3

SEAN

Infiltrating the conference wasn't hard. We simply made a phone call and things began to happen. This was Tasmania after all, and the globalists hadn't yet completely succeeded in creating an atomised world of mistrust – the conference itself, of course, was to be one of the biggest steps in doing so. Well, we would see what we would see, and based on what we learned, determine a plan of action.

So, I simply phoned the little office in Battery Point from a payphone, pretending to be the vice-principal of a leading Hobart private school, a co-educational one (the very one my parents had sent me to before moving to East Lynwood, in fact). As to the name I gave, it was a real one, just in case they should think to check, and I think I did a reasonably good job of imitating that man's placid voice, sounding suitably unctuous and globalist in the process. Indeed, so upper-middle class did I sound that the hag on the other end instinctively warmed to me, recognising me as one of her own.

I had heard all about the conference (I said), and wished to nominate three students of exceptional promise as *youth delegates*. They would be in year twelve next year (unlike Tasmanian government high schools the private ones go up to the twelfth grade), and due to their popularity and the consequent influence they had on other students, a glimpse into the future Tasmania could only do them, and those around them, good.

"Oh *yes*," she cackled. "By all means, yes. A fantastic idea. I never thought to have youth delegates...but you've already sorted it out for me, ha ha." And so it was done, with a simple phone call. For this was still the old Tasmania to some degree, even down to the minds of those who wanted to change it for the worse.

I was then invited to send the students in question for a 'chat' and authorisation at the Battery Point building. It would be strange, literally returning to the scene of our crime, and in daylight I imagined the building would appear more sinister, but we needed those student passes. I had thought of claiming that Aloysius was sick, and taking his pass *in absentia*, but if she insisted he go alone there at any point it would be an even greater hazard. In any case, it seemed unlikely she would remember his appearance from the lingerie shop (he had a pile of underwear over his head at the time, after all) so we decided to risk it. Coot himself was sufficiently paranoid, however, to get a cheap haircut at Spazzo's Shearing Shed in order to change his appearance a bit. School uniform wouldn't be expected, of course, as it was summer holidays – which saved us the trouble of breaking into the school's repository and stealing some!

We were greeted at the door by the same hag Coot had recently shadowed, and he was right – she did indeed remind me of Ms. Lindley from East Lynwood. I now suspected these types were dotted across the landscape, like ossified scarecrows.

To my horror, she looked long and hard at Coot as we went through the door...but the mild frown soon disappeared from her brow, as if a certain word she had been searching for had eluded her, and she was content to let it go. There was an air of overwork about her, in any case, and so probably little danger she would give it further thought.

"So," she said, as we sat around the table in the library room. "You must be Jonathan, Karen and Russell, if I got your right names from Mr. Hargrave?" We nodded, beaming at her. We wanted to come across as enthusiastic, and ever-so-slightly awestruck, but not to overdo it.

"We're really grateful for this opportunity to participate," said Maddy. Coot, too nervous to speak, sat grinning appropriately. I got the feeling she was slightly puzzled by our personalities, even when acting, but she said: "I thought it was a good idea to have some youth delegates. It was something I hadn't previously...considered. But here you are, and you can help spread the word to the next generation." Was it just me, or was there a very faint distaste in her voice as she pronounced this last word? Although it was difficult, I did my best to act submissive and humble, remembering how these egalitarian types loved to wield the whip. She demanded to know more about us, and Maddy and I gave the life stories we had prepared, dropping details of all the globo-projects we were involved in, besides more ordinary interests (cricket for me, clarinet for Maddy), and she nodded mechanically at these. Then, however, she turned her attentions to Coot.

"And you...Russell?" she said, almost seductively. He looked taken aback. His mind had been wandering (dreaming of bare breasts he said later), and now he was snapped out of his trance by this leering ferret whose eyes seemed to drill straight into his head.

"Ah, yeah," he stammered, forgetting his cover story entirely. "The *round globe*, that's for me."

"The...round globe?" she rasped, her frown reappearing. Perhaps Coot was trying to summon up those lost breasts, or perhaps it was an honest attempt at adopting a globalist persona. In any case, I had to step in quickly to allay her suspicions.

"Russell here has big travel plans," I said. "He's been planning his pre-uni gap year, and he's going to visit every continent, in order to research how diversity can better be promoted *here*." Or something like that. It worked, anyway, and to my relief she didn't press him any further. She even looked a tad impressed.

"Well, you'll have to excuse me, I'm very busy at the moment organising the conference. I've prepared these for you." She handed us three 'youth delegate' security badges...exactly what we'd been hoping for...then she bid us a curt goodbye, and returned to her work.

We were in!

*　　*　　*

On the way 'home' (does anyone really have one?) I was looking in a bookshop window in Sandy Bay Rd., when someone gently elbowed me. I turned to see a familiar face – it was Japhrey, my artist acquaintance from East Lynwood. He nodded at Coot (still downcast after his botched performance), and I introduced him to Maddy.

"So, you're in the smoke, too," Japhrey observed. "What are you doing lifewise?"

"Oh, you know. Just plodding along, like Jesse James."

He laughed. "I'm on the dole myself. Youth allowance, it's called. Parents kicked me out, but they signed the papers luckily. I'm getting on well with painting, though. Someone even nominated one of my pieces for this new gallery that's opening soon." I assumed he must mean the Lafayette Gallery, a new art museum currently being erected in the middle of Hobart. The *Messenger* had been full of nothing else for weeks now.

"That's great," I said, and Maddy nodded in agreement.

"Do you think we could have a look at the painting?" she asked in all innocence, and I expected him to exhibit an artist's secrecy. But he casually said: "Sure," and took us back to his flat in the CBD, up some metal stairs in a laneway near the Fiddle and Dish. He led us through a very messy lounge room, past a shy female flatmate who stared at us like a cat, then into his studio, where numerous canvasses were covered with old dust sheets.

"*This* is the piece," he said, unveiling one. "It's called 'Eternal Youth'."

And to my surprise it was a painting, brilliantly executed, of one of my childhood heroes – none other than Tintin himself! "Surrounded by his symbols," Japhrey explained. Yes, there in the swirling melange of figures and scenes was the redemption of Haddock on the *Karaboudjan*; the apocalyptic prophet of 'The Shooting Star'; the triumph over the crime lords of Chicago; the ice cave in Tibet (symbolising Tintin's loyalty to his friend); and the eerie Inca mummy crawling through the window. It was all there, swirling like a dream from the ages – from Tintin's fight against Marxism to his death by 'modern art' in the final unfinished adventure.

This last seemed particularly poignant. These capitalist Damien Hirst types had accomplished what even the 'commie scum' had never managed – to completely crush the spirit of youth, embodied by noble Tintin. I hoped it wasn't an omen for the outcome of Japhrey's artistic mission...

After we had admired the masterpiece for some time, he unveiled the series of paintings which I described near the start of this memoir. He was currently engaged on the seventh and last of these, and only showed us the six completed ones (I later saw the seventh under very different circumstances), which took our breath away. I don't know how long I stood there admiring them, but it felt like a fertile eternity.

When we finally emerged from our trance, Japhrey was no longer around. His flatmate had vanished, too, and the place appeared to be deserted. We departed silently, pulling the front door shut behind us, and feeling like we had been penetrated by a tempest from another world.

*　　*　　*

The week leading up to the conference was a strange one in Hobart. Things seemed edgier, even for summertime. More drunks, more arguments, shrieking mothers, cops everywhere. Perhaps nature was showing these signs of tension because she knew that *significant events* were about to take place. Signs had been seen. The apparition of a giant needle freak wallowing in the fountain at Franklin Square, and a ghostly viking ship sailing through the fog at Lindisfarne. There were strange flashes of light on the Demesne and Mt. Nelson. Battlements were raised, consciousness altered. Maddy gave me the sweetest looks, eyes raised to my face amidst her curls, sure in the knowledge that although things were about to change forever as we stepped on the public stage for the first time, we would nonetheless always be true to each other.

Olivia was a distant memory now, a faint sour taste that faded further with each of Maddy's sweetening kisses. The fair one had betrayed me (had betrayed her own ancestors, in fact)...and so the Dark Redeemer with her pale face and black curls had stepped forward to turn the spiral around. I don't expect you to know what I mean...but perhaps you do.

*　　*　　*

The day before the conference we received summonses in the mail (Coot's came care of the drop-in centre where he showered, as he was sleeping from house to house). Our stupid lack of watchfulness that night on Sandy Bay Rd. had cost us, but there was no point regretting it now. The court appearance was set for a week's time, but for now we had a conference to crash, and needed a good night's sleep.

The big day dawned, and my head felt funny – inflated with something thin, like an old copper balloon. A cup of tea over breakfast solidified it somewhat, then we headed out to meet Coot.

The three of us arrived at the conference centre some fifteen minutes early, and there was quite a crowd milling around in the foyer and the main hall. There must have been a few hundred people there. Displaying our badges, we proceeded to mingle.

All of Hobart's proud aristocracy were hobnobbing it there, but from the tones and figures of speech I gathered that most of the attendees were actually from the mainland. I had expected that. What stopped me in my tracks, though, was the sight of a familiar figure...Ms. Green, who had expelled me from East Lynwood. Her arm was no longer in its cast, and she was walking around with the most treacly, ingratiating look on her face, so that I gathered she was a small fish here. I nudged Coot, who had spotted her also. There probably wasn't too much danger of her 'unmasking' us, but it was best to steer clear of her regardless.

The bell rang, and everyone rushed to fill the seats in the main hall. Ms. Green was near the front, so we were forced to sit down back. Luckily there was a PA system and we could hear the speakers just fine. I still didn't know what we were actually going to do. Coot expected that I would somehow disrupt the proceedings, and was waiting to follow my lead. But I felt more inclined to take notes, then plan guerrilla raids for afterwards. If we caused a disturbance here, it would not be newsworthy, and we were relying on the media to communicate our feelings (hazy though they may have been) to the masses.

As I mused thus, a man mounted the podium to introduce the conference – and there proceeded a spectacularly dreary set of speakers.

The first three were male, though distinctly unmanly. Two of them used the term 'whitebread' liberally and disparagingly when talking of Tasmania's future (as something to avoid), and combined it frequently with the word 'monoculture', although it would be hard to imagine a more lily-white and monocultural crowd than they. Perhaps I'm prejudiced because their verbal unctuousness formed such a negative contrast to the laconic demeanour I myself wished to cultivate, but I honestly had to choke back a burning cry of rage when they described my beloved Tasmania as a 'cultural lab'. I understood that they allowed it to be a microcosm of the West, a Lilliput if you will. But lab??? What kind of fucked-up plot were these globalist Frankenstein half-men hatching?

I glanced at Coot to gauge his reaction, but he just looked bored out of his mind. A fire was smouldering in Maddy's eyes, though, and she looked at me like she wanted to fuck me, a sure sign she was angry.

Then Angela Russell-Smythe, the first female speaker, came on. Young by the standards of the conference (late forties), she utterly electrified the audience. The title of her speech was "Does Tasmania need a UN intervention – or can we intervene ourselves?" (the 'we' denoting that she was born in Tassie, though she had lived in Sydney for decades).

"So *does* Tasmania need an intervention?" she thundered from the pulpit. In answer, she launched into an epic speech about her fabulous life in Sydney, and how her friends had pitied her so much when she recently made the 'momentous' decision to return to the island of her birth that they sent her 'aid packages' in the mail. Tasmania was the 'third world', they warned her...away from the centre of things, and populated by 'bogans'. Worse, it was whitebread, a monoculture. (A culture in other words, I wryly thought).

"Luckily, though," she continued, "the island is *changing*. The Lafayette Gallery is opening next week," (enthusiastic applause from the audience) "and high-end tourism is on the rise" (a smaller burst of applause). "So perhaps now I can tell my Sydney friends to stop sending aid packages..." (delighted laughter, but also scepticism: "Oh come, not yet, surely!")

Another voice yelled: "The Lafayette will be the *existential salvation* of this benighted island!" Russell-Smythe grinned, and motioned with her hands to calm the excited audience down.

"Of course there are still wrinkles to be ironed out," she sighed, plucking at her cashmere top. "For instance, the low percentile of overseas-born on the island is deeply disturbing."

"Hear, hear," yelled an old snoot.

"But I'm sure that can be *fixed*. Perhaps if we apply concertedly to the federal government they may see fit to increase our immigration quotas."

"Oh yes, *yes*," screamed a grey-haired lady in front of me, sounding on the verge of orgasm. "We are *cosmopolitans!*" (Her eyes nearly popped out of her head as she uttered this last word, and being a bit hazy about its meaning I resolved to look it up when I got home. It seemed to inspire a sexual and religious fervour in the old woman in front of me, so it must be something powerful.)

Russell-Smythe rambled on for a bit longer about her vision for the 'New Tasmania'. Every 'cracked voice' must be given a place in the choir, it seemed. I wondered idly if my own Black Metal rasp would receive a seat, then realised instinctively that it wouldn't. What this woman meant was *pliable* voices...I was learning to read between the lines of establishment speech.

Then she finished with an extraordinary rant about a strategy of 'shaming' those who didn't fit in with her vision. Sounding for all the world like a biblical prophet, she boomingly insisted that "all the dinosaurs be shut off the ark..." An interesting way of putting it. Well, it felt good to be tyrannosaurus for the day.

But now the thunderous applause was dying down, and the final speaker before lunch ascended the pulpit. This one was Godfrey Nussbaum, art critic for the Hobart *Messenger* no less. He looked the part, with horn-rimmed glasses and a black skivvy, but for an arts type, he wasn't particularly creative – most of his speech sounded like a re-recording of the first four. There were the joys of 'cosmopolitanism' (that word again), the need to confront 'bogans', and banish the 'whitebread'. I could see that Maddy and Coot were bored shitless by now.

Where he *did* get my attention was when he spoke of mainlanders referring to Tasmania as a 'beggar state' which took more than its share from the Australian Commonwealth. One third of the Tasmanian population was on welfare, it seemed. Well, we would have a look into that, and perhaps we could come up with some ideas to do something about it. Economic autarchy might be something to be considered.

Then Nussbaum related his horror at a recent survey that showed Tasmanians were taking pride in *not* being educated. Well, to be honest, if being 'educated' meant being like the speakers there that day, I couldn't say that I blamed them.

Finally, after reiterating Russell-Smythe's strategy of shaming those who didn't fit in with the 'new vision' (but at the same time somehow letting in 'every cracked voice'), he introduced a special guest...no less than Peter Winslow himself, owner and curator of the soon-to-be-unveiled Lafayette Gallery.

The applause eclipsed even that given to Angela Russell-Smythe. Winslow smiled self-depreciatingly and stepped up to the podium. It was hard to make out a lot of his speech due to orgasmic audience noise, but I did catch his final sentence, something to the effect that the Lafayette Gallery would "affirm life by undermining the reasons you have to lie to yourself." Then he pulled aside a large piece of silk, under which was a painting from the museum...a sneak peak of what was to come.

The painting was a well-executed one, and showed a woman in business dress, standing on a building site and holding a shovel full of small jagged rocks. She was about to thrust them into the gaping anus of a man (also in business shirt) who was bending over a pile of rubble. After a few embarrassed titters, the audience went wild. Angela Russell-Smythe came back on stage and wrung Winslow's hand warmly.

"So good to see some *culture* in the wasteland of Tasmania!" she grinned, and several hundred baby boomers agreed with her (I recognised a man up the front that Maddy and I had robbed a few weeks back). I glanced around at the others. Maddy was scowling, but Coot could hold back no longer. As soon as I looked at him he burst into a howling fit of laughter. It was infectious, and Maddy and I soon caught it. But fortunately the general tumult drowned it out – to all but those sitting immediately around us. The grey-haired 'cosmopolitan' lady turned around and gave us a severe look.

"*That* is *art*. Can't you get that through your thick, barbarous little skulls?" She was completely outraged that we had laughed at the arse-shovelling scene! I wasn't going to be drawn into a debate on what constituted good art, but simply said: "I agree with you, it's fantastic. And what does it do for *you?*"

Here she looked flustered...like several other female boomers of my acquaintance, it seemed that she didn't like being questioned.

"It's not what *I* think," she snapped scornfully. "It's what the artist intended."

"Well what do *you* think the artist intended?"

"Why don't you ask them?" Dripping with sarcasm, but it was a sarcasm of fear, absolute terror that her mask would slip.

"Would you say that it affirms life?" I asked casually.

"Yes," she said, jumping at the lifeline. "By undermining the reasons you have to lie to yourself..."

Winslow's words had imprinted themselves on her as they had with me, though less critically in her case.

"So, man is just an anus...an alimentary canal...a shitting machine," I nodded. "Well, fortunately for us we've read Plotinus and Schwaller de Lubicz, and know better." She looked at me with deep suspicion, but her eyes were opaque, not deep. I stared straight into them, and she couldn't meet my gaze. "Some even say that man *creates* value, and what's *created* can never be a lie. As you boomer cunts are about to find out," I added with a feral snarl, and it was lovely to see her shrink away from me. Luckily for her, the lunch gong sounded.

"We can go now if you want," I told Maddy and Coot as we filed into the crowded foyer, and they were only too eager. "I got what I wanted, and the best course of action seems clear to me now. There's just one more thing we need to do." I whispered something in Maddy's ear and she nodded.

We approached Peter Winslow as he stood drinking his wine and schmoozing with the other movers and shakers. Here was the guy who handpicked the art, I thought...the curator. In the last year or two I had noticed the term 'curator' had become so widely applied that it even extended to someone who organised a pub rock concert. The 'curator' was now deemed more important than the mere bands, artists etc., and certainly more important than the audience. The triumph of the middleman was almost complete, in every walk of life.

That was one of the things we were rebelling against.

I stood politely near Winslow, waiting for a gap in the conversation. To my surprise, he was discussing the work of our good acquaintance.

"My step-daughter's been badgering me to put something in by this Japhrey Small fellow. She loves his work, for some reason. Shares a flat with him. I can't stand his stuff myself. I showed it to Godfrey here," he gestured at the *Messenger* art critic, black skivvy man, standing next to him. "*He* can tell you what he thinks of it," he laughed.

"Oh *god*." Nussbaum rolled his eyes. "Absolute bloody kitsch. You wouldn't *believe* how bad it is." Those around him tittered.

"Oh why *not*," rasped one old buck-toothed slag, "give some local artists a go. Doesn't matter if it's not quite up to scratch."

"Scratch? This guy's not even in the *ballpark*." I couldn't believe my ears. Were they really talking about Japhrey? I know art is in the eye of the beholder, that you can't make a horse drink etc., but this was ridiculous. I was standing with my mouth agape in shock, staring into space...when Winslow turned and asked me if I wanted an autograph! The curator as idol...

Luckily Maddy was thinking quicker than me, and said: "Oh, you could give us something even better than an *autograph* Mr. Winslow." I swear she even batted her eyelids as she said it, and the old goat was immediately aroused. "We were wanting to write an article about the Lafayette for our school newspaper, you see. The first issue of the year comes out as soon as class goes back, and we thought we could include a special piece on the gallery. Hobbiton's...I mean *Hobart's*...existential salvation, as someone here today put it. So we were wondering...if the three of us could have a sneak peak inside the gallery, perhaps even a guided tour...before the press deadline for the issue, which is next week." She was a great actress, and her performance was greeted by an array of "Absolutely, why not..." "What a *wonderful* idea!" "It's *so* good that you're reaching out to youth, Peter...they're the future, you know." *Your future ruin*, I thought grimly, Wotan raging in my veins. But we were now free to carry out our final piece of reconnaissance, before Operation Götzen-dammerung began in earnest. The twilight of the idols was near at hand.

*   *   *

I later looked up the term kitsch, and found it to mean "considered to be in poor taste because of excessive sentimentality." Some artists (Odd Nerdrum, for instance) had even adopted this term as a badge of honour (to the further disgust of their already hostile critics), and I felt that Japhrey could profitably do likewise.

But Japhrey's work was not *really* kitsch, unless by 'sentimentality' one meant any kind of strong human trait, as love, honour, strength of will, melancholia, etc. And if *those* are 'excessively sentimental' then count me a sentimentalist. But what's in a word?

I also looked up 'cosmopolitan' and found it was used chiefly to mean "someone who is at home everywhere." So what it really meant was: citizen of nowhere. These cosmopolitans were the original Nowhere Men, as Maddy put it (she was always citing Beatles lyrics, for some reason) and the name stuck.

We were at war with the Middle Men, the Nowhere Men.

*   *   *

First we had to face the courts of law, however. I had a big speech prepared about how our knives were defensive, not offensive, and what kind of society would punish a young man for seeking to protect himself etc. (all true), but my court-appointed legal counsel strongly advised against it (even though I could tell that he sympathised), because the magistrate would never wear it, he said.

"Law isn't about justice, or very rarely," he said. "It's about the smooth maintenance of a system."

"So they want people to helplessly rely on the authorities for protection?"

"Yes, yes..." And of course he was right. So for pragmatic reasons I swallowed my pride and confessed I was a bad boy...a youthful indiscretion, and it wouldn't happen again.

Maddy did likewise. She really *was* a superb actress. The two of us were let off with a verbal warning and no conviction.

Coot wasn't so lucky, however. It seemed there were other charges pending against him that he hadn't told us about...possession of a controlled substance (from his druggie days), a drunk and disorderly, two loiterings, an assault, and something called a public order offence (he had urinated on the front door of the police station).

"You are a serial pest, Mr. Coot," croaked the magistrate, and sent him for a two week spell at Blue Tier Juvenile Detention Centre, three hours drive north of Hobart. A short sharp shock, intended to scare him into reforming his character, I guessed. Unless Coot managed to escape, he was out of the game for the time being. I gave him a look that said "Bad luck old boy," and as the cops led him away he grinned, and mouthed something like: "I'll be back."

So Maddy and I alone were given the tour of the gallery. We made an excuse for Coot, saying he had sprained his leg in a rock-climbing accident, and then we were invited to imbibe the stifling atmosphere of contemporary art. Winslow was otherwise engaged, so we were shown around by a tall girl with a freckled face. The building itself was striking, and even extended underground...it felt like entering an Egyptian tomb from the Valley of the Kings. The ambient lighting was fantastic and gothic, lending itself well to moments of contemplation. The only problem was, there was nothing suitable for us to contemplate. The art was dreary...it wasn't even confronting, in a shock-the-bourgeois kind of way. It *was* bourgeois. There was nothing remotely transcendental about this collection of mass media rearrangements, contorted car parts, depictions of famous historical figures engaged in sordid sex acts, and so on. Forget about Entartete Kunst, this was *Langweilige* Kunst.

And yet the girl who showed us around...her eyes seemed to glow in heavenly rapture. I tried to work out why this was. Could she see something in the art that I couldn't? But as she prattled on about Mr. Winslow this and Mr. Winslow that, I began to fear that she had fallen victim to the cult of the *curator*. It wasn't the artwork itself that excited her...it was the fact so much of it was collected in one place, and with a *curator* no less. This, to her, was Art – a lifestyle, an image. My heart went out to the poor, deluded, gentle creature. I don't mean that in a patronising way. I had actual tears of pity in my eyes...my soul was profoundly moved, much more than it ever could have been by the artwork itself.

But as numerous philosophers have pointed out, misplaced pity is a great wrong. We were about to enter into the central chamber of the museum, when she suddenly gave us a cold look and a patronising warning: "I hope you kids realise how *lucky* you are, seeing our prize exhibit before it's even open to the public..."

Oh, we were aware all right, we assured her, and thanked her reverently for taking the time.

And what did we see in that grand central chamber, that holy of holies?

Why, nothing less than a gigantic fibreglass turd...

*   *   *

Yes, I assured myself, tapping it. It's fibreglass all right.

"That's a really big...piece of shit," rasped Maddy. She was trying to choke back laughter, but the museum girl didn't hear...she was in another world, clearly enraptured by the turd. Well, maybe not the turd itself, but the fact that it *existed*, was Art.

The phrase 'museum piece' kept repeating itself in my head for some reason. The room began spinning. Then something came to me – the beginnings of a really good plan. A way to genuinely *give* something to society by combatting the cancer that was attacking it, turning negative into positive. Negativity itself could be *used*, a kind of fertiliser, manure (but not fibreglass)...

Well, if this seems a bit abstract, you'll soon comprehend what I mean.

*   *   *

I was a bit worried that, well...you know how subjective these things can be. I was concerned we had something *wrong*. Japhrey's art was exciting, riveting, profound and mysterious, while the turd art at the Lafayette was boring and completely lacking in transcendence. But the art mob seemingly had it the other way round – so who was right? There were more of them than us, numerically – so did that mean *we* were mistaken? Were we ignorant, uncouth, philistine yokels? I wanted to go back and have another look at Japhrey's work, just to be sure my feelings were absolutely clear.

We knocked, and his flatmate opened. Japhrey was out, but she recognised us from the other week and gladly let us have a look at his paintings, except for the one he was currently working on.

She stood there in quiet rapture, admiring them with us.

No, I certainly hadn't been mistaken. This was art one could go into battle for, risk annihilation for. It was worth infinitely more than every piece in Winslow's cruddy gallery put together.

"Am I to understand," I said, turning to the quiet one, "that you are related to a certain famous curator?"

"My name's Michelle," she said. "Peter's my stepfather, not a blood relative. I don't think he likes me very much." She seemed so nice that I found it hard to credit, but said: "Have you had any success persuading him to accept Japhrey's piece?"

"He's not going to show it," she sighed. "He's agreed to include some local art...just not this. Japhrey's very depressed about it. He's been drinking a lot." I didn't know what to say. I muttered some feeble words about courage, and there would be other galleries in the future, better ones, but her wan smile was so softly sad that I had to leave.

"What an absolute cunt," said Maddy when we were outside. "Winslow, I mean."

"Yeah, and he has the public in the palm of his hand. The art critics too, of course. Godfrey Nussbaum can't write a sentence without singing his praises...that is, unless he's bagging out the *old* museum. He really hates that place. Come to think of it, maybe we should go there. My enemy's enemy, and all that. We could at least have a look."

"All right..." So we headed down to the old crumbling building near the docks, which I hadn't visited since early childhood. Nothing had changed there, and even the smells visually evoked a world I thought had been lost forever. Evoked, yes, but not summoned. The truth was over the horizon, out of reach. I sat down on a bench, and grasped at it. Then there was a warm flash behind my eyes, and suddenly I understood. The world of forms, of dreams, was behind us, but could only be grasped by moving *forward*, on the long spiral climb towards the pole star. It might be many lifetimes before I got there. But there was no going back to the entrance of the maze – that way was closed, even if starlight continued to filter through it.

Maddy tapped me gently on the shoulder. I had been sitting motionless for ages, she told me, and it was nearly closing time. We wandered through the museum's chambers, looking at fossils, relics, Victoriana. Although it wasn't a way out of the maze, it was still good to know this place existed, a thorn in the side of the Godfrey Nussbaums of this world. And then there was the crusty curator, a delightful old duffer who was always making some reactionary statement in the letters section of the *Messenger*. I heard that they only printed his letters because he would walk the two blocks to their building and raise a ruckus if they didn't.

Then I saw it...

Near the exit a large notice had been pinned to the wall. The museum was to undergo extensive alterations, it said. In a year's time it would be completely refurbished. Future exhibitions included one called "Hobart Afresh: Rebranding a Colonial City in a Global World." Maddy laughed at this last tautology ("So what shape do they *think* the world is?"), but to my lasting horror, the notice had been signed by none other than that same reactionary duffer whom Godfrey Nussbaum was constantly attacking in print. He had caved! Or was he on their side all along? I've said it before, and I'll say it again: Never trust a fucking conservative. They're in lockstep with the Left...you just can't tell at first because they're several paces behind.

On the way home I bought the *Messenger*, only to find it was a special double issue devoted to the Lafayette Gallery, whose imminent opening was supposedly throwing the populace into a state of orgasmic anticipation (which populace?). The state government had proudly announced subsidised airfare deals for museum visitors from the mainland and overseas, and tourism was expected to massively increase as a result.

I thought that I would give the Lafayette's curator one more chance to stop us attacking. I phoned the gallery and (in my guise as school reporter) insisted on a short phone interview with Winslow himself. After being put on hold for half an hour, there was a slightly cranky sounding 'Yes?'

I didn't beat around the bush. Word on the street had it that a prominent local artist, Japhrey Small, had been rejected by the gallery. Didn't he find that Small's work exhibited a remarkable quality of transcendence? Winslow became angry. He scoffed at the very notion of 'transcendence'.

"If you want that kind of mumbo jumbo, go to the local Steiner shop. This is an *art* gallery."

"So you won't consider including his Tintin painting?"

"He doesn't use Tintin to undermine illusion...he uses Tintin to *foster* illusion. So fuck him. Anything else?"

I hung up on the drug-addled boomer, clearly not the young man of promise he had initially thought me to be. Well, I'd given him a chance.

Before our war campaign began, I took a bus up to Fern Tree and went for a walk in the rainforest alone. Maddy pouted when I announced I was going without her – my constant companion – but I needed to clear my head. I kissed her brow and promised to make love to her as soon as I returned.

At the higher altitude of Fern Tree the air was very clear, even in the gloomy path through the rainforest. My sweat chilled in the breeze, and it felt like my head and neck were covered in a thin layer of crystal. Perfect for thinking.

To my surprise, however, I found I could *not* think, not in a rational way. I had been running on pure instinct since that morning on Myrtle Hill, and when I tried to think, all that came was a whirlwind of archetypal images.

Then the physical wind picked up as I emerged from the trees onto a wide open fire trail. I couldn't dwell on what I was getting into. I just had to trust to the divine wind, to wait and see where it was blowing me. I wished I could have left Maddy out of it, but she was so devoted, and would never consent to be left behind. Her kind of loyalty was so rare in this throwaway age that it made my heart melt. At least I would protect her as best I could...

Then a forest raven alighted on a nearby rock and fixed me with a beady eye. "Are you ready?" he seemed to say. "*Croak.* Are you ready?"

Nature, the universe, hungers for us to give it meaning. But our capacity to do so has become clouded, and that is why a great awakening is required.

I was about to become an alarum.

*　　*　　*

Godfrey Nussbaum was annoying to follow. After he left the *Messenger* office he kept darting in and out of shops to look at clothes, books, sunglasses and whatnot, until we thought he would never get home. Once he stopped to have a screaming argument with someone over his mobile phone, while we huddled at a nearby bus stop, pretending to be waiting. Then a bus pulled up.

"Wrong route," I said apologetically.

"It's the *only* route for this stop, mate," countered the driver.

"Ah...wrong bus, then." He looked at me scornfully, and drove away. But now Nussbaum had finished on the phone and was walking with surprising speed towards Battery Point. I had a suspicion he would turn out to live there, and I was right. He entered a beautiful old house overlooking the river. Not bad digs for a guy who only wrote a newspaper column once a week. There was a silver Mercedes in the driveway, but fortunately for us he preferred to walk to and from the CBD. Well, we would be back here tonight, and Mr. Nussbaum would get a little surprise...

*   *   *

We had a nasty surprise of our own, however. In his column four days later he referred glowingly to the 'spontaneous street art' which had appeared all over his home and Mercedes. The words 'kitsch' and 'derivative' had been spraypainted numerous times, with big arrows pointing to the front door where he lay ensconced...and he *approved* of this!

It seemed he believed this prank had originated with his colleagues. His grovelling response in the *Messenger* reminded a bit of Shostakovich's subtitle for his Fifth Symphony (written at the height of the Stalinist purges): 'A Soviet Artist's Response to Justified Criticism.' But Mr. Nussbaum had no gun pointed at *his* head when he wrote of the "breathtaking originality" and "contrapuntal ellipsis" of the spraypaint artists whose work he now vowed to "preserve forever" on the front of his house.

So the system had co-opted our first mind-expanding prank, and in a way we hadn't expected! We would have to try harder with the next one, then...

*   *   *

Angela Russell-Smythe lived in Leslie Vale, a semi-rural area not far from Hobart. Her address was easy to find...unlike Nussbaum, she was in the phone book. We took the bus to Kingston, and walked from there to scout around a bit. As I had suspected, Leslie Vale suffered a

91

distinct *lack* of the 'diversity' Russell-Smythe had preached a need for at the Future Tasmania conference.

Ah well, the revolution would swallow its own.

*   *   *

We tested her first, as this one was going to be a bit brutal. We had to make sure she was absolutely a worthy target. I phoned her from a payphone, under the pretence that I worked for Anglicare, a Christian organisation whose main aim was settling migrants from various African countries into working class areas of Hobart. Russell-Smythe's plummy voice warmed considerably on hearing this.

"Oh, Anglicare does *such* a good job," she gushed.

"Thanks, but there's a small problem we were hoping you could help us with."

"Oh? Moi?"

"It seems the residents of one of our target neighbourhoods are getting up a petition to oppose settlement there, on the grounds of cultural incompatibility, social problems and the like."

"*Bogans!* Cultural incompatibility," she snorted. "As if those types even *have* any culture. Well, I'm not sure why you need *my* assistance. Just get onto the *Messenger* editor. He'll smear them as ignorant yokels, and shame them into acquiescence. You *must* be aware of the tools at your disposal. If that doesn't work, bring the law down onto them. Hate speech and so on." Interesting the things you learned. But now for the test...

"Yes, but that wasn't exactly what we needed your help with. You see, we were wondering if we could settle one of the more...difficult families...at *your* place. After all, it's quite a big house, and you're the only one living there. It would set a *great* example for the bogans, if a member of Tasmania's elite..."

"Elite?!" she spluttered in horror. "I'm not part of any elite, you're just parroting what the extreme right says." (Actually, we had researched her online and found that she had family ties to *both* major political parties, as

92

well as to the third biggest party, the Greens). "Anyway, I have to go. I'm very busy. I'm sure someone else can help with your request." She hung up.

"Yep," I said to Maddy. "Definitely worthy."

*　*　*

Russell-Smythe's key aim, as outlined in her conference speech, was an 'intervention' to 'shame' those who didn't 'let in every cracked voice,' and we were determined to hold her to this goal. Applied to Tasmania as a whole, it would be a rape of the island's subtle spirit, but applied to those who preached it, it was justice itself. Not that justice was our exact aim – our aim was some kind of awakening that would lead to a renaissance of the human spirit. To this end, we would intervene and shame her.

The flyer we printed said *strictly* no show before 5pm, as before that the house would be locked and there would be no free booze. Party night was this coming Saturday, as in an online interview Angela had mentioned that she always spent Saturday evenings in her gazebo (in summer) or her study (in winter), without her mobile phone, for a quiet meditation on the state of the world.

Our first stop was the city's only gay bar. We stepped under the greasy rainbow flag and entered what looked like a normal pub, with a handful of middle-aged men staring sullenly into their drinks, and some weak pop music playing on the jukebox. All very 'gay', but Maddy soon perked things up.

"Guys, we're having a huge *party*," she announced, "and we'd *love* to have a lot of LGBT people. Everyone knows you guys party the *best*. And there'll be no bogans, don't worry...it's a bogan-free zone!" The party animals muttered to themselves as they looked at the flyers, of which she handed them a dozen each. "Make sure to give them to everyone you know, guys. Even email your friends from the mainland...plane fares are really cheap at the moment because the new museum's opening. All right, see you at the party!" They murmured appreciatively as we left – it seemed we had won them over.

So next it was off to one of the more 'bogan' pubs in town, to spread the word there. We were in luck, as besides the garden variety bogans there was also a member of the 'Devil's Disciples' motorcycle club, a true one percenters outfit. He was pretty keen on the idea of the party, especially when we told him there would be "lots of good-looking chicks", and said he would give the flyers to his fellow club members, only not to invite any 'Satan's Soldiers' members or there would be "fucking bloodshed." We assured him that we wouldn't, then went straight round to the Satan's Soldiers clubhouse on Bannockburn Street, grateful for the tip.

The place was locked up, but there was an elderly (fifty-something) bikie on the bench outside, smoking a cigarette. He took some flyers, and said he would tell his colleagues about it.

And then we went to a certain housing block (I had been there once before) where a large number of African immigrants were housed. These were the guests of honour, of course, and most of them looked overjoyed to be invited.

After that we handed the flyers to random teenagers in the CBD, and they, too, were most enthusiastic about the party. Then, after robbing a boomer couple on the way home, we settled down to relax and unwind after a good day's work.

*　　*　　*

We arrived early for the party, and true to the injunction on the flyer there was no one here yet (incredible, given the margin of error involved). We cut the phoneline to the house, then peeped round the back. It was a largish block, at least twenty acres, and up on the hill we could see the famous gazebo, and a figure with its back to us...perfect. We went into the unlocked house to look for her mobile phone, and soon found it on the kitchen bench. As we had expected, it had video capability, so I pocketed it. Then we threw open the front door, and settled down to await the throng.

First to arrive, at five on the dot, was a group of swaggering teens clutching a five-litre goon and a slab of beer as if they were magical talismans.

"Where do I chuck these?" said the sweaty one who had carried the slab. I nodded towards the big double fridge. His girlfriend looked around cynically.

"Pretty posh place. Isn't anyone else here yet?" But as soon as she said it, a car purred up outside the door. I went out to check. Unfortunately there was no wind to block out the sound of the engine, a flaw in my plan. Angela was still up in the gazebo, but stirring. Fortunately another car arrived straight away, and so besides the teens in the first car (who vaguely knew the bunch already in the lounge room) there was now a car load of obvious and incredibly drunken homosexuals. These weren't ones I recognised from the bar, so word must have spread.

"Hey guys," Maddy said. "There's a big king-sized bed if you're having trouble keeping your hands off each other."

"Oh *yes*," one of them said, and tittered. "Maybe you could *video* us?"

"Only if you're good," said Maddy, and that sent him off into spasms of delight, just as another car pulled up. Yet more rowdy teens hopped out. I could see Angela hurrying down the hill.

It was all out of our hands now, I thought. I strolled back into the lounge. "We should act as unobtrusively as possible," I said to Maddy.

"Except when we're filming her," she countered with a grin, and we didn't have long to wait.

When I say Russell-Smythe *stormed* into the house, I'm not exaggerating. Her dark crimson face looked for all the world like the famous red spot that rages on Jupiter. As she swooped into the room I thought: "She's going to kill us all."

It was magnificent.

"What the hell are you people doing in my *house*," she bellowed. "Get out now or I'll..." She stopped suddenly, red face quivering...she had *heard* something. And in the eerie silence after the thunderclap we could all hear it too...a truly *disgusting* series of sex noises coming from the master bedroom.

She raced in there, primed to kill. Maddy and I followed warily with the phone-camera. I didn't have the stomach to look into the room (not out of privacy concerns, as the gays had left the door wide open before beginning their orgy), but I got some very juicy close-up footage of Russell-Smythe's face shrieking: "You sick *faggots*...you revolting fucking *poo pirates*," etc. etc. Her progressive friends would probably disown her when they heard that kind of language – but perhaps *they* might have reacted similarly under the circumstances? I felt a brief pang of pity for poor Angela, but crushed it. I was giving her what she wanted, after all...diversity. So fuck her.

And here was more diversity brewing. Several carloads of Somalian men (no women) had arrived, and a few of them had seen what was going on in the master bedroom. One of them began speaking in tongues, while another tried to exorcise the demons of "faggot witchcraft" which had infested the room (one of the gays was pleading with him to join in the orgy as he did so). A stern older African was lecturing Angela in a booming voice: "This is your house? You *permit* this? You *permit* this?" She exploded in rage, and I got some great footage of her liberating her repressed illiberal emotions, by calling him a "foul, lying coon," and a "boot-lipped, bulging-eyed pickaninny."

The old man looked truly shocked, and turned to me with a dignified gaze. "She is a witch," he said, with sadness in his dark eyes. "She is *possessed*." I gave him a look of sympathy, then headed back to the lounge, where more teenage partygoers were arriving. Maddy opened the huge mahogany liquor cabinet, and there were whoops of joy. Lots of expensive looking wines and spirits, mostly still in the bottle, but a few in fine crystal decanters. The horde seized the latter first and started sculling them, before smashing the decanters on the kitchen floor. Things were really getting rowdy, and it was then that the first group of bikies arrived.

Although one of them was muttering something about "niggers", they didn't seem like they were in a particularly violent mood. That would change, however, when two more carloads of obvious gays pulled up, and the bikies started jeering at them. But the queers, counter to stereotype, were armed and ready for a fight, and what's more there were eight of them, and only three bikies. Knives were flying out of kitchen drawers, as people armed themselves with anything they could find.

Things get a bit blurry after that...I can't remember if the rival bikies arrived *first*, or if the brawl between bikies and Africans over a perceived insult occurred before that. In any case, we saw Angela fleeing the house on foot (her Mercedes Benz being hemmed in by Harley Davidsons), having discovered the phone line was severed, and presumably on the way to a neighbour's house to call the cops. We made our own way to Kingston on foot, pausing only to hide in the bushes as a veritable fleet of flashing police vehicles wailed past (I counted three separate paddy wagons). All in all, it was a good night's work.

The next day we uploaded our footage to a popular video-sharing website. We titled it: "Prominent leftist Angela Russell-Smythe snaps, makes RACIST, HOMOPHOBIC remarks."

When we checked back a few days later it had had over two million views! Beneath it were thousands of comments like "Wow! This bitch must really h8 diversity!!!" "Kill this whore NOW pls" and "Racist scum like this should be slowly tortured to death..."

Shortly afterwards, the video was mysteriously removed from the website...but too late. Angela Russell-Smythe wasn't just the talk of Tasmania, but of effete types the world over. And nothing more was ever heard from her in public again.

*　　*　　*

Then Coot was back in town, having done his time. He looked a bit grey around the muzzle after his experiences there, but although the security was somewhat lax (he said), and a ninja like himself could have escaped at any time, he chose to sit it out and start afresh with a clean record.

The media had said that the police were now looking for 'persons of interest' who had handed out flyers for a party in Leslie Vale which had gotten out of hand, so I figured it would be in my interest to ask him what youth detention was actually like. He told me a sad tale of a place where there were neither ideals nor idealists, and where the pecking order was based on who had committed the most base and trivial (to my mind) crimes. I wondered if I would have the strength of body and will to "take over the joint" if ever I went inside...perhaps I could lead a ragtag army of society's refuse against the boomers. But tush, I was dreaming, and there were other tasks at hand.

Coot was envious when he heard about the prank we had pulled on Russell-Smythe. He wanted to be right at the centre of the next one, he said...so I told him what I had in mind. This time it would be an attack on an institution rather than a person...on the turd-art gallery in the centre of town.

I had recently been reading a book on medieval alchemy, and it seemed that shit was actually a symbol for the first stage of the alchemical process, Nigredo: blackness, putrefaction and death; pure matter, prima materia. It was from shit that true gold was made – philosopher's gold, not the material 'gold' of the banking establishment.

So with that in mind I failed to see why the Lafayette Gallery, with a giant turd as its focus, couldn't produce a kind of spiritual gold whose gleam would snap the Tasmanian masses from their trance and turn their rapt and newly-awakened attention to higher things.

The next day was spent at an internet cafe, putting together a press release. We used the Lafayette's logo as a masthead, but with *our* phone number attached. We wrote whole paragraphs in professional 'artspeak' (a style quickly gleaned from other online press releases), giving biographical details for a rare hermit artist of our own invention, called Alphonse le Coq. We made out that he was a modern Schwarzkogler, and subtly implied that anyone who hadn't heard of him wasn't 'clued in' and was, by implication, a bogan.

And *then* we announced he would be giving an Ultra Rare, Very Special PERFORMANCE in four days time at the Lafayette, and that all media were invited to attend. We emailed the press release to every single daily newspaper in the English-speaking world...with the exception of the Hobart *Messenger,* due to its close links with the gallery (they might smell a rat).

So for the next four days our 'field office' (i.e. the flat) was busy answering phone calls from as far afield as America (the *New York Times* was *very* interested, as the Lafayette had already acquired a cult reputation overseas, and then this mysterious artist...) No, we couldn't reveal the nature of the piece, we told them. It would be unveiled only at the time of performance.

The *Times* promised they would send a photographer (our juicy artspeak had primed them), and so did several other 'prestige' newspapers. Everything was set for the big day.

*   *   *

We arrived at the museum early to scope the situation. Maddy waited in the spot we had prearranged with the press (just out of sight of the staff in the foyer), while Coot and I went inside. The smiling girl in the foyer handed us a map of the (fairly complex) building, and we set out to find a suitable room for Coot's performance. Eventually we found the perfect space – a gallery in an obscure corner of the building, empty except for a large white pedestal about a metre across, on top of which someone had left an empty fried chicken bucket. I threw it aside, then Coot mounted the pedestal to prepare for his act. (It was only later we found out the fried chicken bucket was actually a valuable artwork).

When I got back, Maddy was already surrounded by half a dozen reporters. That would do – we didn't have too much time before the museum cottoned on. The others would just have to miss out. The *New York Times* guy was there, at least – I could hear him talking to Maddy, saying it was great the gallery was employing people so young. "In the New York art scene it's all ageing boomers like me, you know."

"Ladies and gentlemen," I announced. "M. le Coq is now ready for his close-up." They babbled excitedly and followed Maddy and I into the gallery.

"But where is Nussbaum?" I heard one of them murmuring. "One of the world's great art critics, and he lives here in Hobart."

"Nussbaum and le Coq aren't on speaking terms, I'm afraid," I said. That got them gossiping all right – an extra spicy rumour to include in their performance notes.

Once we were out of sight of the map girl (the journalists had declined to take maps; one of them had actually said "that's for the plebs"), I hurried them along.

"Faster, please," I urged. "M. le Coq is very regular in his bowel habits." That threw them a bit, and perhaps they already sensed this was to be an *explicit* piece of performance art.

We entered the barren gallery, where they were greeted by the sight of Aloysius Coot's hairy arse (I noted that he had picked up the empty chicken bucket to use as a receptacle, adding a further touch of his own to the artwork we had planned together). They lifted their cameras on cue and began clicking furiously as the first turd dropped in the bucket. I don't know what Coot had been eating, but it stank. Maddy and I backed out into the hallway, gasping for breath; the journalists seemed to positively revel in it, however.

Then, to our alarm, a staff member walked in to see what was going on. *Oh no, this is the end of our prank*, I thought, but to my amazement she merely nodded and walked out again, humming under her breath. To her, it seemed, the sight of someone taking a shit on a pedestal was no more unusual than, say, the vulture made from empty jelly packets in the foyer, or the used condom swastika down the hallway. Just the sort of thing you *should* see in a temple of art. And as Coot wiped his arse and left, refusing all autograph requests, I began to suspect that this in itself could actually impede the success of our alchemical experiment...

*   *   *

Unfortunately, I was right.

The papers all wrote positively of it as expected, but to my immense annoyance the *museum itself* actually went along with it – just like Nussbaum after we had spraypainted his house. And the Lafayette weren't even blustering – they actually assumed that Alphonse le Coq was a real artist, who had chosen not to tell them before staging his piece. After all, if the *media* were covering it, it must be genuine.

So we were forced to step in ourselves and begin the process of alchemical fermentation. We sent a press release to all the same newspapers *explaining* the prank, and signing it (for we needed a name that could be readily identified) as 'the Hungry Wolves of Van Diemen's Land'. (Van Diemen's Land being the old name for Tasmania, back in the days when it was a notorious British penal settlement).

But did they bite? No! Every single paper, to a man, *ignored* the press release. I don't know if it was out of embarrassment (to admit they'd been fooled), or a belief that the hoax statement *itself* was a hoax. In any case, we were forced (with extreme reluctance) to send it to the conservative publication *Parabola*.

Now, I don't really agree with the old Arab saying that "my enemy's enemy is my friend," but in this case our enemy's enemy could at least serve as a temporary ally. And sure enough, *Parabola*, after briefly interviewing us on the phone to verify our statement, ran the story with gusto, making it the next cover piece of their monthly magazine.

'Excremental Art: Our Fine Arts Institutions Exposed!', the headline screamed. Then followed ten pages of what I thought was mostly huffy-sounding wank about 'Frankfurt School degeneracy', 'cultural Marxism gone mad', 'dripping wet psychosis' and so on – but it got people *talking*, and that was the main thing. The conservatives (liberals, really) thought our stunt was the best thing since sliced bread. A pity for them when they found out we weren't exactly on their side – then they would throw us under the wheel, no doubt, joining forces with the same 'progressives' they were now attacking. For the time being, however, they thought we were kosher.

Following our article was a piece from an American guest writer about how Martin Luther King was actually a *conservative* (next month, no doubt, they would be claiming Che Guevara as one of their own). These people were obtuse all right. Since 1789 they had always been ten steps behind the 'progressive' faction, and after those ten steps they morphed into them – today's 'leftist' agenda was tomorrow's 'conservative' agenda (and thus the communist sympathiser King had really been a 'conservative' all along). In short, conservatism has *nothing* underlying it, nothing eternal – it is pure nihilism, and only a hypocrite would pretend otherwise. At least the leftists are more honest about their ultimate aims – many of them freely *admit* they want a globalised totalitarian society where everyone marches in lockstep, monitored at all times by the global State. Conservatives work towards this goal too, only they won't admit it, not even to themselves. And by refusing to provide a proper opposition to the Left they are *traitors*. It's not too strong a word.

Anyway, a 'culture war' was now raging throughout the blabbering classes of both 'left' and 'right', particularly in the illusory realm of the internet.

The sole leftist to take our side was a well-known 'laddish' comedian from Sydney, who hailed our prank as something akin to Duchamp sticking a moustache on the Mona Lisa. He was immediately shot down by voices on his own side: "Don't sanction their appalling ignorance." "Duchamp was a *legitimate* artist, these people are just teenage bogans!!!" (It's always amusing how self-professed leftists are concerned about the concept of 'legitimacy' when it suits their agenda to be so, ignoring it at all other times).

Well, lots of people were talking about us, as we had intended – but where were the intelligent people, the *perceptive* ones? Not spouting off on the internet, that was for sure. We felt certain they were out there, however, and that it was just a matter of time before they would contact us and form a *new creative elite*. The hour would produce the man.

But alchemy was a dangerous thing, and who knew what we had unleashed?

The media were already announcing a criminal investigation into the destruction of the fried chicken bucket (Coot had scrunched it up and tossed in into a bin on his way out), which, it now emerged, was worth over $50,000, and obtained only with great difficulty by the Lafayette, outbidding galleries in Los Angeles and Paris. Fifty grand for a paper bucket? Well, it was all about context, you see. The artist had deliberately arranged it on the pedestal (built especially for the purpose) as a statement of something-or-other.

Well, I was *glad* Coot had shat in it, and resolved never to pay the bill, even if it meant prison time.

These boomer cunts would soon see what their world of shallowness had unleashed – the Hungry Wolves of Van Diemen's Land!

4

MADDY

We were hoping for a big influx to our cause, but in the end we only got two. Quality over quantity was our watchword, however (oh how we despised the Reign of Quantity!), and the important thing was their energy and enthusiasm.

Dianne was a stay-at-home mum. Her boyfriend Mark was a philosophy postgraduate at the University of Tasmania, so he had a lot of conversations with Sean that went over my head. He hated the university, though; he called it a sterile wasteland full of talkers, and pretty much implied there were a lot of GLC-types there, mainly in the faculty.

Their child, baby Varg, was six months old and full of smiles. He was adorable, and intelligent-looking like his parents. Mark emphatically didn't want Baby Varg growing up to inhabit a world full of multicult-consumer zombies, and I think having a baby was what separated him from his fellow students...it made him think about important things like the future of society, while the rest only thought of their careers, or (in a few sad cases) had even been indoctrinated with the doctrine of globalism.

We were able to educate them a bit on how globalism worked, especially after our experience with the GLC. It was a smoke and mirrors thing ("Like the wizard of Oz," as Sean put it), with one public figure pronouncing that "Globalism is inevitable!", and everyone else taking up the mantra because, with all the smoke and mirrors in effect, *they couldn't envisage an alternative*. We explained that our main role was to smash the mirrors and unmask the wizard, and that we were currently doing this by means of outrageous pranks and stunts. Dianne and Mark were only too keen to join in, in any way they possibly could that didn't endanger the baby. We assured them we would arrange things so as to keep little Varg out of danger, and immediately set to work to dream up new pranks.

We began receiving our first death threats at this time, as a journalist had published the 'Alphonse le Coq' press release online, including our home phone number. Although these were nothing compared to the amount of threats and insults we would receive at a later date, it was still annoying to be woken up at 3am and have a conversation like this:

"Is that the *art vandals'* number?"

"No, it's the discerning critics' number."

"Oh bullshit. Don't lie to me, you filthy little *art vandals*.

I'll tell you this. You're going to die a miserable death. You will drown in your own blood, you vile philistine slut. And then we'll dig your corpse up and *kill it again*. JUST DIE, YOU CHEAP WHORE!"

"All right, see you later mate."

"Don't call me *mate*, I..." (hang up)

No, I wasn't scared of these sadistic authoritarian types, especially not with Sean at my side, but it did disturb me that anyone would take the time to be so petty, instead of actually learning from what we were trying to do.

It was around this time, too, that a pompous writer called Richard Kopf began attacking us in print, calling us "a moral cartoon for the millennial generation" and other rude things like that. We later found that he was intimately connected to various globo-currents, but at the time we only knew that he was angry with us for *showing things as they actually were*. His big trip was acting as a spokesman for the long-dead Irish convicts of old Van Diemen's Land, and we identified with that, for sure, because Sean had convict blood as well – but he was going about it the wrong way. Shouldn't the convicts be *attacking* the prison establishment, rather than identifying with the gaolers who had mentally enslaved them?

To be honest, we considered Tasmania's beginnings as a prison colony to be highly fortuitous for our project – a symbol that we would be helping people all across the world break out of a mental prison. Tassie was also once known as the Apple Isle, which we naturally identified with Avalon, the Isle of Apples of Celtic legend. And as for the *wolves* of Van Diemen's Land, well, this clearly referred to the extinct *Thylacinus cynocephalus*, or Tasmanian wolf – another victim of homogenisation and 'progress'.

In this regard, too, it was significant that around this time we had a chance meeting with an old acquaintance of Sean's. A short, stocky, snub-nosed-looking guy tapped him on the shoulder while we were standing looking at pictures of Europe in the window of a travel agent. Sean looked blank, then gave a flicker of recognition, and his eyes narrowed angrily.

"Well if it isn't 'Johnny Boong'," he snarled. "I wonder how tough you are when you're not with your *friends*. Maybe we can find out, and put your head through this window?" (Sean later explained that 'Johnny Boong' was one of a group who had bashed him in East Lynwood...but for now his old acquaintance seemed genuinely hurt).

"Fair go mate," he said. "That was a long time ago. I don't even hang with those guys anymore, and I'm not called Johnny Boong."

"Well, that's something."

"My real name's Troy Partridge...I changed it from Troy Johnson after my stepdad left. So what have you been up to?"

Sean looked at him warily, but said: "Conjuring. Magic tricks, aimed at changing public consciousness."

"Fuck, that's pretty heavy. I've been discovering my ancestral heritage." It was then that I noticed his t-shirt, which said 'Tasmanian Aboriginal Pride' above a picture of a clenched fist. Looking pointedly at this, Sean came right out and said:

"I hope it's not too rude, but given that you can't be more than one eighth aboriginal..."

"One sixteenth."

"...one sixteenth aboriginal...what makes you identify with *that* part of your heritage, more than, say, the other fifteen sixteenths?"

Troy scratched his jaw, and said: "Fair question. I do respect the other fifteen sixteenths, but, you know, I've always been known as 'the Abo' and 'the Boong', so that's the part I came to identify with. There's no full-blooded Tasmanian aboriginals left, as you probably know...our culture was almost completely destroyed by the British imperialists. So now we're trying to reconstruct it."

"And what would you say to someone of English stock who was trying to reconstruct *his* pre-imperialist culture, for instance?"

"What do you mean?"

"I mean, someone who was trying to look into the original cultural and spiritual forms of his people...the *indigenous* English culture and spirituality."

"How long ago was that?"

"A long time...over a millennium. But in some ways, it's like the blinking of an eye."

"Fuck man, that would be even harder than what *we're* trying to do."

"But you don't have any problem with it in principle?"

"Nah, why would I? Good luck with it."

"It's just that I get the feeling we're going to run into opposition on it. Some people of my acquaintance would probably say it's 'racist'."

Troy looked puzzled. "How can it be racist? You're not hating on other races?"

"No."

"Well, it's not racist then. No indigenous person I know would say it is."

"Well, it's not them I'm bothered about."

We went and sat in St. David's Park for a while, and Troy pulled a couple of longnecks of beer from his backpack and we shared them. He told Sean about some of their classmates from East Lynwood, and it appeared many of them had gone badly in the last few months...drugs, mental illness, abortion. Only 'Johnny Boong' with his inflated sense of racial pride had pulled through. I think that that, more than anything, determined us to try the 'way of the ancestors'. If it worked for him it could certainly work for us, and we needed all the strength we could get. We parted with him on friendly terms, and not long afterwards Sean said: "I think it's about time we called a press conference."

After discussing it with Mark and Dianne, however, we thought a video on the internet would spread our message more effectively. They, too, were interested in the pre-globalist English religion and its gods: Woden, Thunor, Tiw, Frige...but ironically, we had to use the writing of the globalist monk Bede to reconstruct them.

We made a video, wearing anarchist-style balaclavas, with a lush glade at Fern Tree as the backdrop. We spoke of our hopes and dreams, and why we were doing what we were doing. We shared our belief that Western societies were on a massively wrong course, and that much of the reason for this was a severance from the unconscious, both individual and collective, and from the gods, heroes and symbols of old. We spoke of how we were tentatively trying to reinhabit our ancestral English religion (remember that 'tentatively' when you hear the media bullshitters describing us as religious fanatics) in an attempt to reconnect with our true nature, with the One, with ultimate reality...

And we told how we were fighting a Kulturkampf against those who tried to block off access to this path, whether they called themselves leftists or conservatives.

We posted the video on the net, and within a few days it got a lot of positive responses in the comments section.

Then there was a curious attack on it in print by a feminist academic called Valma Grim, a descendent of one of Tasmania's oldest colonial families. After viewing the video, she had come to the strange conclusion that we were 'neo-Nazis' who had invented a 'fake religion'. Despite her delusions, the *Messenger* had given her half a page to air her ridiculous views...even more ridiculous in light of an article she herself had written in the *Messenger* just a few weeks earlier, praising a Chinese temple (built in Tasmanian colonial times by economic migrants who had come to mine gold), which she spoke of reverently as having a mysterious aura of the 'ancestral sacred'.

So, given that we ourselves were reconstructing the beliefs of our sacred ancestors, shouldn't she be praising us? Sean suspected it was because we were Anglo-Celtic rather than, say, Chinese...although her calling us 'Nazis' was apparently based on our rejection of both leftism and conservatism ("I know of another man who claimed to be 'beyond left and right'," she raved, "and *his* name was Adolf Hitler!")

When we researched this academic, we found it was rumoured that her family had committed appalling massacres of Aborigines in colonial times – and so it seemed that her own anti-white animus may have sprung from a *personal sense of guilt*, something like the 'original sin' of the Christian church.

We wrote a letter to the *Messenger* pointing out the inaccuracies of the column, and putting some hard questions to Valma Grim. Among others, we asked:

- How are we supposed to understand the racial 'Other' without understanding ourselves?

- If all ancestral cultures have value *except* those of white people, and if all cultures consequently have the right to existence and an identity *except* white people...then how are white people supposed to become 'mixed' all by their lonesome little selves?

We thought these were fair questions – but the *Messenger* refused to print them. We phoned the letters line to ask why our missive hadn't appeared, and the woman who answered was evasive. It was out of her hands, she said...a matter for the editor. Was there a number we could reach the latter on? No, there wasn't. He was incommunicado to the public, just in case he should be swayed.

So Grim could write half a page of lies against us, but we couldn't write a single word in our own defence. It was to be the first of many instances of duplicity by the minions of that vile little rag (which somehow managed to combine the worst elements of a right-wing tabloid with those of a left-wing broadsheet, in the same paper!). We thought of marching in there and nagging them to print it (like the curator of the Hobart Museum was wont to do), but Sean said that in our case they would probably just call the police.

Indeed, part of our problem, he felt, was that we *weren't* simple reactionaries like the museum man. Like Socrates, we posed difficult questions, and the establishment didn't like it.

Anyway, we were now ready for our next naughty prank.

A boomer-led 'multicultural' festival was happening in Hobbiton, and we decided to go as the Nowhere Men. The name served two purposes – it highlighted the absurdity of the 'cosmopolitan' identity (or lack of identity) that so many boomers subscribed to, but it also referred to the fact that we, as young Anglos, were not officially supposed to have any identity at all.

We showed up with a blank flag (made from calico), and drab, nondescript clothes we had found in op shop bargain bins. We were all dressed that way, even little Varg, and it looked quite comical. Boomers began to stare at us as we stood there with our calico flag, singing 'Nowhere Man' by the Beatles at the top of our lungs.

"We are *cosmopolitans!*" screamed Sean, and received warm smiles from the boomers around us. But then we started handing out flyers: copies of the letter in response to Valma Grim. Not many stopped to read it, but there were puzzled frowns from those who did. Perhaps we were sowing seeds of doubt with regard to the whole globalist enterprise, but I didn't have much hope in that direction. Instead, what we did was to stir up a hornets' nest.

We were getting ready to leave, and handed two of our last flyers to a couple of young people. One had a t-shirt with the words 'Born Against' written on it, while the other's contained a word that was strange to me at the time: '*Antifa*', followed by 'Melbourne Chapter'. They looked energetic and rebellious, so I thought they might prove open to our message. Fucking hell, was I ever wrong!

After they had gone some fifty metres, one of them must have actually read the flyer, because I saw them have an animated discussion, then turn back. They marched right up to Sean, who had handed the flyers to them, and screamed right in his face: "You fucking Nazi scum!"

Sean was somewhat taken aback. "I'm sorry?" he said.

"You're those fucking Van Diemen's Wolves. Don't deny it you snivelling little fascist turd!" I had to laugh at the description 'snivelling' as applied to Sean, and Mark and Dianne chuckled too, perhaps at the way the guy's eyes were popping out of their sockets. But now that I looked at this person closely, his face had something ever-so-slightly *wrong* about it, although not something I could exactly put into words.

"Don't you fucking *laugh* at me, you bigoted shitmuncher," he replied. "Go back to where you came from, you slimy inbred white trash fascist piece of shit..."

"My home's right here," said Sean, trying to keep his cool. "Unlike yourself," he added, looking pointedly at the fellow's 'Melbourne Antifa' shirt (we would later find out that 'Antifa' was short for 'anti-fascist', and that it was a worldwide, loosely-connected organisation with branches in most large Western cities; the state government's new subsidised airfares must have brought them down to Tassie).

"If you're referring to the article in the *Messenger* that falsely claims we're fascists..."

"I don't *need* the newspaper article, I can see from the piece of paper you handed us...your own words."

"Eh?"

Now the weedy one with the 'Born Against' t-shirt chimed in: "You're claiming an identity for yourselves based on white supremacy."

"Oh, what a crock of garbage," exclaimed Mark. "Where does it say that? Point to the words."

"It's the *general tone*," yelled the first one. "It's obvious." He had such a smug look on his face that I wanted to smack him.

Then Sean said: "It's obvious that you're a liar, just like Valma Grim. There's *nothing* in our worldview that implies 'white supremacy' as you put it. What we're trying to do is help our people to find their core nature. The last thing we want to do is lord it over other races or cultures. The only 'culture' we feel hostile towards is the cosmopolitan one, because it's fake. It's a mockery of true culture."

"Race and culture don't exist you moronic dickhead...science has *proved* it. It's a social construct, designed to promote the supremacy of massive bogan rednecks like *you*, you stupid shit." Was he trying to provoke a fight in order to get Sean arrested, or was he just a very rude little brat?

Then Mark said: "Okay, mate, you go on up the road to the Tasmanian Aboriginal Centre and tell them their identity is a lie, based on a social construct. I'm sure they'll be pleased to hear that."

"That's *different*," spluttered the brat.

"How?"

"They're an oppressed minority, not part of the dominant culture like you."

"Oh I see, so a culture is only real if held by a certain numerical amount of people, and as soon as that number exceeds, say, fifty percent, the culture suddenly becomes a *lie*, henceforth to be forbidden."

The two Antifa looked daggers at us. "Okay, you bogan shit," sneered Melbourne t-shirt. "If you want your white Anglo culture, then be my guest. Go wallow in your KFC and McDonalds and Miley Cyrus, and all that other fantastic white culture...and *go fuck yourselves* while you're at it!"

"If you'd actually listen to us," said Mark, "you'd realise what you're talking about is the cosmopolitan anti-culture. What *we're* doing is trying to get our people to take on an authentic culture..."

"*Your* people! The fact that you even say that *proves* you're a racist." Mark started to say something else, but he cut him off, saying: "No, I'm not arguing any more with Nazi white supremacist scum. *No free speech for fascists.*"

"No free speech for fascists!" echoed his friend.

"We'll be back," said the first one over his shoulder as they stalked off. I wondered what he meant by that. Why would they be back if they hated us so much? We were soon to find out...

An elderly lady who had witnessed the argument was just telling us that she thought the Antifa were "very rude", when we saw them coming towards us through the thinning crowd. There were nine or ten of them, all with similar punk or Antifa shirts (one of them said: 'RABM: Red and Anarchist Black Metal'), and haircuts ranging from dreadlocked to shaven. Two were female, although one of these could almost pass for male as she was big and ugly, with a shaved head. I instinctively targeted her as 'mine' in the brawl I knew was coming.

At least three were carrying makeshift weapons – one a plank torn from a picket fence by the look of it. I could see the rusty nails sticking out as they swarmed on us.

Mark turned to Dianne and motioned her to get baby Varg out of there. She disappeared at once and thankfully the Antifa didn't pursue her. They were upon us, and it was four of us against more than twice that many of them. They were armed, and furthermore had no conception of a fair fight. I'm just telling you so that you know what these capitalist-sponsored (we later found out) *thugs* were like. And what would you have done if you were in our shoes – turned the other cheek?

The butch bitch was one of three who went straight for Sean. I grabbed her by the hair and put my arm round her throat, freeing Sean up to deal with the others. I could see Mark and Coot grappling with other Antifa. Coot had a highly enthusiastic gleam in his eye – he was tasting battle at last. This was what he'd been waiting for the whole time he'd been working with us. Then Butch wriggled free from my grip, as people around us shrieked 'help!', 'call the police!' and things like that. And then she was on top of me, pummelling me and screaming 'Nazi whore!' at the top of her lungs. Then my anger truly kicked in, and I smashed her in the nose. She rolled off and slowly stood up, with her hand to her bloody nose, looking very wobbly indeed.

"You shouldn't have done that," she stammered. Then she yelled: "Fuck you, Nazi slut!" and limped away. I turned to look for the other female Antifa, but she must have fled too. Then I saw Coot on the ground, being kicked and beaten with sticks by three Antis. Sean and Mark had just finished fighting off their own antagonists, and rushed over to deal with the coward scum. I managed to help by grabbing a weapon from one of them, just as he was swinging it back to hit Coot. Then Sean smashed him in his ugly face and he turned and fled. The other pair must have realised they were now in a *two on two* situation versus Mark and Sean, and so ran like the pussies they were.

We knelt down to see if Coot was okay. He was unconscious, but breathing.

"I'll call an ambulance," said a nearby boomer, looking shocked. Luckily the ambulance got there very quickly, and after we helped load Coot in, we took off before the cops arrived.

We visited the hospital later that day, and to our relief Coot was in a stable condition and awake, although his speech was slurred. For now, though, we had to find Dianne and Varg. We went back to the flat near the Uni that she shared with Mark, but she wasn't there. Then, just as we were discussing what to do, in she came holding the sleeping baby.

She had taken refuge in a shop, but an Antifa fleeing from the fight had either followed her in there or found her by chance, and threatened her, despite the fact she was holding an infant.

"It was scary," she whispered.

The middle-aged shopkeeper had apparently stepped in to help her out. "Don't you realise this is a *Nazi?*" the Antifa had spluttered incredulously.

"I don't care if she's a Moonie or a Mormon...you will not threaten a woman in my shop, you despicable little mongrel! Let alone one with a baby..."

"It's a *fascist* baby!"

"Hold on...isn't that a Communist symbol on your t-shirt? Don't you know those bastards murdered fifty or a hundred million people in the last..."

"Oh, fuck you," the Antifa stormed out in a huff, tipping a rack of merchandise over as he did so. It was clear the man's shop was now a possible future target for them, and Dianne told him so.

"Not to worry, love. I'm not afraid of rats like that. Now, I'd better escort you out of here in case he's lurking in ambush." He left the shop unattended and walked her to the bus stop, even waiting until the bus was there. And so, with the help of a good citizen, Dianne had escaped the clutches of the horrendously misnamed 'Antifa', who in defiance of their moniker seemed to behave much like the vulgar, distorted image of classical fascism. So sad to see youthful energy harnessed in the cause of globalism...

*   *   *

Even though we had already experienced their perfidy at first hand, Sean and I could still scarcely believe it in the morning when we saw the *Messenger's* front page.

'Neo-Nazi Violence at Peaceful Harmony Festival' the headline screamed.

Apparently a gang of 'Neo-Nazis' (for so the *Messenger* asserted we were, despite having our phone number to confirm otherwise) known as the notorious 'Hungry Wolves of Van Diemen's Land' had attacked a peaceful group of 'anti-fascist young people,' who had been minding their own business in an innocent, youthful, lamblike way, and had not only *brutally beaten* them, but had also committed 'violence against women'! There was a close-up photo of the butch slag, with blood pissing out of her nose (had they gone straight to the *Messenger* office after our confrontation?).

There was *no mention whatsoever* of the fact that I, a fellow female, had been the one who had smacked that woman's nose. Anyone reading the *Messenger* article would have jumped to the conclusion that the Wolves were a bunch of brutal *male* thugs who went round bashing girls. These journalists were bigger liars than the Antifa themselves!

Starting around 10am, that day set a record for the amount of phoned death threats we received in a single day. Around twenty calls all up...and now the phone-threateners were all calling us 'Nazis' instead of 'bogan philistines' as before. Oh well, variety is the spice of life they say. Some of the calls were even international, judging from the foreign accents and long-distance echoes on the phone line.

To think that, in our innocence, we actually contacted the *Messenger* in an attempt to set things straight! After putting us on hold for some time, a staff writer interviewed Sean on the phone, assuring him that his version of events would be used to balance the story next day. But of course they didn't use it at all. Next day was more of the same, complete with a editorial denouncing 'the menace of National Socialism.' Apparently "the vicious ghost that Churchill and Roosevelt thought they had laid to rest for ever has *once more resurfaced*, in our far-flung corner of the former British Empire..."

Godfrey Nussbaum joined in, too, in his 'Arts Watch' column. He must have been waiting to have a crack at us ever since we'd been revealed as the true instigators of the prank on his house, because he wrote: "I, a proud Jew, have already been the victim of attempted terror by this vicious Nazi street gang! I had to install a new alarm system, and even buy a watchdog. I live in constant fear they will attack my house again..." Oh Godfrey, you're really not worth it...and we're in gaol now, so you can relax, you squalid little man.

After that we went to an internet cafe and tried to post a comment on the online version of the *Messenger*, giving our side of the story. We spent quite some time composing the comment, choosing our words carefully so as not to be unfair to anyone, not even the Antifa. There was nothing in the comment that could be regarded as offensive...and yet it was deleted within seconds for "not adhering to community standards." (Interestingly, one of our few supportive phone calls came from a lady who had witnessed the fight at the festival, and had also tried to clear our name with a comment on the *Messenger* online...she had the very same experience, with her comment also being censored for "not adhering to community standards." And later down the track, when our identities had already been revealed by the media, we ran into Troy Partridge, who told us he had phoned the *Messenger* to put in a good word for us and had been completely ignored, even after they had verbally assured him that his quotes would be included).

While we were there we did some research on 'Antifa', and found that the movement had originated in Germany, where it was sponsored by the federal government, allegedly to fight any resurgence of postwar Nazism at street level. In practice, however, the Antifa were hostile towards *all* forms of German identity (including things as innocuous as traditional Christmas markets), and despite the occasional bit of anti-capitalist rhetoric (in pursuit of a 'radical' image) they were clearly cheerleaders for the open-borders policies of international capitalism.

The Australian Antifa were much the same, only not officially sponsored by the government. We found an article, however, which linked them to Sheldon Albright – the same multi-billionaire financier who funded the GLC and many other globalist front groups, some of which had initiated coups against 'recalcitrant' governments in the Middle East and the former Soviet bloc (recalcitrant meaning 'only partly friendly to globalism', as opposed to 'completely friendly').

This Albright was clearly a dangerous individual – much more dangerous than his hired goons of Antifa. As to what motivated him we had no clue – maybe he was just a born arsehole? But although we didn't know why this rich old Nowhere Man wanted to erase all the world's unique cultures and religions in the name of global capitalism, it certainly broke our hearts to see the same outlook in people our own age. What had gone wrong in their lives to make them embrace pure evil?

*   *   *

We went to visit Coot in the hospital, bringing him some inspiring books to keep his courage up. He had been moved to a different room. Although fully conscious, he had some broken bones and internal injuries, so he couldn't leave his bed. That was okay, as there was a nurse he had the hots for, and was working up the courage to ask her to have sex with him in the hospital bed (ever the gentleman).

He told us something that shocked us, though. Two Antifa had located him in the hospital and had attempted to beat him up...but he had managed to pull the emergency alarm, and they had scurried away like cockroaches. After that the staff had moved him to a more secure room. Was there nothing these Antifa slimebags wouldn't stoop to?

*   *   *

Then the TV show 'Island Watch' contacted us. The weekly Tasmanian current affairs program wanted to give us a chance to get "our side of the story" across. Uh huh, we had heard that before!

"Why should we trust you when the other journalists have lied about us?" I asked. "The aim of our group is to change public consciousness...and how can we do that when the public are being lied to about the very things we represent?"

"I understand that," said the slightly drunken-sounding voice on the other end. "But you can trust us. We're more professional than some of the...politically motivated types in the print media. Our show is purely about issues that affect Tasmania, and even though you're a bit extreme, we still think you deserve a chance to put your point of view across. And if you're not really Nazis, as you claim you're not, then the public need to know that."

After some hesitation, we decided to trust him. Even if they lied about us, surely it couldn't make things worse than they already were. So we rocked up to the station around 2pm for an interview.

As we entered the building, we ran smack bang into two Antifa! Three burly security men were escorting them from the building. One spat at us on the way out. "No free speech for fascists! Hate speech is *not* free speech!" You know, the same sort of crap, but the security men were there to prevent an altercation.

"We know who sponsors you," I yelled after them as they left. "Sheldon Albright, the bigshot capitalist..." They snickered.

"Well good on him, you inbred fascist slut! At least we don't worship *Hitler*." I found this amusing, as I had barely given Hitler a single thought in my entire life.

118

We were ushered into the 'green room', where the show's producer (the same one who had phoned us) told me the Antifa had been invited to put their views across, and that we would now have the opportunity to do likewise. He said he would only interview two of us.

After consulting among ourselves we decided that Mark and Dianne would handle the interview. Dianne was the most feminine of us, and Mark was somewhat less grim-looking than Sean, and so would hopefully give the public more sympathy. I held the baby while they were daubed with make-up and led into the studio. Varg was very well behaved, perhaps because he could hear his mother's voice coming from the next room.

The interview went like this, from memory:

Interviewer: So, you're not neo-Nazis?

Dianne: No, definitely not. We don't trust centralised government of any description, fascist or otherwise.

Interviewer: You see yourselves more as pranksters.

Mark: Yeah, for sure.

Interviewer: You don't seem to like multiculturalism very much, though?

Mark: Well, mass immigration is something the baby boomers wanted, and something they got. Our generation has a different perspective. We think it's a form of cultural vandalism that dilutes, and ultimately destroys, *all* cultures, via the melting pot strategy. It's a tool of multinational capitalism, and its ultimate goal is to erase all organic group identities in pursuit of a unified planet of mindless robotic consumers.

Interviewer: And what direction would *you* like to see society take?

Mark: Well, not the one it's currently taking. We don't have all of the answers, but we're posing some pretty important questions.

Interviewer: So what was the cause of your fight with the anti-fascist youth group? They say that you provoked it...

Dianne: They're liars. *They* were the ones who started the violence, and they even threatened my six-month-old baby. I have a witness to prove it – the guy who runs the Smallworld Collectibles shop in town.

Interviewer: Thanks, we'll certainly contact him to confirm it if possible. Now, what happened after they attacked you?

Mark: We beat them and they ran, simple as that. (Laughs) There were twice as many of them and they *still* ran. Cowards.

Interviewer: You're not afraid of them?

Mark: No way. We'll *never* back down.

Interviewer: All right, well, that wraps it up. We've got what we needed, thanks very much.

Dianne: Wasn't it a bit short?

Interviewer: Well, we have to fit the story into a six-minute timeslot. But you made some pretty telling points, and hopefully the public will now have a better understanding of what you're all about.

Dianne: Okay, thanks for that.

We left, marginally more optimistic about the future. On the way home we saw Ade and Helen, and they crossed the road to avoid us...I had almost forgotten they existed.

*　　*　　*

The section, when it went to air three nights later, wasn't just cunningly edited...it wasn't just distorted...it was outright LIES. We watched it at Mark and Dianne's place, staggered in disbelief at the perfidy of the producer.

First, the Antifa savages came on, presented as victims from start to finish. There they were, walking along minding their own innocent business, when a gang of Nazis (who had come to disturb the peaceful multicult-harmony love-fest) began to yell vicious insults at them, perhaps because of their t-shirts (which only referred to social justice and equality for all). The meek Antifa ignored these insults, and so the Nazis set on them and began to beat them up. The Antifa were unarmed, of course...unlike the Nazis, who had knuckledusters and clubs.

Then the picture cut to Mark: "We beat them and they ran, simple as that," he laughed. The camera zoomed in on his chortling face, then cut to the interviewer (wearing different clothes to those in which he had actually interviewed us), who said: "So when you come across people whose opinions are different to yours, your first response is to bash them?"

"Yeah, for sure," nodded Mark.

"And the fact that the public doesn't approve of what you're doing, does that give you pause?"

"No way. We'll *never* back down."

Then the camera cut to Dianne, who to our utter amazement was presented as an Antifa! Her jaw dropped as she saw how her performance had been utilised:

Interviewer: So it was the Hungry Wolves of Van Diemen's Land who started the brawl?

Dianne: "*They* were the ones who started the violence, and they even threatened my six-month-old baby."

Then the man from Smallworld Collectibles detailed the incident that had occurred in his shop...but he didn't give a name to either group, so the audience was led to believe it was the Wolves who had attacked a young *Antifa* mother. It was amazing, incredible. Such brazen lies. *How could they get away with it?*

Then the camera cut to our old friend, the American chicken bucket artist, who gave a big sob story about how the Wolves had 'desecrated' one of his most passionately-wrought works of art ('wrought' being his word).

And to cap it off, there was a short interview with the novelist Richard Kopf, the same one who had called us a 'moral cartoon' in print.

"We don't need these types in Tasmania," Kopf frowned. "We need to move *forward* as a state, and these horrible reactionary elements are holding us back. Where is the love, I ask you...where is the love?"

It was ironic, this globalist dick calling *us* reactionaries, and especially so because his last book (*The Stolen Dignity of Ulrike Kühn*) had been about a woman falsely accused of terrorism...by the media! We vowed that the next target of our prank campaign would be him...

Then there followed on the TV such a string of mentally retarded *garbage* as I could scarcely begin to describe. It was a real eye-opener for Sean and I, because we didn't have a television, and neither of us had watched it much when growing up. But the shows of our childhood seemed positively mind-expanding compared to this stream of ads for vapid reality shows and excruciating gossip about airheaded celebrities.

Was this what people really *wanted*, a string of robotic pop stars bouncing up and down, always on the same spot, like monkeys? Hadn't the man in the street been *hypnotised* to desire this, if indeed he ever wanted it at all? It was the only possibility that our inborn optimism could accept.

But now the mass-hypnosis machine had persuaded the public that we were brutish thugs who attacked babies. Perhaps it was time to see the wizard (the wonderful wizard of Oz) and to unmask him...

*　　*　　*

The public hate campaign against us now began in earnest. Firstly, Mark was recognised by the university authorities and received notification in the mail that he would no longer be welcome at the University of Tasmania. That same day, however, a prominent academic, Professor Vickers (Mark's thesis supervisor), went public with his doubts about the official story, primarily because he recognised Dianne from the interview as Mark's *girlfriend*, not his victim. Then all hell broke loose. The vice-chancellor locked Professor Vickers out of his own lecture theatre, and there was talk about his taking 'early retirement'. A mob of students 'organised' to harass him (again, so sad to see the young doing the bidding of the washed-up boomers), and the airwaves were full of their plaintive, sonorous chants: "Say it loud and say it clear, fascists are not welcome here!" etc. etc.

122

All because the good professor had merely doubted the official story. (He was, of course, branded a 'conspiracy theorist' for questioning it in the first place.)

Then the guy from Smallworld Collectibles managed to contact us by phone (his call sneaking through between a foreign death threat and a local one), just before we took the phone off the hook for good. He was understandably outraged at the way the media scum had used him, twisting his words to mean the exact opposite. But although he sympathised with us, what could he do? Complain to the press council on the mainland, he supposed, but that would take ages, and the process was probably rigged.

Then someone published our home address online. We never found out who it was...perhaps someone in the housing department who had access to it, or someone else entirely. Perhaps the Antifa's master Sheldon Albright had done it. The point is, it happened, and the first we knew of it was when we were sitting having a beer together after the stress of the previous two days, and heard a murmur of voices.

"Light's on, must be home," someone yelled, and the fine hairs on the back of my neck stood up. Sean went to the window and peered out.

"Antifa," he growled. "Twenty or thirty of the slimy cunts."

"What do we do?"

"I'd be inclined to go down fighting...if it weren't for my love for you. I have to get you out of here..." There was banging at both doors of the unit, so they already had it surrounded.

"We'll *have* to go down fighting, my love," I said, trembling with fear, but determined to be brave and worthy of Sean.

"Hey fascists!" boomed an ugly, brutal, stupid voice outside the door.

"Haven't you forgotten the balcony?" Sean winked at me. "There's a clear leap to the next unit. We'll live to fight another day, c'mon..." He herded me onto the balcony, accompanied by a sound of breaking glass that signified the Antifa had gained entrance...then, remembering something, he lightning-bolted to the bedroom and returned with a backpack. "I nearly forgot, Coot left this here."

The bag contained a primitive harpoon, a throwing net, and some ping-pong balls with pins sticking out of them (the latter were our impecunious ninja's equivalent of shuriken).

We peered over the concrete edge of the balcony. It seemed a long gap to the next residence (home of our alcoholic neighbour), but theoretically I could jump it. In the gap between the units three Antifa were milling, and one looked up, as if sensing our dark presence.

"There they are!" he yelled to his crooked companions. "Up on the balcony!" Antifa were all through the flat by now, and Sean turned the key in the lock of the balcony door, shutting off access unless they managed to smash through it, which was certainly possible. More were filling the alley, and a chant went up: "*Bash the fash...bash the fash...bash the fash!*"

"Get ready to leap," Sean said. "It's our only chance." I nodded. He turned to the Antifa fascists below and addressed them, like Mishima on the balcony of the Tokyo military headquarters...and to similar hoots and jeers.

"We're *not* fascists," he yelled. "And I don't know why you persist in saying we are."

"Bull*shit*. Fascist scum!"

"Kill the Nazi pigs. Drag them out and *kill* them." I genuinely thought they would. In fact, I know they would have. It was surreal...

"What we *want*," persisted Sean, "is a return to an organic, poetic, spontaneous way of being, in harmony with the patterns of our unconscious, both individual and collective. We want to undo the mistakes of the past few generations."

"Fuck off, fash! Hail Bomber Harris! Burn Dresden again, burn it *again*..." These human insects clearly weren't going to listen. The ones inside were battering at the balcony door, buckling it out of its frame, while the ones below began to pelt Sean with pebbles from the garden. One hit him in the face and left a welt.

"All right, you asked for it," he snarled, gathering up Coot's throwing net and dropping it over the edge, which caused audible consternation below. Peeping over, we saw we had caught two of them in it, including the one with the tatty ginger mohawk who had yelled obscene comments about fire-bombing. Then Sean picked up the pin-studded ping-pong balls and began to pelt him with them. Mohawk screamed, but doubtless less than the victims of Dresden.

Then Sean flung the harpoon (really just a sharpened stick on a rope) at him, but unfortunately missed. Then he rose up onto the balcony (magnificently, I thought) and leapt down onto the next roof. He held out his arms to catch me, and so I gathered up my courage and did likewise, landing just next to him as he steadied me. Then we ran across the roof, down a drainpipe, over fences, through gardens and lanes, and across roads and streets...until we were out of earshot of the bestial, lunatic Antifa.

*　　*　　*

Now we were homeless again. Not wanting to burden the young parents Mark and Dianne, we tried Japhrey and Michelle's place, and they kindly let us sleep in their lounge until we could find somewhere else. (Coot had crashed there periodically before his hospitalisation, apparently). Michelle was easy-going, and as long as Japhrey had his studio to himself, he didn't care how crowded the *rest* of the flat was.

Next day we visited our student friends to tell them what had happened. On their laptop they wryly showed us the *Messenger* website. Our identities (Sean's and mine) had been completely revealed by the media. And some guy called Thomas was dominating the online comments, claiming he knew Sean from East Lynwood, and that he was "just a silly bogan, nothing more." ("To think that I once helped him out," Sean mused sadly). The theme was taken up by other of our middle-class detractors, and we were subsequently known as "the bogan Nazis" or occasionally as "the Nazi bogans." Funniest of all, a charity had been started to pay for the restoration of the artwork entitled 'Dawn of Reason' (but known to us as 'the cardboard bucket Coot had scrunched up after shitting in').

Now that we were supposed to be 'Nazis', the conservatives of *Parabola* were also denouncing us, just as expected. A prominent Sydney right-winger now screamed in print for our immediate arrest under terrorism laws.

And the day after that, the *Messenger* got hold of a scandalous story about *me*, in which I was held to be the chief instigator of a transphobic hate crime, namely my 'attack' on 'Rex'. I wondered at whose instigation (and how?) this story had been dug out. One could witness my own mother on the television, denouncing her daughter for the edification of the viewers...but I doubted she was the one who had first made it public.

*   *   *

Amidst all this chaos, we decided to play a prank on Richard Kopf while we still could, before we were gaoled, killed or worse. And it did in fact turn out to be our last prank, although not a particularly mirthful one.

I remember walking to Kopf's house in the melancholy twilight with Sean, Dianne, Mark and Varg. There was already something about it that felt like the end of an era. Two people sneered as they walked past us, and Sean later told me they were Olivia, his former beloved from East Lynwood, and her boyfriend Kim. Even in the twilight I could see that she looked like a cold-faced little tart.

We reached Kopf's house in West Hobbiton (everyone knew where it was) and posted our flyers all over his white picket fence, and the fences of his neighbours. They consisted of fake news headlines we had printed out: "Kopf Joins the Klan," "Kopf Revealed as Granny-Groper," "Kopf Robs a Dildo Shop," and things like that, just to let him know what it felt like to be misrepresented by the media. And then we left, heading back to town.

The Antifa were lurking near the entrance to the rivulet track, almost like they had been waiting for us. There were only six of them this time, but in the near-dark we didn't see them until they were almost on top of us. Their sneers turned to leers in the superconcentrated final mist of light.

"It's the fassscisssts," hissed one, stepping forward with a Gollum-like grimace. Sean's eyes were smouldering, ready to bash these grotesque creatures who only attacked in packs. Even six against one wouldn't be enough to save them, and they must have sensed it...because all six instinctively moved to surround Dianne.

"Hey, back off," she snarled. "Don't touch my *baby*." "It's a *fascist* baby," one snickered, closing in on her tightly. "Nothing to worry about."

Sean, Mark and I stepped in to kill them, but two of them were actually wrenching the baby from her arms, while the others formed a scrum around them, trying to block off access. Dianne was screaming. I gouged one of the Antis eyes from behind, and he let out a girlish squeal, but I couldn't get through the scrum, and nor could Sean and Mark.

"Go back to Melbourne you deranged *freaks*," Dianne screamed.

"*We're* at home anywhere," one of them yelled. "Anywhere there's fash like you who need a lesson..." Sean smashed him in the face...but it wasn't he who was trying to grab Varg, who was now bawling at the top of his lungs.

"Help," I screamed (who to, I don't know). The Antis sensed they were outnumbered (only six males against four of mixed gender, after all), and one of them yelled: "Let us go, or we'll hurt the baby. *I mean it...*"

Dianne screamed again, and suddenly, like a neon will-o'-the-wisp, the red and blue lights of a police car flashed smoothly around the corner. The Antis seemed to panic, pulling harder at Varg.

And then the beautiful baby's cries *suddenly ceased* as he flew with a sickening thud to the concrete with two Antis on top of him...Dianne let out a cry of such mournful intensity that even the scum must have realised they had gone too far.

All six bolted, melting instantly into the darkness of the rivulet track, while we knelt around the baby in disbelief.

"Call an ambulance," I screamed at the cops, who were moving oh-so-casually towards us. But baby Varg would never move again.

5

SEAN

We passed the point of no return that night. The nightmare of sitting in the police station, waiting to give statements, while Mark and Dianne were grilled in separate interview rooms, I remember it so very well, imagining I could still hear her despairing wails through the shuddering soundproofed walls.

To say the police were unhelpful is a grotesque understatement. To begin with, *Inspector Tippett* had been transferred to Hobart (which explained my sighting of Olivia earlier that evening, like a bad omen before the tragedy). He remembered my name from East Lynwood, and insisted on interrogating me personally. After a few cursory questions on the topic of the murdered baby, he passed straight to the real core of their investigation — the vandalised chicken bucket. How had we done it, he wanted to know...who had been the one to actually scrunch it up, and who had defecated in it? Could there have been anti-Semitism involved (the artist was half-Jewish apparently), making it a *hate crime?*

Needless to say, I laughed in his face. "Hooked any kids on drugs lately?" I sneered, and he lost control and smashed me in the solar plexus. He was enraged, for some reason...his subordinate, playing good cop, had to hold him back. He didn't entirely succeed, though, and I was struck several more times over the course of the next two hours, it being apparent that I wouldn't answer any questions other than those related to the *killing of a baby,* which they didn't seem terribly interested in. Being handcuffed, I couldn't fight back, but I did spit and snarl a lot.

Eventually they had to let me go, after warning me not to leave town any time soon. Maddy was waiting for me outside. She had been summonsed for a hate crime of her own (her defensive action against the transexual), and would have to face court early next month. It was clear they were desperately seeking evidence to charge me with something similar.

"They didn't even care about Dianne's baby," Maddy sobbed.

"I know," I said, comforting her as best I could. It was surreal, unbelievable. There was something so obviously *wrong* here.

We agreed there was no going back. We were certain to end up in detention, possibly in adult prison, and if that was so then we might as well give them something half decent to put us in there for. Accordingly I went hunting all over Hobart during the next couple of days for Antifa, with every weapon I could lay my hands on hidden under my coat. I admit my intention was to kill several of them in reprisal. But no one knew where they were, and I was forced to concede they had all skipped town.

We visited Mark and Dianne, but they were too upset to speak to us. Worst of all there was *nothing* in the media about the death of Varg...the *Messenger*, the TV, the radio, all alike were silent. There was plenty more about the chicken bucket, though, and its artistic significance, and more demonisation of Maddy, complete with a mugshot from the police station, so now she would be recognised on the street and her life was genuinely in danger...

Beneath that we noticed a story about a man who had been sentenced to two years in prison for defending himself with a walking stick against a home invader. The *Messenger* thought the sentence was a good thing, and said so in an editorial ("No one, barring the appointed police, has the right to take the law into their own hands...") The man had injured the burglar slightly when fighting him off, you see.

The burglar was also caught and given a suspended sentence, but the defender received two years of actual gaol time. An increasingly common story...but what caught Maddy's eye was the name of the magistrate. It was the same one who had sentenced Packo to only *eighteen months* for knifing an old man. As the legal counsel had told me at our first court appearance, self-defence was now considered a worse crime than an unprovoked attack. Those coward boomers again, trying to drag everyone down to their own level. I still remembered Ms. Green's words: self-defence was a "grotesque act of violence." Well, we would see about that. Someone was going to pay for what had happened to Dianne's baby. I thought of pursuing the Antifa to Melbourne and confronting them there, but for all I knew the ones who grabbed the baby might have been from a different city.

And then it hit me. No doubt you, dear reader, have seen it all along – but I swear it only hit me then, with full conscious force, who the real villains of this piece had been from start to finish...those lying, cancerous dogs of the mainstream media!

And they had vast segments of the populace in a puppet-trance, thinking their propagandistic simulacrum had something to do with reality!

Now it struck me fully – I could get partial revenge for the killing, while still carrying on the original mission of the Wolves, namely to wake the people up from their delusional sleep.

*   *   *

We didn't want to bother Mark and Dianne any further at a time like this, but decided to visit Coot in hospital to say farewell. He could walk limpingly now, and was almost ready for discharge, but was stunned when he learned what had happened to the baby. We told him we were embarking on our final mission, from which there might be no return. We had nothing to lose in terms of heavy gaol time: 'hate crimes', a concept unheard of until a few years ago, were now considered the worst crimes of all (although Orwell had predicted them somewhat with his notion of 'thoughtcrime').

As we told Coot this, he picked up a piece of paper from the small table beside his bed. It was a summons, served on him for a hate crime.

"Apparently one of the Antifa I hit before they knocked me out was a homosexual...not that I knew it at the time."

"Is he still around?"

"He was from Adelaide, the cop who served the summons told me. They'll probably fly him back down to testify."

"You're fucked, then."

"In the same boat as you."

"Maybe you should come with us."

"Wouldn't miss it."

"You know a bit about explosives, don't you?"

*　　*　　*

Nietzsche famously warned us to beware of those in whom the will to punish is strong, but this wasn't punishment it was education. After familiarising ourselves with the magistrate's face by attending a session in the public gallery (where Maddy attracted stares and scowls), we waited until he emerged from the court then followed him in a taxi from the nearby rank, tailing him to a fine old house in New Town.

We kicked the front door in, just like a real home invasion. What we failed to take into account, though, was that the hypocrite would own a handgun. That there was one rule for him and another for Joe Sixpack was predictable really, and why we didn't foresee it I can't for the life of me now work out.

Anyway, he swung the gun to his shoulder as he saw our grim faces drifting towards him in the hallway. We dived aside, panicking, and he missed, his bullet smashing plaster out of the wall instead of flesh from our bodies. Luckily my reflexes were on fire, and I was waiting around the corner of the passage to wrench the gun away as he stalked into view. I pulled it from his hands, but the hot barrel surprised me and I fumbled it to the carpet. He dived for it, and the three of us piled on top of him, determined to teach him some English common sense. His grey arrogant face was stretched tight as he screeched at us: "What the fuck do you *want?*"

I hissed back: "We want you to feel what it's like, the urge to defend yourself."

"*What?*"

"Why did you sentence that man to two years for doing what you just did yourself?" But if I had expected him to reason or reflect on his hypocrisy, I was sorely mistaken. He laughed in my face, completely at ease with his double standards. It was the accepted thing amongst a certain section of the judiciary now, and nothing, not even torture, would ever make him admit that it was wrong. He revelled in it, delighted in it...it was almost admirable.

Then he lunged for the gun, and Coot tussled with him. I don't know exactly what happened, but it ended with our magistrate taking a bullet in the leg. He screamed and writhed in agony. This man was incapable of learning anyway, so I told Maddy to phone an ambulance for him. There was nothing more that could be done here.

"Where's your car keys?" I yelled. He pulled them from his pocket and threw them at me, grimacing in pure hatred.

"You'll never get away with this, you puritanical little shits," he panted.

"We don't intend to," I growled, leaving the scene.

I opened his silver Mercedes and we screeched away. I could barely remember how to drive (having had only two lessons shortly before leaving East Lynwood), but the precision German car was so smooth to handle that I had a lot of fun trying. We headed towards the CBD via backstreets, sirens caterwauling in the hazy background.

We had ruled out mounting a *Wizard of Oz*-style attack on the television towers on top of Mt. Wellington, as they were so huge that we didn't even know if we *could* blow them up...and besides, satellite TV would still work. So instead we were concentrating on a more realistic target – the *Messenger* building, in an all-out assault. Now we had a gun it would be even easier.

We waited until midnight, when the morning edition was being prepared for print, then hammered on the front door like demons, until a security guard came.

"We want to see the editor," said Maddy.

"You're those...no, of course you can't see him!" I had little choice but to level the gun in his face.

"Take us to him *now*. No funny business or tricks."

He put his hands in the air, although I hadn't asked him to, and said: "All right, buddy, take it easy...I'll take you to him, okay?" It was just like a gangster film...

We went up two flights of stairs and along a darkling corridor, before arriving at a door marked 'Barry Smart (Editor).' The well-mannered security guard even knocked for us, but I spared him further formalities by turning the knob and marching to the desk where a thin bestubbled man in a pink business shirt was sitting. When he saw the gun he began to visibly quake.

"What do you want?" he stammered.

"We have some alterations for tomorrow's edition," I said. "You will carry them out as instructed, or boom-boom stick go bang-bang, and off goes your head." Maddy snickered. I waved the gun at the security guard, who appeared to be sneaking off: "Stay in range, thanks mister."

The editor muttered some cliche like "You won't get away with this," right before I pistol-whipped him and told him, with a dark purple bruise on his cheek and tears in his eyes, to lead us to the newsroom. Then I handed the gun to Coot (although I later regretted this) and told him to keep it trained on both of them, so Maddy and I could have our limbs free for various endeavours, while the semi-crippled Coot held our best weapon of war on the enemy.

We strode through the double doors of the newsroom like cowboys entering a saloon, and the force of the displaced air made the entire room, some dozen people, turn to look.

"All right folks, you can see that my comrade has a 9mm pistol pointed at the head of your esteemed editor and his minder...so stop what you're doing instantly and hands in the air, please. I won't say it again. Anyone who attempts to use a mobile phone or similar device will be severely punished. Gather over there." I pointed to an empty part of the room. "Stand in a line, with your hands on your heads, where I can see them." They obeyed silently, other than a whimpered "oh my God" from one of the female workers.

"Now, who's in charge of the print layout, or whatever that kind of thing is called? Tell me quickly." A bald, vulture-faced man raised his hand.

"I'm the Chief Design Editor," he said nervously. "If it's me you want, then let the others go."

"No chance of that. Now, I want you to delete every single page in the paper, except for the cover. I repeat, the whole newspaper should be blank...apart from a big banner headline that reads: 'WE, THE MASS MEDIA, ARE A PACK OF LYING TURDS.' No, change that to 'WE, THE MASS MEDIA, ARE A PACK OF LYING, VERMINOUS FILTH, WHO APPROVE OF KILLING BABIES.'" Nervous looks among the whole pack of them.

"Come, we understand that you're angry," said one, in a patronising boomer voice, "but..."

"Shut up," said Coot, and pointed the gun at him. He whimpered and puffed, eyes to the floor, looking like he needed to go to the toilet.

"Someone," I said crisply, "made an actual decision not to print the story about our friend's baby being killed by the corporate-sponsored Antifa thugs. So *who was it?*" Silence. Then another boomer in a pink shirt (it seemed that most of the males there were wearing them) said:

"The role of our newspaper is to uphold community standards." Can you believe it, there was a tone of offended dignity in his voice when he said it! This boomer was actually getting on his high horse with me...

"Community standards," I shouted. "Murder or manslaughter of an infant..."

"Yes, community standards," said a woman huffily. "We don't like you, or the things that you stand for. And why should we tarnish the reputation of anti-fascist young people just because of something that may have been a simple mistake?" It was incredible...even at gunpoint their arrogance couldn't be quenched. Would they ever let go, these grey turtle-faced creatures? Would their stranglehold on the Western world ever cease? I was beginning to think they were immortal. Maybe I would shoot one and find out...

But now they were debating among themselves, over technical details of the case, and the definition of community standards...as if we weren't even there! Coot was beginning to look nervous, and Maddy was shaking her head in disbelief.

"*Whose* community are you talking about?" I shouted. "There are others in the community, other than your kind and what you wrongly imagine others to be! Who consulted the community on the issue of mass immigration, to take one example? Hey, come to think of it, why don't we include a section in tomorrow's edition on how the 'socialists' of the GLC and Antifa are sponsored by a billionaire *capitalist* named Sheldon Albright, whose business concerns benefit immensely from an open borders policy? Don't you think that's something the community should be aware of?"

Now there were *very* nervous looks from the staff. The editor himself muttered: "You don't want to go there..."

"Yes, we do. Also in tomorrow's edition, we'll add a call for a genuine *community* debate, town by town and suburb by suburb, on issues of identity, globalism and mass immigration."

"You *don't* want to go there," he repeated, shaking his head sadly.

"Yes, we *do*. Now, who's the online editor?" One of them grudgingly put up his hand. "Log into your computer, and start a new article. It should be the first article anyone sees on the *Messenger* website." He did so, and I handed him the letter we had taken from the GLC (so long ago it seemed), signed by Albright. I had kept it in my wallet, one of the few things to survive our forced exodus from the flat. I then instructed him to scan it, and that the scan itself should be the body of the article. I also instructed him, very forcefully, to leave the comments section unmoderated...as even though few people would be logging on at this time of night, we planned to keep the siege up for as long as possible.

But already sirens were wailing, and a glance out the window from a darkened side room told me that the police and anti-terrorist squad were gathering outside. Someone must have phoned them from within the building. Oh well, they would have to bear with us. Several phones began to ring, including mobiles, but I instructed the hostages to ignore them.

Then it occurred to me that the scan alone might be a bit obscure for most readers, so I added an explanatory paragraph about how our 'left-wing' enemies (including the ones who were openly trying to remould Tasmania in their own image) were actually bankrolled by big business. Not to mention the irony of 'anti-racists' being sponsored by Sheldon Albright, a confirmed Zionist who had given millions to the racial-based regime in Israel. I didn't know if the sleeping masses would care, but I wrote it anyway. I could hear someone jabbering on a megaphone outside, something about having the building surrounded, but I shut it out.

"Shouldn't we add something else?" said Maddy. "A memorial to our little murdered comrade?"

"Yes, for sure. You," I motioned to one of the senior journalists. "Type as I dictate. An epitaph for the potential in the world that you've crushed."

"That's not fair, you can't blame..." began a female reporter, but Maddy screamed and smacked her hard in the face, stunning her to silence.

"Hey, you can't do that," snorted another, with a condescending frown on his white-browed head. Even at gunpoint they felt they had a divine right to lecture us. Like I said, it was almost admirable in a way, but I fear the earth grew tired of it.

"Pistol whip the next one who speaks out of turn," I instructed Coot, and he nodded. We were getting things done now. The din of the phones, ringing nonstop, made me tense and intolerant. I spent the next fifteen minutes dictating an obituary for little Varg, with some vicious barbs directed at the journalists and senior police who had conspired to cover up the crime. Then I checked that he had rendered it properly, edited a couple of typos, and put it up.

There were more noises outside, and I thought perhaps the time was ripe to pick up a phone. What do you know, it was my old friend Inspector Tippett...hardly the best person to carry out a siege negotiation I would have thought, but that was Tasmania for you. I told him to go fuck himself, and hung up. Then I looked up some live news sites online, and sure enough the story had been picked up all around the world. *Live Media Siege!* Predictably they were slanting it as negatively as possible, and one American news host was praying for the safety of the 'brave Aussie journalists'.

The bonus, though, was that the *Messenger* website was getting a lot of hits, and one mainstream outlet even mentioned the murder of baby Varg as a possible(!) source of our grievances. There was *no* mention of Albright, however. I guessed the globalists would have no hesitation jettisoning their Antifa shock troops if need be (the revolution eats its own!), but you would literally have to kill them before they would betray one of the inner circle. Indeed, I clicked back onto the *Messenger* website and found that while the baby Varg article was still there, the Albright one had completely disappeared.

"What perfidy is this!?" I roared. But then I realised that no one in the newsroom could have done it. Maddy, looking over my shoulder and seeing what had happened, said: "It must have been hacked from outside." The pink-shirted editor started to say something, but Coot pistol-whipped him and (as I later learned) broke his jaw.

Then a young female hostage put her hand up, shyly. A tag identified her as Anita, cadet journalist. She only looked about nineteen, but it wasn't just her age that made her seem out of place...she also had an honest face. After being given permission to speak, she said: "I could help you type the article up again." There was a hopeful note in her voice, and I realised suddenly that the poor sweet creature had Stockholm syndrome!

I didn't have much time to reflect on this fascinating phenomenon, however, before the lights went out. Someone had cut the power from outside, and now the room was lighted only by the glow of computer screens (laptops, with reserve batteries). And then the doors were kicked in, and strong light flooded our retinas.

"Put your hands up," screamed the special weapons operatives, who were sufficiently good at their jobs for us not to have heard them coming upstairs. Their machine-pistols were trained on us, and it seemed our only choices were to surrender or go out in a blaze of glory.

Looking at Maddy, I quickly opted for the former, as I knew she would follow me, and I couldn't stand to think of her fair body riddled with bullets. She slowly put her hands up too.

But Coot didn't.

He chose immortality, raising his weapon in defiance. I heard that his body had to be identified from dental records. The sight of my comrade's death filled me such all-encompassing rage, that I actually changed my mind and resolved to die myself if I could take just one of them with me in vengeance...but it was too late, and I was knocked to the floor and pinioned, then handcuffed and punched several times in the stomach.

Our rebellion was over, and what had it achieved? At the time it felt like nothing...

*   *   *

I will gloss over the terrible treatment I received during interrogation. Needless to say I am allowed no contact with my beloved Maddy, but a silver cord connects us forever, no matter how far apart we may be in physical space.

They put me in the adult prison, naturally. My first act there was to kill Packo with an iron bar in the weights room; after that I was moved to solitary, where I remain at present. That's fine by me, as the general population is apparently none too fond of 'terrorists'...and such the lying media are once again calling us. Thanks to the 'Left' we are here in the first place; thanks to the 'Right' they will test new vaccines on us, and never let us out.

With my ridiculous 'trial' approaching I have been forced to visit Dr. Halvorsen, a cynical and jaded psychiatrist. And as I am desperate not to be classified insane and thereby pumped full of drugs, I have agreed to write this memoir. Maddy is writing one too, Halvorsen informs me. She is loyal and will never betray me, and my only wish is to be buried next to her when I die...

I must thank the shrink for wrangling it so that Japhrey was allowed to visit, and to show me the final painting in his now completed series. I saw it, that black rock, glistening and wet. The pyramidal certitude, obsidian finality. The return to pure Form. It haunts me still.

As for Coot, he was given a pauper's grave...but his real monument is his deeds, especially the way he pulled himself up from a self-destructive lifestyle into noble action and a hero's death.

That, too, haunts me still.

*　　*　　*

The night I killed Packo I had a terrible dream. A hideous female corpse was floating towards me through a closed window. Calling itself 'Bonna', the corpse kept insisting that *it* was the real rebel, the real iconoclast. Its face had the same grim, sickly look I had observed on USA establishment figures, and I believe that it was the baby boomer generation incarnate...utterly enslaved to globalism, yet still desperately wanting to be seen as 'edgy' and 'rebellious'.

But now news has reached me, via Halvorsen, of the Wandervögel-like movement called the *Wolves of Joy*, springing up around the world, and inspired by the Hungry Wolves of Van Diemen's Land. Anita, the former cadet journalist, has told whoever will listen our real story, and the way the media covered it up...and it turns out that people are believing her. I guess too many have had similar experiences of their own for them *not* to believe it. So even though I never replied to her in the flesh, Anita is now our greatest comrade. Yes, Stockholm syndrome is certainly an interesting phenomenon...women clearly respect force and action, despite what the feminists say.

But the Wolves of Joy are more *positive* in outlook than we ever were. Their spontaneous acts are not attacks on the present system; instead, they are building a new one in its very ruins. They speak the language of the birds, and so the authorities hate them, regardless of their approach…but how quickly they are spreading!

And they don't talk, they *do*. One could say the religion of the Wolves of Joy is 'positive action,' forging, through symbols, a new and better Zeitgeist…

The Wheel turns!

AFTERWORD

by Dr. Michael Halvorsen

Now that the trials are over, the reader will perhaps join me in expressing puzzlement over many of the contradictions embedded in the preceding narrative; the inconsistent usage of the political markers 'left' and 'right', for instance, even down to capitalisation; or the strange insistence on the word 'transcendent'. I believe Kant defined the latter as 'beyond the possibility of human knowledge', but I'm not at all sure what the Wolves mean by it.

And again, simplistically attacking an entire generation, yet simultaneously appropriating some of that generation's most revered cultural icons – Tolkien, Hermann Hesse, the Beatles – yes, we boomers worshipped at the altar of those artists in the 1960s and 70s, though some of us may have forgotten it.

I personally find Sean, though likeable in some ways, to be extremely arrogant, almost to the point of megalomania. But what would I know? For I am merely one of the hated boomers.

Others may, more charitably, describe the Wolves as simple idealists. One can read, for instance, in the preceding pages how Sean, while still a child, found the real world didn't mesh with his fantasies of 'warriors' and 'transcendence'; just as the beautiful Olivia Tippett, at a later date, didn't mesh with his ideal of femininity (an ideal that could be best described as 'complete and utter loyalty'); but the less physically attractive Madeleine *did*, because she understood the ideal.

Sean dismisses me, in his own words, as a jaded cynic, and perhaps he is right. But I would remind him of Mencken's classic definition of an idealist: "one who, on noticing that a rose smells better than a cabbage, concludes that it will also make better soup…"

On the other hand, I find the Wolves' criticisms of conservatism fascinating, and cogent. I am professionally acquainted with Sean's father (who like Madeleine's mother publicly disavowed his child during the trial), and believe him to be a cretin.

But how far does Sean's hatred of globalism, for instance, stem from a merely *personal* dislike of ageing leftist battle-axes like Green, Bannock and Lindley, embodied finally in the hideous dream-apparition he calls 'Bonna'? (He also told me of another dream, in which his future self was busy denouncing its own youthful acts of rebellion. Sean argued back with his future self, shouting: "Even *you're* against me, you decrepit old cunt!" I didn't know whether to laugh or cry.)

Any sympathy I do have for the Wolves fails to encompass their acts of violence: Sean's slaying of 'Packo', the assault on a public magistrate, the treatment of Angela Russell-Smythe (hypocritical as she was), or the robbing of 'rich mainland boomers'. Yes, I do understand that youth unemployment is high, and yes, it *was* my generation that offshored the jobs...but surely there has to be a better response?

Regarding the Wolves' negative approach to mass immigration, well, at the start of his memoir, Sean expressed a desire for mental patients to run free in the streets. He is clearly not adverse to danger (to put it mildly), so simple xenophobia can be ruled out as a motivating factor. The late Aloysius Coot was obsessed with Japanese ninjas. But were their stated motives for opposing cosmopolitanism also *valid* ones? Does the mass immigration 'melting pot' really mean there is *less* diversity in the world? The reader must make up his own mind...

In any case, their trial was a farce, and even those hostile to the Wolves have voiced suspicions that the verdict and sentences were preordained. Sean and Madeleine were not allowed to testify, and their memoirs were declared inadmissible as evidence. I don't believe that such severe sentences (life without the possibility of parole, in both cases) would have been given to the rebels of the 1960s! The response is inappropriate, and avoids addressing a fundamental issue: namely, how to deal with the growing numbers of alienated young people who couldn't give a fig for the values of 1968.

As for Mark and Dianne, they, too, are now in custody, awaiting trial for 'belonging to a terrorist outfit' or somesuch. I myself have been visited by soft-spoken bureaucrats with federal badges, who warned me in the strongest possible terms against publishing these memoirs. Well, I will publish and be damned. Australia is still a liberal democracy, at least in theory.

I visited Mark for the first time yesterday, and found him to be a well-mannered and highly educated young man, thoroughly familiar with European cultural figures like Guénon, Éliade, Spengler and Schmitt. Yet this cultured youth expressed a barbaric desire not only to murder members of the Antifa cult (described in these pages), but also to spit on their mutilated corpses.

I agree, for my own part, that the Antifa are deeply fraudulent, and that the media's characterisation of the Wolves as 'fascist' is sheer bosh. Pundits like Valma Grim have inferred that anti-Semitism played a role in the Wolves' outlook, as with some others who claim to be anti-globalist or anti-cosmopolitan. I will only say I have never known them to make *overtly* anti-Semitic remarks (their tirades against the "filthy rich Zionist pigfucker" Sheldon Albright are neither here nor there), and I believe we must take their stated motives at face value in this regard.

But a question Mark put to me is worth repeating. It was this: "Why can't those who support globalism for idealistic reasons realise that bigwigs like Albright are pushing it purely as a means of gaining *power*, and that the only thing 'global governance' will achieve is putting more heads in a single basket for these very wielders of power to cut off?"

I was unclear on how to respond to this. If Mark is right, then no one of a liberal persuasion should be an internationalist; and that is a disturbing thought. But when future ages judge us, it may be that the things we think so terribly 'moral' now are seen in a different light entirely...

I sometimes feel a strange desire, a wish that Sean and Madeleine had gone ahead with their original plan of taking out the transmission towers on top of Mt. Wellington. I can't help thinking that a year without the idiot box might have done Tasmania good.

But what is happening when I succumb to this desire?

And why do I shudder when I hear the words 'Wolves of Joy'?

The Heretic Emperor

CONTENTS

PREFACE

To penetrate the mystery that was Maximillian Scarlotti, we have been forced to draw testimony from a wide disharmony of sources. After absorbing these discrepit portrayals, the reader will be better positioned to understand how disaster unfolded. Those who have ears, let them hear.

For we *Weltverbesserer* (or 'globalists' as our enemies like to call us) the lesson must be learnt and learnt well if our project is to blossom again, no matter in what far future. For although we lost a mighty battle, the war goes on and on.

Even so, two things have of late changed the battlefield beyond recognition, the first being the Grey Death. The other, of course, was the strange life of our even stranger adversary, Maxi Scarlotti – the one who managed to pull the rug from under us when we were in a seemingly unassailable position – something that must never be allowed to happen again.

The most revealing statement we possess from the hand of Maxi himself is a written testimony from his early years – the first document presented in this portfolio. From thence, other voices will take up the tale.

\- Elmer J. Cohen
(former) Special Advisor to the
(former) Unicursal Curia

1

THE TESTIMONY OF
MAXIMILLIAN SCARLOTTI

I am leaving tomorrow, so I wish to put my thoughts in order. It seems to start with the dream. While I have had many recurring dreams since early childhood (like that of the empty Sears building in Chicago full of cobwebs in the moonlight, now a dangerous wreck), the one that came to me three times of late at Sterns is markedly different, due chiefly to its visceral intensity. On waking each time, I *felt* the strips of flesh under my fingernails – my own flesh.

In this dream I am a child of six or seven, but strong, almost as strong as a man already. And I am springing at a warrior twice my height – a tall German.

I am leaping, attempting to kill him. The scene is a castle where he has imprisoned me, and while the prison is a luxurious one, I hate him for it. I try to tear his flesh, but he beats me off with ease – so I turn on myself, ripping at clothes and skin with sharp little fingernails, gouging red and jagged stripes into my chest. Some of the onlookers are shocked, but for others it merely confirms the rumours, for it is whispered that I am the son of a butcher or a demon...that my birth was public, like that of Antichrist. Some say I am the Antichrist, but I don't believe it.

Then, I somehow know *that later the same year this tall warrior will already be gone to his long home – cut down at a place where Hannibal once decimated the armies of Rome many centuries ago. For some reason, this strikes me as profoundly significant.*

Then I awake, clawing at my chest. I feel the deep gouges in my flesh, but this is illusory, as my nails are perfectly blunt.

It was this *dream* that first encouraged me to explore outside the confines of Sterns, making a solo voyage into the African darkness that is darker yet by day. There had been

nothing technically impeding me from doing so, for at Sterns, a blind eye is traditionally turned to students who feel the urge to sneak out on surreptitious weekend missions, taking only a handgun for protection, in order to observe what the school authorities call 'unredeemed humanity' – Homo sapiens bereft of the blessings of the World State – but it had never interested me before; so here I was, doing it for the first time, two months before graduation.

The nearby market town, Masongo, is the centre of a lively region near the the edge of the Kenyan highlands. Despite the thin air, a thick and macabre menace permeates the atmosphere of the town, rolling down its grenadine, garbage-strewn streets, and forming a sinister cloud in the centre – the marketplace, scene of violence as often as commerce.

On the occasion of my first visit I was witness to the spectacle of a small truck, creaking as it wobbled beneath an enormous pile of garbage, crashing, as if in slow motion, into a tree stump on which stood a hatchet-faced baboon.

The chained yellow monkey, buried under such a vast tract of refuse, could scarcely have survived – it must surely have suffocated under the avalanche of filthy plastic bags in the time that its owner spent screeching and booming at the truck driver, while his woman looked on from across her ugali pot.

Then, two mottled black urchins attempted to pick my pockets as I watched the conflict unfold and almost made away with my precious handgun...and while fending them off, I noticed something damnedly strange: a white man was staring at me. An old white man with a long beard, who clearly had nothing to do with Sterns. Indeed, his steely blue-grey eyes were like nothing I had seen on this planet before, and I couldn't meet that winnowing glance for long...

But when I looked again, he was gone.

Then a brawl flared out across the marketplace, and a lynch mob began to coalesce, with the aim of stringing up the hapless baboon-killer, so I left the stench of 'unredeemed humanity' for the more civilised surroundings of Sterns.

On returning, after the usual infection check pertaining to such expeditions, I headed to the television room to unwind. A spell of passive voyeurism would soon help me to forget the *real* Africa.

And there, just outside the door, standing with folded arms, was Tegg. A quiet, dreamlike girl so utterly different from the other students that I still have no idea how on earth she ended up there. In the nearly two years since our mutual arrival at Sterns, I had scarcely given a thought to her sweetly freckled face (like that of a highly intelligent yet timid marsupial mouse), but now something happened – she *looked* at me. It was a look that signified something, I knew not what...which made it the second significant glance I had received that day.

I smiled frigidly back, not wanting to betray the sudden upsurge of feeling in its pristine private nest (where I naturally expected it would stay), and she bit her lip as if working up the courage to speak – but as I couldn't bring myself to slow my steps (O utter fool!) and, as no speech was forthcoming, my locomotion carried me cruelly onwards, into the darkened opium den of the television chamber, where a dozen students stared fascinated at the news, which showed footage of mass demonstrations now taking place across Europe.

"Fresh protests yesterday against the Archetype in Hannover and in Mainz," intoned the reader, over footage of frenzied parades where dreadlocked Antifa mixed with sharply dressed yuppie careerists, all of them screeching "*Smash the Archetype! Smash the Archetype!*"

The kids in the TV room were grinning excitedly and saying "This is *our* work!", high-fiving each other and so forth. And I should have been part of it too, but something in me felt cold. I returned to the corridor...but Tegg had gone. In her place, now walking rapidly towards me, was Tricia Philips, my affianced. Normally Tricia's perfect, blandly symmetrical face would have put my doubts at ease, but today it had the opposite effect, thrusting my nerves into overdrive. It felt as if her visage was sucking out all my remaining calm and using it to feather her own enervation – just a cosmetic layer, of course, as there wasn't a bone of doubt in her.

"Hey, the sex room's free if you want to," she breathed, with a half-smothered yawn. At eighteen, sex had already become something mechanical and joyless for her.

The sex room at Sterns is a sterile, comfortable chamber with controlled lighting, filled with various dispensers of prophylactic and lubricative substances, birth control manuals (as if we could forgot the constant lectures!) and so forth. Senior students, even faggots, are encouraged to form heterosexual 'partnerships' to further their career ambitions among the unenlightened – nothing to do with love, of course (not that love is forbidden, just no one at Sterns believes in it).

Anyhow, Tricia is something of a traditionalist, that is to say, one who favours retaining the *form* of open marriage for strategic reasons – as against the faction who think its usefulness is played out. But the thought of her lying naked on a rubber-coated mattress beneath the Warmth Lanterns, her genitals coated in some sterile, factory-flavoured substance, making small talk about our upcoming final exams as I tupped her, filled me with a vicious sunburst of claustrophobic quease.

"I'm not in the mood," I stammered.

"That's fine, Maxi," she said. "Maybe later...or we could listen to the Storyteller instead."

"Okay," I agreed, relieved. It wasn't like Tricia to suggest the Storyteller, who held court here of Sundays like a blind poet of yore (not that he actually *was* blind, but he gave that impression for some reason)...in fact she had never shown the slightest bit of interest in him before, but end-of-year madness was upon us all it seemed, even stolid Tricia. And as we were walking down the corridor holding formulaic hands, she asked what I had been up to.

"I went out into Africa, alone," I murmured.

"Oh, wow. I still remember the time *I* went. Late last year, with Seth and Jemma. It *stank*. Never again! Interesting place, though."

Tricia and I had been an 'item' since January, and indeed, as star pupils of our year it had always been more or less expected that we would form an 'alliance with benefits', so to speak, and that we were destined for big things – but now, as we entered the Storyteller's chamber, I suddenly felt very small and uncertain.

The talker was there, telling his audience of three (now five) a horror story – at least that's what I think it was supposed to be. His dark eyes sparkled in the glow of the brazier as we sat in the silken darkness listening to his recitation of an epic about the war and suffering caused by 'Kshatriyan aristocrats', who as our teachers never ceased to remind us brutally governed the world in days gone by, and "that's why we're in the mess we're in now," etc. etc. But the Kshatriyas weren't wrong to want order, they assured us – it was simply the wrong *kind* of order. They were an elite who brought suffering as well as greatness.

"Our goal is a world completely *devoid* of suffering," the Storyteller reminded us.

"But why, then," spoke a voice from the shadows, "does Mr. Snow *[The PE and martial arts teacher at Sterns – E.J.C.]* make us *suffer* so?" There were chortles. The voice belonged to Bryn, something of a class clown. Back in first year, he had been considered somewhat suspect due to his obsession with Hermann Hesse's 'glass bead game' – something he vocally intended recreating. Hesse, of course, is now seen as a 'proto-fascist' (despite his pacifist beliefs) by dominant taste setters.

But the teachers must have seen *something* in Bryn, for they kept him at the school despite his raving. And their foresight proved correct, for in second year Bryn had become considerably more orthodox. Now the other students could relax and laugh at his jokes, because he no longer mentioned the insufferable German romantic. And the Storyteller, too, politely chuckled at Bryn's remark.

"Mr. Snow teaches you pain," he said, "so that others won't be able to. We must be *strong* if we are to eliminate strength, and suffering along with it..."

And so here it was that my own thoughts began to coalesce.

I was already beginning to feel that, at Sterns, the atmosphere of an idealist project was a superficial one.

Not only that, but deep down I was beginning to sense it was the *wrong* idealist project.

*   *   *

Next Saturday, I went back to the township. All was as before, and the mess was such that you couldn't tell there had been a riot and a lynching. To my surprise, a strange black *gamin fee* approached and beckoned me to follow him: "Mistah Kurtz, he want see you now," he whispered, and I laughed out loud in spite of myself.

I followed him on what turned out to be a ten mile trek through the countryside. There were no adventures on the way, despite my apprehension of lions...or worse, an armed gang of the kind that occasionally raided from across the Somalian border. There were only the vultures, staring mournfully from baobab trees...and then when we finally turned off the dusty track, walking across grasslands for the final mile, a serval cat grinning at us from its shelter in a hollow log. Then night emerged, swiftly and brutally, all becoming a blur except for the cave ahead, a silver spray of glowworms irradiating its mouth in the thickening dark. I shuddered, wondering if the old man was home (for I had known from the first, of course, where I was going). The *gamin* turned away, plodding emotionlessly back the way he'd come, and so I stood alone before the dark gate to mystery. Two Anglo-Nubian goats paced impassively in a nearby enclosure – the old man's source of milk, no doubt. How did he guard them from predators, I wondered idly.

"Well, are you coming in or not?" The deep-crusted English-accented voice boomed out at me from another plane of being. I shivered and made my way into the cave, ducking to avoid the hanging rock at the entrance. His eyes were glittering in the near-dark of the atrium, lit only by a flickering glow from a chamber further back. Into the latter he led me, and we sat before an open fire in the middle of the craggy cavern. The cave smoked, although a chimney hole of sorts in the roof provided minimal ventilation.

"I won't beat around the bush," he growled. "I have a gift for sensing past lives of others. And as I was wandering the world, rather close to one of those indoctrination centres where future evil is trained and directed, I suddenly sensed the presence of *greatness*. Of a powerful spirit from the past. I don't know *which* spirit, but a great one. And so I nested in the area, hoping for this reincarnation to show itself. And when I saw you in the market, I instantly knew it was you. So overwhelmed was I by the feeling of world-historical greatness that I withdrew in shock.

"But it didn't take me long to recover my senses, after which I set a few of the local urchins to watch for your reappearance...for, with my persona, it was easy to make them fear me, the powerful 'white warlock', and they obeyed on pain of death. They think nothing of a ten mile trek through the bush, either. I could sense your presence for nearly half an hour before you finally arrived, you know."

I was taken aback at all this, yet unsurprised. *There were the dreams.* But I said nothing of these. Instead, I asked what he actually wanted, and he calmly smiled.

"To set you on the right track. To free you from the grip of evil. I know all about that *institution* you're embroiled at." Rapidly, with hypnotic voice, he began to expound his doctrine of *esoteric ethnopluralism*, talking of fractals, of hundred-armed swastikas and thousand-branched candelabras.

And I listened in the glow of the moth-spangled firelight, taking it all in. I will remember it until my dying day.

"Evolution springs from a silent centre," he intoned. "From the unconscious of God. It is the duty of our Order to help that centre grow into a multifaceted labyrinth."

In spite of myself, I was thrilled that he had said *our* Order...that *I* was included in such a grand and secretive project. Enrolment at Sterns was supposed to make me part of an elite, but it had always felt hollow – and here, now, finally, was a *real* elite, one I could be proud to fight for...no matter that no normal person, when gazing on my corpse, would even know I had belonged to it!

"And so, needless to say," he continued, "for those of us who want to *increase* the diversity in the universe, the doctrine of globalism is anathema, the ultimate evil. The multicultural 'melting pot' destroys the earth's myriad of unique cultures by depriving them of authority, assimilating them to the global fast-food anti-culture..."

I had heard this argument before, of course, from a member of the cult known as Wolves of Joy (I think everyone now knows of *them*), and had dismissed it with a counterargument of my own. But somehow it was different hearing it in a firelit cave in the African bush, with the mad laughter of hyenas in the background like nocturnal spirits of unrest.

Nevertheless, determined to show the old man that I had thrown in my lot with the Sterns globalists for entirely *honourable* reasons, I reiterated the counterargument forcefully...

"If you give authority to *all* the 'unique cultures'," I said, "it will result in war and suffering, and then in the smaller cultures being swallowed by more powerful or persuasive ones, until few, or only *one* are left. Thus, globalism is inevitable, and so we should we seek to attain it by the shortest possible path, the way of *least* suffering, rather than that of war, conflicting nationalisms, regionalisms, tribalisms and so forth."

"I anticipated you would say so," he smiled. "For that is what your Jewish teachers at Sterns have taught you to..."

"Not *all* of them are Jews," I interjected angrily.

"No, not all of them, to be sure. I believe at least one of them isn't. And I'm impressed enough by their argument to expound to you, right here and now, the second and more esoteric doctrine of our Order. The doctrine of *Imperium*."

"What's that?"

"I mean that the periphery cannot hold without a strong centre whose force guards and protects the many-faceted paths."

"You mean a kind of globalist anti-globalism? With a central body at the top?"

"With a *single* body at the top – an emperor, Imperator."

"But who's to say he won't become corrupt, and bring in the melting pot anyway, with greater force than even the Unicursal Curia would be able to?"

"That is why he must be a *man*, not a council or committee. Because a man with the right training can keep himself pure, whereas a council cannot."

"And how on earth do you propose to get this hypothetical princeps to attain power in the first place, let alone keep it?"

He smiled again.

"I already said that I sense greatness in you, and can help to bring it out. The rest is up to you."

I shuddered violently at the enormity of what he was saying.

At dawn, he led me outside to see the Morning Star.

"Our sign," he said, bowing his head in reverence. "The symbol of our Order."

As if by some illusion, that cold sigil now seemed more remote than the fixed stars themselves, and an indescribable loneliness stabbed me in the guts.

"Please, let this cup pass from me," I murmured, but the Morning Star said nothing in response.

*   *   *

The first person I saw on my return was Tegg, who was waiting by the school gate as if looking out for me. In fact, she *was* looking out for me, and when sighted, it seemed as if she was struggling with herself.

"So *there* you are," she stuttered. "You know, they're already talking about sending search parties out. You'd better report to the director's office at once."

The freckles on her face were like the stars of the Milky Way, scattering my heart to the far void...such cream of sweetness, such aching melancholy. I knew now it was the face of my astral beloved, *but how had I failed to recognise her before?* Surely I must pay for this transgression...

There was an unspoken bond between us, and I wondered if she, like me, bore the mark of Cain. So I asked her outright:

"Do you ever have strange remembrances?"

"What do you mean?"

"Dreams you were once...someone else."

"Like reincarnation?"

"Call it that if you want."

"I'm not sure. If I *have* lived before then I'm not sure if I'd *want* to know."

"Why not?"

She paused and considered a moment before replying. "Do you remember Kyle?"

"Hopkins, who got expelled in first year?"

"Yes. Well, he claimed he was pursuing a philosophy of total awareness. Total consciousness at all times...or something like that."

"I remember now. He said it was compatible with the teachings of the school, but they didn't believe him...and perhaps it wasn't."

"Yeah, perhaps...but what I mean is, I'm not sure if I would *want* to have total awareness...as there's no light without shadows..." Her face, half-shaded as she said it, was like a drawing from five hundred years ago, an etching from one of the masters beyond time.

Then our conversation was interrupted by the arrival of several teachers, and I was summoned to the director's office for an explanation of my night out of bounds. So I made up a lie about spending the night with a disgusting black prostitute, which they thankfully accepted, officially admonishing me not to do so again.

Good...they believed my mission was merely one of cavorting with 'dark and comely maidens', and so (after an additional check-up for venereal diseases) it was back to the usual routine, only waiting for a chance to speak with Tegg again.

I was disappointed, however. She didn't show her face in coming days, not even in the classes we shared. I found myself worrying she might be ill, but was unable to bring myself to mention her name aloud, or enquire about her to anyone. It was a long week, long and cruel.

*　　*　　*

Kyle Hopkins and Bryn Sturgess were certainly not the only ones to have come under suspicion of harbouring unorthodox beliefs during my time at Sterns. Even a prominent teacher had once been relieved of his post after it had been revealed he was secretly a worshipper of Cthulhu, and working with the globalists because he thought it the best means of setting Cthulhu free. (But was he kicked out because he was wrong, or just honest? These kinds of ambiguities have contributed to my growing distrust of the Sterns brand of esotericism...no such haziness surrounds the clear and manly doctrine of Esoteric Ethnopluralist Imperium!)

As I write, my mind flashes back to my own Idealism Test, administered days before my sixteenth birthday, the final hurdle before gaining entry to the most elite school in the world. I clearly remember the examiners stressing to me as stringently as possible that true Illuminism was something far beyond the ludicrous 'clocks forward' mentality of the Skull and Bones Society, the latter being an item of priceless comedy for the staff and students of Sterns. *[The Skull and Bones, famous yet secretive fraternity of Yale University, allegedly have their clocks set forward as a sign that they are above the common herd of humanity. – E.J.C.]*

Even more did we chortle at Ellison Plugg, that chubby and drug-crazed American preacher who attained to stellar heights of fame by making wildly exaggerated claims about the Unicursal Curia. His bellicose claims that a chemically sedated and microchipped populace is both the aim of the Curia and its means of attaining power were always good for a laugh, made all the funnier because, while the spittle flies from his mouth and while he screeches and fulminates, he remains blissfully unaware that the Curia are the ones lining his pockets via sponsorship deals, and misdirecting him to describe them as a 'German Illuminati Death Cult'. We know in practice, of course, that such drugging and microchipping would be too difficult logistically, even if desirable – which it *isn't*, as it would

165

make for subjects who couldn't appreciate the high wisdom of their rulers.

But in some ways, I have come to realise, the attitude at Sterns *is* like the 'clocks forward' mentality they claim to revile, just more subtly rendered. For while claiming to be world improvers who care boundlessly for humanity, at bottom I believe they still *see* the latter as cattle...and that's not how I see it at all, for *who would want to live in a world of cattle?*

In the week after my conversation with Tegg, I had a very memorable class with Professor Levin, in which these hints and suspicions suddenly coalesced into total conviction.

Levin is a man who tries very valiantly to get his students on side, but only partially succeeds; that is to say, his attempts to come across as foppishly self-mocking may appeal to some, but leave others with a faint feeling of disgust. Levin makes constant snide remarks about his fellow Jews, as if trying to convey that he is not as heavy-handed as some of his compatriots. This had unforeseen consequences, however, during the lesson in question, when some remark of his (giving some of his students the feeling that Jews were no longer a *completely* taboo topic for open enquiry) led to a heated Q and A session on why the student body of an apparently globalist institution like Sterns was so overwhelmingly white, with mainly Jews for professors.

"Why are there so many Jewish teachers here, but no Jewish students?" someone asked. I noticed Levin's forehead covered with tiny beads of sweat – either the question *was* unwelcome, or he had now arrived at a foreseen but important hurdle in the course of the curriculum. Either way, he tried to make the best of it. He began with a humorous anecdote ridiculing British Israelites and Black Hebrew Israelites. *[These are movements who claim that white and black people respectively are the 'true Jews', while the Jews themselves are 'Satanic imposters'. – E.J.C.]*

"You know, with the information at their disposal, you'd think these people could take the time to actually *read* the Old Testament, particularly the Book of Esther, and find irrefutable proof that the Jews of today are one and the same as those of the Book," he chuckled.

"But what has that to do with Sterns?"

"Everything," he said mysteriously, and launched into a lengthy tirade about the current strategy of the Curia and its feeder institutions such as Sterns. There was an ongoing conflict between two parties (those of us who had already heard rumours of this felt an almost sexual thrill on hearing it expounded explicitly for the first time).

One party, the Wobblers, believe that it is crucial to steep the Western world in a cultural atmosphere of 'no rules'...so that there can consequently be *no rebels*.

The other group, the Blades, oppose this, because it means the only rebels will be those who advocate *rules* (i.e. fascists, and others who believe in any kind of irrational national structure). For this reason, they want to retain 'structure' but keep the rebels harnessed solidly to the outlook of the 1968 generation. The difficulty in this, of course, is that it is now almost impossible to convince the average person that 68er ideals aren't the status quo – for indeed they are, and this explains the rise of the Wolves of Joy and similar groups.

The professor then revealed that he, and most of the other teachers at Sterns, are in the Blades camp, and the Curia as a whole is also leaning in that direction, chiefly due to the dangers inherent in the Wobbler approach.

"But the Blade strategy means we need idealists to carry our work forward. And you guys were picked *precisely* because of your idealism. I can't emphasise it strongly enough. My Jewish brethren can talk all they like about *tikkun olam*, but when it comes down to it, white people (and maybe a few East Asians) make the greatest idealists. So here we are, harnessing that idealism in the service of goals worth achieving." He rubbed his hands together, and cackled self-deprecatingly.

It was difficult to know if he was insulting his 'brethren' and complimenting us, or the other way round. There was often a strong ambiguity about the way he talked. Nevertheless, he had explained the absence of Jews in the student body to the satisfaction of most of my peers. Only Bryn looked a bit sceptical...maybe he was having a reversion.

As for myself, I was seething with disgust.

*　　*　　*

I made my second trip to the Old Man's cave that weekend, leaving in the early morning so as to return before nightfall. It was important not to arouse any further suspicion.

The Meister was in a pensive state, but pulled himself out of it, seemingly as eager to teach as I was eager to learn. He lapsed back into deep thought, however, when I told him of Levin's conversation. After lengthy silence, he observed that it would be far more worrying if the Wobblers were to gain ascendency.

"A world without possibility of rebellion would be far more dangerous than one in which the opposition is phoney," he pronounced, "So the Blades have effectively sealed their own doom. No matter how many idealists they enlist, the Curia will find it impossible to convince young people that globalism is anywise edgy or rebellious. We've already seen how fast the Wolves of Joy have grown in the past decade. All we have to do is take their immature rebellion, and transmute it into an Imperium. An alchemic act, for which the strictest spiritual discipline is of the utmost."

He then taught me a set of spiritual exercises, which I won't divulge here, but which have given me the great reserves of strength I will surely need for the task ahead.

The afternoon wore on, and I took my leave of the Maestro, raising my hand in salute as I left.

"Remember the Morning Star," he enjoined.

But I didn't tell him about Tegg, whose face was the starry void itself.

*　　*　　*

168

These exercises, which I had only just begun to practice, soon helped me to pass my end of year exams with unheard of brilliance – perfect marks in *every* subject. And not just perfect – I demonstrated political, administrative and military strategic skills of the highest order, giving wonder to those who had set the very questions. I plumbed the depths of scenarios they hadn't even dreamed of. Nothing like it had ever happened in the ten year history of Sterns, nor ever will again. Although I was already the best pupil in my year, this was something altogether unexpected.

One teacher wanted to retest me. The others declined, but only after lengthy interviews and discussions in which they probed my sudden über-brilliance, satisfying themselves that it wasn't ephemeral. And it wasn't, for the Old Man's exercises allowed me to tap into deep wells of the unconscious.

"The Caesars were said to have matured early," muttered one professor, scratching his wizened head in confusion.

I had a robotic 'celebration fuck' with Tricia, already sensing that I had earned her lifelong enmity for outperforming her so overwhelmingly in the exams, but it wasn't something I gave much thought to.

And then came the most incredible news of all. The Praesidium, created to replace the old EU by the Unicursal Curia (itself, of course, having replaced the old UN after the latter had become too hostile to the land of the Dead Sea), was now looking for a new and *youthful* figurehead to give it renewed propaganda appeal in a world where the Wolves of Joy are a serious spiritual force. And in light of my stunning results, would I take the job?

Again, this was something unheard of in the history of globalism. For an eighteen year old boy to be chosen as Executive Commissioner of a major world body...

"I'll be a politically active EC," I warned them (don't say that I didn't!), "and certainly don't intend to sit on my backside."

"That's fine," chortled the representative. "We know your values are sound. If you can't trust a Sternsman, who *can* you trust?"

And so it was decided. The Morning Star moves in mysterious ways.

*   *   *

Who giveth with one hand, taketh away with the other one, however. It was only the next day that I learnt of Tegg's suicide. She left no note, nothing.

Her body was flown back to England before I even heard the news. It is still a wondrous mystery to me. The other students, having barely spoken to her, scarcely reacted, other than with a faint contempt for an ill-timed act that soured the mirth of graduation (and infinitely deepened the gulf between them and me). My journey to the obscure side was now complete.

The deep shock brought on an illness which lasted a week, of which I have no memory, and when I recovered it was like the rebirth of spring...my beloved's face was now emblazoned on my *inner* being, my true being. And that's where it will stay. She is more real now than she was in life. There is no more grief, no more tears. I fight for *her*.

It only remains to mention my return to the Old Man's cave for advice...it was empty, of course, there being no trace he had ever lived there, or even existed at all.

And now I realise for the first time that, in material terms, I am completely and utterly alone. So I offer a prayer to the Morning Star, whose light now illuminates the astral face of my beloved, and go on my way. Tomorrow, my new posting in Europe begins.

I will go.

And see.

And conquer.

And may this record stand witness as to the seriousness of my endeavour, to be made public only in the event of my death.

: Maximillian Scarlotti : Dawn :

2

THE TESTIMONY OF
KARINA SEDLÁKOVÁ

My first impressions of my boss were that a new sun had risen in the sky, wearing a subtle and slender mask of gold, and had descended to bless and protect me. I had always waited for this.

My mother told me from the earliest I can remember to "never trust a man," and although over time I came to hate my mother, this piece of advice stayed with me for the most part, against my better wishes – for, unlike her, who was beaten regularly by my Communist tyrant of a father (so she said) before he finally left when I was a baby, I am not actually *afraid* of men, and never have been. No, it is my own sex I fear, with its vague mushiness, never quite gelling with the bright-clear golden image of God I have in my head, and which I was never taught.

I don't fear men – I understand them. But I don't trust them, either, because that which I *understand* is not in keeping with the bright golden head of God either, which *dazzles* and is inscrutable.

The Chief is in keeping with it, though.

I fell in love with him from the first moment he walked into the room. Despite the fact that he was eight years younger than me, I knew him instantly as my Lord and Master – also, that I could never say so out loud, or he might vanish.

"So you're my appointed PA," he smiled, and bright rays of purifying light filled the labyrinthine crevices of my heart. Weeks earlier I had received word of winning the position as his PA...and he was, of course, the talk of Prague. For years the public in many countries have been

171

moody and rebellious; not just the Wolves of Joy (yes, they exist in our country as in others) but also vast brigades of internet trolls taught the public to see that everything is moribund: the Curia, the Praesidium, even Capitalism itself.

And perhaps it *is* moribund. I don't know, as politics is not my strong point. I am good at observing the politics of others, however – as that is their 'idea', just as my idea is the Golden Head of God. And as my aim is the intensification of my idea, so too is theirs, perhaps, in their own manner – and it didn't take a genius to sense the heavy air, crackling with discontent.

So Maximillian Scarlotti was installed as Executive Commissioner of the Praesidium, to give a sense that youth was in the ascendency. There was now talk of a 'European Springtime'...and although I think most saw this as phoney, it is undeniable that the Chief was seen as a heartthrob by many women and girls – so perhaps the bold gamble paid off? Partly, at least, for everyone knows it is the female sex that, in our day, sets the mood of 'public opinion'.

But other women admired him merely for his 'good looks' – which is like admiring the sun for its roundness, not for its golden scorching fire. Was I, alone of all women, the only one who saw his inner searing flame? That I would like to believe, as it justifies what I am about to do.

Well, when the Chief first arrived in Prague, he was obsessed with the legend of the Golem. He had read Meyrink's famous novel on the aeroplane, and asked if I had also – so I said yes, and bought a copy that afternoon, perusing the strange story for the first time. Next day I started a conversation, based on my experience of the book. He had read it for the *second* time that night, it turned out – O golden coincidence!

"Miss Sedláková," he said, with intensity barely concealed beneath his formal politeness. "Were you aware that Karel Čapek's play *Rossum's Universal Robots*, also written here in Prague, has many similarities to the legend of the golem? The golem is a man of mud, just like a robot. But, you see, at the end of the play, something occurs that its creators never envisaged. Life always finds a way, and that is what these Curia types will never understand."

"I have read the robot play," I said (truthfully this time).

"And to think this was once the city of *alchemists*," he snarled. "Is their robot-golem a reaction to that, from those afraid of fire? The Curia think *I* am a Golem, you know...a mud-man to clean up their synagogue of Saturdays. Ah well, they'll soon see that they've bitten off more than they can chew, like the sorcerer's apprentice."

"He who manages to bind the golem and refine him will be reconciled with himself," I said, quoting Meyrink to him, and no one can guess my inner turmoil and fluttering heart – but on the outside I was all polite coolness and efficiency, even managing to keep my poise as we read a little from each work, comparing the inner meaning of both authors.

It was unusual for the Chief to engage in such a seemingly frivolous exercise – he was a highly driven young man – but he seemed to place great significance in the golem legend. At the time I didn't understand why, but now that my head is clear it seems that he didn't want a world turned to mud. He believed in a soul. Did that put him at odds with those around him? Yes, of course...

He engaged in plenty of frivolities *outside* of work, however – and indeed, was expected to. Several times he asked me to accompany him to those decadent parties where the elite unwound.

"Please help to keep me sane," he said. "You're level headed, and I need that in this nest of smiling vipers."

But who can soothe the sun? Anyone who has *been* to one of those parties, can see in their minds' eye what they are like. Full of insane phoney gurus, selling spiritual remedies for all the problems of the multiverse, brought there for amusement by hardcore Praesidium types, but sometimes a novice is taken in and must be disabused. The Servitor Kult was one such, appearing on the scene around this time, but it was more of a trend than a 'kult' – a set of wealthy feminists who suddenly found it cool to be submissive because they thought that no one had done it before, and because they *could*. So they became 24/7 subs (on finding the right master), and played the role enthusiastically. The Curia's Department of Culture issued an official warning against the Servitor Kult, but only a half-hearted one. There were even one or two Curia women involved in it, at least for a few months, before the next trend came along.

And so the Chief was introduced to a Servitor called Darla Shaw, the widow of an ultra-rich currency speculator who had since reverted to her maiden name. She was a smooth operator seeking a harsh master, to keep up with her friends. She was all over the Chief in an instant, and he seemed to enjoy her attentions, despite the fact she was nearly twenty years his senior.

He asked who she was (it was part of my job to be his social navigator), so I whispered her life story into his ear. By the end of the evening she had formally knelt and 'submitted' to him...there were wedding plans afoot, and he had already dictated to me a curt dismissal note for his former betrothed, a Ms. Tricia Philips. He married Darla later that week in a small private ceremony at a country estate outside Prague. His affections for his new bride were not entirely genuine, however. He dropped hints (to me, at least) that he had married her mainly in order to have access to a private fortune (she having inherited the majority of her late husband's wealth, which was valued in the tens of billions).

"I don't enjoy money for its own sake, Miss Sedláková," he told me. "But it's an important resource for my mission." I nodded politely, afraid to ask what his 'mission' was. Later that night I witnessed him whipping his new wife with a curtain rod, and as she writhed in ecstasy beneath his blows, I wished it was *me* that he was beating...but I don't think that's what he meant by 'mission'.

Next evening I accompanied the two of them to a performance of the Czech Philharmonic Orchestra at the Rudolfinum. It was Beethoven's *Triple Concerto*, appropriately enough. The pianist, a thirty-something Chinese with hair that flopped around his face, was a known hater of the Praesidium, and his angry klavier-hammering deadened the impact of the piece. The interplay with the other two lead instruments became a grim battle, but at the same time it helped me to think. It was then that I realised Darla was no *real* threat to me — not a spiritual threat, as only *I* perceived clearly the true inner greatness of the young Octavian. But I longed to hold him in my arms all the same, and this desire has never let up, not for an instant.

After the performance, a man with thick eyeglasses whispered to the Chief of a confidential meeting, one where he would learn something to his advantage. Two days later I was present at this meeting.

"I trust Miss Sedláková implicitly, her discretion is absolute," the Chief said, causing me to glow with pleasure...and even now that I am leaving this world, I maintain this discretion, and will burn this note when my thoughts are collected. *(The note was found unburnt...either she forgot, or the pills kicked in quicker than she intended. — E.J.C.)*

"We know the entire Arts allocation left over from the old EU has just vanished — forty million esperos to be precise — but we don't know where to," said the bespectacled little fellow, and the Chief promised he would look into it promptly.

"I only have the name of a Belgian hedge fund, but there's no hard *proof* linking them with the disappearance of the money," the fellow said. "Just someone who may have known a someone, and so forth. Here's the address and suite number." He scratched something onto a slip of paper.

So next week, the Chief and I flew to Brussels. On the surface it was an educational tour to see how the city had fared after the EU bureaucracy had been dismantled and revamped in Prague. Since its decommission as de facto capital of the EU, Brussels had been trying to reinvent itself as a 'vibrant, cosmopolitan city', just as Bonn had done after German reunification. The only problem was that, with every city now billing itself as vibrant and cosmopolitan, tourists stayed well away. Vibrancy is also also an anonym for 'high crime', and Brussels did not disappoint in that regard.

The glass-honeycomb tombstones of the old European Quarter with its bilingual signage soon gave way to neighbourhoods where an overlap was in place —

tongues of the demographic wave, soaking the shores of reason. A decaying, Islamified city, and despite all the noise, an empty feeling underneath, as empty as the cube of Kaaba. The further you walk, the wave actually seems to ride out, like the tide going out before a tsunami. Once the Chief was spat at, and his bodyguards were forced to protect him from what could have been an unpleasant incident.

"And this was once the hometown of that noble reporter Tintin," muttered the Chief. "He would be no more at home here now than would an alchemist in latter day Prague."

After we had walked another few blocks, we reached our intended building – a bland new edifice with a convoluted façade.

"Now," said the Chief, "it's quite possible that certain heads in the Praesidium or Curia know that we're here, investigating this lead, and I want to send a message to them that I'm not a man to trifle with." He instructed his bodyguards to be very rough indeed with the hedge fund's investment manager. "It's something the Curia probably hasn't anticipated. I want it to be crystal clear who has jurisdiction in Europe. Also, I won't tolerate corruption in my fief."

His bodyguards nodded eagerly, but I was surprised. As Executive Commissioner he certainly had powers, but *controlling* the entire European treaty zone? I shivered, suddenly afraid for him.

We quickly found the correct wing of the building. The hedge fund, Gaumont Capital, was listed at the entrance, but the front door was locked. The Chief rang at the buzzer and announced that he was an envoy from the European Department of Culture, who had urgent news to impart to a Mr. Michael Crossley. A minute later a short man in a suit, with slicked back hair and an old-fashioned nose ring, came to the door and ushered us in.

"I'm Crossley," he said in a working-class English accent when we had reached a private office. "Anything the matter?"

There soon was, and he crawled around the floor gasping for breath as the Chief's men smacked him around. "What the *fuck?*" he kept repeating, at weird intervals. "What the fuck have I *done?*"

"Just tell us what happened to the money from the EU Arts Grant."

"Wait...let me guess...someone in Prague told you this...a man called Bernard something."

"Never mind *how* I know."

"Wears glasses, a squinty-eyed bloke. White, but looks like a Chinese moonfish. Big sticky-out ears." An exaggerated but recognisable depiction. "You fool," Crossley snarled. "He's misdirecting you. *He's* the one you should ask about the culture budget. I fucked him over in the past, and this is his revenge on me. He probably feared that with your energy you'd soon be onto him, so he put you on a false trail. All the while he vanishes off to Russia or someplace."

"You're lying."

"No!" There was desperation in his voice, and he really sounded like he meant it.

"Then what will I find in suite 5C of this wing?"

"N-nothing. That's our old office. We moved to *this* suite a few months ago."

"Give me the key to the old office, then. I know you still have it..." It was a bluff, and didn't work, so the Chief had to recourse to brutality. After they had beaten him within an inch of his life, he finally retrieved an electronic key from the top drawer of his desk, where there were several.

"You can't get away with this. I don't care if you're the Executive Commissioner of the whole fucking world. I have rights..."

"If you tell anyone, you will suddenly cease to exist. And no matter where you hide, we'll track you down."

We marched to the suite, which was empty, but a padlocked trapdoor in the corner drew our attention. The toughs smashed the lock, and we walked down some stairs to find a long, carpeted passage under the ground, like something out of a spy novel.

One bodyguard had a torch, and we followed the passage for what felt like miles. The carpet ended, then our footsteps echoed on clacketty concrete floors. There were no side tunnels. We reached a winding metal staircase going up, and climbed the rusty edifice before reaching a small, dingy chamber with a wooden boarded ceiling, apparently a dead end.

We tapped the walls for secret passages, then realised that there was actually some kind of trapdoor in the ceiling. The bodyguard-built-like-a-mountain pressed his hand against it, and before long there was a splintering sound and it gave. He boosted one of the others up to see if the coast was clear.

"A room without doors," he said. "Just a filing cabinet in the middle." The mountain hauled us up, one after the other, and stayed on guard below. The Chief opened the venetians and peeped out the window of this strange doorless room.

"It looks like we're back in the old EU Quarter," he exclaimed, and was right. The room seemed suddenly filled with ghosts, the dreary shades of the politically correct era.

The filing cabinet wasn't locked, and contained a single file. We stood, sat, and squatted patiently while the Chief perused the contents. His eyes grew wider the more he read.

"It isn't tens of millions, it's *hundreds of billions* of esperos that were siphoned away," he whispered in a shocked voice. "And not just the Arts fund, but *most* of the revenue from the old EU."

One of the bodyguards frowned. "Siphoned away where, Chief?"

"I don't know. But Bernard Sauveterre must have been trying to warn me. I should have realised that nothing I learnt during the *Triple Concerto* could be false...only understated," he murmured. "Because three is the magic number."

And then, as we returned to the chambers of the hedge fund, we found that the staff had vanished, documents shredded, computers taken and furniture overturned. And someone had called the Brussels police, who were nonplussed.

"What 'as 'appened 'ere?"

"A crime that can never be atoned for," muttered the Chief.

The mirror-glass on the building opposite now showed a dead city, drained of its last protective energy.

*   *   *

Back in Prague, the Chief walked around with a look of fire. He contacted his Curia liaison, and told him about the Arts money (*not* the larger amount – here he winked at me with a fire-swirling eye), and next day attended a meeting with some people from the Unicursal Curia. They asked what he was going to do, and the Chief said "Well, what do *you* suggest?"

"Perhaps a press conference is in order. You must let the public know of this urgent matter at once."

"Good idea," said the Chief, but they couldn't decipher his secret smile.

At the press conference the Chief spoke as follows:

"If I was to announce to you today the disappearance of a large sum of money from the coffers of the old EU...you would be incensed...but I can now reveal...that it is in fact, a...much...*larger*...amount...of..." He spoke at a funereal, drumrolling pace...this was deliberate and calculated, I knew. He told me later, but I already understood. Before further words could emerge from his mouth there was a flurrying of feet, as advisors pretended to whisper in his ear. Someone came to the mic and told the journalists the Executive Commissioner had "urgent unforeseen business, and the press conference must be postponed until tomorrow," then he was whirled out in a flash, leaving his loyal PA behind. I knew what had happened, of course – but was he doing it to test the Curia's resolve of letting him serve his term, or for reasons of justice? (It really *was* a large sum of money.)

I didn't see him until work the next day, when he took me aside and told me in greater detail what had happened.

"I was slapped back, as expected, Miss Sedláková," he said. "It's what the espionage crowd call 'limited hangout'. I was *meant* to find out about that Arts money,

179

and to let the public know. But they didn't foresee that Bernard Sauveterre would tell me more than instructed. He has recently disappeared, needless to say." I shivered – but at the thought of the grey-suited corpses grilling the Chief, like dirty clouds encrusting the sun. (I felt bad for M. Sauveterre of course, but that was purely abstract.)

Next day the conference resumed, and the story of the Arts money was given out to the press, with promises that it would be "looked into severely," with no stone left unturned. That was enough to get them gossiping, accusing and pontificating, ensuring of course that they would never actually muckrake into the real truth of the matter. Limited hangout, indeed.

That evening I walked alone through the Old Town of Prague, fantasising about what the Chief was doing to his wife. I couldn't live without my sun, and here I was in the moist, clammy labyrinth, with no way out, and night closing in. I ran home sobbing through the cobblestoned streets, and cried myself to sleep. Oh, why couldn't I be a man and die a hero's death? To burn my face in the flames...

But next day I was basking in warmth again – the Chief instructed me to accompany him on a weekend trip to Munich, where a high-ranking member of the Curia had summoned him to a secret meeting. As we boarded the plane for the short flight, I felt blessed to be alive.

From Munich airport we took a taxi to an Italian restaurant in the university district of Schwabing. The man from the Curia, with a very Jewish-looking face, was waiting at the table he'd reserved for us in a quiet corner.

"Do you like the choice of establishment?" he asked.

"Seems nice enough."

"You don't recognise it? This was *Hitler's* favourite restaurant, you know, in the days when he resided in Munich."

"Really. And why did you want to meet here in particular?"

"Well, Munich in general tends to make me reflect a lot on the past...and this place in particular has that effect." He sighed. "You know, if only Hitler had looked favourably upon the mixing of races, we really could have made use of him."

"It's only his opposition to miscegenation you have a problem with?"

"That's it! That was his problem entirely...not the whole cattle car thing. Now, let's see, I'll have the *coda alla vaccinara*, please." We placed our orders, and chatted over trivial things until the meal arrived. After the repast and a bottle of good Puglian wine, the Curia rep got down to business.

"What I am about to tell you is strictly in confidence. It does not have the official sanction of the Curia, but there are those of us who think you should be on board with it, and we are in the majority." He then told the Chief that, although the Curia distrusted him as a result of the affair of the EU coffers ("and, because we distrust *everyone*," he added with a smile), they nevertheless valued highly his magnetic force and proven leadership ability.

"Combined with your youthful energy, it makes you a veritable *Übermensch*, if you'll excuse the expression. And we would be very foolish indeed not to utilise your talents and persona. We need all the help we can get right now!" I noticed that he didn't say what would happen to the Chief after his 'help' was no longer required.

"How do you want to utilise me, then?"

"Well now, I take it you know our esteemed North American Executive Commissioner...your counterpart on that continent, the delightful Anita Jokum?" A sarcasm, surely, as Ms. Jokum was not only physically repulsive, but had an aggressively self-righteous persona – a real do-gooding harpy.

"I know who she is."

"Well, without mincing words, we wish to be rid of her. Her belligerence has become an embarrassment, especially in the USA, which despite its economic decline is still an important country for us. And Anita Jokum has nearly everyone there against her.

"It goes without saying that rightists hate her – pushing a 2010-style political correctness in the 2020s! – but she has also alienated large swathes of the left with her outspoken support for female genital mutilation, despite her claims to be a radical feminist. Not that the American left are especially valuable to us at the moment, mind you...no, the most pressing task at hand is a final crusade to stamp out Islamic fundamentalism, and for that we need to temporarily dispel the resentment of the American Right. We want a showdown, a real clash of civilizations. A last day in the sun for the hamburger-eaters of Flyover Country, before they disappear forever into the melting pot of that good night." His cynicism chilled even me.

"But the Curia or its predecessors *created* fundamentalist Islam," I interjected, unable to help myself, although the Chief had not given me permission to speak.

"Yes, of course, Miss...uh," he said frostily, "but it has outlived its purpose. Like many ideologies we created for strategic reasons, its time is now up. And besides, it has gotten somewhat out of control of late, in case you haven't noticed."

"And Jokum is impeding its demise?" asked the Chief.

"Massively. She just won't be budged on her attempts to appease the fundies, for reasons of her own trendy vanity...a position that scarcely has any traction anymore, not even with the far left. Seriously, can't you feel it in the air, Scarlotti? There has never been a riper time for extreme Islam to perish. *Kairos!*"

"So what do you want me to do?"

"We want you to be our new North American Executive Commissioner, of course. Your talents would be far more valuable over there at the present time."

"You could order me to."

"But it's very difficult for us to stand down an EC without a valid reason, even a continental one like Jokum, let alone the EC of the Praesidium...which technically isn't even in our jurisdiction."

"Technically...but you *could*, though."

"We would prefer it if you didn't give us any reason to."

"Well, there's the Brussels thing. No doubt the reason you want me out of Europe in the first place."

"Come, let's not talk about that. Will you be our man in North America?"

"I'll consider it."

"As EC, you'll need to portray yourself as more right-wing than the current US president. Above all we want you to gain the allegiance of the military, which we will need for our Grand Crusade. And of course your secondary mission will be to bolster the Curia's power over the US as a nation state. Also over Canada and Mexico."

"Sounds simple. Is that all?"

"Ha, I knew you were the right man for the job! Another bottle of wine, please, waiter. The Chianti this time, I think..."

*　　*　　*

After that, it all seemed to happen so fast.

Anita Jokum was forced to stand down over a sordid sex scandal. You saw it on the gossip shows, no doubt...the video shot in an expensive brothel showing its employee (a mulatto girl) threatened with clitoridectomy by Jokum if the former didn't bring her to climax in time for her committee meeting that afternoon; not to mention footage of Jokum whipping the unfortunate whore with a riding crop, hollering that she would "tan her nigger hide back to the sugar cane fields" if she didn't admit that "niggers are superior to white liberals like me. *You are the master race*...just admit it, you lying slut..."

"Please, stop hitting me so hard."

Of course there was no proof that the brothel itself released the footage...normally such an incident involving a high-ranking Curia official would have been covered up immediately, but *someone* apparently wanted it released. That, along with other tidily leaked 'incidents', brought about the downfall of Anita Jokum. Maximillian Scarlotti was appointed Interim Commissioner , pending immediately.

The Chief then let it be known he was sponsoring a law and order campaign aimed at stamping out the Knockout Game, a sport that had been growing in popularity for two decades, and which had now reached unprecedented levels of brutality. The sport, also known as the Polar Bear Hunt, invariably involved a group of young black men approaching a solitary white victim, and seeing how quickly they could knock him (or increasingly *her*) to the ground.

Death on impact was considered a high score, but there were other ways to amass points, such as creatively kicking the victim to death, or varied mutilations.

The media had been instrumental in covering up the existence of this sport, but the more victims there were, the more people knew of it...so finally, despite the best efforts of Anita Jokum to play things down, Euro-Americans had begun to reach boiling point.

Into this tense pre-storm atmosphere flew the Chief. He travelled to Philadelphia, myself at his side, to be photographed with Knockout victims who had survived the experience, and thereby immediately endeared himself to a large segment of the population.

As expected, this provoked massive violent protests from the far left worldwide, especially in Europe where he was still officially EC.

Something we *didn't* expect, however, was that the Reformed Ku Klux Klan (now open to members of all races and sexual inclinations) would also protest against the Chief for "inciting disharmony among the community of the nations." A group of Reformed Klansmen actually burnt a huge wooden rainbow outside the hotel in Fishtown where we were staying...it was an eerie sight, those hooded figures screeching about 'social justice', while the black police moved them on.

After that we were driven to Rockville, Maryland (a suburb of Washington, D.C.), where we attended a meeting in a nondescript office building with a blustering gentile neocon who thought he was more important than he actually was. I can't remember the details, but apparently the meeting was successful.

Then we crossed the Potomac into Arlington and met with some senior military figures, and that seemed to go well too. I think the Chief wanted their support over and above that of the current US president – the line between nationalism and globalism becoming ever more blurred. You remember that President Hodge's election over the Democratic incumbent in 2020 caused the worst Black and Hispanic riots in US history...but he has since proved a more malleable figure for the Curia, ironically, than Anita Jokum herself.

Nevertheless, the Curia needs a *real* captain at the wheel for the coming Crusade, and that's where the Chief steps in...

So, shortly afterwards he was formally appointed North American Executive Commissioner. He never set foot in Prague again after his first day in the USA, and when I went to his office to report for work one morning he was gone...whisked off somewhere and given a new PA. So now I am back in Prague, which is a living tomb without him.

Time for my last lines: I am going to God now, and if I return to earth, let it be an earth where my golden template has triumphed.

Let me stare untrembling into the face of the unconquered Sun.

(Karina Sedláková was found dead of a sleeping pill overdose in her apartment near Wenceslas Square, Prague. – E.J.C.)

THE TESTIMONY OF
MAJOR GENERAL JOHN C. FRAMPTON

Dear Marcus,

It's been too long, hasn't it? I guess you know how busy I've been, but now that I finally have some time I'll try to fill you in on what has been happening. I can't posit every detail, for security reasons of course, but will simply endeavour to run you down on the main cut and thrust.

You've heard all about the Crisis, and you've also heard, no doubt, how I was assigned as Scarlotti's liaison to the Pentagon by the former Secretary of Defense (on the recommendation of the Joint Chiefs of Staff). I was surprised that their recommendation was accepted, especially given my previously expressed (albeit cautious) optimism as to the man himself. I expected they would want someone more cynical, but apparently I was wrong.

Things have sure been getting strange in the Beltway of late. Those conservatives who were most vocal these past few years in their opposition to the Curia have now suddenly decided they want Scarlotti as their head of state over that "miserable son of a bitch" Hodge (as one of them described him to me in private).

"Pity he (Scarlotti)'s not eligible for president, as foreign-born," growled another. And I'm not talking Paleos, Libertarians or White Nationalists (whose ranks are swelling fast enough), but your common or garden Republican. It shows how deep the distrust of Neocons is right now – especially ironic given that Hodge's biggest election promise was to *counter* the power of the Curia, something he has singularly failed at. I almost suspect the Curia are using the two as rivals, to find out which is best: the unpredictable genius (Scarlotti) or the dumb puppet   (Hodge).

Scarlotti's swearing-in was a real eye-opener. I don't mean the austere public ceremony – there was also a lavish *private* do, up here in Manhattan, and I tell you I couldn't have dreamt this thing up. Scarlotti actually *prostrated* himself before the current head of Curia, donning a yarmulke before 'singing' a two minute piece of gangsta rap (which presumably they made him memorize in advance) about pimping someone's sister out for KFC and crack. He was toasting shalom and shaking his rump like a goddamn baboon, can you imagine? I don't know how that would gel with his public opposition to the knockout game – is it actually some weird initiation rite, or do these Curia bastards just have a *really* sick sense of humor?

Anyhow, over the subsequent week I got to know Scarlotti about as well as anyone *can* know him, but he still remains an enigma to me. About the only sign of humanity I saw in him was when he learnt that his former secretary in Europe had taken her own life – he seemed depressed, then; but the next day was sanguine as usual.

Then came the Crisis.

It's hard to tell it objectively from my own standpoint, as I was in the thick of it, carrying messages and intrigues back and forth like the god Mercurius. My time was spent in a dizzying oscillation between the skyscrapered canyons of Manhattan and the domed velveteen skies of Arlington. I found myself longing for change, and when a middle of the road guy like me starts to feel that a revolution might be good, you know the country is in serious trouble – that is, if it even *is* a 'country' any more. Scarlotti will either save or damn us. Or maybe both.

I don't believe the Chiefs of Staff share my musings in any sense, but the sheer *hatred* they've developed towards Israel is striking. Their talk is now of not wasting another single bullet on the 'parasite state' (as many now call it). And these were men handpicked by the Curia!

I won't say any of them have gone as far as to express sympathy for the Palestinian cause, as that would be out of keeping with their character (and mine), but distrust of Israel, yes...that's now the glue keeping our military united, from the lowest grunt up to (and there's no point hiding this now he's gone public) the former Secretary of Defense himself.

"$10 million a day to that shithole," was the comment he was forced to resign over, caught by an open mic, but I could tell you other, more extreme things that he said in private. And again, this was a man who had been picked by the Curia, *founded* by all accounts because the old UN was too anti-Zionist.

So what did the Joint Chiefs of Staff want from Scarlotti? Simply his assurance that America won't be bogged down in another Zionist war without honor. And to our surprise, Scarlotti readily agreed to this.

"I have big plans for this world, gentlemen," he said, "but Zionist wars aren't among them." So he gave us his word of honor, which still counts for something among the military, if not among politicians.

This greenlighted us to give the flick to Hodge, that dumb shill of a sock puppet who has been worse than disappointing. He spluttered and raged, both privately and publicly, but was helpless to prevent something that could never previously have been imagined, let alone thought possible – *the direct allegiance of the US military to the Curia*, freezing the President out. In our age of blurred jurisdictions and ambiguous globalization, however, no one should have been surprised at how easily it was pulled off.

The central committee of the Curia themselves, of course, claimed to be opposed to Scarlotti's actions – but were they? Perhaps by the *motives* of the Chiefs of Staff, who had such a disturbing change of heart (was it the 'OpenBorders4Israel' campaign, or the neverending sea of atrocities?), but Scarlotti himself assured us they would leave us alone, as long as they thought he was using the military for their bizarre project of "stamping out extreme Islam" (more on that later).

Scarlotti is energetic, even his worst enemies concede that, and he immediately commenced to "make the forces strong again," succeeding alarmingly in the task. His first act was to expel cannabis users and the overweight, which immediately reduced the enlisted ranks by half. Then he weeded out all those belonging to the Crips and Bloods, for presumed disloyalty, reducing the remainder by nearly half again.

Then, he did something more controversial. He announced his intention to ban women from serving in the armed forces proper, instead proposing the creation of an auxiliary services branch, as in the WWII days. While I don't know of any *man* in the forces who would be opposed to this in their heart of hearts, many let their token protests resound in the media for fear of not doing so. And then came the protests from the far left. Yes, the anti-imperialist, anti-military-industrial left are currently having conniptions because the fairer sex *may* be removed from frontline combat ops, proving officially that the world is now *beyond* being 'beyond satire' and has in fact become a neverending satire in itself. But of what, I don't rightly know.

Anyway, with the ranks of our regular forces down to 28% (19% if his female policy goes through), Scarlotti had to explain to the Curia how he would be able to persuade America to go a-crusading. But although the ranks have been thinned, morale is now at an all time high! I almost think Scarlotti could persuade the general staff to commit to *anything*, even if he reneged on his promise not to lead us into any more Zionist wars!

At the time, he confided to the Joint Chiefs of Staff (via myself) something which is no longer a secret, that he has been recruiting a legion of bloodthirsty pirates from the Horn of Africa to serve him in the capacity of a private army, undisciplined but incredibly fierce, thanks to his wife's considerable fortune.

And in the midst of all this, he somehow found time to embark on a pet project of his, the establishment of a university whose aim is to develop something called the 'Glass Bead Game'.

"Yes, I know the game is only supposed to be a metaphor for creativity, Frampton," he told me. "But I'm interested in whether *the attempt itself* might not revivify Western culture." And then he launched into a long and confusing ramble about hieroglyphs that stood for multiple things; for instance, certain musical chords and the chemical structure of Portland cement. I didn't pretend to know what he was jabbering on about, and still don't.

But then came the second Crisis. I was standing by Scarlotti's side when his wife fell to the assassin's bullet. I have seen men die, but never a woman, and it's not something I will ever forget. I remember her trying to form some last hissing words, which never emerged. She looked at Scarlotti as if begging him to rescue her, before her eyes went away to the dark beyond. Scarlotti was weeping, yet rigid and composed. Was the bullet meant for him? Who fired it? Still unanswered questions...

After this, he became understandably more cautious, expending much effort in creating what he regarded as an invincible bodyguard. By now the leftists and their media enablers were inciting serious mass riots against him, mainly because of his attempts to stamp out the Knockout Game. He adroitly used the Baltimore riots as an excuse to bring down martial law across the continent, something neither we of the forces or, I believe, the average Joe, were particularly enamored of. But we didn't know what he would do with his temporary discretionary powers! You've seen for yourself the laws he has made – making left-wing race-agitators live amongst those they claim to be helping, for instance. We've all been waiting a long time for that one...

Naturally, the Curia were incensed. They must have felt like Frankenstein, with the monster they created now getting well out of hand. All the more so when he disappeared for a week and came back with a blushing new bride – no other than Kahina Tate, daughter of Mohammed Tate, emir of the Provisional Emirate of Northern Iraq and Syria (PENIS).

Despite his Arab first name, this post-ISIS emir is as white as a swan, a blue-eyed blond originally from the High Atlas (said to be of Berber stock, with an English father that he never knew, and, I suspect, a healthy admixture of Visigothic blood). This icy warlord has done much to heal and reorganize the war-ravaged lands of northern Iraq, and is much hated by the Curia as a result. In some ways he seems a kindred spirit of

Scarlotti, so perhaps it should be unsurprising that they formed an alliance, though for the life of me I couldn't tell you how it came about; Scarlotti likes to play things close to the chest.

The wedding was a signal to the Curia – they immediately began to hook their claws into India and the Russian 'dissident' factions. Perhaps they are biding their time, waiting for Scarlotti's predicted mideast war absence (which he *did* promise) in order to check his power here in the US.

And this week, Scarlotti has announced (allegedly against the wishes of his father-in-law) the creation of a new homeland for the Palestinians, a plan to help them to self-sufficiency in a fertile region made empty by the Iraq wars. Israel is *livid* at this, proving beyond all doubt (to myself at least) that they enjoy brutalizing Arabs (besides needing them for menial labour), and Scarlotti told them so in as many words.

"You'll just have to learn to live *without* servants," he bellowed at the Israeli envoy. Due to this, I like him immensely, but there is still a feeling of ambiguity at the bottom of my heart. I'll say it again: Scarlotti will save or damn us, or both.

At least we now live in interesting times once more...

4

THE TESTIMONY OF
OLENA PETRENKO

(via extracts from her journal)

Childhood is bound like the Gordian knot with my memories of the Black Sea, and I still feel its waters welling up within me today. Sometimes these waters are leaden, as grey as the military ships that sail on their curved expanses, and sometimes they are blue as pigmented cobalt. Then would come dusk, when I would sit and watch the seabirds waver to shore, flitting from open waters to the quiet empty vastlands in darkening spaces behind me, the same birds Ovid once saw during his exile, perhaps; and the same waters the Argonauts crossed searching for the fleece of renewal.

And out in the distance, invisible, the towering heights of Caucasus, where once-bright memories of the fire-thief have transmuted into something weird and many-faceted, and beyond these, pitch-black Karabakh in dolorous Armenia.

But king in my mind are legends of my own land – those of the mighty Bogatyr, so nameless and dread, whose Arrow brought war and suffering. He commanded his sons to throw this Arrow into the depths of the Black Sea, for they lacked the strength to wield it themselves, and that is why its waters are always restless.

And just lately, it seems, the Bogatyr has returned. [...]
These last few years, until yesterday, everything has been so empty in Kiev, falling into a void. The old places that once meant much to me seemed drained of blood and meaning, like a plastic bubble-pack sucked out with

a ridiculous vacuum. Even the mysterious fire of metal bands I used to admire was gone, and in interviews they now seemed empty imperialists.

But Kiev wasn't always like this – it once felt full of mystery and promise.

Was that just an illusion? Either this mystery never existed (then whence comes my memory of it?), or it *did* exist then disappeared (then why and where did it go?); and either way there is something unknown, unseen at work. A god or a demon mocks me. The only other alternative is that 'I' myself don't exist, but I can't accept that. So I would sigh, and say "the season of autumn is upon us," and other precious things like that, and my mother would look at me like I was mad.

"Why don't you follow your sister?" she would badger me. "She makes good money in America." But I shot her a look of withering scorn every time she broached this hated topic, although it failed to silence her. Nothing did...except when I would bark back, nagging her about Natalya's upbringing, and then she would take on a look of pouting indifference, pressing grey lips together til they were greyer still, an ashy tight communism. It seemed the world now *belonged* to people like her.

Then Anna, who I hadn't seen in ages, phoned and asked me to come to a hall in central Kiev and hear a speech. It was the North American Potentate for the Curia (or something like that), she said...and I told her coldly that I had no interest in such things.

She laughed and said: "This one is different," then hung up. I didn't know if she referred to the speech or the man, but her tone had struck me dumb with curiosity. So I went, endeavouring to see what was on the cards.

I had no idea that the fire would return to my heart last night!

The Bogatyr (for so I now think of him) was visiting Kiev with his Praetorians, the elite bodyguard he had created after his wife was assassinated, by a bullet said to be meant for him, and he was here to negotiate. He doesn't wish for open war, yet refuses to guarantee or confirm the new Ukrainian constitution until his authority in this land is recognised.

However: I didn't care about any of this. I only cared for his electrifying speech.

In his speech he *talked* of the Bogatyr, speaking openly of a Slavic legend that until then had gone unspoken in my heart, but instead of destroying this myth, *his* light seemed to make it grow! I feel sure he is sent as an Avatar from our gods...perhaps the Avatar of the entire Slavic folk, though he isn't Slav himself.

"*My* imperialism embraces ethnic and regional differences and boundaries," he thundered. "Unlike the phoney imperialism of Sheldon Albright, that traitor to humanity, with his open borders madness..." That drew a rousing cheer from the crowd, as Albright is powerful and supremely hated. And then the Bogatyr denounced some of our own Ukrainian nationalists as dupes, playing into the hands of Curia and Albright.

"But you're part of the Curia yourself!" someone shouted.

"I AM the Curia," grinned the Bogatyr. "And don't let anyone tell you otherwise. But now I am steering it in a *different direction.*"

How firmly and adamantly he stated this! And I knew that here was a man to be trusted, an agent of the virile gods themselves. And Anna thought so, too, as she danced towards me through the crowd, her face aglow with the flames of future.

"And well," she shouted, "wasn't I right to summon you?" I laughed merrily, taking her hand and leading her through the throng to somewhere we could talk more peaceably, but when we reached the park around the corner, the words just wouldn't came...only tears at our own rebirth.

And when I got home, I thought how flabby my drunken father looked compared to the Bogatyr. I had a sudden feeling he was already dead, and that if I planted a tree atop his grave, it too would grow to a living death, and so on for seven generations until, finally, a green sapling would emerge from the shadow of its petrified forbears...seven generations to break down the corpse.

But for me, the lightning is shaping a different world entirely.

[...]

Now many Ukrainians are volunteering for the Bogatyr's 'International Brigade' (even this name infuriates the Unicursal Curia, who seem to believe they have a monopoly on the international) and also the more elite Praetorian Guard. I myself have volunteered for the women's auxiliaries, and will learn in two days if I am accepted or not. Even if rejected (unlikely, as I am sound in body and soul), I will find some other way to help the Bogatyr to glory. But I very much wish to be accepted for the auxiliaries, as part of their task is spreading propaganda, which appeals to me immensely. Although the Bogatyr encourages traditional roles of wife and motherhood, I feel I can contribute in other ways at this point, and it seems that so do many other young women...the Bogatyr is loved!

[...]

Yesterday was the proudest day of my life – accepted into the brigades of Bogatyr! – but my mother had to sour the taste with a shallow argument, repeated from the propaganda of the Curia news machine:
"He will betray us. He is negotiating with Russia, to lock us into a definite sphere of Russian economic influence..."
"And, what if he is? He has extracted a guarantee from the Russians to leave Ukrainian *culture*, including neopagans like me, alone. And do you honestly think economics is more important than culture?"
"You can combine them. Your sister is in the movies, for instance…"
"In *porno* movies, in Los Angeles."
"At least it's money."
"It will destroy her soul, if she still has one."
"You are a vicious girl. I am ashamed of you."
"Well, at least I'm not corrupt." And then she snorted like a pig, leaving the room.
Truly, she does not understand.
She understands *nothing*.

[...]

The Bogatyr is succeeding in driving a wedge between the Ukraine administration and the 'official' Curia, but he has been less successful in the west and south Slavic lands. So now the Curia begins to play the role of mediator between the 'Bloc' (Croatia, Poland etc.) and the Bogatyr. It is difficult, because there has been a resurgence of the Western style 'left' in these countries: marches against the Archetype begun in Germany have spread outwards...but not to Ukraine, thank the gods!

Meantime, my parents try every trick in the book to make me quit the Brigade. They even cut me out a newspaper article about a big pagan festival in Lithuania, hoping to entice me there and away from Bogatyr...but my fealty to him *is* paganism in its purest state, somewhere flaccid festivals cannot pierce. For he is the Bogatyr.

And I am distressed, too, because I sense my parents' emptiness...how awful it must be for them! I wonder what they will take with them when they depart this plane of being? Just wasted time, dank and crumbling...

There was a moment only yesterday when I wondered if they might be right, and maybe *I* am going mad...and then I returned to the Brigade, and realised without doubt *we* are the sane ones!

In the end, they will see so too.

[...]

Arguments coming thick and fast now. Myself and mother, Bogatyr and Curia, each reflecting the other.

My father's depression and alcoholism are now established beyond doubt, and he is increasingly comfortable with them – until someone cuts off his supply of vodka, of course. I wanted to, but couldn't. Too soft and afraid of hurting him, but more damage to him in the long run. So should I steel myself to the task, worthy of Bogatyr?

Then, these constant fights with my mother on her raising of Natalya, my sister's little girl. Mother is determined to surround the infant with the worst of Western trash, and with newfound strength I berate her:

"What is the purpose of these dolls?"

"To play with, of course."

"Do they *look* Ukrainian, with their plastic eyes and muddy features blended from every race on earth?"

"Please don't tell me you're a racist as well as unpatriotic!"

"What? Racist *and* unpatriotic? How is that possible?"

"We know you are unpatriotic because you follow that awful Scarlotti...and you're racist because you also appear to have a problem with certain dolls..."

"They are disgusting. They're not a *real* race, they're artificial."

"It's such a shame you feel that way. They are what every normal girl plays with."

"And who's pushing them? The Curia!"

"I don't understand your politics."

"I just want every people to be proud and free...and Imperium guarantees that."

"I'm sorry, my girl, but you are racist and unpatriotic, and I scarcely recognise you any longer. I really don't know what has happened to my second favourite daughter."

Insults aside, she had everything the wrong way round, just like we were in mirror-backward universes! But as she said her piece, something boomed from the TV news which caused me to quiver in trepidation. The game has now begun in earnest:

"A spokesman for the Unicursal Curia today announced the organisation's official severance of North American Executive Commissioner Maximillian Scarlotti, who, however, is refusing to stand down, claiming that he represents a made-up fantasy body called the *Multicursal* Curia. This deluded man's ravings have caused great sadness to the world body, and to the humankind it represents."

So now the Curia and their controlled networks (in other words *all* the networks) were busy denouncing the Bogatyr as a 'traitor'. Israel was displeased with him, despite his avowal of 'the rights of peoples' (what does

that matter to them?), and the news footage showed
many Orthodox Jews wailing and gnashing their
teeth...as if anyone cared! So now "war is declared,
you'd better come down," and the world stands blinking
on the razor's edge. Will the Bogatyr's sons find strength
to wield his arrow?

[...]

I wanted to take mother to the Black Sea, so she
could sense the Bogatyr's rebirth for herself, but her eyes
clouded over when I told her of the legend. "Oh, that
old story," she said woodenly, and I knew then, finally,
that she is lost. I wept for her soul, and at the end felt
closure. There is nothing I can do for her, her soul will
drift to mist, so just find comfort in that. The real world
now is Brigade, and my happy friendships therein.

And now I know I possess the strength to launch legal
proceedings, to take my sister's child away from its
grandparents' care.

It will be a Brigade baby, and facilities will be
provided for it. Legends, too, more nourishing than
milk...for the Bogatyr is rising.

5

THE TESTIMONY OF
HARLAN COAD
(via his journal)

Cobain Day in Aberdeen today...hooray.

The first Cobain Day I really remember was the big one, the time it was made an offical public holiday. But Hoquiam celebrates it in April, a different day to us, and someone on the Aberdeen council said that made it too close to Hitler's birthday. That's when the trouble started, and the deputy mayor of Hoquiam was stabbed in the arm so the dark blood gushed.

After recovering, he apologized for his microaggressions, and Cobain Day had been a pretty quiet affair ever since. Hoquiam council now spell it Kobain Day (as 'Kurdt' sometimes spelled his own name that way), but there has been no more violence.

I always feel cynical around this time. Except for the ritual hymn 'Something in the Way' at the bridge-sleeping ceremony, they never even play the guy's music, and the whole thing seems like a big wank-fest. But I would hate for people to think I'm down on the guy. Besides the fact that Naomi likes him, he also had a good effect on at least one 'alienated loner' I used to know – Dobbin. The Nirvana song 'Tourettes' encouraged Dobbin to take up painting, and maybe he would be dead now if it wasn't for that. But Dobbin is the exception, not the rule, and hardly anyone listens to that kind of music anymore. The only thing that matters to most people is that drugs are *fully legal* in Aberdeen this one day of the year, and that's why I'm sitting here smoking a joint under the bridge as I write.

Soon a dozen others will be here for the bridge-sleeping ceremony, when the mayor lies down symbolically in the freezing mud...but I'll be well gone before then. I might walk over to the most recent statue, the one started four years ago that was never finished (and probably never will be), half-formed, with birdshit under its eyes like crocodile tears. Honestly, it looks more like Gollum from *The Lord of the Rings* than Kurt. They say they stopped building it because the tourists stopped coming – but I don't remember a time when they actually did. Even the 2017 ceremony was just a local affair.

And now, ten years later, the whole town seems empty. Naomi is gone, and we're all devastated, especially me. I really want to marry that girl, and I only realized it after she was gone. She's probably in some library in Olympia right now, working on her thesis. No, wait, she hasn't graduated yet, she intends to write a thesis on Kurt *after* she graduates...now I remember. She's the only one I know who's literally obsessed with our town's tutelary spirit, old murdered Kurt. He'd be sixty if he lived today, and hardly anyone here remembers him as a real person – if he ever actually was one. Some folk even think it's a conspiracy and he never existed at all. Not my grandmother, though – she thinks she may have seen him once, around 1986, cutting his toenails in the main street, just a couple of years before my mother was born, and before he was famous.

Mom, who's still politically correct years after it went out of fashion, once made a remark about how she read 'In Bloom' is an ironic song, and it was even more ironic that jocks would sing along to it when it was really an attack on them. That's what she'd read, anyway.

But as she said it, Grandma looked thoughtful, as if remembering an old crush.

So, I used to fantasize that Kurt was actually my grandfather, which would be better than the truth.

But I have to admit I find it hard to grasp the guy. Could he actually have been a real person, and if so then why did they make a fucking statue out of him?

These questions will probably never be answered...

Dobbin is joining the Dreamers and Poets Brigade. I record a conversation around the dinner table for posterity...the weirdest one ever, in which I saw a whole new side to Grandma.

Grandma: "What is the Dreamers and Poets?"

Me: "It's part of Scar-Lo's International Brigade."

Mom: [Snorting sound.]

Grandma: "And what is the International Brigade?"

Me: "It has generous wages, but tough training and discipline. The Dreamers and Poets is for artists, though, and it's more lenient. Scar-Lo is trying to get them to join in the fight against globalism or something. I think he's hoping to attract the Wolves of Joy. I dunno if they'll bite, though."

Mom: "If you had ever buried your own child, you would hate and despise that kind of horseshit." [She actually said horseshit.] "Scarlotti's a troublemaker."

Me: "You don't still blame me for that?" [It was a reference to my twin sister Kathy, who died in early childhood, less real to me even than Kurt]. "What's that got to do with Scarlotti?"

Mom: "How many children is *he* going to kill? He's making war."

Me: "Isn't war better than tyranny?"

Mom: "*Harlan!* What's gotten into you?"

Me: "The Curia have gotten out of hand. They're pushing everyone around."

Mom: "Maybe that's because they're trying to stamp out racism, sexism, transphobia…"

Me: "They're just words, Mom."

Mom: "You wouldn't say that if you saw a person of color being bullied…"

Me: "I don't think I'd see that, because they're more likely to be doing the bullying."

Mom: "*Harlan!*" [Nearly choking on her GMO salad.]

Grandma: "I'm afraid he may be right. Haven't you heard of this knockout game business?"

Mom: "A vile myth of the corporate media."

Me: "No, the media did their best to cover it up. But what's any of this got to do with Scar-Lo? He supports the right of *all* peoples to exist and thrive, doesn't he?"

Mom: "Yeah, separately, in little Nazi enclaves."

Me: "No, he's said there can also be mixed enclaves for people who want a multicultural homeland."

Mom: "*Everyone* should have a multicultural homeland."

Me: "So it can be as soulless as Seattle?"

Mom: "Aberdeen is more soulless."

Me: "How come it inspired Cobain to write his songs, then?"

Mom: "He hated it here. That's why he moved to Olympia."

Grandma: "I'm afraid that's not strictly true. He moved to Olympia because of pussy."

Mom: "*Mother!*"

Me: [Snickering.]

Grandma: "You shouldn't be so uptight, dear. Anyway, it was *politically correct* pussy by all accounts...the kind Olympia is famous for. So you can relax."

Me: "And what do *you* think about Scar-Lo, Grandma?"

Grandma: "Everything is so dreary just now, Harlan. Maybe you should join the Dreamers and Poets brigade yourself. You've done some writing, haven't you?"

Mom: "*Mother!*"

Grandma: "Put a sock in it."

Mom: "Encouraging him to join a fascist cult!"

Me: "I guess I'll see what Dobbin thinks of it."

Grandma: "Isn't that a bit insipid, waiting for someone *else* to test the water? Where is the fire of youth?"

Me: [Blushing bright red.]

Mom: "I can't believe I'm hearing this. In my own house."

Grandma: "It's a rented house. And if you believe Harlan has any prospects in a world dominated by the Curia, then you're out of your fucking mind, girl."

Mom: [Storms away from the table in disgust.]

Grandma: "Just consider what I said, Harlan. You have to grasp the nettle if you want to be happy. My

biggest mistake was not realizing that in time. There's
still hope for you, though."

So I went down to the basement and put some King
Diamond onto the antique turntable ("*Grandma, welcome
home!*") to thank her for her honesty. (A more entertaining
singer than Kurt, IMHO).

[...]

Forget Mom's fascist paranoia about Scar-Lo. I met
my first *real* Nazi today. Not a German one, though. He
was from a group called North West Front, and called
himself a 'white nationalist', but they're the ones the
media call Nazis, right?

Anyway, night was falling over Aberdeen and I
decided to take the bus home. The bus was nearly full,
and this large stocky man in a camo jacket sat down next
to me, that is, in the aisle seat opposite to my aisle seat,
and I had a sudden vision of blood. Everything seemed
to go red. Then, half a minute later, he got into an
argument with the couple in front of him, who were
talking about President Hodge.

"I think the president is doing his best in a tricky
situation," the man was saying.

"Lies!" bellowed the Nazi. At first I thought he was
drunk, but his speech was clear, just highly exuberant.
"You've been listening to the Ziomedia, haven't you?
Hodge belongs in a mental asylum, along with his
corrupt cuckservative lackeys."

"No offence, buddy, but I was talking to my wife, not
to you."

"Well, we're in the end times, pal, so no need to stand
on ceremony. I won't apologize for speaking my mind,
that's for damn sure." For some reason I was anxious to
defuse the situation, perhaps because his bellowing was
interrupting my lovelorn musings about Naomi.

"Do you really think we're in the *end times?*" I asked
politely.

"Hey, buddy, this could be the last bus ride we ever
take."

"Why...is there a bomb in your jacket?" I chuckled
nervously.

"Do I *look* like a terrorist?"

"Um…"

"Oh, so you think I look like the *media* type of a terrorist, is that it? Always a white man, isn't it? So utterly realistic…" His vocal chords dive-bombed with sarcasm. "No, if *I* had a bomb we'd all be fucking dead by now. I don't mess around. Lucky for you, though, I'm the honorable type. I only kill with fists, knives or guns, and only then when absolutely necessary."

I believed him. And then he started telling me about his organization, which I admit made me a bit uncomfortable. The other passengers were doing their best to ignore him, glancing timidly only when they rose to get off the bus.

Put bluntly, the guy aims to set up a 'White Republic' here in the Pacific Northwest, but amidst all his political talk I learnt something highly interesting: it seems that his people have offered Scar-Lo the 'Honorary Presidency' of their North West Republic.

"He's not WN strictly speaking, but he stands for the *rights of peoples,* including whites."

I was all like 'whoa', but inside I felt far less cynical, even touched. Sometimes I wish I had the 'alphaness' of these people, any of them! Scar-Lo, the Nor'westers, the Wolves of Joy…hell, even my **PC** mother has more balls than I do. Grandma was right, perhaps it *is* time to grasp the nettle. But how do I do it?

The bus was getting closer to home, and by now it was nearly empty.

For some reason, I asked what he thought of the Wolves of Joy.

"Unreliable," he snorted. From his talk I gathered that the Nor'westers were more conservative than the Wolves. Also, the Wolves originally started as a rebellion against 'boomers', who are now dying off and irrelevant…or that's what the Nazi thinks, anyhow.

"Look I'll admit that the boomers squandered a lot," he said, "but you have to move on, and besides, later generations aren't any better. A lot of the gripes about boomers have to do with them locking up all the wealth, and those kinds of materialist concerns are beneath the dignity of the North West Front."

"But the Wolves themselves have transcended their anti-boomer origins, haven't they?"

"Maybe," he muttered.

"And they're anti-colonialist, and so are you."

"Maybe," he muttered again.

My stop was coming up. It was the last stop, and I realized in horror that he must be getting off here too! We stepped off the bus, out into the rotting night. He walked along with me for a bit before I got the courage to say: "Uh, do you live round here?"

"Huh?" He looked round, confused. "Truth be told, I don't even remember where I was going..."

"We're right on the edge of town. If you wait on the next street there'll be a bus back to Cobain Plaza before too long."

"Nah, think I'll just walk. I'm an animal, really, I feel cooped up on a bus. Not even sure why I was on it to begin with." And with that he turned and trudged across the vacant wasteland to the next street, right though a big clump of *stinging nettles*.

My time approacheth, surely...

[...]

The trip to Olympia was hardly what you would call a success. I wanted to win her over with words...words of steel, words of adamant, words of barbed wire and monkeys' brains...but I couldn't even find her, and the events of the world kept impinging. I wandered around the campus of the Evergreen State College in a daze, for I don't know how long, as afternoon turned to night, and then a security guard approached shining a torch into my face.

He said: "I won't bother asking you for ID as it's clear you're not a student...now scram, or I'll hold you til the cops get here. And you don't want *them* to get involved."

I'm not sure how he knew that I wasn't an Evergreen student...maybe your physiognomy changes when you take classes there...but I left before this shambling ape tossed its nose further into my field of flowers. I'm the last person to cause a scene.

So I caught a bus downtown and checked into a hostel. The TV in the foyer blared out some unexpected news: a serious outbreak of Ebola had occurred among Scar-Lo's troops. I still don't know what to think of Scar-Lo, but the news depressed me in some phantasmic way.

I got to the twelve-bed dorm, and some guy had put a tablecloth round his bunk (I could see his dreadlocks poking out), and was smoking a substance that smelt like burning cowshit. That depressed me still further, so I went for a walk outside to collect my thoughts.

On the dark street at the other side of the block I rounded a corner only to have more torches shine into my eyes, this time from what turned out to be two black cops. I answered their grim questions submissively, half-paranoid they were telepathic, and knowing they were waiting for the slightest excuse to beat me down. Eventually they got bored, so I hurried back to the hostel, relieved to have escaped unmaimed.

The next day I returned to Evergreen in full sunshine, mingling with the collegiate body in a spirit of friendship...but they seemed very sedate compared with my image of what college students are supposed to be like. Maybe they all had hangovers? I got some odd frowns, particularly from females, increasing my paranoia that my physiognomy really *did* look out of place, and, after one last look around for Naomi (there wasn't any sign of her), I'm sorry to say that I fled that sterile place, heart pounding with fear.

I thought of having another go tomorrow, so paid for one more night at the hostel. This time the TV in the foyer announced that Scar-Lo himself has contracted Ebola! There is chaos, apparently, and no one knows what is going on.

Although I can't compare my miserable problems to Scar-Lo's, this certainly matched how I felt.

Back in the dorm, the stinking hippy had moved on and his bed was taken by two Chinese girls (not lesbians, just top and tailing) who had left their evening dinner (raw fish) on the table with flies crawling all over it. This didn't seem to bother them...but I confess I went to the john and puked everywhere (probably a reaction to my horrible day, not to the flyblown fish). Anyway, next morning I decided to leave the disgusting city of Olympia, which makes Aberdeen feel clean and welcoming by comparison.

What did Kurt see in this dump? Grandma must be right, the guy must have moved here for 'pussy' as she delicately put it. As for Naomi, who am I kidding? I love her, but she's better off without a loser like me. Time to move on. A fire of pride now burns inside me, even stronger than the pangs of unrequited love.

The morning paper in the foyer told me that presidential forces are now seeking to regain control of what Scar-Lo dubbed the 'American Protectorate,' now that he himself is out of action and almost certainly dying.

It seems Scar-Lo has alienated the right-wingers lately by raising taxes to pay for his Brigades, although he also put an *extra special* tax on 'rich leftists', which caused a lot of hysteria. So nearly everyone is against him...all the blabbermouths, anyway...what a guy! On my way back to the Aberdeen bus I heard some snoots outside a posh café making catty remarks about him, and one of them called him an 'ignorant redneck'.

Hold on, this guy is supposed to have been the greatest scholar of his time! I'd hate to know what these snoots would say about *me* behind my back.

[...]

Scar-Lo has recovered!

The doctors are announcing it as a virtual miracle, as it seems no one had ever made a *full* recovery from such advanced Ebola before. People are now saying he is chosen by God, or the gods, or providence, depending on their beliefs.

Tonight he made a televised speech about a dream he had, when the virus was at its worst...a dream where someone sang to him about the legend of a king and a roofing tile. That is to say, in the dream he was a king of some sort, richly clad, and sitting in a beautifully decorated hall...but a singer was singing him the legend of *another* king, who lived a lot earlier. This earlier king had been warned by an oracle that his great task in life was to fight against an *Iron Empire*. He wasn't fazed by this however, as in his heart it coincided with his own more selfish goal – creating an empire of his own.

So he invaded the lands of this Iron Empire, taking a couple dozen war elephants along with his massive army (and this led Scar-Lo, in the dream, to suspect it was *Hannibal* being sung about...but, as if in response, the singer stressed that this was a full generation before Hannibal was even born).

Then the king offered the Iron Empire peace terms, but they were rejected...so the cup of peace rose in the air and was spilled, and the Moon State then abandoned their own alliance-negotiations with him because his empire-ambitions would bar them from gaining land of their own. And then, the fought-over Lands themselves started to rebel against him, so he had to resort to force and dictatorship to keep them in line. These heavy-handed measures proved so unpopular that the Lands turned against him even more, so that his sun was in eclipse and battles not going his way. Then, after a final struggle he withdrew from the Lands forever, leaving them for the Moon State and the Iron Empire to squabble over.

But his own dreams of empire wouldn't fade, so he turned to another land – the Rugged Peninsula – which he tried to win control of. But resistance was unexpectedly strong, and his own son died in the retreat. Then voices warned him to flee to the woods, but instead of listening to them he chose to interfere in the quarrel of an ancient city that had nothing to do with him. And while he was there, some decrepit crone threw a roofing tile at his head, knocking him down, and a solider finished him off from behind, beheading him.

On waking, Scar-Lo immediately realized that the king in question was some guy called *Pyrrhus of Epirus*.

"Was that who I was?" he asked his viewing audience. "Once I was told (if you believe in such things) that I was the reincarnation of a powerful leader from the past. And now I believe that it must have been Pyrrhus. The Iron Empire, of course, being Rome.

"So I have made a cursory study of Pyrrhus' weaknesses, in order to avoid them myself. His main shortcoming was his tendency to spread his battles too wide, and a failure to band with his enemies against the Iron Empire. For instance, he should have worked harder to cultivate an alliance with the Moon State.

"I swear that I will work harder on my own alliances from henceforth...and if I fall, it will not be from hubris.

"Pyrrhus also had money problems because of his habit of hiring expensive mercenaries, and this, again, is something I can relate to. So I am now calling on all idealists to flock to my banner for nominal wages, in order to build a better world..."

So, now the International Brigade is being flooded with applications – including the Dreamers and Poets, of course, for many artists are fascinated by Scar-Lo's Dream Speech.

The Curia, on the other hand, are using the the speech to convince people that he's insane. They have even announced that the Crusade Against Wahhabism is no longer important, and that the only thing that matters is Scar-lo's standing down and trial for Global Treason...

[...]

A lot has happened since the last time I picked this journal up.

Civil War has come to America, and much of the country is back under Presidential control, but the Nor'westers have seized some big tracts of land in Washington and Idaho (though not as much as they expected, apparently). I have witnessed things that would have made my hair turn grey if it wasn't already dyed green, and I can hear my mother moaning and cursing the fact that she has lived to see such times. Grandma is more cynical, taking it in her stride, just as I would have expected.

Around ten minutes after learning from the TV news about the Civil War, I heard actual shots fired, and later that night we witnessed Presidential soldiers, then Nor'westers, driving through the streets of Aberdeen in open-topped cars. I was stoned, which made it worse, so that it seemed like the cars were the ones in charge...their headlights were cold, mean eyes, and the drivers were their helpless slaves. And they were all going off to a big battle somewhere near Kurt's bridge.

Mom and Grandma were both drunk and arguing about some trivial thing from ten years back, so I went down to the basement and smoked another joint. Then I stretched my limbs and contemplated what the hell I would do if either side won. The alternative, of course, would be a draw, in which Aberdeen would be utterly annihilated. Would Kurt have liked that? Would it be *his* revenge, like Frances Farmer's on Seattle?

The Presidentials will surely win, though, I thought, because they have more troops and resources.

But then, the Nor'westers are more tenacious because they are fighting for an ideal.

I wished, and not for the first time, that *I* had an ideal, too...but all I could see in front of me was the face of Naomi. And with Olympia probably still under Presidential control, she must be in hell tonight, writhing under the jackboot of the enemy.

That thought surprised me...what was lurking in my unconscious, that I would so readily think of Presidentials as 'the enemy'? Wasn't I always raised to think of *Neo-Nazis* as a menace? And the Nor'westers will probably crack down on marijuana if they ever take over, making my own life emptier than ever...

I had a sudden vision of them, these Nor'westers...grim-faced elementals, men of wrath, all lined up like square-jawed mannikins, staring with hard contempt at the decadent liberals of Cascadia, of whom they would certainly number myself as one. Laser beams would shoot from their eyes, obliterating us all, making a dirt patch in which they could grow corn and start from scratch, or something, with all decadence erased. Hey, that might be the best solution. Isn't decadence the root cause of depression – the depression that afflicts so many of us around here – and isn't depression a sign of unworthiness? And isn't unworthiness another word for *unworth?*

So come on, men of oak, blow us all away!

But fuck, fuck, fuck, something in me wants to keep living...

And again, I see Naomi's face before me, stretching out into the far distance.

[...]

The guns are tapping out their autistic messages again...but why do I get the strong feeling that the Nor'westers have won?

[...]

It's confirmed: the North West Front has taken Aberdeen and Hoquiam, while Olympia and the Seattle region remain under Presidential control.

So I'm cut off from Naomi, probably for good.

[...]

The square-jawed mannikins have taken over, and they have been ruling Aberdeen better than people would have thought. They have acted to stimulate independent trade and bartering, and have also set up a simple welfare system for those who have lost their livelihoods due to the war (which is quite a lot of people). My family is scraping by okay, but I have been drafted for the town labor brigade, and have to spend six hours a day, five days a week repairing damage from the Battle of Aberdeen. Other than that, my time is my own. It's not so bad...

One thing that will *not* be fixed is the varied assortment of Cobain statues – in fact we have been tasked with pulling them down. One of the first acts of the Nor'westers was to abolish Cobain Day, which wasn't much of an issue with the populace, although not everyone is happy about its replacement holiday – Hitler's Birthday. But we all get double rations on Führertag, whereas all we got on Cobain Day was the right to smoke weed in public, and a general feeling of malaise.

The colored (Black and Hispanic) population has been transferred to the Presidential territories in exchange for certain square-jawed prisoners held in internment camps near Seattle. I thought this would raise some protests, but no one seems to care, except for my mother who mutters harsh words over it.

I find myself constantly wondering what Naomi is doing. Is she humming a Nirvana song and waiting for better times? Has she found a sweetheart, or perhaps gotten engaged? I'll probably never know. She stopped emailing anyone I know in Aberdeen ages ago, and it's now illegal to send emails to Presidential territory (though they have no way of policing it). I don't know her email address anyway, and even if I did, you need some kind of special dongle to get the internet now, which we don't have and can't afford.

The Nor'westers seem serious about moving to a barter economy, though it's being done in dribs and drabs and I'm not sure how long it will be before the money stashed under Grandma's mattress is declared worthless. Oh well, we struggle on.

[...]

Scar-Lo himself has been to Aberdeen!

He was invited as a guest by several of the patchwork of mini-states that constitute the North West Republic, and though he declined the honorary presidency, he chose to accept the invitation to visit. And by doing so he has apparently earned further pariah status as a 'Nazi' by the 'international community' (i.e. the Curia-controlled media), who have declared him even worse than the elderly Vladimir Putin...but hardly anyone takes the 'international community' seriously any more, and those who do waste their time gossiping in cafes in Seattle or Portland, and aren't much threat to anyone.

I actually attended the speech by Scar-Lo, right near the ruins of my old smoking spot, where the Kurt statue that was never finished has now been carted off to landfill. I wonder if the seagulls still fight over who gets to shit on it?

It was surreal seeing a celebrity in the flesh. I didn't have a very good view, but it was obvious how different Scar-Lo looks in real life than on the TV...more fragile, somehow, as if burdened with the weight of the

212

world...and perhaps he is. There is a flame beneath the surface, however, that aroused my awe and, I'm ashamed to say, my envy. Why does my own flame find it so hard to catch hold and illumine the dazzled shell in which it burns? Are some flames purer than others, or do they burn with a higher heat? I would give anything to know.

Scar-Lo's speech was mainly about autonomy, and gained a rousing reception from the crowd. Everyone who saw it seemed electrified afterwards, though I don't know how long that will last. I have to admit my own feet are kind of skipping...Scar-Lo must have some magical ability, a power to motivate crowds.

He is also very intelligent – much of his speech about economic autarchy and regionalism went completely over my head. But he stated very clearly that while he didn't agree with all the views of the Nor'westers, he now recognizes that they have set up their own state and are creating a unique culture for the non-metropolitan parts of Cascadia.

"The Puget Sound area will remain a Free Port under Presidential control," he roared, "but in the areas outside of it, the North West Republic is here to stay. I recognize it unconditionally, giving it an honored place in my coming Imperium!" There was a wave of raptured cheering and applause...and so I think the residents of Aberdeen have gotten used to the idea that they are part of a new nation. It didn't take them long. American flags have been banned, and many are already flying the North West flag in their front yards, though it isn't required by law. Aberdeeners are adaptable...

But what happens now that Scar-Lo has gone away? Who will motivate us tomorrow? It remains to be seen.

[...]

A talking head, some guy who used to be a 'Catholic traditionalist' but who publicly renounced religion and threw in his lot with the Curia, has declared that the Curia would have *revoked* its fatwa against Scar-Lo if it hadn't been for his diplomatic visit to the North West, which apparently put him beyond the pale.

Malicious bluffing swipe? Would they *really* have rescinded the declaration of heresy?

Then I could have seen Naomi again...

But I doubt it. These people are liars through and through.

So I lit some incense and visualized her instead.

And now Scar-Lo has sent communications to ALL world leaders, asking them to pick sides between him and the Curia.

So that's it.

World War Three is coming.

I have to cross the Great Divide and see her, just once...once would be enough.

I think that Grandma knows how I feel. She hasn't said anything directly (how could she, as she doesn't know specifics), but she talks about roses being the finest flowers because they're harder to pick, and about life being what we make of it. She is encouraging me, despite the danger, or so I choose to think.

Something is awakening inside me. Is it courage?

[...]

Here I am, betraying my new country for the cursed Presidential Territories, all for the love of a girl who probably barely remembers me. I'm a fuck-up, but a happy one at present. If it's all an illusion, then let me enjoy it while it lasts.

Aberdeen to Olympia is fifty miles as the crow flies, and it felt good leaving in the morning before Mom or Grandma were up, after first filling my backpack with food and plucking a flower from next door's garden, knowing that I might never see my hometown again. I couldn't find a rose, so I had to make do with some saggy pink mongrelly weed, with bugs crawling all over it. Then I got a bus to Cosmopolis and started hitchhiking.

The traffic is much thinner than it was before the new Civil War (or 'War Between the Hates' as some wit dubbed it). On the other side of the road some guy was hitching in the opposite direction. There were big gaps in the traffic so we got to talking, and I told him I was seeking love in the east.

"Heading out west myself..."

"How come you don't get the bus through Aberdeen and Hoquiam? There won't be many cars going all the way through."

"Don't have a penny to my name."

"Hardcore! So where are you trying to get to?"

"The sea. I've lived within ninety miles of it my whole life but never seen it. What a joke! World war's on the way, and I have to see the ocean before I die, man. It'll be *immense*." I was silent, not knowing if he meant the ocean, the experience of seeing it, or his impending death. Then a car stopped and picked him up, and it was then that I realized the *only* cars passing were going westwards. Was there some conflict in the borderlands people were fleeing from? Although it is a cliché to gulp nervously, I did so.

But ten minutes later a car finally came the right way, and stopped. The wiry fellow who opened the door had a hardline stare, and his face twitched as if there were strange electric pulses running through his body. He said he was going as far as Porter, some thirty miles down the road.

"Awesome," I said, jumping in. "That gets me most of the way there."

"And where is *there?*" he asked as we screeched away down the road. (I was glad there was so little traffic because his driving was already making me nervous.) I didn't want to say Olympia, so I muttered the name of a town south of Porter, and he laughed.

"You can't fool me. I know you're headed into the Hodgelands."

"No, no..."

"Yes, yes. It's written all over you. Soft little lank like you couldn't hack it in a White Republic. Oh don't worry, I won't tell. I ain't on anyone's side. I'm just a mercenary. I kill for *money*. Principles can fuck themselves, har har har." (I can't write his laugh down properly, it was a kind of gargling growl).

Well, I won't lie, I was starting to get a bit scared. Historically there have been a lot of serial killers in this area, like Billy Gohl, and the Green River Killer, and this guy seemed like he would fit their ranks well. Then he said: "Take a look in the glove compartment." I did so, and saw a pistol with a silencer which looked suspiciously like a replica, but as I know shit all about guns I couldn't be sure, so I shut the compartment nervously.

"The Silent Killer they call me," he leered. "I take out who I want to take out, Presidential or Nor'wester. But don't worry, pal, I won't kill you. You're too soft-looking to be worth it. Bet you're one of those crinkly-eyed potheads, ain't that right?" He seemed certain, so there was no point arguing. I merely gave a nervous laugh.

"Course you are," he said with condescending pity. And then, true to his name, the Silent Killer passed the rest of the journey in complete silence, the better to hear my heart beating with fear over the engine noise.

I was ready to grab the gun at any moment, just in case he tried reaching for it, but to my relief he was true to his word, and dropped me outside of Porter, giving a sardonic salute by way of farewell. I sucked the oxygen in deeply and gratefully.

After walking a couple of miles down some backroads, I found myself in the Capitol State Forest, a big tract of woodland with four-wheel-drive tracks and hiking trails running through it.

I trudged through the forest for at least two hours without coming across a single soul. Then, during a rest on a tree stump to eat, I heard the sound of female sobbing in the distance, and had a sudden vision of Naomi, so I walked cautiously towards it. A girl around my own age was sitting on a mossy log and blubbing, a bottle of cheap wine her only companion. I approached deferentially, and asked timidly what the matter was.

"I'm crying because Jake, m-my boyfriend, is in Olympia. We're separated *forever*. And I've vowed to pine away near the border."

"Well, I'm going to Olympia myself, to see my...uh, a girl I know. So maybe we could go there together."

"No...like I said...I've vowed to pine away."

"Oh."

There wasn't much else to say after that, so I went on my way through the forest. She seemed taken aback as I

walked off, but aside from an intensification of her
blubbing, said nothing.

Should I have handled the situation differently? I'm
not sure what I was supposed to have done...I was hardly
going to throw my arms around her neck and implore
her, was I?

Anyway, in the late afternoon, I finally began to
approach the borderlands. I paused to look at the
handdrawn map I had copied from a real one in the
library, and as I stood there trying to make head or tail
of it, afternoon gradually turned into twilight. I decided
on a path, and after walking for fifteen minutes I
stumbled on a cache of abandoned logging equipment
on which two weird children were playing a game that
seemed to invoke the souls of the dead.

"Three nights spent in the house of death," they
chanted. "To tame wild wisdom's breath..."

And then a ragged old man, apparently their
grandfather emerged from a nearby shack, and asked
who I was. My instinct told me to trust him, so I said I
was trying to get across the border to Olympia (but not
the reason why). It turned out he was a *smuggler*, and
offered to take me across with his run of goods that very
night! I was in luck.

The goods, it turned out, consisted of packages of
compressed marijuana. I asked how many times he had
done the smuggling run, and it turned out this was the
first time! Still, he seemed like he knew what he was
doing.

Our adventure took us four or five miles through the
moonlit woods. At one point we came across a female
trapper, who turned out to be a Nor'wester setting traps
for enemy soldiers (they were old-fashioned steel raccoon
traps).

"And what if you get one of our own by mistake?"
asked Gramps.

"Then I'll drag him back to the bedroom," she
grinned, "and have some fun while I heal his mangled
foot."

For some reason I thought she said 'heel' his mangled
foot, and that her traps were therefore particularly
vicious. Even after realizing I had misinterpreted, I

noticed that she had a slightly sadistic leer about her, so I kept walking, and Gramps soon followed. She didn't twig to the possibility we might have been smugglers.

The next folks we came across were from the Presidential side, and it now became clear that the old man had made previous arrangements to bribe them (presidential troops being notoriously corrupt, unlike the NWers). And to cut a long story short, we got through. I farewelled Gramps and made my way towards the city of destiny.

So that was the story of my adventures in no-man's land. Now it's dawn, and I'm lying by a muddy stream outside Olympia, hiding from patrols, with freezing northwest rain coming down on the back of my neck like tiny heroin needles. So here's a big hearty 'fuck you', Kurt, from the muddy banks of an unnamed creek (not the pathetic Wishkah). You had nothing to whine about, but I expect your ghost has faded by now...there are other spirits on the march.

[...]

Well, I managed to penetrate Olympia without anyone asking me for papers. The city is almost free of soldiers, because they've all been dispatched to the borderlands. Even so, it seems like a place of faded glory. The student types seemed even more sedate than usual, as if struck by the fact that everything they believed in the past has now been invalidated.

I walked past the hostel on the way to the campus, and it was shut down. Not surprising, really, as these aren't exactly prime tourist years that we're living through. But *I* felt like I was in Paris in the Spring, and my heart was beating rapturously.

I strolled down the Evergreen Parkway and finally arrived at the campus. There was no extra security as I had feared, but glossy flyers were posted everywhere, with messages like:

SEE SOMETHING, SAY SOMETHING: REPORT ANY *SEPARATIST* TALK ON CAMPUS.

Another one said:

ANTI-GLOBAL SPEECH IS NOT FREE SPEECH.

And my favourite:

MOCKING YOUR ELECTED REPRESENTATIVES HELPS THE ENEMY.

The word 'enemy' had blood dripping from its letters. At least the no-nonsense Nazis in Aberdeen don't resort to that kind of cheese…

I now reached the gleaming new student dormitory building, and milled around until someone came out of an electronically locked door, passing in quickly as he did so. Then I sat still as a mouse on a sofa in the foyer, wondering what to do. Should I knock on every damned door? There must be hundreds of dorms in this massive building.

I got up intending to do so, and then…I saw her. She entered the foyer with a tall black guy and a couple of skinny white chicks. She was looking very skinny herself…the campus diet, no doubt. I walked across to her.

She glanced at me with a kind of tired sneer…then looking more closely, her eyes narrowed with confusion.

"*Harlan?*"

"Yep."

"Are you at college now?"

"Nope."

"Then what are you doing here?"

"Uh…" I glanced at the black guy, who was doing his best to give a 'I be wise patriarchal nigga, you want me deal with this skinny white dweeb?' kind of look, but thankfully she said: "I'll catch you guys up." She was probably embarrassed they had to see me at all. The football scholar nodded, and sauntered out the door, his two 'bitches' giving me curious looks on the way out.

Naomi said in a cold voice: "Well, do you want to come up to my dorm and explain things?"

"All right."

A plush elevator, then a walk past a lot of doors, and we were in the room that she shared with another girl, who fortunately wasn't there, discussing things. But I couldn't melt the frost from her voice, no matter how hard I tried.

"You mean you crossed the border *illegally?*" Her eyes bulged out. "You fucking *idiot* Harlan. It's lucky I've known you so long, or I'd report you to the authorities, for sure."

Even as she said it, I noticed a poster above her bed with two crying children under a Mexican flag...the poster said 'No one is illegal.' And on her chest of drawers was a sticker celebrating 'Open Borders Day' (which fell near to the Hoquiam Cobain Day). But although Naomi has turned into a hypocrite, I felt I could still save her. After looking round at the photos on the wall, which were mainly of her in compromising positions with people of both sexes, I turned to her and said: "I love you."

She gave me a look of what can only be described as murderous hatred. For a moment I thought she was going to call campus security, but then she took cold pity on me.

"Go back to Aberdeen, Harlan. We don't want dreamers here. Look at the trouble they cause – look at Maximillian Scarlotti."

"Wasn't *Kurt* a dreamer?"

"I'm not a fan of Kurt's...I'm no longer writing my thesis on him."

"Why?"

"He liked guns too much. It didn't sit right with me as a gun control advocate."

So, she had become a true conformist, one of the dreaded campus normals!

"But you already *knew* he liked guns."

"It came to overshadow his more progressive qualities for me...there was a point when it became too much. *He wasn't the person that I needed him to be.*"

I felt a sudden flash of rage, against her and against Kurt, and I believe I began yelling incoherently. Then Naomi said calmly but firmly: "If you stay, I'll have to report you." So I left, and found this little closet at the end of the hallway to write my diary and to let off steam.

What the fuck did I come here for? This icy bitch who looks at me with the eyes of an enemy? How could *this* have been the girl I had fixed in my mind for so long?

She isn't, of course, *but where did that girl go?*

And now I have a vision, for the first time in months, of how my twin sister died.

I was five years old, sick with an infectious illness. Mom still lived with my drunken father at the time, and Grandma offered to take my sister back to her place so she didn't get sick also. But on the way there was a car crash...which Grandma survived and my sister didn't.

And Mom still blames me for killing her, because *I* was the one who got sick.

Oh shit, now there are footsteps outside the door. Cobain, it is *you* Naomi has betrayed.

[Coad was taken to an internment camp near Bremerton, WA, and terminated by lethal injection for wartime espionage. — E.J.C.]

6

THE TESTIMONY OF
DR. ADRIAN SAVAGE

Rendering this report in plain language (avoiding psychiatric jargon as much as possible) should be relatively easy, as existing medical terms are completely useless when describing Johnny 'Buffo' Stokes, who, psychiatrically speaking, is a law unto himself.

Of course, I understand the distrust of headshrinkers and their jargon. There are more psychiatrists than ever in the military at this point. Many of the 'mental health community' found themselves out of work after Scarface's selective editing of the forces, but under Presidential rule they have been reinstated and reinforced. Not that this was entirely unwarranted – there is an increasingly fine line between the soldier given leeway to kill and the soldier who is court-martialled or put in a loony bin *for killing*, and the stress for grunts who constantly make these kind of calls is enormous (though this may change with the gathering intensity of the war against Scarface, where, I predict, increasingly, anything will go), and then, of course, there are the psychiatrists needed for the *children* of the military – lots and lots of them.

So with our numbers swollen like never before, it should perhaps come as no surprise that an anti-psychiatric movement has emerged in the forces. One of its founding members (who blew his own brains out after the First Battle of Damascus) even had a slogan: 'mental illness is a myth'. Now that's going *too* far...

Anyway, back to the report. I was assigned to Buffo as part of my research fellowship, sponsored by the The Reverend Dr. Martin Luther King, Jr. Institute for

Psychiatric Medicine. The topic of my research was, and still is, the problem of difficult-to-diagnose battlefield trauma, and Buffo seemed a case in point.

The shrink originally assigned to his case made a cursory diagnosis of symphorophilia (a condition whereby sexual arousal is achieved by witnessing disasters, in this case the carnage of war). But this proved not to be the case at all – the cause of Buffo's agitation not being sexual in nature, at least not *directly* so. Nor do I believe it to be any kind of PTSD. I can only report what I have observed at first hand. His condition is truly a mysterious one.

On first landing in the Middle East I reported to a Combat Stress Control unit on board the non-commissioned hospital ship USNS The Reverend Dr. Martin Luther King, Jr., where Buffo had been brought for an evaluation before being released back into active duty (he was too valuable to spare for long, even with his curious condition). I was briefed on board ship, then flown into the combat zone to begin my fellowship. From that point, I was on my own.

I found Buffo in an urban part of the southern Iraqi war zone at the break of dawn, heading off for a morning snipe. Snipers usually work in two-man teams, with a shooter and spotter taking turns to avoid eye fatigue, but Buffo didn't need a spotter or flanker...he had eyes of steel.

While Buffo was the PS military's best sniper by far, beating Chris Kyle's record (with over 240 confirmed kills), his mental instability had become the subject of concern. Any other soldier with his stress levels would have been relieved from active duty, but, as I said, Buffo was too valuable to spare. And while emotionally troubled soldiers can endanger the mission, that wasn't what bothered Buffo's superiors...the fact is, they were concerned about the possibility of him defecting to the other side.

So I approached him, still considering how to initiate conversation. What would be his attitude to having a shrink attached to him for large parts of his day?

As it turned out, I needn't have worried. He seemed eager to welcome me, shaking hands vigorously when I told him who I was.

"I fucking hate sand niggers," he grinned (those were his exact first words to me), "but I *love* homosexuals. If you're gay, then you're alright with me."

"I'm not...gay...actually."

"Oh. Are you some other kind of LGBTTQQIAAPCINDNQQINBTSAO?" (He had actually memorized this now outmoded and faintly non-PC acronym, pronouncing it clearly and distinctly for my benefit).

"No."

"But...you're *tolerant*, right?"

"Well, sure...I like to think of myself as a tolerant person."

"Alright, doc, that's just as well. If there's one thing I can't stand it's homophobes. Now sand niggers..." He stared off in the distance, as if scouring for the enemy.

"Yes?"

"They should all just die. Because they hate faggots. Gays, I mean. I wish I was gay myself, but unfortunately I like women too much, ha ha." As he said it, I was reminded of that unfortunate historical figure Kurdt Kobain, who had also apparently wished himself to be homosexual. I didn't bother telling Buffo that the term 'gay' had been banished from progressive circles for quite some time, and was now considered as quaint and patronizing as 'negro' once had been, before it was replaced by 'black', then 'POC', then 'nigga', then 'negar', then 'blackamore'. (And recently, of course, 'negro' has again become the sole polite term.)

But although Buffo was uneducated, and could not be expected to keep up with such limber subtleties, in his own way he had a flexible mind...although I could sense, too, a certain level of aggression inside him, and steeled myself in case it should come to the surface. Typically, solider stress occurs due to easily understandable factors — combat fatigue, or a 'Dear John' letter from a girlfriend. Buffo's stress, on the other hand (and it was palpable), had a completely unknown cause. I was determined to get to the bottom of it, although I realized

I would have to take things at a relaxed pace, approaching the matter subtly over the course of several weeks or months.

While Buffo's love of all things 'LGBTTQQIAAPCINDNQQINBTSAO' at least demonstrated a patriotic loyalty to the values of the Presidential States (so much that I wondered if his superiors might have jumped the gun somewhat in fearing he would defect), I couldn't deny that there was a paradox at the heart of his persona that I had yet to get to grips with.

Well, after some more conversation on the topic of 'sand niggers', he bade me follow as he went to set up his sniping post, and we entered a house in darkness. I sat quietly in a dark corner while he arranged things (avoiding being sighted is a real skill, as you can imagine). In the dust of the clay shelves in my desolate corner I imagined I could see the remnants of the countless races and civilizations inhabiting this fruitless and eternally fought-over part of the world, this land between two rivers. Then, as Buffo adjusted a curtain, I had a strange vision in the sudden sunlight that I could see dawn coming...or was it actually sunset? Everything seemed red, murky, ominous.

"Scarface's supposed to be arriving in this part of the warzone soon," Buffo growled, keeping his voice low. "I can't wait to have a crack at him." I said nothing, doubting he would get the chance. Security would be intense – the leader of the reactionary world had already been hit by stray shrapnel soon after his arrival in the warzone, thus earning (from progressive troops) his nickname of 'Scarface'.

Scarface has been smeared massively by our propagandists, who claim that he rapes and beats his wife, and worse things. And Buffo eagerly joined in the smears, adding that Scarface was a 'homophobe,' who deserved to die a slow death because of that. I thought I would use the opportunity to subtly probe the sniper on his knowledge of world events.

"So, I hear Scarface is supposed to have fallen out somewhat with Mohammed Tate," I casually remarked.

"Ah, they're all cut from the same raghead cloth," muttered Buffo as he 'zeroed in' his weapon (military jargon for the process of adjusting his weapon's scope for accuracy at a specific distance).

"Well, yes, they're still fighting on the same side, no matter what their personal differences may be," I admitted.

"And our side can certainly learn something from that kind of pragmatic approach."

"The only thing I learn from homophobic sand niggers is *shooting skills*," grinned Buffo. "Moving targets are always the most educative."

I nodded, not wanting to antagonize him. His anti-Islam sentiments were somewhat misplaced, however – the Curia cared not a whit now for their former anti-jihadist crusade, their sole focus being on killing Scarface. Perhaps they had even tried to bribe Emir Tate, but for now, at least, he was still nominally on his son-in-law's side. It was rumored, too, that the Curia were going to launch a concentrated attack on America's 'North-West Republic', though this had yet to be confirmed.

But none of these delicate issues clouded the mind of Johnny 'Buffo' Stokes. He continued to set up his nest, putting a finger outside the window to determine the wind velocity, air temperature and humidity. He was certainly an expert at his job. I attempted once more to engage him in conversation, remarking briefly on the decentralized nature of fourth generation warfare, and the complex, shifting alliances between the clans of the local area (having been briefed on this at the hospital ship), noting possible similarities to the famous Iron Age battle in which Pyrrhus of Epirus had died.

"Better get your roofing tiles ready, then," chuckled Buffo. So, he was familiar with Scarface's famous 'Dream Speech' at least, and thus not completely ignorant of world affairs. From that point on he would refer to his sniping bullets as 'roofing tiles', and then 'rofling tiles' (as he would be rolling on the floor laughing when he finally killed Scarface, he said).

Before I could make further conversation, there was a flurry at the door, and we both wheeled round in alarm, Buffo reaching for his rifle. It turned out to be a false alarm, though – a camera crew had burst in on us.

I imagined Buffo would be incensed, but he merely demanded to know if the crew were homophobes. When they assured him they weren't, he proceeded to grant them an interview, on the sole condition it would not be broadcast for twenty-four hours, thus preserving the location of his current sniper's nest. A live interview, of course, might give his position away to the enemy. (Something that really irritates me about the current war is the constant presence of the media. I have personally witnessed an armored camera crew running alongside soldiers and insurgents during a pitched street battle, and boy did they look ludicrous. I even heard of an actual firefight between rival camera crews in a different part of the warzone.)

I chatted briefly with the camera crew about the terrorism, not officially sanctioned by either side but an increasingly common phenomenon among civilian combatants (car bombs being a lot cheaper than standard military equipment). As for the official troops, in general they fight with much the same weapons as in previous Middle Eastern wars, with the much-vaunted sound weapons and EMP (electromagnetic pulse) tech still at the experimental stage, and not likely to put in an appearance on the battlefield anytime soon.

I learnt little that was concrete from Buffo on the first snipe, however, as his chatter to the journalists consisted entirely of various inanities, and I felt that if I made any inroads at all into his character, they would be slow ones. Only the coming days would tell if I could forge real tracks.

Next day came news, however.

He of the shrapnel-ravaged visage had arrived in our part of the warzone, as part of a greater tour giving motivational speeches to his troops. Buffo was like a child at Christmas, bouncing around so much that I thought he would piss his pants. When he finally managed to utter a coherent sentence, he confessed himself *desperate* to be the one to put a bullet into Scarface. I told him not to submit to false hopes, as his nemesis was likely to be surrounded by vast cordons of security, but Buffo ignored me, rocking back and forth with glee.

That night I had an interview with his immediate superior, Lieutenant Jonathan Briggs, who I tackled on Buffo's chronic Islamophobia (a court-martial offence, incidentally, which in his case was overlooked by an army desperate to keep such a lucky-charm killing machine within its ranks). Apparently this was the cause of friction with some of the other troops, who were themselves strictly gagged from expressing similar sentiment about the Religion of Peace (in fact, the very term 'Religion of Peace' has recently been banned by the military, due to the fact that some incorrigible rogues had been known to utter it sarcastically.)

Briggs was a soft-spoken man, and shook his head sadly as he told me that Buffo not only *denied* being Islamophobic, but had once had said (in the same breath as expressing a wish to "exterminate all Muslims") that he "will *kill* anyone who thinks that I'm Islamophobic." This kind of doublethink is marvellous to contemplate, only adding to the depths of Buffo's mystery.

Two days later, he walked up with a gleam in his eye and beckoned me aside, confiding that representatives of the Curia had just approached him brazenly inside the warzone (above his superiors' heads), and asked him to undertake the very sniping mission he had so longed for – his target being Scarface himself.

"They showed accreditation," he said, "so I know these boys are genuine." I couldn't be sure that he was telling the truth, but played along to keep him onside.

"That's great," I said. "And when will you carry out the mission?"

"Right now," he said. "They've told me about a farm house where I can get a clear shot at the place Scarface will be at eighteen hundred Juliet, this very evening, do you understand? I'm gonna be the most famous goddamn sniper in history!" I heartily congratulated him, wondering if perhaps the Curia really *had* approached him. He then made it clear that he wanted me to accompany him, as a witness to the mission. Under the terms of my fellowship, I could hardly refuse.

We were provided with a detachment to secure the building, indicating that there *were* higher-ups involved, and that afternoon, to cut a long story short, I found myself crouching on the dirt floor of a decrepit outbuilding, on an ancient wheat farm that had somehow survived all the various Iraq conflicts, waiting for Buffo to take a plug at Scarface. A successful shot could win the entire war, since it was only Scarface's organizational genius that allowed the disparate anti-Curia forces to unite and gain the upper hand.

The tension was unbearable, and our eyes were drawn irresistibly to Buffo's eye, glued to the scope of his M2024 rifle. He would only get one shot; there was no possibility of relocation. If Scarface occupied the position he was meant to, then that shot would be just under a mile, and as Buffo had made over thirty of his kills from further distances than that, he was certainly in with a chance. But his bullet would be in the air for nearly four seconds before finding its target, losing much of its kinetic energy on the way, and many things could happen in that time. Scarface might move in an unexpected direction, or a cross-breeze could divert the bullet from its trajectory. And although the air was still and sultry, there were untold dust-motes in these camel lands, making zeroing harder to achieve.

Then, at last, the moment came.

"I can *see* that sumbitch," Buffo murmured, "so it's now or never."

He squeezed the trigger almost sexually. The four seconds of tension felt like four long minutes...and then he let out a groan of scorched despair, deeper than I have ever known human tongue to utter.

"And why did he wanna move *that* way for?" he sobbed uncontrollably. "What in the blue hell did I do to *deserve* it?"

Things sure were glum around the base that night. I visited Buffo in his tent, and on entering heard him mutter something about "killing homos"...but I must have misheard him..."killing homophobes," it most likely was. In any case, he had taken his failure to heart, and now seemed to think that Scarface was operating under some kind of divine protection.

"Is *God* a homophobe?" he asked me in all seriousness, and when I failed to answer he began to mutter curses, at one point expressing a wish to snipe the Almighty. He was slowly becoming more crazy-eyed, and his circling movements began to remind me of a cat chasing its own tail.

I assured him anyone could have missed the shot at such a distance, with a four second gap between firing and striking, but he wouldn't listen to my reasoning so I decided to let him be. There wasn't any point in increasing his agitation.

But he didn't want me to leave. He swung round and grabbed me by the collar, his moon-face grinning ineffably into mine. One second it seemed there was a great mystery behind his countenance, the next I felt sure I was gazing into a void – empty tiger-like teeth hanging meaningless in mid-air, covered in blood-flecked spittle, concealing nothing underneath.

Which glance was right?

"All right, Buffo, it's been a long day," I said, "and I'm going to go get some sleep now, okay? We can talk further in the morning." Slowly, as if engaged in a pointless ritual, he released his grip on my shirt and gave a weird sigh.

"I thought I saw you falling, Doc," he said in a tired voice. "Today, I thought I saw you falling and you couldn't get up. I kind of wanted to help you, but couldn't. I don't rightly know *what* was happening."

Needless to say, I hadn't fallen that day, and Buffo was now beginning to officially freak me out. Professional as I was, I thought it best to depart his tent without further talk, in the hope that he would be less disturbed in the morning.

I slept uneasily, waking half a dozen times with lukewarm fragments of dreams crawling behind my eyeballs. In one of these, I dreamt I was asleep and couldn't wake myself up...I was yelling really loud, but couldn't get myself to hear.

In the morning, I began to ask myself just what the hell I was doing in Mesopotamia.

The afternoon brought further news, however...after the latest attempt on his life, our intelligence services had learnt that Scarface had now flown to the opposite side of the current theater of war – to Syria, heart of the Provisional Emirate, no doubt to meet with his father-in-law, Tate, to further discuss their differences. And it looked as if Buffo was going to be flown there, too, to have another shot at the bigtime, and naturally I would be obliged to accompany him.

So we left next morning. On the flight, I had a disturbing vision of my patient as a Little Lost Lamb who just wanted to be loved, but this was swiftly replaced by the sight of his hands stained purple with blood, and I started to wonder if my own sanity was slipping. I couldn't worry about such things, though...I had a job to do.

It was several miles above the desert that we first heard news of attacks by combined Curia armies on the nascent North West Republic in America (and Buffo muttered something like "Good riddance, homophobic *freaks*"). Then there was another message – insurgents had just killed Dano DeLacey, the world's most famous transexual solider. This predictably sent Buffo into conniptions. He turned to the nearest person, a lieutenant of Arab extraction, and started on a rant about "goddamned dune coons...can you believe it, sir?" (The Arab lieutenant nodded sympathetically.) This proved to me beyond all doubt that "sand nigger" for Buffo was a mere abstraction, not a term of actual racial vilification. Good, I was making progress...

The steward brought us trays of roasted chestnuts, which I thought was an odd thing to serve on a flight, and I tuned my headset to the announcements (on every channel) that DeLacey's funeral would be shown live on all networks in America...but that furious arguments had broken out between varying factions of transexuals, feminists, anti-militarists etc. as to the significance of the event. I asked Buffo where he stood on these issues, and he became confused. I noticed the empty look in his eyes again, and so changed the subject.

Then the plane descended. There was a dazzle from the tarmac, so that it seemed we were entering some shimmering hell, and my head began throbbing with a persistence scarcely to be endured. I clenched my teeth, determined to present a face of complete normalcy, although my tongue felt like it was coated with a silvery substance like mercury, and my innards performed a twisting dance of slow strangulation. I hobbled downstairs onto the tarmac, and slumped into the waiting jeep with something resembling gratitude.

We were ushered into a small field office, whose atrium was covered with pictures of homosexual couples kissing and fondling, and notices saying it was a court martial offence to remove or deface them. I was shown to a small room, where I lay down to take a quick nap, hoping I would feel better on waking. But just as I was fuzzing off into dreamland there was a knock at the door, pushing electric barbs into the backs of my eyes. It was Buffo.

"I'm going on a mission now, doc," he said. "Thought you might like to know."

"Of course. I'll come along. Just let me get dressed, and splash some water over my face."

"As you wish, doc."

But when I finished, he was nowhere to be seen. A search of the field office and surrounds revealed no trace, and I went back to my room, scratching my head with puzzlement, and for other reasons.

An hour later, I learnt he had gone out *sans* permission, to try to snipe a unit said to be directly from the fief of Mohammed Tate. The latter, though white as the driven snow, was an arch "dune coon" to Buffo, confirming my tentative view that my patient was a mere solipsist...but that would be too easy a diagnosis, I thought, and surely not worth an entire fellowship.

I waited for further news of Buffo, mulling over the possibility that the Curia had approached him again in secret with a new location for Scarface.

I read up online about the latter's father-in-law, who had started out as a semi-romantic Turpin-like camel thief, but who in the chaotic last days of ISIS had emerged as a powerful warlord, and eventually the emir of a secular provisional state, which despite (or because of) occasional heavy-handedness, had been greeted with immense relief by the ISIS-ravaged denizens of Syria and northern Iraq. Initially the Curia, for whom ISIS had become a liability, had welcomed Tate's rule, but they soon turned against him when he revealed himself as disturbingly competent and efficient. And now it looks as if our side's strategy is to try and drive a wedge between Tate and his volatile son-in-law...but so far this has not been a success, for there is every sign they will be reconciled, and even their present rift has not hampered a united war effort.

I stood and looked at the little bouncy Syrian clouds, wondering idly if someone like Buffo was, after all, for the best in the best of all possible worlds...and then dismissed the idea as supremely ridiculous.

A sergeant approached and informed me that a detachment had been formed for the purpose of locating Buffo, and (for reasons still unknown to me) I immediately volunteered to be attached to the unit. After some initial hesitation I was given the green light to go with them, possibly into a combat zone. I should have been greatly afraid, but in fact I felt calm, even confident. My presence would give the mission a touch of class, I foolishly thought.

We sailed out like Argonauts into Syrian dirt, and I listened idly to the talk of the troops as our jeeps bumped along...it seemed that they had mixed feelings at best about the famous sniper, and not a few jokes were made at his expense – including malicious ones. But what did that matter to me? My job was to analyse Buffo's mind, not to assess his popularity.

Then, after twenty minutes or so, we entered al-B___, a smallish town, where we left our jeeps under guard while we combed the place on foot. There had been insurgent activity here in the last week by jihadi rebels (sworn enemies of both ourselves and Tate). Mere amateurs compared to the ISIS of old, of course, but still potentially dangerous. And, what do you know, as we neared the far end of town, a dozen or so men with black masks, wielding submachine guns, turned the corner, coming face to face with their American enemies. There was a standoff, both our commander and theirs seemingly frozen and unsure of what to do.

Just as the situation seemed to be devolving into stalemate, however, something unexpected happened –

a platoon of Tate's troops entered from another branch of the intersection. They weren't even supposed to be in this area. Now we were caught between the devil and the deep blue sea...

The spell was immediately broken, and a three-way fire-fight ensued. Despite being armed, my first act was to dive into a pile of rubble, avoiding the bullets that were flying in every possible direction. After cowering in the rubble for what may have been ten seconds (but felt like a lot longer), I suddenly heard a familiar and greatly-loathed voice.

"Doc," it hissed. "Get out of my line of fire, damn it!" And an arm reached through a window and pulled me back into a semi-ruined building. It was Buffo, of course, and he was far from pleased to see me.

"I had everything under control," he growled, "until you clowns made an appearance. I had a clear shot at Hani Fakhoury, who's an important commander in Tate's army."

But even as he scolded me there was a deep booming blast outside, and the walls of the building seemed to collapse around us. I huddled on the floor, losing consciousness. When I came to, it was in a strangely darkened room.

"Where are the lights?" I muttered.

"It's getting on towards evening, doc," came the voice, "and not much light gets in through the airhole."

"Airhole?"

"Yeah, that's right...we're trapped in here, in case you didn't notice. But don't you worry. There's a tiny shaft in the rubble where the air gets through."

"My god...what will happen to us?"

"I don't rightly know."

"Are you *sure* we're completely trapped?"

"Course I'm sure." He sounded mildly offended. "I've checked thoroughly. Someone heard me yelling though the airhole, though...so if our boys capture the town, someone'll *prolly* see fit to rescue us. But if the sand monkeys take it, well..."

I suddenly became dizzy, and he passed me a small flask.

"Go easy on the water, doc. It's all we got. And dark's closing in. If we're rescued it won't be til morning, so ease up. Don't chug so, damn it. What're you so nervous of?"

How could I tell him that night was falling, night was falling? The ruined walls seemed to close in around me, and I put my face to the airhole, sucking the dusty air which felt infinitely cleaner than the miasma surrounding Buffo in the claustrophobic gloom.

"Don't you have a light?" I muttered. "Don't soldiers carry torches?"

He giggled. "No torches, doc. No light tonight." It was a new moon, too, I thought with a shudder. A wave of cold seemed to billow up from the floor. I was in my tomb, it seemed, my very own precious tomb, and there was *no way out*.

"Now...let's play spin the bottle."

Did he really say that? To my horror, I actually heard the sound of an empty plastic bottle being twisted round on the fragmentary floor. "So doc, we play it like this...the one the bottle points at has to tell the *truth* about something."

"How can you see the bottle?"

"I can feel it, and it feels like its pointing at *you* as a matter of fact!"

"What...do you want to know?"

"I wanna know if you support freedom, doc. Good old American *freedom*."

"I, er..." Thinking frantically. "Yes...as long as it doesn't involve hate speech."

"That's right, doc. Hate speech is *not* free speech." (Parroting a now ancient and meaningless slogan.) "You support *true* free speech, then...which never includes hate speech?"

"Uh, yeah, sure."

"So...you don't mind speaking *freely* about why you think the way I use 'sand nigger' is an abstraction?"

Shit...he'd been reading my notebook. How had he done so? It must have been when he came to my room, and I'd turned to wash my face.

"The thing is, doc...I ain't never *said* the words 'sand nigger'. Never in my life. I don't use hate speech. I'm starting to think that *you're* the insane one, doc."

I cast about desperately for a way to change the subject. I suddenly realized that I didn't know where my gun was, and had little hope of finding it in the dark.

"Uh, isn't it my turn now to spin the bottle?"

"We're not playing that game any more, doc. We're playing the *faggot game*." Oh shit, he was going to try to rape me, I thought, groping about me for a weapon. My hand found a good-sized chunk of jagged concrete, and I clutched at it desperately.

"This is how the faggot game works, doc. You are *always* playing the game...and if you think about faggots, then you lose. And I'll blow your fucking brains out!"

"*What?* How on earth will you know if I'm thinking about...homosexuals?"

"You must've thought about them already, doc, because you mentioned them! Now, where's my rifle?"

"No!" I screeched, moving towards him with the chunk of concrete, fully intending to brain him.

"Haw haw haw...just a little joke, doc. All right, let's play another game..."

Another one of his stupid mind games followed, I don't remember which. The rest of that night is a terrible blur. Trapped underground with a madman, whose madness followed unpredictable patterns. And he never slept...

Yes, I know psychiatrists aren't supposed to use terms like 'madman', but it's okay because I'm no longer a registered psychiatrist. They stripped me of that privilege right after I grabbed a gun from the staff sergeant of the infantry squad who rescued us, and proceeded to shoot up the Combat Stress Control unit.

I write this report calmly but under armed guard, as the radio outside informs me that Buffo has just been awarded a Medal of Honor...not for his high number of kills, but rather for his aborted attempt on Scarface's life.

And I wait, and wait.

And all I can see is Buffo's empty visage in front of me, while bullets fly behind me out in camel lands.

So say goodnight to the West for me, please, and don't forget to turn out the lights.

7

THE TESTIMONY OF
MOHAMMED AL-ZAHABI
(via excerpts from his journal)

The lustre of the room was wonderful. This was the high point of my life, there could be no doubting it, and yet something was still lacking. I continued to play the dutiful poet, modest yet manly, while they went on congratulating me. My lesser part basked in it, just as my higher turned aside, with idle wryness, to contemplate the mystery of why the hole in my soul continues to wax larger.

But even my basking lesser part regarded them as philistine lunatics. For years, had I not turned out the most exquisite poems on love, philosophy and eternity, and with no recognition? Now, with one idle satirical verse about the creature called 'Buffo', I am suddenly admitted to the highest circles of war-ravaged Damascus, with old Colonel al-Ahmar proclaiming me a 'national treasure'.

It wasn't that my poem is a bad one – the taut construction of the verse, so different to my usual sinuous style, hints at new and previously unforeseen directions, new mimetic prisms for the Levantine Arabic dialect itself.

But it is no *achievement* – for with the subject being what he is, the satire virtually wrote itself. Syrians, to a man, believe Buffo to be a *faggot* (the Curia-aligned armies are riddled with such – maybe that's the only thing that keeps us fighting them). And while homosexualism doubtless happens here to a certain extent, too, it is not in the public square as with the broken, dying West, and many praise Allah for that.

In keeping with this theme, there was a point during the evening when someone turned on the TV to catch al-Akbar's latest war speech...for the great one has recently attained fluency in Arabic, and for some reason (good taste?) has chosen to learn the *Egyptian* dialect, and those present were curious to see how he handled it. (I confess the Egyptian dialect my own favourite, and intend to write poetry in it myself some day.)

But we didn't hear the results of al-Akbar's linguistic striving, because the Mossad were once again broadcasting gay porn into Syria, on all channels. Each time we counter their jamming technology they upgrade it, once more subjecting our populace to the visual sewer. If they seriously think they can destabilise the Tate regime in this way they are gravely mistaken, as it merely turns the populace further against our 'esteemed' neighbour (whom no one doubts is behind the spectacle).

I took advantage of the loud expressions of disgust to leave the party early, playing the part of mysterious poet vanishing into the night. There was little chance of the military men taking my reticence as a sign of weakness, however, for they knew I had proved myself in war (in the splendid First Battle of Damascus) with the Dreamers and Poets Brigade, which, along with the International Brigade, has now been given official recognition by the Emir.

Having recovered from my war wound, the time was now right for me to volunteer for the new front: Cairo. (It was while waiting for my application to be considered that I wrote the idle poem on Buffo that has made me, overnight, into an unlikely celebrity.)

But a fire burns inside me. As poet, I have always had to write in code (a code of words and symbols, of course...not a mere cipher like this journal), and all due to Islam – the religion of submission – from which I must hide my true feelings, my dreams across the waters.

For my allegiance is not to Allah but to the *neteru*, the great gods of Egypt, who existed before Ibrahim left Ur, and who exist still, giving lifeblood to my poetry. I give allegiance especially to the goddess Seshat, my true mistress, whose gift to me is that no woman shall ever have hold over me. Seshat, the goddess of history, who opens the doors of heaven...her spotted cloak the night sky, the stars, the leopardine world of poetry.

I remember well the trite tears of Rima, that beauteous wench I strung along these past six weeks in Damascus. I still hear her pitiful wailing, so fake-sounding to my poet's ear. I cast her off like so many dead skin cells, just as I have cast off so many others during my years as a soldier.

For in my sickly youth, with an artist's shyness and frail physique, I was scorned and rejected by these whores...and now am seen by the same empty vessels as 'desirable'! That is not due to my inner worth, though, but solely to my status in the Dreamers and Poets Brigade, much as I am now famous for a poem I consider a mere trifle, while my true work goes unnoticed and unappreciated.

So yes, I take delight in leading 'respectable' whores into thinking I like them, only to abandon them at their most vulnerable, when most deeply in love with me, for revenge is sweet, and I would not be a *man* if I didn't long for vengeance, pulsing and hot.

The price I pay for revenge, of course, is celibacy. Even masturbation is forbidden, because to do so I must conjure up the image of a woman in my mind's eye, and I will not give them even that pleasure. My semen is for the blood only, an offering for the goddess Seshat. That's how I write my poetry, the finest poetry in any Arabic dialect, and if the goddess leaves then my gift, too, will vanish.

But just lately, I have noticed a hole in my soul, which is growing undoubtedly larger. And for the first time since my youth, I am afraid of the future.

[...]

An even higher point of my life has come.

Al-Akbar himself saw fit to present me with an award for my little poem!

While no surprise that he would appreciate a work denigrating his would-be assassin, it is still a great honour that he would choose to confer the prize on me with his own hands, because he is *founder* of the

Dreamers and Poets Brigade, and has done so much to restore the ideal of the Warrior Poet.

He presented me with a large copper medal engraved with semi-mythical figures from the past: T.E. Lawrence, Yukio Mishima and Henry Howard, Earl of Surrey. I received this medal with reverence and gratitude, studying al-Akbar's face as he presented me with it, but gleaning little from the shrapnel-scarred, careworn visage. This man is inscrutable, a mystery to myself and to others. Does he, like myself, have a Seshat in his soul, driving him to greater and higher deeds?

After the ceremony, I was privy to a game of chess between himself and the Emir. The latter lost, of course, and his facial expressions were far easier to read than those of his son-in-law. During the game these two giants casually discussed philosophy and architecture, and while they didn't say anything particularly profound, it was stimulating and inspiring to listen to.

Towards the end, they resumed negotiations which must have started earlier that day. It says much for al-Akbar's respect that I and several of my fellow Dreamers were allowed to be present without so much as a security pass. The key to these negotiations, it seemed, was the atomic bomb...for as a 'floating government', al-Akbar has so far found it impossible to get his hands on one, but believes he will lose prestige if he doesn't do so.

The Emir, on the other hand, is fervently against this devil's weapon (a Jew's weapon, he calls it), but al-Akbar is worried that, if the Curia are defeated, the Samson Option will be pursued. There are also rumours an extreme Islamist sect may have attained the bomb, but no one knows anything concrete, making the world situation murkier and more amphibious.

Despite al-Akbar's lust for the bomb, he reminds me greatly of Neferirkare, that gentle Egyptian king of the fifth dynasty who forgave one of his ministers for an accidental transgression of sacred ritual. I wonder how someone like al-Akbar, clearly a Dreamer himself, has attained the level of power he has? He is a paradox, like the Bennu bird, the lord of jubilees, who is self-created and renews himself like the sun...like Atum, too, who made union with the feminine principle within himself, making love to his hand (or shadow) and creating divine children from loneliness.

And I, too, am lonely, even with the goddess within me…but my poems are my children. And although al-Akbar is rumoured to have an illegitimate child (the Emir's daughter having proven barren), I wonder if his *real* child is not the new world he is creating?

After the ceremony, I gave my medal and prize money (a bag of specially-minted gold coins) to a beggar in the street. There was an eerie sunset, and I am trepidatious as to what I will find in Cairo if allowed to proceed there.

[…]

I have been given the green light (along with four of my comrades) to travel to Cairo. I feel revitalised, like an ice age has ended. My limbs fill with relaxed energy as I plan what I shall do to those verminous fanatics currently raping the ruins of the sacred land of Kemet. This multicursal war has now truly become World War III, with only China and Russia refusing to pick sides. (Despite the Chinese making tentative overtures to al-Akbar, they are probably waiting cynically to see who is the victor. As for Russia, her motives are more mysterious.)

But I care not for such trifles – the excitement of the search is within me. And whatever I seek, I feel I will not find it in the squalid ferment of Cairo, but rather in the shifting desert sands. Time shall tell…

[…]

My blood has nearly boiled dry with the horrors I have encountered since arriving in Kemet (still glorious even in utter ruin). Cairo itself is vandalised by a vicious mob of Somalian mercenaries, and the worst of it is that they are ostensibly fighting for al-Akbar (not one of the great one's finest decisions). These 'allies' are agents of chaos, emissaries of Set. Far worse than the tomb robbers of old, they have literally *destroyed* ancient tombs and carvings in the suburbs of Cairo, as I saw with my own eyes on my first patrol – witnessing such an abominable act of desecration at a recent excavation near the temple of Ra-Atum at Heliopolis.

I turned to my brother Akram, a master weaver and Sufi, and my eyes filled with tears, before I hurled a grenade and blew at least five of the goblin-faced fiends limb from limb. Brother Akram shook his head sorrowfully, but did not take me to task for my act of fury, which anyone with a soul would have to admit was merciful, although not just – for justice would surely decree a slow and agonising death by torture for these wretched half-men.

A tourist plaque landed at my feet after the explosion, and I picked it up and wiped away the intestinal residue of one of the swart-skinned pirates, before perusing it. It spoke of the 'changeless valley of the Nile,' something I knew to be a gullible deception for tourists – for there are no changeless societies. It is true that Egypt changed more slowly than our own barbarous age, but it changed nonetheless. There is a world of difference in tone and form between the third dynasty (when the legendary Imhotep walked the earth) and the fourth, that of the mysterious Khufu and the pyramids of Giza. Likewise, between the fifth dynasty (the Sun Kings and their solar temples) and the sixth (when Osiris began his dominance) there is little comparison.

There are no static societies. What the Germans call 'Zeitgeist' is a very real phenomenon, and Seshat is its mistress. And while history rhymes, as they say, it never repeats.

Still, a successful society in my opinion is one that slows down the chaos as much as possible, and judged by that standard, Kemet was far greater than anything the present has to offer (although we may yet see what happens if al-Akbar wins the war).

Our modern attempts to kill change are pathetic, as exemplified by the Aswan High Dam, which so conveniently did away with the Nilus flood, and that was when Kemet truly died, for not even the coming of Christianity and Islam had such destructive power, *creating* Chaos in the name of destroying it.

Now I have been assigned guard duty at the Cairo Museum, which had already been trashed a generation earlier by the blasphemers of ISIS, doing the work of Set under the name of his bitterest enemy, the golden goddess. And now their successors continue the evil work, but thankfully under different names.

Before taking our places, we were given a short (too short!) tour of the ground floor of this incredible museum, and I saw for myself the hauntingly lifelike eyes of certain Old Kingdom statues, something no other culture has managed to replicate, ever. But unfortunately, the building has become a haven for Western tourists, who know the heavy guard here affords them protection from murderous pirates, and who walk past the most amazing relics with looks of smug and wooden blindness, their eyes deader by far than those of the statues. One of them actually snickered at me as he walked past.

"It's one of Scarlotti's men," he said to his companion. "What's a white supremacist doing *here?* Everyone knows Egypt was created by negros..." I laughed out loud at the fraud of this 'Black Egypt' theory, which he had fallen for even in spite of the statuary around him...and also at his description of me as a 'white supremacist'. For while I could probably pass for a southern European, I never thought of myself as anything other than a pagan Arab. The tourist, on the other hand, could easily have passed as a rotting corpse.

[...]

So it has begun again.

Her features, too, are fine like a European's, but her skin is copper. Not from the climate, though – it is the copper of love. The sign of ancient Kemet, the joy of living.

My first glimpse of her was a shoe, sticking out of a doorway. She was being raped by two Somalian savages, and they would doubtless have killed her afterwards had

I not blown their minuscule brains out with my automatic.

I have hooked her in already, earning her devotion through sheer gratitude by saving her life. Naturally, I have been nothing but chivalrous in my actions since taking her under my wing (all her relatives in Cairo have been killed in the war – so much the better), and of course, when the time comes, I will joyfully abandon her.

She is a rare find, changing from Hathor to Sekhmet as she menstruates, but I believe I have the measure of her. All that is required, as usual, is self-control and patience. Just a little patience...

[...]

I took her for a camel ride in the Western Desert, outside of Kemet, in the Red Land, the scorpion land. We had armed guards for the journey – it is still possible for Dreamers and Poets to obtain such a privilege, al-Akbar having ordained that our kind are to be respected.

Things are very different out there in the land of Set, where the sky is that solid dome which gave birth to the monist heresy. A land of blood and brains and chaos, but also a place where heroes are engendered. The spirit of the heretic pharaoh Akhenaten (whom I believe to have been the son of a proto-Jewess) is said to haunt this desert eternally. His ghost would be the most terrible thing I could possibly come across, and even the thought of it makes me shudder intensely.

But her lithe and sinuous beauty took my mind away from these things (it is only fair to admit I had an erection for much of the journey.)

On returning to barracks in Cairo she hinted that she wanted me to enter the secure room in which she is ensconced, and while I managed to smile and refuse, my body gave greater resistance than I am accustomed to.

This one, I fear, is not going to be easy.

[...]

My beliefs have been made public – not something I intended. During a patrol, we came across one of the

New Gnostics, a heresy that grows rapidly in the chaos of wartorn Egypt (I believe they have little in common with the gnostics of antiquity.) This cretin was preaching his vile belief, worse than Islam in my mind, that there is nothing but an *elemental malice* behind the universe, and that all that we hold good and beautiful will ultimately prove illusion, being created in the first place merely as a method of torment (once we have grasped the truth) by this same elemental malice.

How does one refute such a repugnant heresy as this? I am afraid that I did so with an uncharacteristic lack of subtlety (what is wrong with me of late, that I can no longer keep my emotions in check?), yelling at the repulsive preacher and calling him a cheap and pox-ridden charlatan who was no gnostic, for he knew not truth.

"And what *is* truth?" he asked me with a caustic sneer. I started shrieking at him about the gods, the *neteru*, the true and noble standard-bearers of the cosmos. And none truer than Maat, goddess of cosmic order, who defends against Isfet, chaos, injustice...Isfet, the invisible thief who sneaks through windows at night filling our subconscious mind with lazy thoughts, with egalitarian and nihilist thoughts. Isfet, the true master of this 'gnostic' preacher, who I now surged forward to punch, while my comrades were forced to restrain me. I can still see his crooked sneer, and I punch the air in front of me.

"Order can't exist *without* chaos," he cackled. "And therefore both are illusion."

"No!" I yelled. "One can't exist without the other, yes, that's why Set originally helped the gods...but they're *not* equal. Maat must be *fought for*. That was the king's role, the pharaoh's role...to destroy Isfet, even if it can't ultimately be destroyed...and that is why he was crowned king."

"There are no kings anymore, imbecile...not even your precious Scarlotti."

"It is the poet who must now fight for Maat, you vermin...and *this* is high religion, not the puerile need for salvation or extinction."

He was leaving, doubtless afraid he would lose face with his followers if I continued to better him in debate.

But I was greatly concerned that his disabling heresies might spread among the young in Cairo and elsewhere, and if my brothers had not fervently restrained me, I would have put a bullet in him, just as I had with the last agents of Isfet I had come across (the Somalian rapists).

But now I had another problem to deal with. My comrades, who were shaking with emotion at this confrontation (which the more orthodox among them would necessarily have regarded as a confrontation between two opposing heresies), now saw me for what I undoubtedly am – an unabashed polytheist. That is a dangerous thing to be in the Arabic world, even in liberal Egypt, and tongues will wag; there is no stopping it. Now I am to be held suspect by Muslims, Copts *and* Neo-Gnostics. That is a pleasure to me, but I must watch my back.

I take comfort in the fact that the *Emir* is now also considered suspect by many for his refusal to seek the Bomb...although I almost wish that he would, for I am loyal to both him and al-Akbar, and have no wish to see them fall out again.

[…]

Already the gossip has spread.

She confronted me about it today, claiming concern for my welfare. My own poet 'comrades' have been casting strange looks at me, and it already feels that I am no longer part of their brotherhood – but if that is so, then *I* am the true poet and not they.

I half expected her, too, to abandon me...but if anything the opposite has occurred. Not only does she say she will stick with me regardless, but has even dropped hints (subtle yet undeniably there) that she may sympathise. Inwardly I groaned, for if true, this will make it harder still to break with her when the time comes, as it must come. And yet abandon her I will, fulfilling justice – Maat.

I spent the night in her arms, but chastely. Even this is a violation of my usual methods, and also very difficult, as she constantly arched herself against me in certain places...not insistently, but enough to make me burn inside.

Corrosion, corrosion, all is corrosion.

Only by resisting it do I create order.

Maat.

[...]

Now al-Akbar has announced that he has attained the bomb, via one of his renegade genius scientists, and peacefully!

Is he bluffing? This man is a chess player, thinking many moves ahead, and not everything he says can be taken as a straightforward statement of fact. For all that, it is quiet tonight in Cairo...I have an unusual feeling that people are *thinking*.

If he *does* have the bomb, what does it mean?

I imagine it as a malevolent sun: Ra's Boat of Millions of Years, only with Set at the helm.

But there is a famous story about the pharaoh Menkaure, who turned six years into twelve by keeping lamps burning at night, thus delaying the death which fate had ordained for him. Perhaps that is what al-Akbar's announcement means – that he is playing for time. Cannon, too, were regarded as demonic five centuries ago, and so perhaps I am merely out of tune with the Zeitgeist?

As for *her*, my resistance crumbled further, so I have removed her from the barracks, setting her up with her own secure house, pulling a few strings in order to do so. I imagine her dancing naked there, alone, and my loins are inflamed. Surely this torment will soon be over?

[...]

Disaster has struck.

The Emir has fallen to the assassin's bullet.

Now I am racked with guilt for being in Egypt, and not in Syria where perhaps I could have helped to prevent it...but no, it is impossible to say *what* I could have done. All I can see in front of me is the slow motion footage from Al Jazeera, showing the Emir's brains exiting his skull in a high-pressure spurt. The projectile, sent by Set, did its job all too well, and the blond beast has fallen. So who will pick up his torch? And what awaits *me?*

I fear the Middle East will be plunged into heavier and heavier chaos, making the current war seem but a trifle in comparison. Isfet, and its emissary Set, are now in the ascendent.

[...]

Sure enough, many of the Emir's men have refused to flock to the banner of al-Akbar's Multicursal Curia (not actually a Curia, of course, but an Imperium...the name is surely a parody), and presumably because their blood has been poisoned by the religion of submission. Now some are flocking to new 'emirs' (pretenders), and others are repudiating them with loud words and many.

All I can do is watch the sun set, and the slow and inexorable rise of Set over Kemet.

Tonight, I am sure, I will dream that I am dancing with a scorpion.

I must go to her.

[...]

I jogged slowly along the bloodstained roads of Cairo, unsure as to what I would find. Brutal machine gun fire dotted the running poetry of my journey through ancient starlight. Every apartment block was a cavern, every house a den of monsters. I saw sights, but they flashed by like apparitions, so I couldn't be sure if they had ever existed.

I saw a man standing *over* his own assassin, one bloody hand holding in his entrails as he made a calm formal gesture with the other, while his murderer laughed and reclined in the alley, gun forgotten next to him, as both basked in their roles in an affable cosmic comedy. It seemed that the murdered one would surely spell some humorous word in his own blood, before finally expiring, but I would never know what it was.

249

Then, further north, I saw a mob (of the kind I detest) clamouring for a leader. They were literally *demanding* that someone lead them, but no one stepped forward for the task. I might have contemplated it myself, but they stank of offal and corruption, so I hurried forward into segmented night, another link flashing in the chain up ahead.

Next I remember, I was actually in *her* neighbourhood, slowing down to a brisk walk, before locating her building with pounding heart.

She was there.

We embraced, ecstatic, and I held her tightly as the sound of gunfire drew gradually closer. Her guards had deserted her. A horse ran past the entryway rolling flame-reflecting eyes...and for the first time, we kissed, our tongues becoming quicksilver, merging in the smoke-stale air, directed by our whims and by the unpredictable rhythms of the gunfire.

But even in my bliss, I realised I had to get her out of there, and that the neighbourhood around the house was now a danger zone. Swiftly we began the reverse journey, along quieter backstreets to avoid the hotspots of violence. My arm was around her waist, which was shimmering as she moved, the last emissary of beauty in this benighted city.

Sights were different in the alleyways, running roughly concurrent with the dangerous routes I had taken on the way out. On a crumbling balcony overhanging the street we were greeted by the sight, unearthly, of an ancient crone watering potted plants from an antique jug whose intricate design made me think of that twisting tongue that had just entwined with my own, and would soon do so again.

I hurried her along, panting, until we were once more in the shadow of the barracks. The guards recognised her, and looked resentful. All their effort spent guarding a womanising heretic (and his whore), while Cairo is on fire! I sympathised, but not too much.

The barracks were deserted apart from the guards, and I surmised that my brother poets were off fighting chaos in the vast urban jungle. This time I was determined to know her carnally, even though it broke every rule of my existence.

I tore the garments from her shoulders and led her into the chamber she had formerly inhabited. Then I lay her down on the bed, pouring oil across her breasts, and rubbing it into her soft copper skin while she stared at me with round eyes, calmly realising that she was being prepared for intercourse. She would neither resist nor enthuse, the gaze said...she was in my hands, and pliable. Her only concern would be keeping my affections *after* the act...and for this reason things might still work, although I had violated my own rules.

I knew her then...and the noise she made was enough to shake the buildings, as was the noise *I* made when I ejaculated – like a rushing geyser of bellowing steam, pent up beneath the earth for a thousand years. My penis, unused to issuing semen in this way, felt scorched, as though something caustic has just passed through it, and I groaned in agony as she rocked gently in my trembling arms.

In the end, she went to sleep on my shoulder, and with some difficulty I prised her away, stepping out the front door to breathe the night air.

The guards had abandoned us, and I could hardly blame them...fancy having to listen to the roaring of rutting elephants while their own families were in danger elsewhere in the city!

But now the thousand and first night had arrived...

I reentered, and she awoke, smiling sleepily at me from behind a soft veil of bliss – which I demurred not from penetrating, ejaculating misery inside her roseate joy.

"I'm going, now," I growled. "And *you* will stay here, worthless cunt."

"What? I am confused...*don't you love me?*" And she burst into tears, exactly as the others had done before her. All so predictable.

But there was something different this time, something about the rote, dulled feeling of my own words as I heaped insults on her. And something, too, about the fury with which she sprang at me, clawing at my eyes at the very moment she screeched that she loved me. I was weeping as I knocked her unconscious, abandoning the barracks, and Cairo, never to return.

Yes...this time something was different.

From whence comes the sudden feeling that the hole in my soul can be *no longer sewn up?*

[...]

Somehow, amidst the chaos, I managed to board a military flight to Damascus...the plane climbs the air even as I write. It is doubtful I shall ever return to Kemet, of which I now realise something *has* survived, in spite of the Persians, the Romans, the Arabs, the Turks, Napoleon, the Curia and the rest of them. For something is still out there, at the edge of the two lands, red and black.

A soldier on the plane dances a crazed Western-style dance (I think it is called a 'pogo'), while his comrades laugh and cheer him on.

I go dizzy at the edges. Can't write any more.

[...]

Last night, my first back in Damascus, I had a remarkable dream. I dreamt that an Islamic extremist faction had nuked the Great Pyramid. In this dream, the pyramid (which has never been proved to be a tomb, incidentally; some believe it to have been an initiation chamber) looked exactly as it must have done during the reign of Khufu, with its limestone casing and capstone...the Benben, perch of the mighty Bennu bird. In short, it looked like a futuristic temple.

And when the nuclear device went off, a *secret chamber* was revealed in the rubble. I woke before I could see what was in it − but I knew it was something immensely important.

I am clutching at it now, wondering what it was...

[...]

I turn the news off and *my dream is true*. It was a premonition, and I am devastated, shaking. The

252

Islamists have actually destroyed that which could never be destroyed. What good is al-Akbar's bomb (even if he wasn't bluffing about it)? He can't bomb them back. The nature of warfare has changed.

But, oh, of all things I have dreamt that might have turned out true, *a secret chamber has been revealed beneath the rubble!* The elderly Zahi Hawass led the inspection party, tottering out on his walking stick in his radiation-proof suit. But there was nothing inside the chamber – nothing.

Hawass wept, and so did I. My resistance to *her* was Isfet, not Maat, for Maat is like riding a wave, or music, and only now do I see this. It is difficult, the way of Maat, even for poets, even for kings...

All I can do now is to go back to Cairo and search for her in the radioactive ruins.

My gnosis...knowing I will never actually find her.

THE TESTIMONY OF
ADAM BRAY

"Ryebread! How are things?"

Those were the words that first indicated I was becoming too attached to the senator, that I was doing my job too well, and that it was probably time to move on. I was looking out for *his* interests at the expense of my own, and that would never do.

'Ryebread', it appeared, was the nickname of one Jed Turner, the senator's liaison with various DC subcommittees. It should have been the first time I had ever heard the nickname, but it wasn't...and for that reason, in spite of the risks entailed, I thought I should probably bring certain matters to the senator's attention. Thus I left the restaurant in a downpour of rain, unnoticed by Turner or his acquaintance.

It wasn't only they I had to fear, however, for the sensitive nature of the information meant the senator himself might very well show me the door, leaving me unemployed, which was not a good thing to be in the Beltway at that time.

The information was as follows:

Weeks earlier I had found a small piece of notepaper in the stairwell to the underground carpark beneath the building housing the senator's office. On it was a scrawled memo which effectively said this: that Senator Edwin Blogue was a confirmed moron, who had been appointed to the senate for similar reasons to Caligula's horse – namely, to show any dissidents that *they* (meaning the Curia) could appoint whosoever they wanted in Presidential America. And to make it doubly clear, Blogue was actually being considered for a position in

President Hodge's new cabinet (now that the laws had been changed to allow the president a third term in office).

But here was the interesting thing: the note was addressed to one 'Ryebread', who had apparently dropped it by mistake on his way down to the carpark. The droll name initially made me believe it to be some kind of practical joke, until I heard Turner addressed so in the restaurant, proving beyond doubt the earnest nature of the note's contents.

I knocked at the senator's door, awaiting the phlegmatic voice to bid me enter. After strangling a brief burst of fear, I gritted my teeth and showed him the note (which I had put in my wallet and forgotten about until this afternoon). He perused it until his jowls wobbled, and for a moment I thought he was going to react with anger...but to my surprise his face assumed a blank look, and he handed it back to me.

"I believe I know who the addressee of the note is, sir...the 'Ryebread' referred to is actually..."

But he held up his hand in a gesture of dismissal.

"These things aren't important," he said impassively. "But, now that you're here, Bray, please tell me what you think of this new dietary plan..." He handed me a printout with the details of some new fad diet, to which I gave a noncommittal "Looks okay", and that seemed to satisfy him. It was a matter of common knowledge that Blogue's struggle with his weight was more important to him than the plight of his people...even so, it was a lacklustre struggle, one he probably knew he would never win.

Next day we were summoned to a meeting of the Senate Subcommittee for Stamping Out Hate, where an important member of the Curia (I forget his name) gave a rundown on events surrounding the Antichrist's alleged obtainment of the Bomb (the recent *actually occurring* nuclear blast at Giza being scarcely mentioned).

After his speech, the assembled senators began to robotically denounce the Antichrist, and none more so than Edwin Blogue, whose protestations sounded so melodramatically fake that even some of the other senators looked at him in fear, as if he might be a Curia spy.

This led them in turn to heighten their *own* denunciations, which caused Blogue to likewise grunt louder, and so forth, in a kind of gathering feedback loop, whose echoed squeals grew so thunderous at one point that the floor began to shake.

I admit there was a moment, just a moment, when I wondered if perhaps Blogue *was* playing some convoluted role as Curia spy, but dismissed it as impossible...unless one meant he was playing the Curia's role neatly by virtue of sheer stupidity. I shook my head, wondering why I even cared about the fate of such a man, who was sure to come to a sticky end sooner or later (for health reasons if nothing else).

Later that day, I remember being present in the senator's office when he was briefed on the Antichrist's work to fulfill his Palestine plan, which was now being thwarted, not just by Israel itself, but also by forces within the Islamic world. The entire Middle East seemed dark on him now, for varying reasons, and the Curia were endeavouring to take full advantage of this. I took in more of all this than the senator, of course, who (as was his wont) nodded off at one point.

After that, we attended the Church of the Multicultural Christ in DC for an evening Holiday Service, as it was December 24th. The reverend had a disapproving look on his face throughout the service, I know not why...perhaps the overwhelming whiteness of the attendees disappointed him. But afterwards he took the senator aside, to ask him how the 'heretic generals' like Frampton (now in prison) would be treated. The Senator held up a puffed flipper to cut him short.

"Please don't ask me for leniency, reverend. Even a man of God cannot sway us."

"Leniency?" snarled the reverend, in disbelief. "I was going to ask you to fry them alive!"

This cute theological discussion was interrupted, however, by a siren-burst outside, followed by angry shouts, and the remaining congregation piled out to investigate.

To the reverend's utter horror, someone had spraypainted the church building, changing its sign to 'Church of the *Multicursal* Christ'. The police had apprehended the perpetrator, having caught him in the act during a routine patrol, but imagine our surprise when we observed the villain was a coal-black negro! This seemed to cause the senator's brain to short-circuit somewhat, and he announced he was making his way home for a festive glass of bourbon and cola...then he actually invited me back to his house, which I had never visited before. I thought it would be impolitic to refuse. Drinking commenced as soon as we entered his limo.

"I hope they horsewhip that bastard," he muttered as we drove off.

"Major-General Frampton?"

"No...the blackamore, I mean."

Sigh. Slow and fat...behind the times in acceptable language. That was our senator.

After a moment of silence he slurped his drink.

"Desecrating the Multicultural Christ is unforgivable," he gurgled, and belched. I had the feeling I was sitting in the car with a distended corpse. Yes...perhaps it was time to move on.

We were driving through downtown DC now, and an old bum rummaged briskly in a bin, searching out his holiday meal. As we passed, he turned to stare, and I swear he could see through the one-way glass of the limo...it seemed like he was looking right at me. He was clutching something he had pulled out of the bin − it looked like a half-full bottle of white wine. I envied his find, which seemed better than the bourbon and cola I was about to drink for career reasons. The wino didn't have a job to worry about, and he looked bright-eyed and bushy-tailed. Still, all in all, I didn't think I would take to the bum's life, mainly because I couldn't stand the cold. Central heating is an indispensable element of my life.

It was certainly warm in the limo, and I began to nod off, drifting into one of those little punctuated half-waking dreams that send electric shocks through the gaps in your ribcage. In this dream, the senator and I were floating through Venice in a gondola, which he was slowly sinking with his weight. I tried to steady him, but couldn't get a grip on his fat rolls, despite the rough outfit he was wearing (made of old potato sacks, I think).

Then it happened – the senator fell, with an abyssal splosh, into the cold-dark water, flipping over the gondola...and I was suddenly catapulted onto the top of St. Mark's Campanile, where I could see, with infrared clarity, the entire city of Venice sinking rapidly into the swamp...little earthen mounds with fires burning atop them, all that was left of the Most Serene Republic.

But out in the distance was a bigger beacon...I strained my eyes, but couldn't make out who had lit it, or even guess why.

Then I snapped to, suddenly remembering where I was. The senator was still muttering about the church vandalism as we pulled up outside the Georgetown townhouse where he lived when in DC, somewhat smaller than his Tennessee mansion. His wife (childless and fatter than he) welcomed us in personally, explaining that she had given the maid the evening off, and that the leave had been of the paid variety. She led us through corridors of an old, elegant house (cheaply and tackily decorated), into a sitting room, where my eye was unavoidably drawn to a signed photo of Johnny 'Buffo' Stokes on the far wall. The senator poured, and we sat morosely sipping our bourbon (and a mint julep for the lady). No one spoke. So much for the festive season.

A second drink livened things briefly by causing the senator to belch loudly, making his wife titter nervously, before silence descended again. But this was shattered minutes later by a frantic hammering at the door. The excited-looking guest turned out to be none other than the usually-sedate Jed 'Ryebread' Turner.

I glanced at him curiously – for now that I knew his secret I half expected his face to look different, but it didn't. It looked embarrassingly mundane, like that of a teacher of dances which had gone out of fashion ten years ago...the workaday Beltway soft-face.

"I was in the neighbourhood when I heard the news myself, and I thought I'd drop by in person to give you a run-down on the *incredible events*...and to wish you a season's greetings, of course."

Blogue sounded distant as he casually asked what the news was. Time to seemed to gather round his ponderous mass like light round a black hole, his coastal edges doing their best to freeze it, and even Turner's professional voice seemed hollow in Blogue's shadow.

"Well, firstly, senator, a sizeable faction of Scarlotti's own troops in the Middle East have betrayed him...completely deserted him, in fact."

"The Antichrist, deserted!" Blogue looked surprised for the first time.

"And not only that, he's been abandoned by his largest unit of Somalian mercenaries. They were lured by the promise of better pay from the Curia."

"That's wonderful!"

"We...I mean *they*...have been working on it for some time. But it's not all good news, senator. Momentous, but not good."

"Well, spit it out, man."

"Scarlotti has fled to the so-called North West Republic."

"*What?!*"

"That's right. He's on our very shores."

The senator sat bolt upright, looking like a rat had just scurried up his ass. I never saw him move so quick.

Next day, December 25, we attended an emergency Senate briefing session, and the feral hordes were out in full force, kept in check only by police guns. And I mean *guns*, not water cannon, as some of these communist and anarchist types were actually equipped with armored vehicles, like something out of an old film called *The Road Warrior*. Aside from a group with signs stating their opposition to 'government microchipping' (who seemed to be shunned by other protesters), I had no idea what the mob was actually against. Were they there to take the side of the Antichrist (which would put them on the side of racism and fascism) or were they frantically urging the government to go to war against him, launching a full scale invasion of the Pacific Northwest (which would put them in the camp of conservative Christian Zionists)? Either way, the stench of their body odor was unbearable. I could smell it through the car's air vents, and it almost made me retch.

The fact that a Mossad agent was due to address the assembled senators may have had some bearing on things – for while Israel is still popular with the Hodge regime (and the aforementioned Christian Zionists), the far left have long been moving towards a more consistently egalitarian position, and now rabidly hate Israel as a result. This is in keeping with the international strategy of the Curia in general (interestingly, because there are a lot of Jews in it), and fewer people now listen to the Right's argument that Jews are *entitled* to hypocrisy on immigration issues because they are somehow 'different' or 'special'. Also, fewer Jews themselves now identify with Israel, and fewer secular Israelis feel inclined to give military service for the benefit of what they increasingly see as a parasitical ultra-Orthodox class. So will the Curia soon make 'Open Borders for Israel' an actual policy? In other words, will the Zionist part of the Curia's project be *abandoned?* Heavy thoughts...

I then realized it probably *was* the Mossad agent they were protesting against, because they were hurling most of their abuse against a group of Evangelicals of the kind who literally worship Jews, and who were hoping to get a glimpse of their hero (the special agent) as his car left the underground tunnel.

It turned out that the agent, David Peretz, was the first speaker, and he briefed us on new evidence from a Syrian double operative which shed valuable light on the Antichrist's bizarre belief system. Apparently, he subscribes to something called 'esoteric ethnopluralism', which Peretz proceeded to elucidate for us. Most of the senators looked baffled at his description of this strange creed, which was utterly beyond their ken – and mine, I admit (Blogue had already fallen asleep). Senator O'Neill, who was recently at the centre of the Four Seasons scandal, until it emerged that one of the prostitutes involved was transexual (and is now regarded as a hero of the conservative movement as a result), probably gave voice to the thoughts of many when he said: "this Morning Star business is surely a sign of devil worship." Those assembled snorted like pigs, reminding me of ancient tales my mother had told me about Senate hearings into 'backwards masking' on old heavy metal records.

Agent Peretz looked down from the podium, smiling at the contentedly self-righteous boars and sows he had just thrown some scraps to.

"Gentlemen and ladies," he shouted. "We have nothing to worry about. The whole *civilized* world is against Scarlotti. He will fall!"

Thunderous applause followed...Hodge's people especially lapped it up (and even Blogue woke and began flopping his flippers together), for they always revel in the straight-talking of visiting Israeli speakers, especially on matters where they wouldn't tolerate straight-talking in their *own* ranks.

But their optimism was badly misplaced.

Over the next few weeks, the news filtering out of the northwest went from worse to *far* worse. Border tensions in that area had never really died down since the uprising, but now that the Antichrist had taken command, Hodge himself had given the green light for an invasion.

He reckoned without the military, however. Now the Antichrist's reforms had been overturned, the forces consisted mainly of fat junkies, mincing transexuals and slovenly gangbangers. As a result, at the Battle of Missoula, the Antichrist actually managed to extend the Republic's borders well into Montana.

Soon after that, he captured several urban areas that had formerly been outside the Republic: Seattle, Olympia, Eugene and Portland. These liberal, pro-Presidential cities must have boiled with rage at such a fate. One celebrity (you remember her, no doubt) was caught trying to paddle a kayak down the coast to California, and was placed on a work detail in Aberdeen as punishment. (After that, no one else tried to flee.)

I remember walking through downtown DC in a daze, trying to digest the fact that there was now a truly separate country on American soil (for until its new leader's arrival, the Republic had always seemed a transient affair to me, and I had expected it to collapse in the next breeze). And everywhere I walked, people seemed to be running round like headless chickens. The crazies were everywhere, or perhaps the new order had *sent* them crazy. One strange beanlike creature was screaming: "I am compelled by law to resist all laws" or something similar, and an aged harridan berated everyone she could on the dangers of "relaxing one's vigilance." The Trots were out in force, too, screeching against Hodge, Nor'westers, and even the Curia itself (which they now apparently mistrusted), but they were just one element in a broken mix. You could feel America's dying breath round every corner you turned.

What was happening in the North West itself, however, was unknown at that point. There was much talk about how incongruous it seemed, a cosmopolitan Nietzschean aristocrat being made president (apparently by popular mandate) of a democratic republic run by hardcore Nazi monoculturalists. My parents' generation, tuned in to Rush Limbaugh, could never have foreseen it. But the seasons they change, and time has a funny way of tilling the soil. My dream of the gondola blazed vividly back to me.

All speculation about whether our particular Antichrist was a 'white nationalist' (he had never claimed to be anything of the kind) was soon answered, however, by the interception of a presidential broadcast, wherein the Antichrist now gave an *actual commitment* to the ideals of white nationalism, placing himself about as far out on the Curia's whackjob-scale as it was possible to go. The Curia gleefully disseminated the broadcast to all the world, hoping to drum up further hatred against their adversary.

But a funny thing happened – now that the Antichrist had declared himself an actual white nationalist, over thirty *non-white* countries rushed to pledge allegiance to him, abandoning the Curia! Apparently he was now seen as having more integrity by virtue of openly working for his own people. To put it mildly, this was something the Curia had failed to predict...

One power which came over to his side was old uncle Chow (smiling China). This wasn't good...but I couldn't drum up feeling enough to care. And when negotiations with the Curia recommenced, the latter were forced to acknowledge him as Imperator over half the world, with

Russia as the only neutral power (the papers, you remember, were signed in Moscow).

More people were rushing about like headless chickens, and frankly this period is a bit of a blur to me. I do remember the stupefied look the senator wore for several weeks afterwards, however.

I also remember our final meeting.

By that time, the senator had reconciled himself to the situation, and (mistakenly regarding himself as something of an expert on Antichrist) believed he would be one of those chosen to negotiate further on behalf of America. For days he had been sitting there, waiting for a call that would never come.

But peace was here! Finally, world peace; though few in the Beltway seemed happy about it. I thought the time propitious, however, so I did it...I asked the senator for a raise.

"At a time like this, Bray?" he spluttered. "What on earth are you *thinking?*"

I left then, with a song in my heart. Multicultural, Multicursal, Christ, Antichrist...let us bide a whiles, part a while...

For a fair maid of England hath told me
That the crows are departed the Tower.
So I'll seek for my bailiwick elsewhere,
Sniffing out some new dungheap of power.

9

THE TESTIMONY OF
EDMUND T. SPITZLER
(via excerpts from his journal)

Dear diary, please excuse my long silence. Dinner with Leonard; discussed new delays in wardrobe, amongst others. Wine from Walla Walla, best available at present, not exactly Hippocrene, and then he showed me the new design for Kundry's Act II dress, which finally looks about right, walking a middle line between underseductive and slutty. I only hope it will be ready for opening night, the only truly important night for all that others may say. Our chief problems lie with the orchestra now (why couldn't it have been Purcell, not Wagner?). Will require general meeting on that, not two crusties roseate with mediocre vino.

Taxi home a nightmare, driver utter Neanderthal. Yes, I know we're not supposed to use that word disparagingly (have read regime booklet showing Neanderthals ancient master race whose blood flows diluted in our veins, Cascadian fruit juice to their exquisite claret), but I don't care. This man looked like what Neanderthal *used* to mean, there's no other way of putting it. Craggen monobrow, sullen insolence...itched to beat him with my stick, but checked self in time. *Remember probation conditions.* Almost regret the day I was given this beautiful ornate walking stick by Marie Lefèvre, descendent of Victor Hugo. Feels like it was made for cracking philistine skulls, and harder to resist doing so than with lesser canes (also, wouldn't have minded giving Hugo a good crack with it).

Returned to my den of splendor to unexpectedly find wayward wife there. Not just *there*, but rubbing herself against me like a cat. How fortunate that I am allergic to felines of all descriptions. Grilled her with suspicious annoyance on why she was acting 'sexy' and 'seductive'. She was forced to confess: had *very* bad news, and wanted to break it gently. I jokingly quoted Hemingway: "What, did you fuck a nigger?"

"*Worse*, from your point of view," she said with a different kind of cattiness, arching finely-combed eyebrows.

"Yes?"

"Two bits of bad news, actually. First, the costumes from Portland were finally delivered...but they went to the wrong theatre."

"You mean…"

"*Whizz* got hold of them by mistake."

"So...that explains the delay. Well, he knows what the Flowermaidens will be wearing. It's not the end of the world."

"No. It's worse than that."

"How?"

"He didn't send them on like he should have...he just threw them in a dumpster out the back of the theatre, and they went to landfill before he could recover them."

"*What?!*"

"Says he didn't realize whose they were...saw them in his office where the delivery men had put them, and thought they were just cheap tat someone had left to be thrown out. Only realized his mistake when he saw the invoice on his desk a few days later."

I stumped around the room, speechless with rage, swishing my stick left and right, and almost thrashing the wife in my blind fury.

"Hey, watch it!"

"He's lying, that philistine...of *course* he fucking realized."

"You don't know..."

"I *do* know. It wasn't just a calculated insult...it was an attempt at sabotaging our entire production."

"Calm down, Edmund, I implore you."

"The truce is over, the rift is reopened. I want revenge...revenge!"

"Now don't go round there. You know your probation conditions."

"*Fuck* my probation conditions. Anyway, there are other ways of taking revenge."

"You should calm down, anyhow, because I told you the lesser news first. The second thing is...*our daughter is pregnant.*" She blurted it quickly, and my anger immediately changed to a feeling of creeping uneasiness. Karl, Stella's steady boyfriend and presumably the father, has gone off on a secret mission of some sort into Presidential territory, apparently with the blessing of Il Maestro himself, and hasn't been seen for two months. Quite possibly dead and, as the relationship hasn't been legitimized by marriage, won't qualify her for widowhood, merely single mother status, which isn't looked on favourably by the regime. Can only hope Il Maestro himself will take pity on her and change her official status somehow...not that she'd care, never has. A rebel, like Wagner...I don't understand rebels. Give me Purcell any day.

"So," I muttered. "I'll be a grandpa."

"You should visit her tomorrow. She's upset. She still doesn't know if Karl is alive or dead."

"Yes, I'll visit."

"You really, really should."

"Yes, I will. In the morning."

"Yes." And then she kissed me, that wife of mine. Led her to the bedchamber for the first time in months. I spare you the details, dear diary, but at 2am feel less desire to swing my ornate stick than I have in...well, months.

[...]

I arrived at the crumbling old wooden house that Stella calls home, expecting to be attacked by bats, ravens or wolves. The darkness seemed to grow as I walked down the path, swinging my stick, and I fancied I could hear the rustle of little people in the bushes. Then Stella opened the door, and all was light. There seemed to be a halo around her visage, tinged with sadness as it was. I dropped the joke forming on my lips about her gothic abode, opting to hug her instead. She seemed more reserved than usual.

We sat in two rickety chairs in the kitchen, waiting for some kind of herbal tea to steep.

"No wine then?"

She shook her head. "Mom told you?"

"Yes. And Karl's the father?"

"Yeah."

"And no news?"

"Nope."

I rolled off some cliched words of consolation. She took them silently, then a spark came back into her eyes.

"It's embarrassing you're looking out for *me*, dad. I'm a Wolf, supposed to be alienated from boomers and all that." I was going to point out that I was born in '81, and by no means a boomer, but checked myself when I remembered that 'boomer' has now become a generic term for anyone over forty. *Everyone* will be a boomer some day, unless they have the good grace to die young. Plus, I sensed a certain self-mocking deceit in her tone, although it was hard to be sure...I've never been sure of anything regarding my daughter, to be honest. She's a strange creature, like all Wolves.

I glanced round the kitchen, but it conveyed little of her lifestyle and beliefs. It might have been that of a psychedelic carpenter, or paramilitary gardening guru. In fact, it was the kitchen of a Wolf of Joy.

"And do you regard the new regime as less hypocritical and corrupt than the old one, my darling daughter?"

"Yes."

"Then why haven't the Wolves disbanded?"

"There's no membership list, so nothing to disband. You're a Wolf by your deeds, and those alone."

"Ah...that's right. *Deeds and death*, your watchword. From Wagner, I believe." Many of the Wolves had nearly abandoned their mission the year before the war, the same year Stella became one of them. That was the year the globalist upper-middle classes began having 'Wolves of Joy' theme-parties, where they would celebrate their own hypocrisy by reenacting pranks from a book called *The Hungry Wolves of Van Diemen's Land.*

"So why didn't you abandon your mission?"

"We realized that if we care what small people think then we're no bigger ourselves, of course."

"But what's your *point* these days? In the North West of all places, which is officially anti-globalist?"

"We must be vigilant."

"Doesn't that bore you?"

"No."

"You need a project...an opera or something."

"Yes...we have a current project, actually. Our new aim is to go to war *for* the Archetype."

"How do you do that?"

"We're still figuring it out."

I left it at that. As we sipped the disgusting tea, we discussed her pregnancy, especially in light of the fact that the new regime is staunchly anti-feminist and frowns upon single mothers. (Il Maestro has respected this, and other North Western tenures, since his coronation as king, despite what his personal proclivities might be). In point of fact, the regime's attitude to women is very much like that of the Nazis' 'Kinder, Küche, Kirche', except with the Kirche scratched out to avoid offending the regime's pagans (whom Il Maestro favours over the Christians, though he does everything in his power to avoid religious discord).

Did Stella have a problem with this?

"No."

No. No matter how 'restricted' women are, she will always do what she wants. Our conversation petered out, and I told her I would return shortly, in spite of my busy schedule, to bring her some wine, so she need never drink that putrid tea again.

"I'm pregnant, dad. No alcohol." She smiled for the first time.

"Oh yes. Well, I'll see you soon I expect."

We hugged once more, and I left. Perhaps this crisis will enable us to form a friendship of sorts at long last. Every cloud has a silver lining. But I note that neither of us expressed any joy in the imminent arrival of a new life in the world. Are we subconsciously afraid? World peace is here, so we've all been told...does peace make us paranoid? Or is there something around the corner, some dreadful, unimagined horror? I wandered the streets of Seattle, pondering these matters, and, even though crime is now virtually zero, I felt glad to have my stick at hand. I seemed to feel a storm coming, though one seldom knows how far off such things are. It isn't *like* me to feel such things...I hope the vile tea hasn't given me some sort of clairvoyance.

To deflect these thoughts I considered the good and bad points of the new regime. Although hardly on its side (or anyone else's) the fact that my lack of strong disapproval in itself seems to cause many so-called friends to disapprove of *me* makes me mildly sympathetic to the regime out of sheer spite. And then there is our sovereign (can it be true?) Il Maestro, who seems like a character from an opera himself...Wagner rather than Purcell, admittedly. (And, how many of the luvvie 'disapprovers' have refused work offered to them by the regime out of principle? None! Hypocrites...)

I do like the dramatic flair with which His Majesty, Il Maestro, has appointed government officials with such ancient, evocative titles: seneschals, justiciars, dapifers, logothetes and so forth. So the Republic and the Free Cities have now become a Kingdom, which itself exists within an Imperium that covers half the world, Il Maestro serving as both imperator and king. His jurisprudence is simple, robust and fair. People are still getting accustomed to such bracing air after decades of being insulated from reality under the globalist patchwork that still covers the rest of North America. But the revival of sacred kingship has struck an undoubted chord in the masses. The Curia fume, and possibly wonder how they turn Il Maestro's centralization (of sorts) to their own advantage if and when he dies.

[...]

Visited Stella again. No news of Karl, but she surprised me in her insight.

While there I couldn't help myself – I launched into a violent tirade against Whizz and his entire stinking production of *Zauberflöte*. I expressed a wish to teleport him naked to the top of Mt. Rainier during a snowstorm, then watch him run jabbering down the mountain, slowly dying of exposure.

"But why does the king want two operas premiering so close together, dad? Surely there aren't that many opera fans *left* in Seattle?"

"He's a great fan of Mozart, while the old guard Nor'westers are far more into Wagner. So it was a compromise."

"Your rivalry with Whizz is political?"

"*Political?* Haven't you been listening? It couldn't be more *personal.* I've hated that rat-faced little squelch since the first minute I ever heard him open his pale, flabbering lips."

"But why?"

"He dared to suggest my production of *La Traviata* could have used some improvements...and even had the temerity to suggest them to me!"

"Is that all? Look, I was thinking of going to *see* his production of *The Magic Flute...*"

"Don't you dare!"

"Now listen, Dad. I read a synopsis of the plot, and it sounded interesting. So perhaps you could tell me a bit about the Parsifal story...then I can decide which one I like best."

"You don't watch an opera based on the *story,*" I spluttered, aghast.

"Why not?"

I looked for the words, but couldn't find them. She let me off by asking about the plot again, which I grudgingly outlined for her, and she considered a while in silence.

I was just about to leave when she sat bolt upright, entranced. It was as if a computer had taken possession of her, and she began to reel out 'hidden connections' (so she said) between the 'inner meanings' of *Parsifal* and *The Magic Flute.* I don't remember all that she said, but it was stuff along the lines of "Klingsor and his Valley of Temptation = Queen of the Night" and so forth...sometimes valid, sometimes forced comparisons. Or maybe she could see something that I couldn't.

"Parsifal has to wander, and Tamino has to find his way through the labyrinth, and Kundry is Parsifal's Pamina..."

"No, that's rubbish. Kundry is *never* the object of romantic love."

"She's not to be loved like Pamina...only compassion can do anything for *her*...in *Parsifal* it's compassion that wins, and in *The Magic Flute* it's courage and wisdom. Parsifal replaces Amfortas, and Tamino will surely succeed Sarastro...eternal renewal, the passing of the torch. But who do *we*, the Wolves of Joy pass *our* torch to? The emperor threatens our inner revolution. Is he in the grip of Klingsor?"

"Isn't he rather Sarastro, the wise and benevolent ruler? There's peace now...people are happier than they were before. Don't you think you're being a bit selfish?"

She frowned. She didn't know. "Power wielded too long can kill you inside," she murmured.

I didn't know what to say to that, and in any case had to leave.

[...]

My daughter may have valiantly and wisely attempted to reconcile two operas vastly different in tone, but I don't care...I will have my revenge over the costumes incident.

Whizz's prize prop, a ruined pyramid, ordered from a firm in China, and meant to be some kind of trendy 'up-to-date' (I hate that) reference to the Giza bombing...well, I had an idea about what might happen to it, based on the oft-repeated story about Wagner's dragon's head ending up in Beirut instead of Bayreuth. But aside from our now infernally unreliable international postal system, what city has a name like Seattle – Seoul? Saskatoon? Sarajevo? Anyway, the firm doubtless knows *exactly* where the opera is taking place.

Then I had another brainwave – I would get the pyramid's dimensions changed from feet to inches (like the dolmen in the old comedy *This is Spinal Tap*). I sent an email to the firm informing them as to the new measurements, but they replied shortly afterwards, confused as to why it should be changed – from metric! Damn. Whizz will probably learn of it now, and beef up his security. Fortunately, I have a trump card.

[...]

Ha! Have done it, thanks to an old acquaintance (who must remain unnamed but is currently a stagehand in Whizz's employ). I possess compromising information regarding his homosexuality (now a criminal offence), and so it was easy to get him to agree to place a specially modified asthma pump, filled with helium, in Papageno's whistle. As it turned out, it wouldn't fit...but he managed to insert it instead into Tamino's magic flute, which turned out to be even more comically ludicrous in its effects. The audience at McCaw Hall (now renamed the Adolf Hitler Center for the Performing Arts) were reduced to tears of laughter. Even the king himself found it hard to stifle a smile, I noted with satisfaction.

Apparently Whizz has vowed revenge.

Well, let him try his best. My stick hand itches...

[...]

The king, Il Maestro, has dropped in on me personally to see how our production is going. He takes a lively interest in the arts, or so he says, especially a Gesamtkunstwerk like that we are engaged on. He is perhaps the strangest person I have met, in that I was never really sure whether I was talking to him, or to someone pretending to be him. Is he a placebo? His visage, scarred as it is, looks young, though his voice has the coolness of ancient marble, the recalling of which disconcerts me.

He mentioned the Magic Flute fiasco. I gave a dignified tut tut, not knowing if Whizz had already voiced his suspicions to him, and assured him nothing of the sort will happen with our more professional production, on which he gave a cold smile betokening aloofness from artists' jealousies and the like. Fair enough...would that we could all occupy such heightened ground. It's far too late for me, however.

272

I thought it best to admit of numerous small problems – not least of which being that our only decent bass-baritone has the flu – of the kind unavoidable when pulling such a complex production together, and he warmed to me more after that.

Our talk then turned to politics, and I must admit that my own problems seem insignificant compared to Il Maestro's. White people of all descriptions are now fleeing here via Canada, risking death and torture to do so, and the erstwhile 'White Republic' (now a Kingdom) has actually had to collude with Curia states in hermetically sealing its borders – to Whites! There is no alternative by reason of arable economy – this particular lifeboat is full – and yet they come...

Il Maestro pays a heavy tribute to the harsh vagaries of existence, but there is no doubt he is more tolerant and enlightened than many of his subjects, and is even attempting to revive his idea of a glass bead university, disrupted when its previous locale fell under Presidential control. And at the former Evergreen State College (now the Ezra Pound College of Liberal Arts) he has employed none other than Gallinule, that open-minded experimenter who wants greater public input on the directions of science. Gallinule's tenure was greeted with *outrage* from the Curia – disproportionately one would think – but what's that here in the real world?

We also spoke of the Wolves, and Karl – the nature of whose mission Il Maestro refused to divulge, although he confided there is a good chance he will return alive (he is now aligned to the king and not the Wolves, which must be unknown news to Stella).

From hints dropped, I believe Il Maestro's plan is to create a truly global Reich as the only way to guard against globalism – the delicious irony of which has filled me with a warmth I have lacked since the last bottle of real claret went dry. But he appears, rather interestingly, to believe himself divinely appointed (i.e. he himself is a man, but the kingship is divine), and thus seems to regard self-willed groups like the Wolves as potentially treasonous.

I pointed out how good-hearted they are (even against my own better judgement), but he went quiet, then indicated to his bodyguards that our conversation was at an end, and left, flanked by two mountainous flunkies.

[…]

Vicious argument between Iain, our concert master (who I know for a fact is part Jew, though I keep quiet about this as there is no proof, and it's not something he would want bandied around in the current climate) and Michael, our Gurnemanz, still recovering from flu, who really shouldn't have been in to rehearsal at all, and who is probably the most sympathetic of our crew to the new regime's ideas. And so the ancient pattern repeats.

Il Maestro now protects Jews from reprisals (in his other lands – they were officially banished from the NW, of course, long before he came on the scene) provided they don't meddle with politics or culture, or have any contact with their brethren in the Curia lands or in Israel (which although not governed by the Curia, is militarily aligned with it, or something like that). Of course, Jews in Curia lands shriek that even *this* is persecution, spreading rumours Il Maestro is committing 'anti-Semitic atrocities', including some rather hideous medical experiments...conversely , however, in the North West, there have been mutterings he is a 'Jew-lover'.

Iain and Michael, who both have to be careful what they say in public, were berating each other over minor details of Il Maestro's attitude to Israel, but there were deeper, unspoken issues at stake, which made it fascinating to watch (in a sadistic kind of way). Part of their argument related to Israel's sudden courting of non-Curia ethnostates. Only a decade ago it was quite common for nationalist parties in the West to express solidarity with Israel, even though the latter only ever repaid their solicitations with contempt. When the NW Republic was first established, its leaders vowed never to repeat such obvious stupidity, choosing to ignore Israel completely.

But the Israeli Right has suddenly changed its tune, making cautious overtures to a handful of non-Curia-approved ethnostates in the Imperium (apparently behind the Curia's back). There is a sense in Israel (among non-hardliners) that the Zionist project is winding down, as the Curia itself abandons its child, despite the former being originally founded by Bilderberg types as a more pro-Israel version of the UN.

Our concert master insists that this newfound regard for other ethnostates on Israel's part is something genuine, while our bass-baritone gloats that it is too little too late, and that the "shitty little country" deserves to die, frozen and friendless.

At the same time, Il Maestro's more relaxed attitude to Jews has created tensions in his own lands, leading to rumours that he covets their money-making skills. This has added to the tensions already present in many of his dominions, where tribalism leads the people to chafe at the very notion of Imperium, and indeed the idea of peace in general. It is unclear how long one man's (admittedly forceful) persona will be able to hold it all together.

Meanwhile, here in the Northwest, someone is writing an epic poem, reviving the form, and our Gurnemanz loves this idea. But my daughter and her friends seem to think the 'neo-troubadours' of Il Maestro's court (modelled on themselves) lack sincerity, having form only. You can't please everyone...

I have heard other, more worrying rumours, too — that Il Maestro wishes to turn away from the world and probe the deepest mysteries of physics and mathematics, and would do so were it not for small matters constantly engaging him, wearing him down. But if he abdicates, what hope for the civilized?

[...]

Sleepless in Seattle. I wandered the streets for hours, hand aclench my firm and cherished stick. The city is so soulless at night...the revolution hasn't gone far enough, as the sense of prim nothingness in certain quarters is still undiminished. At times like this I feel like a dissenter, a dissenter from everything. Not a rebel though...never a rebel.

Some oldster moaning about 'chemtrails' asks me for a dollar, still legal tender in the royal domains, increasingly rare in rural regions, and I give it him to shut him up. The incident seems completely void of sense and depth. Then I pass a so-called 'eccentric' called Dr. Moon, sitting on a front stoop teaching invented languages to a decaying leaf. That, too, lacks depth and sense.

This kingdom we inhabit – how long will it last, when all the civilizations of history have eventually ended? Ours hasn't even created a unique culture of its own – just rehashing Mozart and Wagner. But again, give it time. It may find its feet after I am gone. That is a sacrifice I would gladly make. History is unforgiving...

And tonight I passed the exact place, Tinders, where I first met my wife. And felt nothing. Everything is turning to plastic. What's wrong with me?

Faces flash in front of me – Chugg and his friends who bullied me in Middle School before I learnt to fight back. Are *they* out there in this plastic city, or did they flee to the Presidential States? So distant...all so long ago. Bullies amuse me now. I'm getting old, and there is little that scares me, not with treasured stick at hand. I swished it at a fence, where faded spraypaint proclaimed that 'Kurt lives', and smiled wryly. I well remember the Cobain killing (suicide it was called at the time), which happened when I was thirteen. Even back then I hated rock 'n' roll, preferring the purity of early music. So here I am doing Wagner, almost its antithesis. And yet, Wagner has a strange purity of his own when all is said and done. Mozart has his moments, too. But I want revenge...

What else did I observe tonight? Oh, yes. Two young men bullying a third youth who appeared to be simple or perhaps autistic. That sort of thing will always go on, whatever regime we live under. I contemplated interference, and eventually decided to crack one of them upside the head, whereupon both immediately fled. Not bad for a fifty-something. Their quarry shuffled off, too, regarding me with fear. I returned home to find my wayward wife there again, but this time felt no desire, nothing.

She had news – that Karl had reappeared, that he and Stella joyfully plan to marry. I wish I could get excited. Karl's mission was successful (he can't reveal the details), and Il Maestro is now considering him as a possible adoptive heir.

I acted happy and such, but feel increasingly dead inside. Maybe that's why good things are happening, and will perhaps continue to happen – because I feel dead inside.

[...]

The big night. Career on the line. King watching, world watching, so it felt. Our bass-baritone recovered marvellously, but that turned out to be the least of my worries. The dive bombers started to circle even before the curtain went up, when we discovered that the water for the lake from Act I had been adulterated with a bright, neon-pink foaming agent. Now I knew for sure that Whizz had procured an inside agent, just as I had managed to do. But who? Hubert, our fat stage manager? Trevor, who was always a bit sleazy? Surely not our esteemed concert master? There was no way of knowing, short of torturing them all.

I had them quickly drain it, making do with a dry lake. Hopefully someone in the audience might read obscure mystical symbolism into that, or something. Then I had the stagehands doublecheck everything, working in pairs in case one of them should be the traitor. I wanted to retreat to my nest, my shell, but it wasn't possible. I scoured the opera house for Whizz (or anyone recognizable as having associated with him), but nothing, just a mess of strange faces splurging out at me.

This double checking was in vain, anyway, as we found at the end of Act I, in the realm where time becomes space, when the mist grew steadily worse. The dry ice machine had been tampered with, creating an impenetrable fog which enveloped the audience, king and all. It was all too much for my poor little head.

To my immense surprise, however, the applause at the end of the Act (contra tradition, I know, but I'm not a Wagnerian) was *warm*. Incredibly, we had gotten away

277

with it, Whizz's sabotage merely *adding* to the audience's experience of the timeless realm of the Grail!

But then came the next act, and at a certain point my brain clicked into gear (I shudder to recall), noticing layered echoes of snickers like ancient starter motors, building incrementally, but it was some time before I worked out what they were snickering *at* – namely, that our esteemed Klingsor had a problem south of the border (I later learned his drink had been spiked with Ellison Plugg's brand of super-strength erectile formula), and that his tights would consequently need replacing. (Our serviceable soprano Ellen, playing Kundry, is unentrancing to look upon, so small wonder, perhaps, that there were snickers.)

Then I spotted him, Whizz, in the second row of the audience, evidently placed so as to get a good view (the acoustics are terrible there). The smug smirk on his face told me everything. I marched up intending to shirtfront him, and beat him with my stick, caring no whit if the king were looking or not (he was), but was preempted somewhat when, grinning inanely, he threw the contents of his wine glass with some vigor into my face. A brawl ensued, not unlike that in a Beatrix Potter story about a fox and badger whose name escapes me, and to my great pride (at the time) and utter disbelief (now) the greater part of the cast joined in, for Whizz was surrounded by a dozen laughing cronies on either side. Several art lovers, who had the misfortune to be stationed in the front row, were enmeshed unwillingly in the brawl, as the orchestra stopped playing, and female screams rebounded. To cut a long story short, Act III was cancelled and Il Maestro was unamused.

And now I have been summonsed for instigating, and for violation of parole – and while my soon-to-be son-in-law will probably get me off, is it really worth the constant degrading lectures from my daughter on "White people fighting over factional trivialities...our undoing as a people"?

Oh yes...I was acting out the age-old drama all right.

I don't care, though. I got him a good one, with the most exquisite stick in the world.

10

THE TESTIMONY OF
MAXINE LEOPOLDINA SCARLOTTI

My dreams are all of fire – mother says dreams usually go by opposites, so does that mean the world will end in ice? With my father listening to his underlings so much, to sly people like Mr. Adam Bray, it would not surprise me if the world ended in ice...

Mother says the wizened Curia vultures threaten father's Imperium once again. In response, he stops treating his subject states kindly, and works towards a military superstate for some "looming final battle". And now, even as he finally lets me take his surname as my own, he pressures me to enter into a betrothal contract with the vile Enzo, a sort of hired killer!

I told father I would rather join the Wolves, and his eyes blazed in rage.

When he calmed down, he told me to "think on it", but his tone indicated he would brook no opposition, and that my 'choice' was not a free one. So, I am resolved to run away.

They say father has actually begun to persecute the Wolves. The legendary outlaw Sean was assassinated in a place called Risdon Prison, and no one has admitted to ordering the killing. At the same time, father passes laws against 'anti-semitism', and although this is aimed only at stopping criminal attacks, it has alienated many of his followers, who think it is the thin end of the wedge for a "revival of Zionist values", or something. It's all very complicated and sad.

Father also says he wants Israel left alone (when even its own citizens are starting to abandon it en masse), because he doesn't want them infesting the West with their 'endless victim swindle' – he wants to use Israel as a stopgap until he can implement something called the 'Birobidjan solution', but apparently this will be extremely difficult.

And now he is launching a massive military expedition against the 'Bloc' (Eastern Europe, that is, not counting Russia), and the Curia are giving him less opposition than expected, because it's more of a *genuine* independence movement (from both Curia and father) that he's suppressing.

And *I* am going to defy him, the most powerful man in the world, and can only imagine two outcomes – death or imprisonment on one hand, or a tearful reunion, with father agreeing to make an 'official' version of the Wolves, although the Wolves themselves will think it is corrupt and refuse to join. But as I'm not exactly the apple of my father's eye, I think the first outcome is more likely anyway.

How dark and tangled everything has become!

Surely it never started out like this...

11

THE TESTIMONY OF
WALLACE TARR

I give this brief remembrance of His Imperial Majesty, Maximillian I. While not a literary man, I will try and paint a picture of His Imperial Majesty as he was in his last days.

My most distinct memory is standing alongside him for nearly an hour as he appeared to contemplate the landscape from where we stood – a barren hill on the edge of the Gobi Desert where a wide belt of green grassland met a neverending sea of brown and sterile sandhills. When he finally moved his noble head, it was to gaze upwards at a flock of overlanding birds flying high above. One of us, Hubert I think, found courage to speak, saying something to the effect that the birds were probably fleeing a distant storm.

And then, in the far beyond, we finally spied the men we were waiting for, changing from motes to full stops and then standing still, hundreds of them, as if contemplating us from remote antiquity. You could almost see their necks craning to assess us, and then, swiftly and silently, they turned and galloped away...just as I had expected, and probably the others too, because nobody raised a murmur. These kinds of fools, who saw only the immediate needs of their tribe rather than the greater struggle...yes, we were well adapted to their sort.

It had recently looked like coming rain (something which apparently never happened at this time of year) but now the clouds seemed to be moving backwards, as if a vast mouth were sucking clean the sky, each cloud detached from the others, shivering and lonely, yet ingested by the same force, so their loneliness mattered not at the end...yet one couldn't feel glad for them. More than one of us had the strange feeling that the sun would not continue to rise over this desert for very much longer.

The emperor, responding to this familiar situation, voiced his opinion that *time never repeats*, and that a theory called 'Eternal Return' is wrong, that patterns really reform slightly different each time, similar but never exact.

"The prison walls which some allege precisely defined, are in fact eternal and therefore impregnable," he stated. "Therefore we should be content with shoring up those walls, like Gilgamesh did at the end of his great adventure."

I vowed to read the story of this Gilgamesh so I could better understand what he was talking about – but one doesn't interrupt the emperor with questions when he is waxing philosophical.

Unexpectedly, though, Hans (who though timid and shy has always seemed a loyal and devoted servant of His Imperial Majesty, at least to myself) did something completely out of character. He not only interrupted the Emperor, but took him to task, speaking in a tremulous voice of prophecy, saying that: "Like Théoden of legend, you need a Gandalf the White to open your eyes, *then* you will find the walls to be pregnable. And the Wolves will return..."

But the Emperor sent him away in a fury, uttering these words:

"I love everything that has ever existed, even my nefarious enemies, so am I not Master of all, never to be defied? What need of breaching walls, when walls are *loved?* Would not breaching them be an act of hatred and malice? Would I not then cease to be Master, and become a nefarious enemy of life itself in my own right?"

And no one could answer these words of His Imperial Majesty.

Then news came in by radio, seeming to kill the moon, which we only then realised we couldn't locate in the sky, although it was supposed to be an Evening Moon. *[He means a waxing one, presumably – E.J.C.].* There had been a nuclear attack by terrorists, though no one was sure who they actually were, somewhere in the wastes of Central Asia – not so very far from where we stood (and so why couldn't we hear the presumably vast report – had the moon sucked it up, and hence been temporarily displaced?).

His Imperial Majesty was aching to hit the trail towards our next battle, but wisely decided to wait for further reports before moving out. These reports, which seemed far-off and near all at once, could be irrelevant or a deadly trap...it seemed impossible to tell which. All we knew for sure was that the situation in camp was very tense, and when at a certain moment I felt drops of rain on my upturned face my first guess was that they were a spray of tears shaken from somebody's head in the darkening congress.

It was just as well that we waited, for over the next week, the news trickled in – a disease, spreading rapidly, which we now know as the Grey Death, its lines of advance largely to the westwards and seemingly avoiding us, but not by much...like the blade of a scythe, hovering for a killing blow that never quite landed, yet making us fear the open skies themselves.

It was reckoned that the nuclear blast had encompassed the site of an ancient kurgan, from which bacteria had escaped that the explosion itself hadn't managed to kill.

So who carried out the attack, and why? Did it matter? Did he who knew have mysterious permission to pass on beyond the plane of bacteria and suchlike obfuscations? The Grey Death, they call it, but in colour-change it is opposite to Gandalf – for where he had turned from grey to white, the disease started out in the latter state...for when slapping the skin of an afflictee with a specialised spatula with a hole in its centre, a small white pustule invariably appears, and then, a few days later, the body equally invariably becomes grey and brittle, dying from within, a coral polyp making the unimagined transition to dried sea sponge, without anyone knowing or caring, or waiting in the wings.

So many 'outbreaks' in the past (swine flu etc.), hyped by vaccine companies to make a quick buck, but this time it was actually real, and horrific, and there wasn't a thing anyone could do about it, not even an explanation. Sickness, dissipation, hallmarks of the Piscean Age, and we are now living in its last gasp, made plaintive solely by intensity, one final wring of the cloth, squeezing out all the concentrated diseased dregs, so that one might say it is the very spirit of disease, while all the time a new world is attempting to be born.

And under the cloth itself, countless lives swirled, stripped to their essence, pared to the Archetype, which no matter how the opposition protest, keeps pushing back. Without it, we would *all* be nothing but grey and brittle sea sponges, and the universe itself would be chalk dust, which no one would see – so in truth wouldn't exist.

And probably just as well this Archetype primes me, sending dreams, which then translate to action. In one, a dry sea sponge embraces a wet fish, both turning to sludge, which is then stored in an exquisite cup, fit for His Imperial Majesty to drink from (if he didn't choose to drink as he does from ordinary vessels).

And when I awoke from this dream, I heard the first report on the final implosion of the 'Smash the Archetype' movement, which had lately spread through the entire world...

The moment of collapse did not come during the long slow weeks when the painful realisation came to these narcissists that they themselves were an archetype. No, it came later – when they realised that they were *a low one*. The pitiful remainder of the once mighty movement can now be witnessed begging for penance, from beggars, on many a street corner throughout the world.

And then I thought of my betrothed, Elanna, whom I will never see again on this side of the curtain. (Already the disease toll exceeds that of the Black Death of the 1340s, and is wider in scope, thanks to jet travel.) And I thought of her warmth, her physical presence, wondering if it was an illusion or whether it had been real. I never realised how good she was until now that she is once more unattainable.

Pity me not, though, for I die among warriors.

Then, after a seeming eternity, the emperor gave the order to move out, for if our troops were affected, then so would the enemy's be. And never was army more ready – we were "harder than Krupp steel," as the saying goes, and fought like men possessed, against a numerically even army which had no chance. It was the emperor's final *human* act – though not his final endeavour. I remember the frenzy as if it were now upon me, albeit felt via another person, an opium penance. I remember the very last time I caught His Imperial Majesty's eye, as we wiped the blood from our skin, panting in confused contamination, staring at a world grown distant and plastic. Whence would new blood flow, giving nearness and depth?

But above all I remember the morning after combat, when I awoke at dawn to see His Imperial Majesty standing still and staring up at the sky, like a prophet of old searching for a silent warning. Then he turned and loped swiftly like a wolf to his campaign tent.

What he had seen, I later learned, was a vision of the Morning Star, whose cold, serene yet steely light seemed to bathe his face even hours later when he addressed us on the matter.

He had found, he said, an old testimony in his campaign bag, which he now intended to make public, having read it for the first time since it was written. First, though, he read from it the record of a dream, in which he had torn and gouged his own skin...reading this, he said, had made him realise that he was *not* a reincarnation of Pyrrhus of Epirus as he had once claimed, but rather of one *Friedrich II von Hohenstaufen*, a medieval German ruler.

"How did I not see it before?" he pondered, realising now that the dream about Pyrrhus had in actuality been someone else *telling* him (i.e. Friedrich II) about Pyrrhus. He was also clear that this past life heritage had caused him to emulate, in various ways, the life of Friedrich II.

But Hans, who had found the courage to return, or perhaps couldn't keep away from the chieftain he both loved and chastised, leapt onto the podium and began to debate with His Imperial Majesty on the nature of reality, reincarnation and the rest of it.

This time, though, and I know not how it happened, their arguments were *reversed*...this time it was Hans who argued that the analogies His Imperial Majesty thought he had found between his own life and that of Friedrich II were not exact, that history doesn't repeat, it merely rhymes, and that the rhymes themselves are irregular, more like blank verse really, and that life is an infinitely-changing fractal, with no exact Eternal Return etc.

And now His Imperial Majesty argued that it was Hans who needed a *Gandalf the White* to awaken him from his slumber, yet closing with mysterious words, said: "I will atone for what I did in that other existence..."

And next day he was gone...disappeared in the deep night, like a seeping shadow. It was a week before we learnt what actually happened. And some have speculated that, having made public and left behind the journal (which he had instructed wasn't to be made public before his death) he now had no choice but to die as a result.

In any case, all the world now knows how he arrived for an unscheduled truce meeting with the executive council of the Unicursal Curia and, using technology he had sponsored or developed himself (and which has still not been made public) caused their heads to literally explode, dying a foreseen death himself in the process (for, of course, his own head exploded along with theirs).

And on his body was found a card with these two quotes:

"He who manages to bind the golem and refine him will be reconciled with himself."
– Meyrink

"At the end of the play, something occurs that its creators never envisaged...life always finds a way, and that is what these Curia types will never understand..."
– Scarlotti

On the back of the card was a single word: "Tegg."
So while a green new world may well emerge from the shadow of the old, I will not myself be here to see it, for the sickness is upon me, and my grey phase begins – already I feel my bones turn brittle.

But I have had the privilege of knowing one of history's greatest lords, and nothing can take that away from me.

Hail Caesar, for those who are about to die salute you!

AFTERWORD

Now that you have perused the material, ending with that terrible massacre of the Inner Council, keep in mind the near certainty that Scarlotti's story of the guru's cave was *invented*, perhaps a safe way of explaining inner impulses he didn't understand, as no such cave was found within a forty mile radius of Sterns, and nor was any student with the name or nickname of Tegg ever enrolled there.

On further investigation, it appears that 'Maximillian Scarlotti' was not even his real name, and that no one knows how he got into Sterns in the first place, the records of his enrolment process having been found non-existent.

Consequently, we *Weltverbesserer* would now be wise to shift our attention to the planet Venus herself, and when we gain the upper hand once more, to form, from existing warheads, a vast nuclear armada to tear her baleful presence from the shivering skies.

- Elmer J. Cohen
(former) Special Advisor to the
(former) Unicursal Curia

Reveries of the Dreamking

CONTENTS

FOREWORD

I

Let me tell you all about my grandfather, Nicholas Lune, who lived during the time of the Grey Death. Or rather, let us contemplate the words of the man himself via his journal that entered my possession on the recent death of my mother, Lune's daughter; a journal I have subsequently edited to remove excess detail, dates and other superfluities, instead dividing it into chapters like those of a novel (which its text curiously resembles).

This bizarre journal is not the only document by Grandfather Lune I acquired, however – there is also a collection of letters, including an intriguing missive concerning an acquaintance of his, a man he refers to (doubtless ironically) as the *Introspector*. So, by way of introducing the journal, I will first summarise the contents of this letter in the hope of putting the journal itself in a clearer perspective.

This 'Introspector' was a reader in Homeric Greek at an institution my grandfather called the University of Sullen Contempt (I have been unable to find out which institute this actually refers to, as there were several universities in the city where he resided). The Introspector's thesis, in spite of an impressive-sounding title, was as utterly superfluous as the exact nature of the research he engaged in.

This, of course, could be said of the work of most students of his time, but what distinguished the Introspector was the complete earnestness with which he undertook his endeavours, an attitude carried over even to his home life, where he arranged his collection of books meticulously, using a spirit level, so their spines were precisely flush with the shelf.

His prize possession was a set of volumes called the 'Britannica Great Books of the Western World', and these were kept on a shelf so high that no one could ever touch them.

It is clear from the tone of my grandfather's letter that he disliked the Introspector immensely, in no small part due to a sizeable chip the latter had on his shoulder over a 'deprived childhood' talked about at great length, with seldom a word allowed edgeways by anyone else. Lune (who by all accounts had a worse childhood, though he never publicly complained about it) doubted the Introspector's sincerity largely for this reason, regarding him as a poseur and probable charlatan.

The Introspector's professed sympathies for the 'Curia' (as Patagonians were known in the days before the Grey Death) also grated upon Lune's nerves...for the Introspector claimed to despise Whites as a group; referred to his girlfriend as his 'partner', etc. etc. In other words, the Introspector was a typical man of his time, and my grandfather, in equal measure, was not.

II

But while my esteemed grandfather did his best to avoid the Introspector, there came a day when he was forced to endure a fresh encounter with him...and somewhat surprisingly, found himself the target of a monologue or rant that was actually interesting to listen to...something other than the Introspector's usual stream of self-important waffle, that is. For, returning from a short holiday during semester break, the Introspector and his girlfriend discovered a *little man* making himself quite comfortable in their rented home.

Their response, not unnaturally, was to threaten to call the police if he didn't leave immediately – upon hearing which the little fellow disappeared, as if into thin air.

After recovering from their shock, the pair commenced examining the house in some detail, straight away noticing that a fire had been lit in the fireplace, and that preparations for a meal were evident on the kitchen counter.

They then discovered that the little man had actually washed their dirty laundry, restocked and reordered the contents of their fridge and, more disturbingly, had *written in their journal*, inscribing at some length in what the Introspector described as 'elegant, courtly and highly poetic language' (although he refused to divulge the exact contents).

On discovering all this, the Introspector had had something resembling an autistic meltdown – only recovering somewhat on ascertaining that his 'Great Books' collection remained immaculate atop its high and dusted shelf.

III

As I said, all this was prior to the Grey Death, at a time when the war between Curia and Emperor was raging in earnest.

Groups of people were singing in the streets, but the Introspector was determined not to let them annoy him. The only important thing was his thesis, which *must* be finished. The behaviour of the singers was noted, of course, but would probably come to nothing.

Before long, however, what appeared to be some kind of *poltergeist activity* began to take place in the house. Again, the Introspector ignored it. The world was entering a time of immense upheaval, but for him it was just an annoyance in the way of completing his paper.

A few weeks later, fighting broke out in the streets. Still, the Introspector put the draft copy of his thesis (on the Trojan War) in his briefcase, and set off for the fortnightly meeting with his supervisor.

The supervisor was affected by the madness of the times, however...and instead of discussing the work at hand, began to speak about his deepest dreams and wishes, and his distant childhood.

The Introspector listened for a full ten seconds, before launching into a two-hour monologue on his *own* childhood; how deprived it had been because his parents hadn't bought him a Britannica Great Books set. When he finished speaking, the supervisor had long since left the room without his noticing, and the boom of distant artillery was beginning to sound.

A clear warning now sounded across the PA system – no one was to leave the campus under any circumstances.

Emergency accommodation had been arranged in the library.

IV

In the library, a hunt was being organised by various students, to eke out Scarlotti sympathisers and members of the Wolves of Joy. The Introspector, with a speech of many words, indicated that he would join in the hunt, but talked so much that he never actually did so. He let it be known, however, that he was unhappy with the rebels, as they had disrupted his thesis – which he now must needs complete at home.

Just then, in the deepest basement of the under-library, a suspicious-looking person was unearthed, and mob values descended. Imagine the surprise of the Introspector when it turned out to be the little man who had broken into his house! The Introspector's face displayed a blank, confused look, as students dragged the little man away to campus police for questioning...

And then there was an earth tremor – or was it more poltergeist activity? – and the entire library collapsed.

The lone survivor related how the Introspector *began to crumble*, just moments before it happened.

She felt sure she was 'allowed' to survive merely to tell of this.

V

My grandfather heard of these latter developments at second hand, because in the meantime he had been drafted into the army to fight in the war against Scarlotti, a war that he had no sympathy for, and when he returned, with artificial legs made of grey, fibrous plastic, he received a phone call which sounded for all the world like the Introspector.

More angry than anything.

He heard that his 'partner' had sold his Great Books collection to a poet who lived in a hut in the forest, *and who kept his hut untidy*.

My grandfather, Nicholas Lune, told him he would look into it...that he would try to find the poet (called Maddem), who lived 'in an impenetrable thicket of thorns, in the unreachable depths of a chasm that howls.'

And not long after that, my grandfather saw a little man himself.

The Journal of Nicholas Lune

PART ONE

1

ACCIDENT

She appeared to me several times, in dreams, during adolescence. I called this figure 'the Friendly Girl'. Perhaps my anima, but I rather doubt it. I always pictured my anima as breezy, slightly cynical (the opposite of myself) and the Friendly Girl was neither of these things.

So who was she, then?

I still see her image faintly sometimes if I shut my eyes. She had red hair, a pale, earnest face, and kept some kind of bug (a stick insect, I think) for a pet. She was always keenly interested in anything I was doing. She wanted to be part of something real, and was always eager to help or play a part. I was angry a lot before she appeared – but the Friendly Girl spread happiness and calm.

And yet, I knew instinctively that I was not the only one she appeared to – like some kind of dream-nurse she did the rounds, and although I wanted to spend more time around her than the others did, when I thought about her too much she ceased to appear, and I knew in my heart this would never come to pass.

For that reason, the Friendly Girl began to make me feel happy and sad at the same time. When she finally appeared again (for the last time, as it happened) an empty steel chamber opened at the back of my mind, and there was a flash like distant lightning. I knew this steel chamber was forbidden me – that I would never pass through it on my march through time.

When she kissed me, the kiss was so warm, fleeting and *real* that I knew it would never occur again, neither in dreams nor in the sunny world around me. I had no idea what struggles were taking place in *her* soul, if she had one, beneath that warm exterior and brightness – but if there were struggles, they weren't mine, and our paths must soon diverge. And I was right, of course, because she stopped appearing to me.

After some time I ceased even to think about her.

A few years later I was drafted to serve in the war against the Emperor Maximillian. Most of this period is a blur, but I recall the accident that cost me my legs vividly indeed, due to the waking vision that preceded it, something I have never known the likes of. (It was the same day I learned, in a letter from an old acquaintance, about the death of the wretched Introspector, although I didn't hear the full story behind that peculiar incident until later.)

I was on watch duty, patrolling a cliffside track, and as I stood looking out across the vast blue Pacific, I felt something I had never felt before, something that seemed to hint delicately at another existence, a place not this place nor *any* place. And suddenly, I was no longer there – I was flying.

The white sun glared off my brow. There were clouds in the distance, choppy grey dragon curls, but I ignored them, staring only at the sea. I peered through its blue, searching for the delicate traces of green, those hidden veins that signalled deep eternal currents, hidden only until looked for. Seabirds wheeled around me as I swooped and dived, dropping suddenly from the sky. The sun filled my wings as I plunged towards the coolness. Water closed round my head, shocking me through, making me gasp, and I found to my surprise that I could breathe underwater. Down through the winnowing currents I passed, to the depths, my flesh melting to nothing as my disembodied senses continued to plummet, and gradually I ceased to feel I was moving at all.

The green veins were all around me, filled with a hidden light, and it seemed they were going to burst, and everything would *change...*

And then, with a shudder, I emerged into bright green Space, a wide open quarter beyond time, where the idea of change seemed utterly meaningless.

I was there.
In a deep, green land.

*　　*　　*

All this I experienced in a moment that could not be measured. It was as if there were two 'me's, one of them now gone forever, while 'I' myself was falling, yes, but not into space – off the cliff.

I yelped in terror as I smashed hip-first against a jutting rock, then rolled and slid and scraped against the stone, scrabbling helplessly towards the deadly rocks below. But halfway down was a jagged, sloping ledge, on which I crashed precariously with an agonising jolt, trying to steady myself, with one knee buckled under so painfully that I couldn't move. How long did I lay there? I fell unconscious, drifted back, then blacked away again. By that time the sun had started to set. I woke again, called, but nobody answered.

There was pain all over, mostly in my abdomen, which felt pressed by a tremendous weight. And then I raised my head, and saw something I never expected to see.

An enormous bird had perched atop me. A sea eagle, I was fairly sure. Its weight was suffocating, and also seemed to be the source of a strange tingling in my legs. I lowered my head and then painfully raised it again. White feathers, dark wings, a solid, deadly beak...yes, definitely a sea eagle.

The eagle glared at me before lowering its head. It tore at my exposed side, now awash with blood. *The creature was tearing at my organs, as if I were some kind of modern Prometheus.* I cried out in fear, and, feeble as I was, raised an arm to scare it off, but it merely continued its measured feast.

Then, there was a searing stab of pain inside me – more pain than I had ever thought it possible to feel. I screamed and flailed out desperately, but the bird merely flapped its wings with an air of offended dignity, and stayed. So I struck again, crying wildly, and finally the bird seemed to get the message. Slowly, but slowly, with a look of cold resentment, it turned on its perch (making me scream again) and then, with rich, aristocratic wingbeats, flapped majestically out to sea. I could see it in the distance, soaring to greater and greater heights...

But the tingling in my legs grew steadily worse. I looked down to see what it could be, and for the third time a thin, desperate screech emerged from my lung pipes...for my legs were crawling with tiny red ants, eating me alive. My stomach gave a violent lurch and I fell from consciousness into a pitch-black swoon.

My next memory is of vivid lights flashing in the darkness, and slowly turning my head, to find myself floating in air, swinging violently with sickening speed, from side to side, as the sound of the helicopter drowned out everything.

I realised I was being pulled towards the deafening roar. *I'll die in the blades*, I thought, before blackness swallowed me again.

*   *   *

There were times in the hospital when I could feel my body shutting down. All energy was expended on willing my very survival. I ground my chattering teeth and pushed myself to live. Sometimes an alarm would sound, and a doctor would come running. Once I summoned the energy to tell him about the bird that had gnawed my innards, but he nodded and said nothing. He seemed to think I had imagined it.

And had I?

The damage to my liver was real at any rate.

Sometimes, at night, behind the soft blip of machinery I could hear the sound of powerful wings; and then I would pull the sheets above my head and wait for morning.

By day, too, I felt constant cries from my mangled body. Both legs had been amputated, and the pain of phantom limbs was dreadful. They injected me with morphine (not enough of it) but what I really craved was sleep.

I also wished for the Friendly Girl, whom I hadn't thought of in years, to visit, but of course that would never happen.

*   *   *

A month later I was finally discharged and invalided out of the army, now the owner of a pair of grey, fibrous plastic legs (the same ones I am leaning on now to write). Made of a light, synthetic substance, with a titanium core, no wiring, and a handheld controller little bigger than a car key, they were surprisingly easy to manipulate. I can even *run* with them.

My phantom limbs have somehow 'become' the prosthetic ones, in ways I am sure were never wont to happen with prosthetics of yore. I have looked into this: after science repeatedly failed to find the 'sense' of the limb in the nerve endings, the spine, or even the brain itself, certain philosophers agreed that the 'limb' must simply be an extension of the basic field of consciousness, by way of which the mind controls the body. So how is it that this new technology has somehow managed to tap into the basis of consciousness itself? None of the manufacturer's public statements have been of any help in unlocking the mystery.

But sometimes, when I walk, I feel a certain queasiness, a sense of something being not quite right. I can't put the feeling into words. I just try not to think too hard about the grey, fibrous plastic of my state-furnished limbs.

I have bigger things to worry about, though, like being alone in the world with neither friend nor family nor employer to care for me. And worse: yesterday I received a phone call from beyond the grave, and I know not what it betokens.

309

2

VISITATION

My previous entry made reference to the phone call I received last month from a man I believe to be dead. I mean, of course, the ridiculous Introspector, whose body was never actually retrieved from the ruins of the library at the University of Sullen Contempt, but who was pronounced dead by relevant authorities after a thorough search of the rubble. One witness attested that his body crumbled to dust, and although this was officially doubted, to me it seemed as likely an explanation as any.

The voice on the phone was stunted in its muttlike belligerence, and there were strange echoes, as if the call came through decaying long-distance cables (which perhaps, in a sense, it did).

He spoke *at* me, so it could hardly be called conversation (whenever I tried to interject he ignored it); but this was how he had been in life, which told me nothing. It was eerie, and also slightly humiliating, being dictated to by a dead man (if indeed it *was* me he was talking to – it occurs to me now that I can't even be sure, due to his monopolising tendencies in speech, that the call wasn't actually meant for someone else.)

His monologue consisted largely of complaints about his girlfriend, who had apparently sold his 'Great Books' collection. The problem was *who* she had sold them to...he wouldn't have minded had they gone to a nice clean home, but the purchaser was someone whose house was in a state of disarray. A kind of hermit-poet who had retreated to the woods in pursuit of his art, who went by the strange name of 'Maddem'.

I will never forget the Introspector's last words:

310

'You will find this Maddem in an impenetrable thicket of thorns, in the unreachable depths of a chasm that howls.'

And then the line went silent, aside from the metallic long-distance echoes which had permeated the entire call.

I assured him, if he were somehow listening, that I would 'look into it,' but he remained mute.

*   *   *

The day after the call I fell into a state of deep melancholia, the onset of which, truth be told, was cause of my taking up pen to anoint this journal. My newfound status as a minor celebrity depresses me, especially given the ridiculous circumstances under which it occurred (I have even heard tell that a 'reality' special about the accident is in the pipes, with some C-grade actor as myself).

But, while you would think I would be grateful to have escaped with my life, the novelty of my new legs and organs having once worn off (which it swiftly did), the world began to fade.

Things that once seemed joyous or colourful now elude me, and wherever I go I seem to hear a tiny, secret sound, like the 'plink' of dull titanium, which says: *there is nothing new in this world, nothing at all, and everything goes around in wooden circles.*

Although *someone* new has in fact entered my world.

She is short, with boyish hair. Her eyes are sunken and her face is pale. The first time she appeared I almost screamed. She looked pitiful – but those eyes held no pity. A cold, inward-falling light clove about her like a mist. I have come to think of her as the Vampire Girl – and am sometimes afraid to close my eyes.

I wonder what will happen if I let her in? How long will it be before she 'feeds'?

I begin to wish I had died back on the cliff.

*   *   *

311

I was contemplating my empty flat when it happened.
('Empty', as in nothing of real value. Even the scarab
pattern on the rug I had so often used as a focus for
meditative endeavours seemed weary, washed out,
drained of meaning.) This time, devoid of effort, the
vision immediately took hold that I was soaring like a
bird. I actually felt it coagulate, like the brief aftermath
of an even briefer life, deadborn from the first.

And then, I saw him.

He was staring at me – the little man.

He looked as if he had just taken in a bountiful
harvest, and was contemplating whether he should pick
up a last stray grain – myself – that had fallen to the
ground. Although not overtly hostile, there was nothing
in his glance that hinted at sympathy of any kind. I had
no doubt this was the same 'little man' who had once
visited the Introspector, and who had by all accounts
managed to escape the clutches of the fanatical mob of
students, but he looked nothing like I had expected...no
garden gnome, anyway. He was clean-shaven, with
neatly-combed hair, and impeccably dressed.

As I stared into his opaque eyes, the thought came to
me: could this be *Maddem?* But I dismissed it – how could
this neat little man, who had left the Introspector's flat
immaculately tidy, be Maddem, the scruffy poet? He
couldn't, surely not. But I wanted to speak to him,
nonetheless.

So I took what seemed like a step towards him. The
step was a *lie*, however, for it didn't do what my brain told
me it was doing – namely, taking me closer to my small
and silent observer. It was not that he had moved – or
apparently not. It was just that my stride had left
precisely the same distance between us as before I had
embarked on it.

Was the man a vision? And yet now he turned, eyes
still fixed solemnly yet uncaringly on my person, and
opened the front door of the flat.

He stepped out of the door, and vanished from my
sight. I quickly stepped after him, but he was nowhere in
the hallway, on either side of the door, and there was no
way he would have had time to escape. *And yet the door*

most assuredly had been opened, which seemed to rule out hallucination.

My plastic legs ran to the end of the hall, where it curved into the stairwell. Sure enough, there was a flicker on the stairs below me...a brief flicker like footwork. So my legs ran after it, and for around an hour became embroiled in a strange, loping chase through the inner city, constantly sighting and losing those flisking steps that always seemed a stone's throw ahead of me, but never once gaining a clear and unambiguous sighting of my quarry (or was *I* the quarry?).

We were now in that amber-lit precinct where the city's business and legal zone merges with the nightclub district, an area where the city's pulse can perhaps be felt more clearly than in other locales. But by now I had lost sight of him completely, not having the merest shimmer for ten minutes or more.

I stopped outside a thrumming pub, where patrons were nervously discussing the latest news – a nuclear blast in Central Asia, carried out by some yet-unnamed terrorist outfit – but this seemed insignificant next to finding and interrogating the little man.

Around the corner from the pub was the famous Pavlova Club, where a sign outside announced that a local stand-up comic was plying his trade. I decided to try in here, as it seemed different to the other places I had been unavailedly looking in.

Inside the club, though, the joke was on me...pure comedic gold as the spotlight was trained on a latecomer, the comedian asking me what I was looking for, the whorehouse? I asked, rather obtusely, if anyone had seen a little man, the size of a leprechaun, run past, and the audience was in stitches – they clearly thought it was part of a staged act. Some heckled me, while others laughed at the surreality of it all.

It was then that I recognised the comedian – the Introspector's favourite, a brown someone-or-other, who four years earlier had made a big trade on his 'I think I saw a few brown people here – at the airport' thing, but now was making arrogant jokes about 'spot the whitey – *there's* one looking for his stunted offspring,' (referring to me as I stalked straight past him into the backstage area), having the audience in friendly conniptions once again, my logic being that if this was the Introspector's favourite comedian, why wouldn't 'his' homunculus have seen fit to come here as well? But backstage was completely deserted.

The old theatre smelt strongly of disillusion, and after wandering for some ten minutes through deserted dressing rooms (if that's what they were) filled with cobwebs and old plastic chairs, I had exhausted both the backstage topography and my own will to search, and despondently decided to head home.

But I had reckoned without my mailbox.

My mood somersaulted sideways as I pulled from it a letter that had not been there when I had checked at the usual time that morning.

The envelope, marked 'high security' (somewhat ironically, as it had been sticking out of the slot for anyone to purloin), was from a senior public official in the government of Mantuaroa, that populous Pacific island known for its biannual Festival. It contained a pre-approved visa, on holographic paper with removable sticky backing, in the shape of a bird, somewhat like an archaeopteryx, I thought...as well as a plane ticket (business class) to the island nation in question, and an officially-worded invitation to the Festival.

Apparently I had been chosen as both a example of the destructive terror of war, and a showcase for the new technological advances being made in the booming field of prosthetics.

And why *couldn't* the little man have gone that way, I thought, before walking out to a public access booth to confirm the details of my flight.

3

ISLAND

On the plane I felt something pulling me back to an earlier time. Just a month ago (it seems like another life) I suddenly felt drawn towards the sea. Green and formless, described in this very journal, but unobtainable now, out of reach. There were the wingbeats, the eagle, too, but something else in the background, very distant, something green.

The vision eluded me.

I glanced at my fellow passengers. Many seemed to be fraying at the edges, and the drinks cart was doing a roaring trade. Important events were at hand, and everywhere I could see the signs of fidgeting and bitterness. I was perhaps the only one feeling withdrawn.

Then, there it was...the island, in the distance, rising like a fortress from the deep, shuddering waters of a dream. It looked bigger than I had expected.

Soon I saw tiny beaches and hidden coves, dark peaks that shimmered in the distance. As the land slowly filled my field of vision, I reached for a brochure from the seat pocket in front of me. With the island itself in view, reading it was somewhat surreal:

The indigenous inhabitants of Mantuaroa are the Mani, consisting of a dozen tribes united only by a common language. The capital, also called Mantuaroa, is the most populous city in the Pacific, larger than Auckland or Honolulu. The island is home to more bird species than any similar-sized area on earth. Wild pigs, while not native, are also very common.

I flipped forward, looking for more info on the upcoming Festival.

The Festival, held every two years, has long attracted visitors from around the world. This month-long celebration has its origins in the harvest of the biennial plant vakka, known colloquially as 'dream root'. Vakka is also the Mani word for a sea-borne type of canoe.

According to anthropologists, the ceremony once culminated in a 'voluntary sacrifice', in which those who volunteered for 'sacrifice' would simply walk away, never to be heard from again. Whether these accounts are true or not, Festival these days is more about life than death, and riotous celebrations take place across the island, from the slums of Mantuaroa City to the heart of the deep green jungle, and from affluent Harbour North to the market villages of the southern hills.

I felt a slight unease, as if something scathing or profound awaited me on the island, something that would take away my boredom, my emptiness, the constant smell of plastic in my dreams. Something that would stave off the girl with rings around her eyes, whose distant presence chilled me to the bone.

The plane was sinking lower and would soon be down to earth.

*   *   *

Many of the passengers were up and scrambling even before the plane had come to rest, despite a clear announcement from the pilot asking them to remain seated. I had seen no sign of human settlement during the descent, and (correctly) assumed the airport must be outside the limits of Mantuaroa City itself.

The terminal entrance was dark, even in daylight, probably as a means to draw attention to two remarkable holographic ads – one showing a negro's head glowing with orange stripes as he raised a can of milk to his maw, calcite teeth gleaming as he threw back his head and drank, the milk pouring downward in ever-changing colours, from paint-white to strawberry to brown. Then I noticed that his face was also changing – from black, to white, to oriental, then finally Polynesian features matching those of the handful of Mani I could see around me. The product under promotion was called *Island Milk*.

The other ad was for an 'erectile enhancement' product called *Plugg's Launch Pills, Super-Enriched*. It showing a rocket belching out smoke, but never quite getting off the ground. Then a face grinned in the moon, a hand reached out sprinkling pills...and the rocket suddenly streaked towards the stars, leaving a silver trail of happiness behind.

Plugg, I recall, had been an American comedian who had faked his own death, then reemerged as a prominent conspiracy theorist, before faking his death *again* (and who knows where he is now).

After walking through customs with nothing to declare, I came to the immigration desk and produced my passport, complete with bird-shaped visa. The official was less than polite, but as two watchful soldiers were standing nearby, hands resting lightly on their automatic rifles, I took it upon myself to be both honest and courteous.

I could see more soldiers milling in the arrivals hall, and wondered idly if the heavy security was for Festival, or if it was always like this. I realised one of them was looking right at me, and gave a guilty jump, despite having done nothing wrong.

But once I was through, things were fine.

As I entered the hall a man approached with hand outstretched. He was to be my official host, and introduced himself as Herb Vickery, First Secretary to the Minister of the Interior. To my surprise he was British, with an upper-class accent and protruding teeth to boot, a caricature made surreal by its actual appearance in the flesh. His creased grey eyes seemed mild enough, in a patronising way, but there was something strange about the cast of his face. I couldn't put my finger on it, though, and cast it from my mind, following him out of the terminal building.

'Lucky you got here when you did,' he told me as we clambered into his grey Range Rover. 'Quarantine laws will be enacted soon, and Festival attendance will be down somewhat as a result.'

'What do you mean?'

'You haven't heard the terrible news? A deadly plague has arisen in Central Asia, apparently due to the nuclear attack – and it's bound to spread throughout the world, here included. My minister will be announcing quarantine measures this evening in a special broadcast. The island will be sealed off to the world for some time – though most of the Festival attendees are already here. Opening Ceremony is the day after tomorrow.'

'I heard nothing about this plague.'

'The rapacity of its spread was only made clear by the Curia this morning.'

'Are most here Curia sympathisers?'

'Lord no. We're Curia-aligned, of course, but there are plenty of Scarlotti sympathisers, especially among the natives. Other factions, too...but let's not talk of that.'

Herb's Range Rover sped along the expressway from the airport to the city. He gave out an endless stream of commentary as we went, filling me in on local events, as well as interesting snippets of history concerning places we were passing through. Suave and good-humoured, he seemed to be in complete command at all times, and although I have a natural wariness of those whose grace seems to come at no real struggle to themselves, I yet accepted the possibility that such grace could be genuine, and was unable to suppress a smidgeon of envy. Herb, in any case, played the tour guide rather well.

'All this was swampland, once. They put the freeway through some six or seven years ago. Local labourers, mainly, and hundreds died. Sank right into the marshes and never came up.' I dimly recalled a newz item in which *Mantuaroa* and *horror* were somehow entwined or interconnected, though I couldn't recall the precise details...presumably this was what it had referred to. I stared at the concrete walls of the freeway, fascinated. The barriers weren't continuous, and through the gaps I could see glimpses of what looked like grassland, but were probably the very marshes Herb had mentioned.

I felt my spirit drifting out towards them, and suddenly they seemed a symbol of my old life. The Friendly Girl was gone, and so was all my youth, sunk down in that swamp, flanked by the bones of smothered coolies...but new life was struggling up within me.

We pulled over the prow of a hill and saw the city spread out in the distance. It was a vast, muddy, straggling sort of town. I thought I could see high-rises in the distance through the smog haze, but before I could blink they were gone behind the hills. Settlements appeared beyond the barriers, however – dilapidated houses with flat tin roofs, on parched grassy slopes. Up ahead on a wider slope I could see what looked like a vast junkyard – a field of scattered scree and fallen monuments.

'That's the autonomous graveyard,' intoned Herb, reading my thoughts. 'It's the biggest cemetery in the city, as it's non-denominational. Many of the poorest citizens bury their dead there. But you don't get much of our local gossip in Sydney or you wouldn't have to ask. It's been talked of quite frequently of late.'

I *hadn't* asked, but put his strange, slightly disturbing comment aside for now and asked why that was.

'Well...*bodies* have been found there.'

'In a cemetery.'

'Yes...but they were found on *top* of the ground, rather than under it.'

'I see.'

Suddenly attentive, I could now see the crumbling tombs and dry, poor soil, a considerable contrast to the swampy grasslands we had passed through. There were black, yawning cracks all across the ground.

'Yes, people have turned up dead. Kidnappings in the slums, or so they say...the bodies found dumped there, thrown on top of existing graves, or left at the door of an old colonial-era tomb, say. It's dampened the tone of the Festival a little.'

'Why were they kidnapped?'

'Hard to say. Those in the shanty towns talk of sorcerers and the walking dead...island legends. And rumours are spreading through the countryside, where the Mani blood is strongest. But it hasn't caused a general panic, not yet. Hopefully the Festival will take people's minds off it.'

'But what do *you* think? Surely you don't believe in sorcerers?'

'I don't have an answer. But some of the politicians in the City Council – the *City* Council, mind you, not the national government – are blaming the killings on the Dead Shadows cult.'

'Is that something to do with neo-gnostics?'

'Yes, it evolved from the neo-gnostics, who started in Egypt around the time the pyramids were bombed. But unlike the latter, Dead Shadows is an *active* cult, aiming to destroy all organic life in the universe and so forth. Ambitious, eh?'

'Ha.'

'Rumour has it that they've infiltrated the national government here, but as a senior public servant I find that scarcely credible.'

'Then it would really be 'the government versus the people'.'

'Yes, very droll. And there are different factions, too, apparently. Some just want to destroy everything that's in front of them, like savage animals. Those would be the ones who had done the murders, if there were any Dead Shadows involvement at all...which I find unlikely, as they aren't particularly organised from what I gather.

'Then there are more advanced factions, which actively support Scarlotti's nascent space program, in order to expand their knowledge to the point where they can...well, destroy the entire universe or whatever it is they want to do.'

'Those are the more philosophical types?'

'Exactly.'

By now we were well into the smog-laden outskirts, and the freeway had merely become a road. The traffic was starting to thicken, and so was the smog. Most of the vehicles around us were buses and trucks, and there were few private cars.

Rows of run-down, colourful houses lined the road, and scrawny dogs lounged on the gravelly footpaths. The sunlight was filtered through dust, and the smog tinged the air an apocalyptic yellow. When the traffic started moving again we passed a large green sign saying: *Downtown 8 km.*

English and Mani were the two official languages, but in the city, Herb told me, the indigenous tongue was rarely heard; English, of varying accents, being the principle form of speech.

The road now swung sharply to the right, and for the first time I could see the tightly-clustered and gleaming high-rises of Downtown up ahead. A bank fell steeply away to the left, and I could make out what looked like a muddy stormwater ditch filled with garbage, following the new course of the road.

'That's the river,' said Herb. 'Not what it used to be, sadly. It gets a bit of backwash from the factories near the sea, besides all the garbage from the drains.'

That's a river? I thought. I could see people down there, crouching in the entrance to one of the darkened culverts that contributed a thin and steady stream of grey to the filthy flow.

'Who are those people?' I wondered out loud.

'Just harmless vagabonds,' Herb said. 'They comb the sewers at low tide, looking for things to use or sell. At high tide the ocean washes in, however, and the water level comes almost up to the road here, rubbish and all.' Yes, now that I looked I noticed a great trail of rubbish spreading almost as high as the road. Then we veered away from the river, and began to approach a strange-looking marble archway, where the road divided into a bewildering series of ramps.

'This is the Strand,' my guide explained. 'It's the main shopping thoroughfare, and it runs on three different levels. Street level and top are where the shops are, but for those of us who just want to get *home...*' (he accelerated as he said this, as if for emphasis) 'the Understrand is far more useful.' The lane we were in plunged suddenly downwards, more suddenly than a road should, and I am not a cautious driver. It was like descending into caramel or honeycomb, while the lanes to either side of us were sucked up into the sky.

Now we were in a tunnel with pale golden lights on the walls, a four-lane road that cut straight under the city. It seemed like we were floating in space, but then we emerged into daylight, with a forty-storey building gleaming blue above us. We had apparently bypassed the whole of Downtown, and the harbour was now visible on the right. A sign informed that we were entering the municipality of Harbour North, which (I remembered from the brochure) was supposed to be affluent, and indeed certainly appeared that way from the large and fashionable houses ahead of us. The harbour itself was beautiful, and could not have formed a greater contrast to the scunge of the so-called river (which emerged at a further point along the coast). There were even a handful of yachts afloat, like scattered tiny feathers on the blue.

On the side of the road, I noticed a group of young people dressed in black. But something was wrong with them. One had a hideously elongated nose, while another was cross-eyed and hunchbacked. A third had a witch's chin, and wizened claw-like hands.

'Dead Shadows?' I asked, somewhat nervously.

'Good lord, no,' laughed Herb. 'Just the 'deformed ones', or so I believe they call themselves. Rich kids mostly, from good backgrounds. They pay to look like that, then they just hang around, trying to shock people, but increasingly failing. Dead Shadows are different. Their leadership may be rich, but they draw many of their followers from among the poor.'

Before long we had arrived at my hotel, and Herb waited while I checked in, then drove me back to his own house for a barbecue.

How long before I can sleep? I thought irritably, feeling sure it would be the soundest sleep I had ever known.

4

DOG

I should write briefly of my experiences watching the giant wall screen at Herb's place, while he and his wife prepared the barbecue. Seldom do I expose myself to the televisual experiments of the Curia, and it was a strange, somewhat exotic experience. I felt (as previously when I had tried it) like a highly nervous person smoking a large pipe of hashish.

Herb's effete teenage son, Thom, was also watching, and I mused idly that, while it was once the children of plebs like myself who watched the most TV, now it was the rich who were more likely to, having seemingly failed to sense they are a doomed class. While the ads played, Thom pulled nervously at his 'Kings' t-shirt. The Kings are a brutal West African gang that he follows onscreen. Such 'tourist shows', as I understand they are called, have become wildly popular in recent years, as global unrest makes actual travel less popular.

Armoured imaging teams, using tiny remote drone cameras known as 'flies', take the viewer inside the violent, gang-controlled regions of Nigeria and Cameroon. Using a touch screen, viewers (or 'zoners' as they are sometimes called) can follow the action from multiple angles while cheering on their favourite gang.

Producers recently introduced democratic elements into the show, with viewers voting on certain conditions and outcomes (a formula made popular by the more traditional 'slave soaps'). In a tourist show, for instance, if a gun battle breaks out between two gangs and fighting appears one-sided, viewers may decide to hit the scene of the fighting with a remote sonic blast, thereby causing an earthquake and greatly enhancing the unpredictability of the outcome.

This sonic technology is still in the developmental phase, and often does not work. (One time, however, it worked *too* well and destroyed several public buildings in Lagos...but as the government there depends on the Curia for much of its income, via the New International Tax Agreement, nary a peep has been raised in protest.) I believe these 'tourist shows' are really the Curia's attempt to show that it has a sense of humour, that it is really on the side of the average Joe. In other words: yet another attempt to quell Scarlotti's growing popularity.

It appears that similar forays are being made into the animal kingdom – for according to an ad, many viewers now keenly follow the wars of two gigantic rat packs (nicknamed the 'Wobbels' and the 'Goggits') beneath the ancient streets of Paris, the tribes being distinguished by coloured dots the viewer sees above each rat.

When ad time was over, a newz show began. To my intense surprise, most of the items concerned a pop star I had never previously heard of. He looked like a savage who had been raised by wolves, but nearly every story was about this creature, whose name was 'Scuzzy', and who was apparently in Mantuaroa for the Festival. His music was actually rather tame in contrast to his wild antics – it sounded like a pastiche of old heavy metal played with the instrumentation of an 80s synth-pop ensemble, which he nevertheless played single-handed with an instrument of his own design called the Rodomontar. Every sentence he uttered seemed to contradict the previous one, to the point where I wondered if *I* was actually under the influence of drugs and hearing things wrong.

Then, in one of the few newz items that didn't concern Scuzzy, several leading experts in neuroscience were revealed to be in town for the Festival, besides, of course, prominent politicians and movie stars from Curia-aligned countries everywhere. The final item struck a more sombre note, however. It concerned Nemet Breisler, the famous computer scientist, who had been missing from his California home for several days.

Then came sport, and Herb, who was passing through the room, let out a triumphant roar when it was announced that the Goggits had prevailed against their rivals in the latest rat-skirmish, slaughtering thousands of their Wobbel opponents in an abandoned water main beneath the Bois de Boulogne.

Finally, the weather, likely to be hot and humid; then after the newz came *Lottery!*, the world's highest-rating slave soap, which I had never seen before.

A precis laid bare the events of the last twenty-four hours. By audience demand, Molly had been taken prisoner again, this time by drug-smuggling Somalian pirates. Les, the midget with rotten teeth, was tied up alongside her, and it was rumoured that he might soon be out of the show. His character was becoming tiresome, running the same disgusting jokes and innuendoes, day in day out. Perhaps the pirates would kill him, while Molly, having survived their tortures, would be rescued at the last minute.

Les seemed to sense his career was drawing to a close. He was straining at his bonds with frenzy, screaming at the pirates, describing graphically what he would do to them when he finally got loose. He was clearly trying to win favour with the audience, and it was a pitiful sight. All he had to look forward to after his fall from grace was a brief retro revival in two years' time, then a final, never-to-be-emerged-from obscurity (lack of talent being an essential factor in the casting of potential slave soap stars). Darkness and failing health would take him. No wonder the foul-mouthed imp was struggling so terribly.

But then the scene shifted, and other characters were shown reacting to Molly's disappearance. Two of them, it seemed, were in collusion with the pirates, while Mantis and Roach were desperate to get back the blueprints Molly had stolen from them and...blah, blah, blah.

Although the show was ridiculous, I felt a sudden inexplicable pang of longing for Molly, even though I knew her to be essentially a whore who had to change her entire personality if the audience so willed it. But by some kind of weird, misplaced chivalry I felt an urge to protect her, and it disturbed me.

I got up and headed for the kitchen to get a drink, but a harsh hissing stopped me in my tracks. Diagonally through the door I could see the towering figure of Herb glaring at someone – presumably his wife, Sally. And if eyes could murder, Herb's would certainly have done so.

'Don't forget your obligations,' he snarled. 'You know what happened last time you disobeyed. You'll go *through* with it, or so help me...' He raised his hand in threat, and I, with my heightened post-operative reactions, moved swiftly and silently back on the carpet, retreating with smooth speed to the living room. So Herb was not entirely what he appeared to be. Somehow that did not surprise me...but what was he, and what did it mean?

Before long the barbecue was ready, and we sat drinking chilled white wine and watching the setting sun. The air, still humid, was made more pleasant by the evening breeze.

Herb's Rottweiler, chained near the back fence, emitted a constant low growl, and after a while, I realised it was growling at *me*. I stared back, and the beast suddenly erupted into a slavering torrent of savage barking that boomed through the surrounding hills.

Despite its iron chain, I flinched, as Herb went over to pacify the brute.

'Seems to have taken a disliking to you,' he said, with a weak, apologetic smile.

I laughed nervously, tapping my plastic feet.

5

JAWBIRD

In the morning, earth-shattering news came from the hotel radio: the inner council of Curia had been assassinated, using fearsome new technology, by Scarlotti himself, who had perished by his own stroke, sacrificing himself in a dreadful gambit aimed at neutralising his enemies.

(Who can believe now, in hindsight, that this man ever actually walked the earth?)

But while my face and body adopted an automatic look of shock and grief (for no matter which side one sympathises with, the news seems to bode ill for the future of the world), it failed to move me internally...and I wondered if the grey plastic of my legs had not somehow also invaded my heart.

A taxi arrived, as previously arranged, to take me to Herb's. The driver, a native Mantuaroan, seemed cheerfully oblivious to the events erupting from his radio dial...and equally oblivious to the road ahead of him (it's a great wonder that I survived the drive in one piece). In his sweat was a world beyond the concerns of emperor and committee alike, yet despite my own feeling of detachment, this was not a world I thought I could ever belong to − I was outside of that, too.

The radio announced that the all-important Festival was still going ahead, despite the political upheavals and the Grey Death. When I arrived at Herb's, he confirmed the same, having just been on the phone to his boss, the minister.

'You can't let these sad events close a Festival that has been celebrated since time immemorial,' he said with a shrug. 'Besides, it would be giving in to Scarlotti's madness, and thus letting him win, even from beyond the grave.

'Let me tell you something, Nicholas; sometime last century there was a female prime minister of Great Britain known as the 'Iron Maiden'. She was said to have performed vaudeville in her spare time, with an act called 'The Powerslave'. A real talent, apparently. But at one point during her premiership, the hotel where she and her cabinet colleagues were staying was *blown up* by a terrorist group.

'Now, rather than giving in to this act of savagery, the Iron Maiden insisted that the conference they were attending should actually go ahead, without so much as a single acknowledgment the terrible event had even taken place. This despite one of her closest friends having been killed in the blast!

'After that, the terrorists pretty much gave up. At least, they ceased to carry out bombings, and concentrated on more legitimate means of airing their grievances.

'So *that* is the sort of steadfastness we must show in the wake of Scarlotti's foul deed. Never retreat, never surrender...'

'Quite,' I said, involuntarily aping Herb's dry manner of speech.

But while the Opening Ceremony was still going ahead, Herb would not be accompanying me. The Mantuaroan government were having an emergency cabinet meeting of their own, which he would be helping to minute, and so he bundled me into yet another car, this time a chauffeured one rather than a taxi. The driver, called Terence, was half Mantuaroan and all muscle. He was to act in Herb's absence as my tour guide...but his monosyllabic grunts served to obscure rather than illuminate any subject I happened to bring up, so after a while I stopped.

*   *   *

The military base where the Opening Ceremony was to take place was located further up the North Shore, outside the city limits, some twenty kilometres from Herb's place.

Only one portion of the massive base had been opened to the public – an enormous grassy field, with a colourful pavilion at one end and a deep blue lagoon flanked by rocky scree at the other. In the vast tussocky space between, large extended families picnicked and played. The murmur of many voices produced a warm expectant tension.

Perhaps due to this convivial atmosphere, Terence found his conversational ability at last. He explained in reasonably good English that the base did not actually belong to the island's official military, but was a private installation owned by someone in Patagonia affiliated with the Curia (or ex-Curia – who knew what was going on in the outside world right now?). This person, whom Terence did not name, was amassing an extensive personal army, and high-tech experimental airforce. And it was visiting Mantuaroa with the blessing of Herb's government (to whom this unnamed 'Patagonian' had contributed a good deal in local taxes – nevertheless much lower than he would have paid elsewhere), ostensibly because he had given verbal promises that his air force would help protect Mantuaroa from attack by Scarlotti, or now that the latter was dead, by terrorist factions.

But these were all abstractions – in the meantime birds were screeching, and drums were throbbing. Around the edge of the field numerous wooden carvings had been placed, half the height of a person, and brilliantly painted, with large, shadowy eyes. Terence explained that they represented the island's many gods and spirits.

Drawing closer to the pavilion, where the air was alive with deafening noise, I could see four larger statues positioned on either side of the main entrance. Terence, raising his voice above the incredible din, explained that they represented the five chief Mani deities.

'But there are only *four* statues,' I yelled.

'The fifth deity, the Bird King, is invisible,' he countered calmly. 'No one knows what he looks like, and even his name is secret. Forbidden for fullbloods to tell outsiders. Even for halfbloods like me, forbidden to know. They refer to him only by English words...*Bird King*. But this Festival began in his honour, for it was he who first brought *vakka* – the dream root – from the spirit world, and gave it to mankind...although he did so in a dream, not realising what he was doing.'

Terence seemed to be warming to me, and proceeded to describe the other four deities. The gloomy figure to the left was Maremare, goddess of fertility and the newborn, but also of the dead, as life and death are intimately commingled. The second was Tuvu, lord of the earth, and also of volcanoes and fire, who inhabited Tuvakoa, the active volcano near the centre of Mantuaroa, and seemed to be many things at once, made of hundreds of red and copper flecks, constantly changing form as my eyes moved across him. On the other side of the entrance was Nawe, mistress of waves and currents. She ruled the waters around the island. Plenty of fish to eat when she was in a good mood...but there was a hint of playful malice behind her huge, dark eyes.

And finally, Nufka, lord of winds, who put the breath of life on all that lives. He looked like a brightly-coloured streak, passing left to right.

As I gazed at these mighty representations of the spirit world, I shivered. They seemed to stare at me from another universe, despite being so closely entwined with this one. And I could almost feel Tuvu's fiery eyes bore into me as Terence ushered me into the pavilion. People turned to stare as I entered. If was as if my plastic legs could be sensed beyond the din.

And now I could see the source of much of the dreadful racket around me. The periphery of the tent was lined with thousands and thousands of birds – all in cages, and all contributing to the general cacophony. Cranes and nightbirds; ducks and eagles; pelicans and gannets; swans; and many, many brightly coloured parrots, all screeching and flapping with abandon.

Steaming hordes of people were thronging through, pushing hard towards the stage, illumined by flickering torchlight up the back. The drumming was throbbing towards a crescendo, but I couldn't see where it came from – it seemed to be all around me. Terence forced a path through the crowd, shepherding me through. I was ushered through an alleyway of foldbacks and wooden barriers, then somehow swept backstage, where someone punched me hard in the shoulder.

A tall, long-haired man was walking past.

'Bionic man!' he grinned. 'They said you'd put in an appearance. Just wait a minute, and then you'll see some *real* technology!'

He disappeared through a blackened doorway, but I knew exactly who he was, of course – the musician known as Scuzzy.

By this time I realised that I had lost my chaperone, Terence. I walked in the direction I thought he might have gone, only to re-emerge in the concert audience through a different entrance. I was caught up in the multitude, and ceased to act of my own volition.

The crowd grew increasingly restless, and began a kind of chant...but then an imposing figure strode onto the darkly glowing stage.

It was Scuzzy, in full battle armour, and he was wielding something – an axe, a weapon, or was it a guitar? Yes, his famous Rodomontar, with inbuilt fan-driven blades, capable of producing a multitude of sounds concurrently – with algorithmic dynamics and counterpoint, so that a skilled operator could essentially become a whole electronic orchestra. And Scuzzy was jealously possessive of its design, relishing his status as the only one-man *live* heavy metal/synth-pop band in the world.

He shambled towards the retro-looking microphone at front of stage.

'Is it ON?' his voice thundered round the massive tent, followed by a torrential cascade of feedback, which set the birds screeching even more. With his foot he stomped some kind of antique reverb pedal, and the feedback looped and echoed for several minutes, drowning even the noise of the screaming crowd.

'Is it *AAAAAHN?*' he roared manically, launching into a peal of insane laughter as he pressed a button on the sinister-looking guitar, causing it to splutter into life like a lawn mower, and as the machine began to squeal, the crowd surged forward with a roar, almost trampling me in the process.

I was forced to admit that his music was a lot more powerful and primal heard live than it had been over the television. Perhaps this was an illusion caused by the fact that it was around a hundred times louder, but I couldn't be completely sure.

On the other hand, he didn't seem as genuine as the original heavy metal musicians our great-grandparents listened to. There was an aura of pastiche about him, and he was essentially a showman rather than an artist...the songs he had penned for himself (like 'The Demon's Name is Flibbertigibbet' and 'Song of the Slowly Advancing Cavalry Retinue') seemed kitsch, lacking soul.

It was certainly *loud*, though.

Many in the crowd had their fingers in their ears, even *between* songs, when Scuzzy screeched and roared (doubtless carefully rehearsed) words about wild birds, and fevered dreams, and smashing open the sky, backed only by the sound of unseen drummers. I then realised that the drumming came from the Rodomontar as well...

'I didn't cage these *birds*, man,' he was snarling. 'And at the end of the show...*I'm gonna let 'em LOOSE...*'

The crowd roared with approval, but I had a feeling they would have roared similarly if he had said 'At the end of the show I'm going to *eat* them, every single one of them...'

Then he took a mouthful of paraffin, pulled a burning torch from the wall, and spewed a mighty jet of flame above the heads of the seething crowd, before launched into another song, his barbarous hair flailing as his head whipped astutely to the hellish din.

But even above the racket could be heard a new sound – a whining, drifting drone. Many pushed back towards the mouth of the tent, taking me with them. In the daylight wall of the entrance, a purple smoke-line trailed across the sky. The air show had begun! Scuzzy stopped playing and launched into a barrage of violent curses, protesting that he hadn't finished his set yet...that the air show wasn't supposed to start for another hour! But the crowd was oblivious as it surged out through the entrances to the field, where many more were milling – those too old or young to endure the vicissitudes of the distinguished musician.

And I, too, hurried out to view the spectacle.

There, in the sky above, were the planes. It was as if the birds in the tent had been caged merely so their mechanical cousins could take over the sky. The experimental air force had to be seen to be believed, and few there that day will forget their attendance. The choreography was impeccable – some craft hovering, while others shot by like whizzing stones. There were cinnamon darts and emerald-green jump jets; orange rotocopters; snub-nosed bombers with red-domed cockpits and bright purple underbellies; olive-green sea-planes and violet-red screamers; fighters in crimson and gold with chestnut circles on deep black delta-wings; pale blue interceptors; black and yellow swarmers; mottled brown spy-planes and iridescent jammers. All the colours of the earth were imitated there, in shapes I had never thought a plane could take, until now.

Sometimes I thought I saw the fierce eyes of the pilots, but this was probably an illusion caused by the streaming sun, and condensed angry flight paths. The dream-splashed planes were everywhere, crossing and re-crossing one another's trajectories...

The crowd loved every minute of it, while in the background Scuzzy's amplified cursing drifted from a now-empty tent. He berated them as fickle and spineless – as philistines, and worse things. But the eyes of the public were fully fixed on the seething, shimmering sky.

I walked with a dull head through the multitudes, picking my way gradually towards the field's far end, where there were fewer people and where I might feel less constricted. I thought I would find a pleasant place on the tussocky grass, and stare up at the mechanical wonders above.

But I hadn't quite reached the bottom of the field when a metallic 'crack' rang out, followed by a thin, unearthly whining. I looked up and saw one of the planes go spinning out of control. A dark shape was ejected as it passed overhead – the pilot. He hurtled violently to earth, somewhere among the rocks, where there was a faint thud and splash. He must have landed in the lagoon, I realised.

My instincts kicked in, and I hurried over the rocks, tripping several times along the way. I could dimly hear the confused crowd behind me, as I threaded through the boulders, my 'feet' squelching down in the muddy froth.

On reaching the lagoon I saw the figure at once, floating face up in the shallow water near the shore. He was very clearly dead, his back having presumably been broken on the rocks.

I looked down at his face. The eyes were open, like the Vampire Girl's. But my trepidation was quickly vanquished by surprise – because the man's head was half-covered by an artificial plate – and that plate was made of *the same grey plastic substance as my legs.*

I had perused a good deal of the medical literature in the days following surgery, but had never heard of this kind of prosthetic technology being used to make a covering plate for the skull.

Then I noticed something dark floating next to the corpse. I knelt down and reached across the body. It was a black, leatherbound notebook – a small pocket diary of the old-fashioned kind. I put it in my pocket without opening it, then looked around at the beautiful green lagoon, so watersure and mysterious. Strange breeds of duck were watching me, clustered up in pairs. Herons and cranes were resettling after their fright at the pilot's intrusion. But I could also hear voices, some of them electronically distorted.

I ran into the labyrinth of scree, then dropped to the ground, creeping slowly, slowly, through the slimy rocks. I crawled for what seemed an eternity before emerging onto grass, with bleeding elbows (I may come to regret having left such obvious traces behind), and was now up against the perimeter fence of the field, on the opposite side of the track where I came in. There were soldiers stationed all around the lagoon, except, as yet, on this side, near to the fence. I managed to crawl down the narrow gully some way without being spotted.

The sky was now free of planes, and evidently the show had been called off. The crowd seemed bored and angry, the atmosphere having been spoilt and polluted by the accident.

But despite my own anxiety, I could scarcely keep from smiling – for Scuzzy's voice came loudly from the tent, still roaring and trashing the stage, oblivious to what had just occurred.

It didn't seem like an act any more. And he made good on his threat to let the birds go. Cage after cage he set free...and while some of them stuck to their confine in a stupor, others took advantage of their newfound freedom. The main entrance to the tent was obscured by a riot of feathers. I walked through it, a feathery powder coating my clothes like the dust in an old spaghetti western.

Scuzzy was nowhere to be seen...but one of the island's famed jawbirds had landed on the mic stand, crushing the head of the microphone with its angular beak.

But the crowd were deprived of this spectacle.

6

ARTISTS

That afternoon in the hotel I sat pondering the contents of the notebook, deep confusion gnawing at my stomach. Had I been seen? Had the pilot been murdered? The newz called it an accident – a small glitch in the design of the new planes, being looked into, which would be completely rectified – but that meant nothing, of course. The pilot, whose name could not be released for security reasons, would be buried in Patagonia with full military honours.

But I had seen what I had seen.

What was the purpose of the grey plastic plate in the man's skull? Were they secretly testing new prosthetic technology on the military? Then it would be understandable that they had kept it under wraps. But before I noticed the plate, something in that pilot's staring grey eyes had filled me with fear. His expression, I now recalled, seemed to embody both resignation and despair.

The notebook was marked, on its first page only, with several lines of neat, cursive handwriting. It seemed to be the draft of a letter, and while the addressee was unnamed, the content was stark and disturbing:

Their goal, as you now know, is control of all mankind. I have <u>seen</u> the rite, empty voice in background. Last Poet followed the Ahu and took the secret stair. Does he know how to stop them?

This latest war will be to seize the Gate. Then <u>no one</u> will get through or escape their coming rule. That actor, master of disguise you call 'The Bird', doubtless knows of this, too.

BTW, if anyone finds this, they've done away with me. You next?

You next. That echoed in my head with compelling clarity. The last two lines seemed to confirm the pilot (if it was he who wrote it) had indeed been murdered.

But who were 'they'? Dead Shadows? Curia? Patagonians? And what was the 'rite' with the 'empty voice in background'? Who was this 'Last Poet', and the 'Ahu'? And what was the 'secret stair', and the 'Gate'? And the 'Bird', a master of disguise who seemingly knew about it...who was that?

And the war? There was armed conflict in various parts of the world, which had only intensified with the death of Scarlotti...did the pilot refer to some local war? There was currently no conflict in the South Pacific I was aware of.

So many questions that couldn't be answered. Or could they?

In any case, I had agreed to once more make the trip to Herb's that evening for a party, where he would introduce me to numerous 'important' people, he said. I wasn't sure what 'important' entailed in this case, but had no wish to sit brooding in the hotel. When one is at a loss what to think, a change of scene is best.

And so I went just as others were also beginning to trickle in. The later they got there, the more expensively dressed they seemed to be. Introductions were made, but progressively became a blur – too many names – and were only made to me, implying the rest were hitherto acquainted.

Many were artists, whom Herb explained belonged to something called the Artists' Guild International, which rang an intangible memory bell for me. They had been invited to the Festival to 'furnish cultural capital', 'garner prestige', or something like that. Not all the guests were artists, however – there were also politicians and military, and the prime minister himself was absent only on grounds of tackling the current crisis.

I sat on one of several couches that had newly appeared in the lounge room, listening to the varying conversations, particularly those of the military men. Much of the talk was of a rumoured coup, and a rebellion brewing amongst the poor. Could this be what the notebook meant by 'latest war'?

I followed the gist, but not the complexities. If a coup or rebellion *was* brewing, it would explain the heavy military presence on the island, more than I would have thought necessary for a tourist event like the Festival. Indeed, I now learnt that the coup threat may have been the *real* reason behind the visit of the Patagonian air force, which would mean it was not related to the death of Scarlotti and the Inner Council, which had taken place only that morning (had it only been *that* long?).

But who would be behind any upcoming violence was never made clear, and something prevented me from questioning them directly. Was it cult members, nationalists, leftists, or Mani tribesmen? Or some combination of the above? Stranger things had happened than such disparate groups uniting.

But while the soldiers and politicians spoke with hushed voices, the artists clearly couldn't have given a damn. They were far too sophisticated to take such rumours seriously. Seated next to me was a tall blonde woman with a massive swathe of pearls around her swan-like neck.

'Hiiiiii,' she said, drawling the vowel to absurdity. 'Soldier, prosthetically enhanced, no? I'm Blinny, Blinny Gunnarsen, young man.' She held out a long, pale claw and gave a prosthetic laugh. Then she handed me a brochure about her latest exhibit, *Plug-ins*.

She had put two racks of electronic devices on a busy London shopping street, with discount prices attached, and an EFT-swipe nearby...and people, unsurprisingly, would pay for them and take them (or steal them).

'But in doing so, they show they're just a part of the system...just ignorant *consuuuuumers*.'

'How would they know what it means if you don't explain it,' I asked testily. I half expected a look of withering scorn in reply, and hints that a mere deformed solider could never follow such grown-up complexities. But instead she turned away and spoke to someone else, completely ignoring my question!

I was at a loss for words, and sat there staring into space. Then a man who went by the name of 'Wakey' came and snapped me out of my trance. More affable than Blinny, he was also eager to tell me about *his* latest work, which consisted of him vomiting on a footpath, then cordoning it off. Each artwork lasted until the first 'philistine' thought to take the rope down.

'In that way, the philistine is drawn – whether he likes it or not – into my art. He becomes part of it...and the vomit part of *him*. Essentially, it is the cosmic vomit. We all spew it. It blurs the boundaries, subverts the liminal...'

'How *fresh* you are, Wakey!' said a listening admirer. 'Your art is always the *best*. So real.'

'I'm moving beyond *real* my dear,' he yawned, 'into unfathomed waters. How good this quail tastes! And now everyone, please fill up your glasses with this magnificent forty year old scotch, and make a toast to our new friend...er...our new friend. A simple soldier, thrust into adventures beyond his making!'

'To...er!'

'To...er!'

I raised my glass of orange juice in return, wondering what on earth they were talking about. Adventures? Were they mocking me? They looked deadly serious.

Then an elderly gentleman tottered up, standing over me in the clear expectation I would vacate my seat for him. When it became clear I wouldn't, he shuffled off, but Blinny, who had once more turned her attentions to me, called him back and introduced him to me. He was Godfrey Nussbaum, apparently a distinguished Australian art critic in his day.

'Do you know, the Wolves of Joy once attacked his house?' Blinny gushed. 'Oh, how madly delightful!'

'They weren't Wolves of Joy,' Nussbaum snorted testily. 'Some other fascist group, then.'

'I have already told you. They were the Wolves of Van Diemen's Land. And they were the original inspiration for the Wolves of Joy, I think. At least, I can scarcely remember it now. So much has happened...' He began to mutter to himself, something about anti-Semites.

'You mean anti-Curia?' I interjected calmly.

'Same difference, young man,' he snapped, then shuffled away again. Blinny had already begun talking to someone else about 'graveyard desecrations', and the 'cult' supposed to be behind them. The sophisticates tried to appear blasé and unsuperstitious, but they also wanted to seem interesting, albeit behind the de rigueur heavy irony. That was the usual formula, no doubt, and they stuck to it.

'Dead Shadows are such an *exciting* prospect,' Blinny said, turning towards me once more. 'They want to destroy the entire *universe!* And *every other* universe as well...what fun!'

Then a sudden blast of inspiration struck me, making my shoulders go cold.

'Do you know someone called the Last Poet?' I asked, trying to sound casual. As I said it Herb, who had just entered the room, seemed to cock his head and prick up his ears. Or did I imagine that? I felt a curious churning in my normally solid stomach. But I wasn't really expecting a response.

'Oh, that's Maddem,' one blimp said.

'Maddem,' I murmured, remembering the Introspector's phone call.

'Yes, silly boy. He called himself the 'final poet', or 'last poet'. Same thing, really, depending on which sense of the word 'last' one uses, of course.'

'Called? Is he dead, then?'

'He went off on a *quest*. But none of us were invited.' There was much laughter at this, and the speaker's pretend disappointment. 'He was looking for some lost tribe who disappeared ages back. An eccentric, you know.'

'Show-off, don't you mean?' said another guild member. Whatever feuds there may have been within the group, they were clearly united in their contempt for Maddem.

'He was a cracked old philistine,' said Wakey, 'who thought he was a poet. Stay away from people like that, dear boy.'

'So you definitely aren't aware of his whereabouts?'

'No, and we don't care,' he snapped. 'Two or three years ago he vanished, and the last place he was seen was right here on Mantuaroa. Said he was going 'beyond' or some such rubbish, and no one's seen him since.'

Taking a further chance, now that Herb was edging away again, and probably but not certainly beyond earshot, I asked if any of them happened to know someone called 'the Bird'.

An Indian artist who called himself Nejit Hopp told me this was probably a reference to an actor called Ramos Passaro.

'*Pássaro* mean 'bird' in Portuguese...a very good friend of mine, you know. Sterling actor.'

'Oh yes, Passaro is superb.'

'Just wonderful.'

'He's here for the Festival, too...frantically rehearsing his latest play at the Regent, downtown...otherwise he probably would have been here tonight.'

'You really are an *amusing* young man, with all these earnest questions,' said Blinny. 'Now I want to introduce you to someone else, so just wait here a minute.' The tedium in her voice as she called me 'amusing' was palpable. She returned shortly, and stood before me with her hands clasped together.

'He will see you in a moment, so he said.'

'Who will?'

'You've heard of Fudi-Da, of course.'

'No.'

She rolled her eyes as if she didn't believe me, thinking it some trite pretence at 'coolness'.

'He'll see you soon,' she repeated, and went to fix herself a drink.

'Who's Fudi-Da?' I said, turning to Wakey.

'The blind seer. Blinny's guru. She brings him to all these parties. In his youth he stared at a solar eclipse, in order to go blind...or so he says. His blindness helps him travel through the spirit world, or something like that.'

'I will 'see' him now,' croaked a voice from the hallway, heavy with irony. I saw a hand beckoning, and followed it into a darkened room, where I could just make out a tall robed figure, sitting on the bed cross-legged. He was wearing sunglasses. One hand perched on a walking stick, and his teeth glowed dully as he smiled and bade me be seated.

'So, this is where I 'see' you, to advise you,' he rasped, recycling his ham-fisted joke on the word see.

'What do you advise me?'

'Student Blinny has told me all about you. You are a young man seeking his path in life. But you mentioned a fellow known as 'Maddem'...is that right?'

'Yes.'

'This is a bad fellow...very unbalanced. Not right in the head, he is.'

'*Is?* So you know him, then. Is he still around?'

'No,' said Fudi-Da, with an irritated shake of his head. 'But listen now. The spirits say you have a great future ahead of you. If you play things right, you can be great artist...maybe even *visionary*, like me.'

'Really?'

'Take the necessary steps, fulfil your destiny! There are those on this very island, currently, who can instruct you.'

'People like you?'

'Yes.'

'I'll think on it,' I lied.

'You do that! And now, something for the spirits.' He held out his pudgy hand, clearly implying that I should cross it with silver. I fished in my pockets until I found one of the crumpled notes Herb had given me for petty spending. But handing it over, I fumbled it, and quicker than lightning, Fudi-Da grabbed at it and caught it in mid-air.

'Special senses,' he explained with a grin. And with that I could agree.

7

FEATHERED DEVIL

In the night I dreamt I was travelling across a vast plain with thousands of shining stars overhead. I was sitting in the back of an open top jeep, but as the vehicle progressed a band of shadow trailed along the arc of the sky, smudging out the stars. *I am leaving tracks on land and sky at once,* I thought. *But what will happen to the stars?*

To find out, I simply ran up to them, roaring as I went. But they weren't stars – they were little crackling eggs. Chirrups and squawks burst forth to welcome my arrival. Then the eggs receded, and a voice rang out with laughter. I realised the eggs were draining into a dark, spinning funnel, and falling, as if through an hourglass.

'There's no *time* left,' croaked a raven from an old blackened stump, and it appeared I was no longer in the sky. 'No time...'

And I knew I had to go. I had never been so sure in my life.

But where did that laughter come from, and why did it shiver so warmly in my blood?

*　　*　　*

I left the hotel at midday, wearing a cap, in the unlikely event someone should recognise me from a newspaper report. No one else was waiting at the bus stop, and five minutes later a chugging bus pulled up. I paid, using more of Herb's money. What I would do when it ran out, I didn't know. Things would have to take care of themselves.

343

The bus sputtered slowly along, meandering through the scenic north shore suburbs. It was a warm clear day, and the harbour looked even bluer than it had on the journey from the airport.

Soon the Downtown skyline appeared, but instead of tunnelling down the Understrand, the bus ploughed straight along the middle tier of the Strand. Having looked at a tourist map in the hotel room, I knew the theatre in question was just off this very street.

The sky was blotted out by the top tier of the Overstrand above, and the footpaths of the shopping strip were crowded. I could see a few 'deformed ones' on the steps of an old colonial building, looking like they were waiting for the end of the world.

I got out in the middle of the Strand, and quickly located the theatre – an impressive but somewhat run-down building, painted in a faded red that looked like it belonged in another time and place, but despite this, blending exquisitely with the other buildings around it.

The doors were locked, and I realised it would probably not open until evening, so I had an hour or five to kill. I walked back to the Strand, crossed it, and headed towards where the map had said City Square was. This turned out to be a large palm-lined space, more oblong than square, where people milled in clusters, and stray dogs lounged unchecked on warm, dark cobblestones. On the far side was a huge building like a cathedral – and in fact it originally had been – but I remembered from the map that it was now the main indigenous temple. It was a remarkable edifice, built in Spanish colonial style, yet now used exclusively for the worship of Mantuaroan gods, which had been revived in the late twentieth century. Given that most full-blooded Mani lived in the countryside, this was more a symbolic gesture than anything. The national flag and city flag hung limply on either side of the soaring temple, cowed by its grandeur.

Turning towards the left side of the square, I saw my intended destination – the National Museum – and it was here I now headed, looking for somewhere quiet and pleasant to pass the time. A special exhibit was on, highlighting a skeletal find known locally as the

'Feathered Devil'. The exhibit was free, so I made my way in, reading with interest about the fossil, uncovered around the time I had been in hospital after my accident.

The dig had caused a minor world sensation. The creature was in fact a very early bird – from the time of archaeopteryx. But its skeleton looked strange, somehow intimidating.

Next to the display case was a very lifelike hologram, giving an artist's impression of what the creature might have looked like. More than intimidating, this was truly disturbing. The feathers were coloured (with artistic license) in every hue of the rainbow, a true Bird of Paradise – but the creature's face did not look birdlike at all. In an eerie way, it looked almost human. I stared hard at it, wondering what it meant.

*　　*　　*

After leaving the museum I sat in a café near the theatre. Here the staff, who had seemed polite when I had ordered my coffee (not excessively friendly, perhaps, but nor were they rude), seemed to change beyond recognition when I asked if I could use the lavatory, the door of which was clearly marked behind the counter.

A simple 'no' would have sufficed, but a shock seemed to stir through them, as though I had committed a serious crime. I could see a shrivelled old woman staring with horror at me from behind a curtain out back, and the younger woman whom I had addressed rolled her eyes with scorn. Then a big man stepped towards me, casting a look of disbelief at his female colleagues.

'Yez, canielpyousir?'

I repeated my question, and they gaped in amazement.

'Are you wanting *everything* in life, then?' spluttered the young woman.

'Does his business in public like a *dog*,' spat the old woman.

'You, sir!' barked the man. 'Do you think we are millionaires? To cover all these damages on the toilets? In fact it is *you* who has money, or you wouldn't be paying for a meal.'

'I only ordered coffee…'

'Just *coffee!* What a *miser!*'

'I told you. Told you when he walked in. A miser, all the way. You can *smell* them.' To my astonishment the man stepped around the counter, one arm held back in a menacing gesture.

'You leave…now. No trouble, of any kind.' The shrivelled old woman limped out from the back with some ancient yellow eggs. They trembled in her withered, angry hands.

I could not believe that a mere request to use the toilet would enrage them so – there was clearly something deeper and darker at work here. Either that, or they were mad. Anxious to avoid trouble, I left, peeing instead in the laneway behind the shop. But later, as the sun was going down, and my footsteps turned towards the theatre, I felt in my pockets for the notebook, and realised I had left it in the café!

I ground my teeth in annoyance, and jogged several blocks back to the accursed place, worried that someone would pocket it. They were just shutting up for the evening.

The girl looked at me like I had crawled out from some dark, stinking hole.

'What does *he* want,' yelled the crone.

'Says he left a book here.'

'A *book?* Can he read?'

'It's a notebook,' I explained. 'I left it on the corner table.'

'And you think it will still be there? You think we don't keep the place *clean?*'

'What's he saying?'

'He thinks we're pigs!'

'Pigs!'

Now the man emerged.

'There is no book here for you sir…you must go elsewhere,' he said in a surly voice.

'Yes, but…'

'Do we look like bloody pigs?' the crone shrieked.
'It might be in the bin.'
'You want to go a-rummaging through the *bin?*'
'Well, would it be...'
'And you call *us...pigs!*' she finished triumphantly, tilting her head with a flourish.
'Don't talk to the pig...you'll end up like him,' snarled the other female.
'You must go elsewhere sir.'
It was that last 'sir' that irked me the most...such a meaningless word in the mouths of these tiresome people.
I had no choice but to sneak round to the back alley, which now smelt like urine, and go through the bins. But there were no bins there — just an old cardboard box full of odds and ends, and no notebook. Then I peeked through the grungy back window. Inside was a filthy-looking kitchen...pigs were *cleaner* than that. In fact I had read somewhere that wild pigs were very cleanly animals indeed.
Then the lights went out. Sticking my head round the side, I observed the obnoxious three locking the front door and trudging along the footpath, presumably to catch a bus back to whatever slum they inhabited.
Fine, then.
After a cursory search for alarms, of which there didn't appear to be any (either they couldn't afford it, or trusted to the heavy police presence in Downtown), I took off my shirt, preparing to smash one of the windows.
Then I recalled seeing a roll of gaffer tape in the box. Pulling it out I stuck it across the window in criss-cross fashion, using my teeth to sever it. I put my shirt against the glass to muffle the blow, and the tape held the pane in place so it didn't shatter or fall. Lifting out most of the window I made my way inside, being careful not to touch the razor-sharp edges.
My shoes crunched on dead flies. To think these filthy people had called *me* a pig! I found the notebook in no time, sitting on the bench behind the counter where they had put it. It was sodden with dregs of coffee, but still legible.

It was then that I noticed a newspaper article, clipped out and framed proudly on the wall. It was a travel feature from the London *Telegraph*, describing this very café, an establishment where people would deliberately pay for very rude service, a new cultural trend – at least it was three years ago when the article was written. Perhaps, given that the place was nearly deserted at the time of Festival, that trend was now dissipating.

The picture in the paper showed the corner booth where I had been sitting, packed with leering 'deformed ones' for whom it had once been a regular gathering spot, the first of its kind on Mantuaroa.

I hurried back out the window, rolling my eyes at my own obtuseness.

8

GHOSTS

Due to this delay, the play had already started by the time I reached the theatre. Even if they were still letting people in, I doubted the money in my pocket would be enough for a ticket, and so yet again found myself in a back alley. The theatre was part of a larger complex of buildings, and there were many doors in the lane. I tried the one closest to me. The rusted doorknob nearly flaked off in my hand, but to my surprise the door actually opened. Only then did I realise that part of me had wanted it not to.

Some concrete stairs led down into a stone hallway, where a chink of light emerged from under a door at the far end. I took a deep breath, then descended, edging sideways down the hall, before pausing at the door and feeling it with my hands. Rusted iron with a ridged pattern, inlaid with what felt like jewels – or bits of glass? No sound emerged, just the faint smell of tobacco smoke.

Then, without warning, the door, heavy as it was, flew open, and I found myself staring half-blind into the face of a boy of around ten, standing unsteadily, holding a lit cigar.

'Hey! Who's at the doo-er?' This voice from in the room was followed by a cloud of raucous laughter, and over the door-puller's shoulder I saw a tableau that chilled my blood. Round a table were seated half a dozen children – just children, but with faces hard and empty. They were playing cards and smoking, with glasses of what looked like hard liquor at their elbows. One chubby kid was sitting in the corner chewing something I guessed to be *vakka*. There was a girl with a thick fur coat, done up like an imitation TV star, fanning herself with a paper fan.

As they turned to stare at me, their looks ranged from condescending amusement to open annoyance to outright hostility. One of them looked especially angry – a short muscly kid in a black singlet, with a dark, craggy monobrow. His eyes bulged fiercely as he glared at me.

'Where you goin' boy?' he said threateningly, stepping forward, not cowed by the fact I was nearly twice his height.

'Wan' drinky?' said another.

I turned and ran, to the sound of their jeers, thoroughly revolted by the scene, intending to go back into the alleyway and try another door, but as I reached the entrance, still ajar, I stopped at the sound of footsteps outside.

Peering out the crack in the door, I saw a group of black-clad men tramping sternly past. Were they police, military, a criminal gang, or what? They appeared to be shepherding someone cloaked in a black hoodie.

Prompted by an instinct I didn't fully understand, I followed them cautiously, pausing as they entered a door further down. When I reached it, I found they had left it unlocked. If I stayed in the alleyway, the card players might emerge, so I opened the door and quickly stepped inside.

It appeared to be the theatre. A sign pointed the way to the dressing rooms. I crept round the corner and ducked into a gloomy little alcove – a cosy niche to wait until the play was finished, or better yet, for the interval, when I would try to corner the actor. But was I likely to catch the Bird alone? I felt a sudden icy sense of solitude, and this in part prompted me to try and get closer to the production itself.

The backstage area was a maze of dark carpets and softly glowing signs. I flitted down a wooden hallway, then heard someone coming and darted under a set of stairs, hiding behind some sort of industrial strength vacuum cleaner. To my surprise, however, I found I could see through a knothole into the theatre itself...it appeared that the hallway I had followed must have run alongside and slightly above the floor of the theatre, between the stalls and the gallery, with an excellent perspective on the action, despite the limitations of the knothole.

It appeared the play had not been running for very long. It was about a haunted house, but the 'ghosts' had been created by means of powerful fans, varied in their direction, creating sporadic currents of air that presumably felt to the audience like unseen spirits were moving unpredictably amongst them. The actors playing 'ghost hunters' (on the stage, and moving through the aisles) could not even predict what they were aiming their weird infrared 'guns' at. Meanwhile, the 'ghosts' were supposed to be entering the heads of some of the team, 'possessing' them and making them do strange things. The paranoia increased, as it became unclear who was possessed and who wasn't. It was all immensely entertaining, no doubt.

The play contained elements of both comedy and horror, and was much to the audience's liking. They were even more thrilled when a familiar figure trod the boards – Molly, the famous slave soap actress.

I recognised her at once, and my heart skipped a beat. I hadn't expected that, and neither had the audience. Then I recalled the hooded figure being hustled down the alleyway – of course, it must have been her. Here she was, playing live before the same public who (some of them) had regularly voted her into all kinds of unpleasant situations on *Lottery!*

As she stepped out on stage, there sounded the chiming of an old grandfather clock, soft yellow lighting showing up its dial in the formerly darkened corner of stage it inhabited. Molly started, as if slapped. And then the merciless lights found out another formerly obscure place – a pit, at base of the stage. I presumed it was some kind of orchestra pit, but there was nothing in it now except a black square.

Then the winds started. They were concentrated in the pit, so wild and frantic that it seemed a mini-tornado was among us, then suddenly they began to disperse, whirling this way and that, all around the theatre. And Molly began to declaim that a massacre had taken place there in the old days, and that now the spirits were finally laid to rest as it were, scattered.

But just as she said it, just as the winds were growing fainter, something unexpected happened.

There was a loud *THUMP THUMP THUMP*, genuinely frightening – the characters on stage looked startled. What special effects were these? The wooded panels in front of me had bulged violently. How had they managed to shake the theatre like that?

Then an interval was announced.

I hurried to get backstage, although I had originally planned on waiting until after the show to accost my quarry, but wanted to get out of that strange alcove where the wood had bulged so angrily. I managed, after a maze of twisty flights, to find myself in an area where a dozen or so people were milling. From the way they were dressed, I realised they were actors, and perhaps a handful of theatre crew. I had somehow managed to find a way, in sheer blind instinct, that bypassed all and any security, and no one gave me a second glance.

The most common expression I heard coming from that room was '*What the fuck?*', repeated variously to the point where it began to grate on my nerves. It seemed they were discussing the incident of the strange thumps.

I looked for Passaro, but in vain. I could see no one there matching the description Nejit Hopp had given me. I crept down a darkened hallway to look for him, then turned a corner to come face to face with

Her.

She jumped.

'Who are you?'

'Shhhhh.'

'Hey...aren't you that crippled solider from the newzcasts...with robot legs or something?'

'Quiet,' I hissed, glancing nervously around and pulling my cap across my eyes.

'What are you doing here? What do you want?'

'I'm looking for the Bird,' I whispered, seemingly no longer in control of my own tongue.

'What bird?'

'He's an actor. Passaro.'

'Ramos Passaro? What are you looking for *him* for? He's an idiot.'

'I'm looking for someone called 'The Bird', and I think it's him. I have to ask him something.'

'What?'

I frowned, and could sense that I was somehow struggling with myself, attempting to hide it even from myself...I had been alone for so long.

Then suddenly I blurted, 'Here!', and thrust the coffee-stained notebook into her hands.

She opened it slowly, frowning. She read it through. I expected her to laugh at me, or call security, but she didn't. Instead she seemed to ponder something.

"This actor, this master of disguise. I think I know who this bird guy is. I mean, a friend of mine might know him. He's mentioned him before. It's not Passaro, it's someone else.'

I thought I was going to have an orgasm.

'Could you take me to him?'

She looked at me very carefully...scrutinising me, I should put it. Then finally, she spoke.

'Let's run away together,' she said in a strange, businesslike manner.

'Uh, yeah?' I said with immense surprise. Despite her fame, I didn't really know her from a bar of soap.

'Yeah,' she repeated. 'Now come on, before I change my mind.' She went to get her backpack and hoodie from the cloakroom, then beckoned me down the same hallway that had led to the knotholed alcove.

'I need to give my minders the slip,' she said, 'once and for all. By the way, Passaro is such a pompous, arrogant prig. It's a good thing the Bird *you* want is someone else.'

But was he? Was she lying? Had she made the whole thing up? I wanted to trust her...

'He called me a second-rate actress to my face! So what? I never claimed to be great at acting, did I?'

'Uh, no.'

'No, of course not. It was just a bit of fun, this play. Supposed to be. To think, I was actually looking forward to it!'

'But what were those thumps?'

'Don't know...maybe the producer?'

'The theatre people didn't know about it.'

'Oh, I don't know then. Whatever it was, I was bored out of my bloody mind. What a prig that Passaro is!' I wisely said nothing, having no wish to spook her, or give her the jitters, before she might lead me to this new Bird, if indeed he existed.

Then she said: 'My life is turning colder, and a shadow seems to fall behind me at all times.'

This was delivered in such a deadpan way, that I thought it was a line of rehearsed script, until I saw her facial expression...and then I understood her a little better, but was unsure how to express it.

'Oh, these stupid fucking actors. It feels like they're dragging me in, sucking me down like a damp, pulling mist. I want to scream but I just bite my tongue. And now...I've finally had enough.'

I could only thank whatever gods there were that I happened to be present on such a night. To my surprise, I found there were tears in my eyes.

*   *   *

I could still hardly believe I was in the presence of the chaotic TV star, and that a certain brittle coldness seemed to distinguish us both from everyone else on that lank, humid island...had perhaps even somehow drawn us together.

It was easy (too easy, I thought) giving her guards the slip, despite that they would recognise her, hoodie or no, the minute they laid eyes on her. Perhaps I would even be charged with kidnapping...

As we hurried through Downtown, she blathered incessantly about the cast of *Lottery!* It seemed she hated most of them. The dwarf was the worst – she wouldn't talk about *him*. The only one she vaguely liked was Tina, who I seemed to remember was a slim, knife-throwing dancer. On several occasions Molly had been injured or violently humiliated but, as she bluntly put it, 'I signed a contract.'

And now, it appeared, she was breaking it.

'So you're taking me to this Bird guy, then?'

'No, I already told you. We're going to see my friend. My only friend. He'll know what to do.' The way she said 'my only friend' made me think she had many such 'only friends', but again I let it slide. For her, everything was falling, there was neither up nor down. In short, she had no centre of gravity. I sensed this instinctively. I didn't trust her, but nonetheless wanted to protect her. Strength surged through my phantom legs as a crudely melted face (a 'deformed one') lurched past, giving us a mocking look.

We had already walked across most of Downtown when she announced she was hungry, and suggested we stop and get something to eat. But this rich celebrity had no money, and I was forced to pay with my pitiful stash of grubby Mantuaroan notes.

We entered, and I walked up to the counter while she stayed near the entrance. Two cops were in there, and they stared at us from the moment we sauntered in. They were Polynesian in appearance, and one of them was truly huge.

The smaller one muttered something. Neither of us responded, but it appeared he had been addressing us, as he now said: 'HEY! I'm talkin' to *you*.'

Molly looked frightened, but continued to say nothing. I had an uneasy feeling.

'What's your name?' said the big cop, walking over and standing above her menacingly. My heart began to pound, and I braced myself, ready for action.

'Hey...I *like* Mantuaroans,' she stammered.

'I'm Tongan, not Mantuaroan, you dumb bitch,' growled the cop, raising his hand above his head, clearly about to rip her hoodie away.

I didn't hesitate. I had already taken such a leap into the unknown, it would be worse now to go backwards than forwards. If her identity were revealed, or we were arrested, things might end disastrously. So I ran across the room and did a flying kick in the cop's back before he could turn – and to my immense surprise he went flying, mountain as he was, into the concrete wall of the diner, then slumped unconscious on the floor.

So my magic legs had come in useful after all...

I didn't have time to dwell on this, however, as I needs must fly at the other one before he grabbed his gun. He took on a startled expression as my invincible limbs side-kicked him in the stomach, and he too fell in a heap like an old bag of potatoes.

'Now *run*,' I hissed, and we ran. A river of black corrosive bile was coursing through my veins. Violence was emotionally heavy, it was overwhelming.

We ran through back-streets of the inner city. Molly was leading the way...at least I hoped she was, because I had no clue where we were. But after a while we began to slow down, and she admitted that she, too, was lost.

Round the next corner, however, we could see the river (if it could be called such) ahead, with a curving concrete bridge across it. We crossed the ditch, its darkened stream below us, black shadowed culverts on its sides.

This was the Southside, more run down. Ragged kids of varied races running around. Thin and dusty streets smelling of milk, unwashed dogs and humid blackness...no shops, no deformed ones.

And then she saw it, the building she was after. It was yet another theatre. At least, the sign said *Theatre of Pain*, but Molly explained that it was actually a kind of club.

'It's where he said he would be, where he hangs out when he's in Mantuaroa,' she said.

'Your friend?'

'My only friend.'

And then we were standing before the huge door warden of the club.

But the man was polite.

'Who yer after, then?'

'We're here for Scuzzy. Tell him 'M' is here,' said Molly from the muffles of her hood. The doorman went to verify.

'Your friend is *Scuzzy?*' I gasped.

She nodded, too tired to give a proper answer. The warden soon returned and let us in. We entered what appeared to be a large, grimy drinking den, with medieval-style wooden tables, so that I immediately suspected (rightly as it happened) that it was some kind of trendy new establishment.

I could see Scuzzy on the other side of the room, but Molly sat us down at a dark corner booth, waiting until he came to us, so as not to attract attention. He was yelling for whisky, but his bellowing seemed contrived, and as he laughed and spoke to those around him, I sensed distinctly that it was all an act...though for whose benefit I wasn't sure. I was surrounded by actors...

He bellowed and roared a bit more, then pretended to stagger across to where we were sitting, gracing us with his rocksterial majesty.

'Howzit?' he nodded nonchalantly to Molly. It didn't seem as if they were close, despite her claim he was her only friend.

'This is…'

'Yeah, we've met. At the air show.'

'Yeah.'

'How'd you like it?'

'The air show?'

'The music.'

'Oh...it was loud.'

'Loud...huh,' he grunted appreciatively.

'Written any songs?' asked Molly, obviously upstaged by our eloquent conversational abilities.

'Well, got this new one. Inspired by Mani tribesman. Western hills. Whole tribe turned against him cos his singing was so harsh. I love it!'

Molly announced she had run away, that is, had officially left the show known as *Lottery!*, and I felt a sense of relief that she probably wouldn't be changing her mind, going back, and having me charged with kidnapping. I was still unsure where I stood with her, however. Then she mentioned our quest to find 'The Bird'.

'You told me about him that time, remember?' Scuzzy confirmed he did indeed know someone nicknamed such, and I felt a twinge of guilt for having doubted her word. Scuzzy then said he would take us to 'The Bird', and instructed us to wait while he went to an antique payphone in the corner. We could hear him making odd sounds and mutterings. Then he came back and told us he had been talking in a special code which 'The Bird' had taught him, using words from several languages, as well as funny clucking sounds.

He had arranged for us to meet the man, whose name was Vonny Moss.

'But even that's not his *real* name. No one knows his real name, probably not even him.' The man was some kind of spy, apparently, and had accidentally let this on to Scuzzy once when drunk, to his later chagrin. But Scuzzy had actually done him a favour, helping him procure a fake ID and Mantuaroan passport for his latest change of identity.

But why had Moss agreed to meet me, I wondered suspiciously.

And what kind of secret agent bungles his identity in such a way?

9

AGENT

The Moss character had arranged to meet us in a park, also on the Southside...but to get there we had to catch a train back to Downtown, then head out on another line. It was a short walk to the station through footworn streets. There were shouts and violent cries in the air on that warm, greasy night. Many drunks were out to mark the start of Festival. A man lurched towards us, but in no mood for trouble I simply pushed him out of the way. His burbled yells tailed us as we wedged through the crowd.

We jogged down a small flight of stairs into a dirty concrete walkway. Scuzzy bought tickets from an old-style machine on the wall, which clunked and buzzed as it spat out three small pieces of cardboard with illegible writing in blurry dot-matrix ink.

We moved through the turnstile and onto the darkened platform. Flickering yellow lights along the ceiling made the dirty walls look sickly and unrested. An old man slept on a wooden bench, but aside from him, no one was on the platform. Then the train came shrieking, piercing the air with white-grey light. The brakes sounded as if they would soon give out, but we boarded, and Molly looked about from under her hoodie, as if re-familiarising herself with something dreamlike and ancient, from before the time of her fame. Scuzzy, lounging confidently, rested his dirty boots on the opposite seat.

The journey was slow, and the train filled up as we drew towards the city. A spittoon near the front of the carriage got spilled at the second-to-last stop, and I looked the other way in disgust.

We alighted at Central, following Scuzzy down a hallway to another platform, which was larger and more crowded. A distorted voice announced that the next train would be arriving in three minutes.

Scuzzy announced he was going to urinate, and shouldered his way through to presumably filthy toilets. Molly and I stood on the platform amid the stench of a hundred sweating bodies, and then it happened – a psychotic-looking man of indeterminate race bumped into Molly, began yammering and screeching at her, beady little eyeballs almost popping out of his shrivelled head. I took it in through the stench and the sweat, and the peculiar Mantuaroan intoxication of the silver, twirling night. My brain was in neutral, but a placid voice thought tiredly: *not again...how many more will bother us tonight?*

But while this languid mind at the back of my head was thinking so, other faculties were whirring into life. Molly was answering the stranger back in a defiant, shrieky voice – so genuinely defiant, in fact, that I felt impelled to sally to its flag. All the anguish of a lifetime seemed doled into that shriek, the verbiage of which escaped me, but the meaning – wordlessly clear. I moved forward to her defence, but my movement coincided with the accoster's pulling of a long and shiny knife. I squared off to him, lifting a leg in the hope that it would tempt him to knife me in the prosthesis, his blow bouncing harmlessly away. But instead, the stranger lunged forward at Molly.

She ducked the knife arm, but couldn't avoid the other, which grabbed roughly at her head, pulling the hood away. There was a gasp from the increasingly panicked crowd.

'It's Molly!' someone needlessly exclaimed. I grabbed the menacing arm...but Scuzzy had returned, and simply clubbed the man over the back of the head with an *iron codpiece*, which he must have removed while peeing. The stunned and howling thug put a hand to the back of his head as his knife clattered to the ground (someone quickly grabbed it), before Scuzzy gave him another whack with the bizarre metal accoutrement, this time knocking him out cold.

'Har, har, jolly good fight, what,' he yelled in triumph, as Molly hurried him on to the just-arriving train. 'I've never been in a fight before and I wish to thank you,' he bellowed. 'For now I am *truly* Metal! I am fucking *invincible!*'

We had trouble keeping him quiet for the remainder of the train ride, and several of the carriage's occupants gave us dirty looks.

But eventually we arrived at the right station, and emerged at street level, looking up to see a brightly lit aircraft overhead, a tiny firefly skimming the firmament. I took this as an omen that we were safe (for now) from unwanted attentions of the authorities, and breathed a sigh of relief. I looked at Molly and she merely shrugged.

The street was only dimly lit, and halfway down the block began a darker patch, lined with the shadowy outlines of shrubs or stunted trees, and looking for all the world like a run-down park. We walked through a gap in the shrubbery and entered the dark expanse, which was bigger than it looked from the outside. Scuzzy seemed to know where he was going.

We crossed the park to a wall of wire mesh and gloomy warehouses, and through the fence haloed lampposts shed a flimsy sheen across, down and into the park.

'This is the spot,' said Scuzzy, sounding unaccountably cheerful. We sat on a bench adjoining a barren flower bed.

'Is he late?' asked Molly.

'No...he's probably already watching us, then he'll suddenly burst from the shadows like the show-off he is.' I stood up and looked around, wondering where this Moss character could be hiding, if anywhere. He wasn't behind any of the nearby trees, or up against the fence.

'There's nowhere he *could* hide.'

But just as I spoke, there was a rustling in the flower bed. I had ignored this feeble garden because it looked so scanty – just a pitiful collection of weeds, with no room for a man to hide without being spotted. But now a figure actually seemed to emerge from the earth itself. The dirt-bedraggled shape rose, like a creature from a cheap horror film, and stood looking around in silent triumph.

'Moss, you dirty bugger!' exclaimed Scuzzy. 'You've sunk to new depths.'

'Got one over on you, didn't I? As usual,' growled the figure in a bellicose voice. 'Not bad for a man in his forties.' Even in the dark and through the dirt, it looked more like he was in his sixties, but I said nothing, as plenty of people lie about their age. And it *wasn't* bad...it appeared he had dug himself a trench in the tawdry soil, covering everything except for the face...a face that looked oddly familiar to me, though I couldn't quite place it. The excess dirt? He explained at tedious length how he had first distributed it neatly around the edges of the flower bed in a small unnoticed line.

Scuzzy let out a long, loud belch, as if there wasn't much more he could really say at that point. But Vonny Moss frowned, raising a finger to his lips. He stepped forward, pulling something from his pocket – some kind of small electronic device. They could see him more clearly now, his drab hair and chubby, nondescript face – the perfect secret agent. Even covered in dirt, he was a marked contrast to Scuzzy, who rolled his eyes as Moss ran the device over me, front and back – some kind of scanner.

'For Flib's sake, Moss...' But Moss put his finger to his lips again and glared at him, apparently angry over the repeated use of his name, even if it was a false one. He then ran the scanner over Molly. Suddenly the device let out a high-pitched tremolo sound.

'Aha! You see?!' said Moss triumphantly. Molly frowned in confusion.

'What is it?'

'Check your pockets.' She did so and found a tiny metal bead, not much bigger than the head of a sewing pin.

'Is it...some kind of bugging device?' she asked, sounding shaky.

'Aha! So you ask my expert opinion now, eh? The 'dirty bugger' who just likes to show off? Give me that...' He prised it from her rudely.

'I didn't call you...'

'No, young woman, this is not a *bugging* device, it's a *tracking* device. And someone, somewhere, right now, knows *exactly* where you are. And, need I remind you, more importantly, that if it was known that *I* was with you, they could also get to *me*...'

He didn't explain how it was possible anyone would know he was with us, but the thought clearly filled him with anger. He started grilling Molly, asking who she was, why anyone would want to plant a tracker on her and so forth. When he found out she was a celebrity, he nearly went berserk. It appeared – oddly, for someone so apparently versed in technology – that despite her being one of the biggest stars in the world this past year or so, he had never so much as heard of her (I only saw *Lottery!* recently myself, of course, but then I am a near-Luddite).

But when he learnt we had a clue about a 'latest war', he became all ears. He read the page from the notebook so intently that I had to badger him to give it back. Finally, he did so, also handing the tracking device back to Molly.

'Ditch it,' he said, 'and we'll run back to my place.' Molly looked at Scuzzy in alarm. He nodded.

'Cat knows what he's talking about. Best do as he says.'

Just then there was a noise on the other side of the perimeter fence, and Vonny Moss nearly jumped out of his skin; but it was only an old drunk shuffling past.

Molly suddenly ran across to him, pushing something through the mesh. 'Want a pack of electronic cigarettes, mister? I'm quitting. No? Put it in your pocket then, and give them to someone else later.' The man took them with a grimace and a nod, then shuffled on his way, now the unknowing object of unknown surveillance.

'Hold on...I forgot to scan *you*,' said Moss to Scuzzy, and did so, to the amazement of the latter when the tremolo sounded again...and to the amazement of *all* of us when it emerged that the scanner had picked up something not in Scuzzy's clothes, but *inside his arm*.

'It seems, my friend, that you are the proud or perhaps indifferent owner of an irremovable biochip.'

'*Indifferent?!*'

'And here I think we will have to part ways. Better one of us goes down than all.'

'Yeah,' said Scuzzy, through clenched teeth. 'You're right about that.' And without so much as a goodbye he turned and loped across the darkened park in the direction we had come from.

'Quickly now,' said Vonny to myself and Molly, and I had never seen an old man run so fast (though he *did* say he was only in his forties). He led us through a gap in the fence, over to where a rusted van was parked near the warehouse opposite. But instead of getting into it as I had expected, he leapt atop its bonnet, then hauled himself onto the van's roof, motioning for us to do likewise. From there he scrambled up onto the low overhang that led onto the roof of the factory.

'No chances. With my dirty face, and your celebrity...the utmost secrecy is called for. We must take the most obscure paths. The situation is *extremely* grave. Please splash your feet with this aftershave, to keep the dogs from our tail.'

'But won't dogs find aftershave even easier to follow than our normal scent?' I demanded incredulously. I felt a bit stupid saying it...perhaps there was some subtlety involved I didn't fully understand. Then it hit me that the dogs wouldn't know to follow the aftershave if they were supposed to be following *us*, of course.

But Moss merely snapped: 'Of course. I was assessing your worth for undercover work. You pass the test. And good thing, because I would have ditched you otherwise and let you fend for yourselves. Now come, let us voyage through the forest of the rooftops.'

Molly tapped her head, giving me a significant glance, but I shrugged, turning to follow our exceedingly odd guide.

The forest of the rooftops ended on the other side of the warehouse, however. We had no choice but to clatter down a drainpipe into a shopping street. Half a dozen people stared as we dropped like monkeys onto the footpath, and Moss made us dart from shadow to shadow, finding any minimal cover we could.

We would wait a bit, then sprint again.

Once we paused in a darkened alleyway while he re-plotted our course, and Molly pulled a taro cake from her pocket and commenced to eat it hungrily. But Moss, annoyed that his 'unobserved cover' might be breached, knocked it from her hand.

'It could be poisoned, you fool...'

And then he made us run again.

*   *   *

When we finally reached his rather squalid bedsit, he sat us down (on the floor) and asked us further questions. It seemed he had genuinely never heard of Molly.

She seemed insulted, but to me it was a sign he was trustworthy...unless it was all an act, but he seemed too nutty for this to be the case (at least, so I initially thought). And he seemed to eventually consider *us* at least partially trustworthy – but not enough to tell us very much about himself.

He admitted that he worked for a foreign government, but wouldn't say which one, nor whether it was one which had been Curia-aligned. He knew enough about current events to inform us that the new Curia-in-exile was based in Patagonia.

Part of his mission, he let it be known, was to gather information on Mantuaroa's power structure, conflicting alliances and special interest groups. One night, it seemed, he had indulged in a cocaine binge, and let this information slip to Scuzzy, whom he didn't realise was a famous musician (the entertainment industry not being 'part of his brief' as he put it).

I mentioned the grey plate in the pilot's head, and showed Moss my own legs. Molly was disgusted, but Moss was intrigued by the grey material, especially after I explained how my legs had seemed to 'become' the prosthetic ones.

And now Moss told us something of interest – it appeared he had known the pilot, who was an undercover agent in the military of the unnamed Patagonian billionaire. He had volunteered to be an experimental test subject in the new air force as a way of gathering covert information, but Moss hadn't seen him since, and was at a loss to explain the grey plate in his head. He asked to look at the notebook again.

'Yes,' he said after re-reading it. 'I am the 'actor' he spoke of. This note must have been addressed to a mutual contact. He clearly wasn't expecting to die in that way. It was stupid of him to write it down at all, but luckily for us the authorities didn't find it.'

'Thanks to me.'

'Yes, thanks to you.'

'And why do they call you 'The Bird'?' asked Molly.

'Because when anyone looks for me, I *fly* away,' he said, with his teeth bared in a strange grimace.

He didn't know who 'Maddem' was, or where he went, but he did know of a conflict brewing between two island nations to the south: Cavendish and St. Vigeans. Perhaps someone was trying to stir up trouble between them, but Moss couldn't imagine why. The dispute was merely over territory, and he knew nothing of the 'Gate' the pilot had mentioned. Indeed, he seemed baffled by the way in which these seemingly fantastical elements had been woven into the normal kind of espionage he was used to.

'I know who can tell us more, though. He works at the university. I'll take you to see him in the morning.' He seemed more sedate now, and went to the kitchenette to make a meal, while Molly and I played cards with his grotty novelty deck, featuring pictures of naked fat women.

Before long, Moss, humming contentedly, brought in the meal he had whipped up – runny, half-cooked eggs on blackened toast, with some kind of coarse herb (cannabis?) sprinkled liberally on top. Starving as we were, we ate it, but it wasn't an experience I hope to repeat.

As we ate, he became more revealing about himself, or so we thought as he spoke.

'I was never successful in the early days,' he drawled in a blasé manner. 'As a young man I staggered through one hideous accident after another, never managing to hold a job or a girlfriend for long.' He almost seemed to be smirking as he said it. 'But one day my maternal uncle, Mr. Phidias Cromfleck, determined to give his unfortunate nephew, myself, a badly-needed break.

'Uncle Phidias was a private eye, and he not only signed me on, but even included my name in that of the business. *Cromfleck and Moss* read the sign on the agency door. He thought that two names on the door sounded more professional, and intended to train me as we went along. 'I'll teach you the detective arts, my boy,' he said. 'And when I'm gone, the business will be yours.' But poor Uncle Phidias little guessed how soon that would come to pass.

'At the time he was working on the Kesserling case, the most famous kidnapping in Mantuaroan history. A wealthy businessman's daughter had been captured by a psychopath. This businessman alerted every detective on the island, promising vast amounts to the one who captured the villain. But Phidias Cromfleck proved more adept than them all. He tracked the kidnapper down in the nick of time – just as he was smuggling himself and his victim on board a freighter, with a huge cargo of seafood bound for Canada. He was climbing on board in the dead of night, hauling himself and his victim (who didn't look to be putting up much resistance) on top of a massive grey hopper being used to load the ship. I tagged along – it was the first case I was involved in, and although I contributed little I was proud to be there for the ride, as my uncle's new assistant. But when Phidias asked me to hand him over his stun gun, something wild took over inside my head. I wanted to impress my uncle, to garner his respect. So instead of just handing the gun across, I carefully took aim myself. I had fancied myself a good shot with an air rifle as a kid...

'Unfortunately that was a long time ago. Rather than hitting the silhouetted figure hauling the businessman's daughter over the rails, I hit one of the cables holding the hopper in place. Under the electronic barrage it frayed and snapped; then two things happened with alarming speed. With an enormous ripping sound, the hopper pierced the hull of the ship, tearing a hole and pushing it down into the water, with the result that the freighter began to sink immediately. And secondly, the contents of the hopper were unleashed, and my poor uncle was crushed to death by eighteen tonnes of frozen octopus and squid. At least I had the comfort of knowing his death had been mercifully swift...

'The kidnapping victim fell down the side of the ship, sliding down the flowing mountain of frozen seafood. She landed straight in my arms, but standing there aghast as I was, she barely noticed me. The kidnapper had jumped into the water and escaped. Shortly afterwards, the girl, who I had just 'rescued', flew to join him at his overseas hideout.

'And that was how I discovered the detective trade wasn't for me. So I became a secret agent instead...'

What could I say to this ludicrous tale? The whole thing was clearly bunk from start to finish, but I was too polite to say so...

It was then that it hit me – like lighting from a clear sky. Like one of those magic puzzles that look an amorphous blur until a picture of a windmill coalesces, and then you can't see anything but the windmill.

He was Ellison Plugg. The conspiracy theorist who had 'died' a couple of years ago.

He must have realised something was up, as he asked why I was staring at him with my mouth all aslobber in befuddlement.

'You're Ellison Plugg!' I stammered.

He immediately denied it.

Then he sarcastically affirmed it, with many a wink and leer.

Then he denied it again, until it all began to seem like a surreal joke.

Even Molly frowned, beginning to see the more-than-resemblance. In an obvious move to divert our attention, he turned the radio on, but what we heard there riveted us even more...Scuzzy was described as being 'wanted' for Molly's abduction!

In a report not linked to the other two, I myself was simply described as 'missing'.

Vonny was suspicious – why would they put out a wanted ad for Scuzzy, with his trackable biochip? Molly wanted to explain things to the authorities, and put

Scuzzy in the clear, but Vonny and I convinced her to wait until we heard more news.

We didn't have long to wait. The phone rang, and it was Scuzzy, calling from a public booth. He spoke in the coded bird-language Vonny had taught him to use. Molly wanted to talk to him, but Vonny wouldn't let her because she hadn't learnt the code.

After a while spent talking in seeming gibberish, mixed with chirrups and clucks, he put down the unit with a grim look. The mystery of the biochip was solved, at least...Scuzzy had gotten drunk at a bar and removed the device by a form of crude self-surgery. The 'irremovable' chip was now floating in the river, but Scuzzy had paid a price...in a terrible state he was. He had lost a lot of blood, and was hiding out with a trusted friend, who planned to help him escape the city.

But he had also heard important news, and that was why he had called. Through his friend he had somehow learned that both myself *and* Molly were now wanted by the authorities. Molly's stardom would not protect her now, for someone high up wanted her for questioning...but about what, he had no idea.

'I'll take you in the morning to my friend, Professor Pommas, at the university, who'll be able to hide you until we can figure out what to do.'

Despite my misgivings, it seemed like he genuinely wanted to help us. Whatever side this quadruple-agent and death-forger was on, it didn't seem to be that of the island authorities. At least that was something.

10

SHIP OF FOOLS

When we awoke, amazingly, it was to the sound of Vonny telling us that 'they' know everything, that we don't have a chance, etc.

I rolled off the coat I was using as a mattress, onto the contents of an ashtray that had spilled on the carpet.

'What?' I demanded, pulling myself to my 'feet'. 'Why are you helping us, then, if we're all doomed anyway?'

'Doomed?'

'Yeah. You were saying…'

'Oh, just muttering to myself. Nothing to concern yourself with. I thought you were both asleep.' Molly yawned and sat up.

'When are we going to the university?' she asked groggily.

'Soon, soon. I could have gone to university myself, you know. But I chose the university of life, instead. The school of hard knocks. And my career path is now in the ascendency.'

'Ascending *where?*' I muttered darkly.

'Well, as my next career move I'm thinking of faking my own death, yuk yuk. Not that I've done it before, of course. And then, maybe I'll become a travel agent.'

Over a breakfast that featured more burnt toast, Moss explained that, although it was risky to visit his contact at his workplace, the latter was less likely to be under surveillance than his home, as it would trickier to install bugging equipment in a public building. That was Vonny's reasoning, anyway. Apparently this man, one Professor Pommas, was suspected by the government of having links to illegal rebel groups, specifically the Wolves of Joy.

'Aren't the Wolves an urban myth?'

'You tell me, young man. Seeing as you seem to be such a know-it-all. Now, I'm going to start my car, so please wait here...the presence of strangers breaks her concentration.' We sat and waited. I kept trying to catch Molly's eye, but she kept looking at the floor, as if second-guessing my intentions.

Splutters came in torrents through the wall, followed by a sound like a dying emu. This cycle repeated a dozen times or more, then there was a violent bang, and a loud but steady purring. It appeared that Vonny's car had found her concentration. He called us out, then opened the back door and lifted up the seat. A storage chamber was hidden underneath.

'One of you can go in there and the other in the trunk. I'm not taking any chances.'

It was funny he used the American word 'trunk' despite his British-sounding accent (Plugg had been American). But by now I no longer cared who he was, or had been. I was just damn sure I didn't want to get into an enclosed space where I might be locked in and taken to who knows where. Molly didn't hesitate, however. She clambered into the compartment, so I found myself, with extreme reluctance, letting Vonny lock me in the boot.

He shut me up in the dark, and the vehicle coughed and jerked into the light.

*   *   *

After what seemed a bumpy eternity, he let us out. He had parked, it appeared, in an obscure corner of campus, some way from any actual building. Molly started to say something, but Moss put a finger to his lips, pointing silently at a dark concrete tunnel on the other side of a muddy soccer pitch. It looked like the entrance to a stormwater drain. Guessing his intentions, I rolled my eyes.

371

'Wouldn't the door be okay?' I asked in a hushed voice. But not hushed enough. Moss shooshed me, eyes bulging. *We're deep in enemy territory*, his face and bearing said. He turned and motioned silently, and we followed with a shrug.

Skirting the edge of the field, he led us into the black, slimy tunnel. He donned what I presumed were a pair of night vision goggles, but he had none spare, so we had to be content to follow his shuffling footsteps up ahead. These sometimes grew hard to discern, even in the otherwise-silent and echoey tunnel. He seemed to be treading as lightly as humanly possible...was he scared of secret microphones even in here? I was beginning to question his sanity.

My sense of time being erratic at best, I couldn't say how long we trudged in silence through that dark, phobic conduit. But at some point a faint source of light began to emerge, and then we arrived beneath a solid metal hatch, which Moss, after standing there for some minutes, lifted, and we climbed a wall-fixed ladder and emerged into a dank and rotting boiler room. How had he known we would come out here? Had he been this way before, or…

But there was no time to think as he hurried us through cobwebs to an antique goods lift, which looked ready to fall to pieces. Moss pressed a button and an ancient panel flickered into life. It jerked us slowly upwards, then stopped, the doors slithering open on some dusty-columned chamber full of broken furniture. Moss stepped onto a solid wooden table in the corner, pushed a barely-visible hatch in the ceiling, and suddenly (quicker than we would have thought possible, even for that scuttling man) hauled himself up into the roof.

A hand extended down, and Molly jumped on the table, allowing Vonny to haul her up. I did the same, finding myself in a square, shiny duct with thin metal walls, clearly some kind of air vent.

Moss pulled the hatch shut tight behind us, but a dimly distant source of light projected through the ducts. Our breathing echoed loudly. Moss pulled a folded sheet of paper from his pocket and waved it in our faces, putting the usual finger to his lips. It looked like a blueprint of the cooling system. But he barely looked at it as he turned on his knees and led us crawling slowly forward.

He's smooth, I thought, the alternative being unthinkable. I was trusting my life to this mad, burrowing animal.

After twisting and turning for what seemed an hour through a labyrinth of culverts, bends and ducts, he brought us suddenly to a halt. Molly opened her mouth to speak, but once again he silenced her. I rolled my eyes. Surely we were making enough racket as it was, clanking around here in the pipes? Moss' paranoia would more likely get us captured than the other way around, and I was also feeling increasingly claustrophobic. But Vonny's hand was resting on a metal hatch. Finally, the office where his contact worked!

He slowly levered at its edges...

But the sight revealed below was not what he had expected. A dozen pairs of eyes stared straight back up at us, while a grey-haired angry woman stood poised on the desk below, holding a broom, perched and ready to prod us. One of her students (I presume this is what they were) called out into the hallway: 'Hey, they're in here! It looks like *people!*'

It appeared that our echoing trip through the air ducts had triggered a campus-wide panic, with students and teachers alike dispatched to hunt the creature or creatures thought loose within the ceiling. Vonny quickly blustered.

'Sorry,' he stuttered. 'Just a routine system check. Your ducts are working fine, thanks. Truly fine.' Perhaps they thought he was an apparition, an animal spirit, some lord of the rats who had taken human form and spoken, actually spoken to them. He quickly slammed the hatch shut, and double-checked his map.

*　　*　　*

Next time he got it right. This hatch revealed hundreds of books, piled in tottering heaps reaching almost to the ceiling. The room was a complete shambles. But no one was there.

Moss helped to lower us down, then dropped down himself. There was barely room to move. He balanced on a chair and pulled the hatch shut, then motioned us to crouch behind the mass of books and wait. But we weren't waiting long. Footsteps clacked outside and a female voice rang out.

'Professor,' it said. 'You missed all the excitement! Some animal's gotten up in the air ducts. A feral pig, apparently. Everybody's rushing around to hunt it.' There was a laugh in reply, and the handle rattled. I looked through a gap in the books as two shapes entered the room − a secretarial-looking woman, and a white-haired man wearing what looked like some ancient Greek or Roman garment; a toga, himation, or something of that sort.

The woman picked up something from a pile of books near the door, then left again, and the professor (for that was who he was, Professor Pommas), left to his own devices, picked a book up, seemingly at random, and smiled a sad but happy smile...a smile that made me think of one I had worn myself when thinking of the Friendly Girl. I felt a sudden sense of unreality. A circle seemed to close.

Then Moss leaped out from behind the books. When the startled professor recognised him, he proceeded to berate him. 'By the shades, man, you might have knocked!'

'Shhh...'

Moss went through the scanning rigmarole; on finding nothing, he asked me to step forward and show Pommas the notebook. Appearing nonplussed as we ventured out from hiding, he took the note and read it, mouthing silently along. A frown creased his brow.

'Where did you get this?' When it had been explained, he pattered urgently up and down, as best he could among the clutter. As he paced he spoke, seemingly to himself, but we heard his words quite clearly. He spoke about the 'Ahu' mentioned in the notebook, a race who apparently once lived on

Cavendish, the island Moss had told us about, which was at loggerheads with the other isle of St. Vigeans.

The Ahu had vanished several hundred years ago, and were said to have taken some 'roads into the sea'. Pommas, an anthropologist, knew much about these legends, but didn't know what 'roads into the sea' meant.

When probed, he thought the 'they' referred to could have been the Dead Shadows cult.

'They have friends all through the government. They have infiltrated every level,' he said, and his tone was not that of a wild conspiratorialist, but of one who had studied and seen a good deal of life. He believed their plans somehow involved taking advantage of the aftermath of the Scarlottian Wars, and the current world situation — conflict and natural disaster alike — to work towards their cherished doctrine of complete human extinction. Death was their delight.

But there was another cult, opposed to them, he told us — and that was the cult of the Bird King.

Several of his students had joined it, he related proudly. The Bird King cult placed no compulsion upon its members, and never sought 'conversions', only free spirits who entered of their own accord. And while the Shadows cult exalted death, the Bird cult honoured *life and death in balance*.

'I am sympathetic for them. They believe in what can never be tamed or trampled. Wherever people think the Bird King is, he is actually somewhere else. Though sometimes, *sometimes*, he coalesces, and his wings converge...and for a brief moment, in time and space, you and he are one...'

* * *

Pommas led us out of the building and bundled us into his car. He had a hard time convincing Moss, who stood for a while gazing wistfully at the air duct, but at long last complied.

Pommas announced his intention to take us to meet someone high up in the Bird cult, but first wanted to stop at his club Downtown, to show the notebook to a contact of his. I shrugged, having no choice but to trust him.

It took twenty minutes to reach the neo-Romanesque building, octagonal in shape, with a dark slate roof, and white-green limestone columns. This was the home of the Gillies Club, or 'Ship of Fools', modelled loosely on the Pall Mall clubs of London. Here the locally powerful could relax in a spick and homely environment, membership being by invitation only; Pommas had been offered it as a Somebody, no matter that his views were at odds with those of many other members. Enemies could meet freely under this roof to debate ideas, and the club, despite its laid-back air, was a hotbed of intrigue.

Pommas opened the front door with an old-fashioned digital key, then stuck his head through to see if the coast was clear. He ushered Molly and I into the ornate entry hall (Moss had chosen to remain in the car), then hurried us up a spiral stair to the left. We emerged on the first floor, and took another stairway opposite the first. He led us to a dingy room with musty furniture, and motioned us to wait there.

'Hardly anyone comes in here...if anyone *does* disturb you, tell them you're guests of myself. I'll be back soon, hopefully with information.' Then he dropped his voice to a whisper: '*Don't talk about the notebook, even among yourselves*'; and left the room.

We sat in musty chairs, awkwardly silent now that we were alone again. I looked at Molly, unsure of what to say...then looked away, in case she saw me looking. I could see she was unhappy. We were certainly on different wavelengths, mine being 'unsettled alone'...but then she jumped up and began pacing round the room.

'I'm going to take a look around,' she said. 'I've never been in a place like this.' (That, or she couldn't tolerate my saturnine countenance any longer.)

'What if Pommas comes back?'

'Don't be so boring.' She was in a fey mood, I could see. And could I blame her? She had gone from a glamorous lifestyle to a world of ducts and sewers, of professors, spies, and dusty cobwebbed rooms. But my pity evaporated when

I looked up and realised she was already gone!

I leapt up. I couldn't let this happen.

I raced to the door, but she wasn't in the corridor. Then I glanced back in the room, and noticed a dark patch I hadn't seen before, in the corner. This was the entry to a narrow wooden passageway. When my eyes adjusted, I saw her up ahead and caught up.

'We should wait,' I started to say, but she brushed me aside. She was brimming with pent-up anger, and perfectly capable of taking it out on me if she couldn't find a better target, so I trailed wordlessly behind, waiting for her steam to dissipate.

The passage became a balcony. A brightly-lit room was spread below us.

Then someone entered, and we froze. It was a man with a balding head and glaring eyes, who paced up and down in agitation.

Molly, retreating further back into the shadows, made a scuffling sound and his head snapped quickly up. We froze again.

'Who's there?' he demanded, staring into the blackness. 'Who the blithering gibbocks is that!?'

He peered and squinted, but the gallery was considerably darker than the room – to him it must be a mere black space at the top edge of the wall. He peered a bit longer, then turned and left the room.

Molly crept forward, more softly this time, and I followed. We soon came alongside another brightly-lit room. This time, two people sat below. I recognised one of them immediately – Blinny Gunnarsen from the Artists' Guild – but the other was a stranger.

We stood stock still, the acoustics relaying their conversation marvellously to us in the top tier. They seemed to be talking about the scientist Nemet Breisler, who I remembered hearing about on the newz at Herb's.

'What did he *do* that was so important?' Blinny was asking, yawning a familiar yawn.

'What did he do? Apart from trying to reconfigure reality into a kind of semantic network?'

'A what?'

'A semantic network – where *everything* can be classified and transferred to other formats. If it's successful, then virtual reality will be...without limits.'

Blinny yawned again. 'You scientists take these things *so* damned seriously.'

'And you artists are a waste of the taxpayer's money...scoundrels.' They smiled and raised their glasses in a toast.

I would have liked to stay and hear more about these 'semantic networks', but Molly was already wandering slowly down the next passageway. I sighed, and followed.

The next gallery overlooked a room filled with old, decaying books (legal volumes, from the look). A stout mahogany table stood in the centre.

I cleared my throat.

'We should go back,' I argued. 'What if Pommas returns and we're gone?'

'I...' began Molly. But the door of the room opened and she hushed herself. Two people entered...and one of them was Pommas. The other was small man with grey, greasy hair and a shiny leather jacket.

'We can talk privately in here,' he said.

'There's nowhere private in this building,' scoffed Pommas. 'Everywhere you go, eavesdroppers!'

'Well, it can't be helped. So tell me more. And what exactly do you want of me?'

'The trip I'm undertaking could be dangerous. I'll be travelling out to Cavendish, as I told you. There are those who might not want me to get there in one piece. For political reasons...but that's no concern of yours. All I need from you, in return for the favour you owe me – and this will make us quits – is safe haven for my friends. I need you to hide them, get them off the island, and fit them up with new identities. I *know* you have the wherewithal to arrange it.'

I was staggered at this. What on earth was going on? Vonny would be pleased at the identity change thing, at any rate...

'Oh yes, and I think I can guess who those friends of yours are, Pommas. Bit bloody obvious, isn't it? The actress and the bionic simpleton. Everyone and his dog is after *them*.'

'Then you'll know how important it is to hide them. And on top of your cancelled debt, I will also give you admittance to our Order...something you have been craving for as long as I have known you...providing you meet certain requirements, of course.'

'Little old me! And I know *your* opinion of my suitability. You must really value these friends of yours, Pommas.'

'It's important they stay alive. Not to mention the ethical issue...they're in my care, after all.'

'All right. You will give me what I have long craved for. Spiritual uplift. It's too hard to resist. So where are they?'

'Here, in this building. Hiding upstairs.'

'Thank you,' said the man, and pulled out a gun with a silencer on the end. Pommas blinked in surprise, and the man laughed.

'I'm afraid, my friend, that there's a contract out on one of them. As for the cyborg, he's wanted by the authorities. And as for your Order...well, I've discovered a greater god. Mammon! I long ceased to believe in your gibberish.'

He pulled the trigger, and there was a sound like a puff of compressed air. Pommas fell to the ground with a choking gasp, eyes rolling. A red hole blossomed forth in his clean white himation. We stood rooted in horror, and Molly made a near-inaudible whimpering sound.

The man dragged Pommas' body to a cupboard and thrust it in. It was clearly a little-used room, so perhaps he was counting on the body staying there indefinitely – or perhaps he just didn't care. He opened the door, scanned the hall, and left the room, never once having considered the gallery above him.

'Run,' I whispered, but there was no need to say it. Both of us bolted down the gallery at top speed. I saw Blinny and the scientist look up as we hurtled noisily past the chamber where they sat. We reached the room where Pommas had left us, then bolted down both flights of spiral stairs. The front door opened from the inside without a key, luckily, and we stepped through, panting furiously. There was no-one in sight except for Vonny, still waiting in Pommas' car.

We jumped in and I described everything that had happened between gasps.

'What did he mean,' said Vonny, 'that there's a contract out on one of you?' Here Molly began to sob, head in her hands.

'It's my agent,' she blubbed.

'What agent?'

'Ward Lardle.'

'The gangster?'

I groaned. That was all we needed.

'I'm sure they would love to kill me,' she sobbed. 'To profit from the death industry generated. Ratings, merchandise, spin-offs...tickets to the funeral...'

Moss had lost his assertiveness somewhat. I prodded him in the ribs, and asked what we should do. Finally, he resurfaced.

'First, we'll hotwire this car,' he snapped. He ripped at a panel next to the steering wheel, and pulled a Swiss army knife from his pocket. After fiddling around for a minute or so, he succeeded in removing the ignition drum from its casing, so it could be turned with a flat-headed screwdriver rather than a key. His knife having such a tool, the car soon roared into life.

'And *now* where?' I yelled.

'A temple, outside the city,' he growled. 'Pommas spoke to me once of its abbess. I'll take you there. In fact, it may be our only hope.'

We took the freeway, then an exit onto a road that soon had us out in the rainforest. We drove some twenty minutes without seeing a single human habitation, and then at last reached a wooden gate set in a long perimeter fence. Vonny got out of the car and hollered – so unlike his usual silent and secretive behaviour that my suspicions were once more inflamed.

Almost at once, two hooded figures glided from out of the foliage. They were carrying guns, but these were not pointed at us. Vonny spoke to them briefly, and they opened the gate. Then one of them led us wordlessly up a muddy track while the other stayed behind, presumably to keep guard. I felt I had no choice but to follow. It was almost as if my legs were walking for me.

I couldn't help but marvel at the big and brightly-coloured flowers that peeped gently out of every nook and cranny of the deep-green foliage. Everything seemed basking in its own languid intensity.

Vonny interrupted my reverie by explaining loudly: 'It's a cult of Westerners... they adopted esoteric beliefs based on *one* of the natives' legends. Shallow, maybe, but Pommas thought highly of 'em.'

Our guides seemed to take no offence, however. They led us to a building with a large wooden balcony made from dark brown canes of the rainforest. The house, if that was what it was, was comprised of different coloured timbers and woven vines. There were gaps between the beams for ventilation. Getting closer, I realised it was actually part of a complex that seemed to wind and stretch through the hills.

Was it one building or many? I couldn't tell.

Then a young man wearing robes of a light material emerged, and beckoned us onto the balcony. He knew about us (he claimed), and had expected us to arrive this very day. He introduced himself as Brother Tarfaxion. The newz was full of our 'escape', said to be arranged with the help of one Professor Pommas, who had subsequently defected with us.

'But that's not what happened at all,' Molly exclaimed. 'Pommas was *murdered* by someone who also wanted to get to us. They're lying about it!'

'Murdered!' exclaimed Tarfaxion, eyes wide. Clearly he hadn't foreseen this. 'That is grave news, indeed. For while Pommas wasn't exactly one of us – he belonged to a different Order – we considered him an important and open-minded ally. In fact he was due here soon, for a crucial meeting with our abbess. He was a learned man, but there were things he didn't know, things she was going to enlighten him on. And now he's gone...'

Then a tall woman with red hair and pale, silky skin sailed out onto the balcony, casting a calm, almost shy glance at we who were gathered there.

'I am Prestal Clare, abbess of this compound, and priestess of the Bird King. Come inside and I will address your thoughts as best I can.'

11

BIRD KING

We filed into a large wooden room ringed by pillars, and carved in a simple, tapering style from hard dark native wood. The floorboards had gaps between them, perhaps for ventilation, and the whole chamber, despite its darkness, had an organic, spacious air. Woven mats had been placed on the floor, and Prestal Clare bade us be seated before settling down herself.

'We were expecting you.'

'From the newz?'

'Yes. But Maddem also told us that some people would follow after him. Around the time the Bird King begins to awaken, in fact. And that time, we believe, is now.'

'Maddem!' I immediately showed the abbess the pilot's notebook.

'Maddem is the 'Last Poet', right?'

She nodded.

'Then what is the 'secret stair'?'

'First I will tell you about a legend, Mr. Lune...a legend that has come to haunt my nightmares.' She laid her head on her hand in such a way that I found it hard to believe she had ever suffered from nightmares. But her brow, furrowed slightly, made her seem human, at least in part.

'Listen,' she said, and the room became still and silent. The light seemed to fade and shrink, as the very colours of nature sank around the abbess. I wavered between rapture and suspicion. I felt I was about to learn something, something very important. But would it be something true, or were nature and this woman in on a double take? I tried to shut out this cynical voice.

And then she began to chant.

The Bloodleach, she sang, was in lust with the Starmaiden...and that was where all the world's sorrow, its turmoil sprang from. But who was the Bloodleach, and who was the Starmaiden?

It all began a long, long time ago. The Bloodleach's real name, if he ever had one, was forgotten. He had desired her, ever since he saw her in the realms outside Saturn, in a tremulous haze of crystalline stars. Her hair shone through the Milky Way like a comet. But she didn't return his feelings, and fled from him. This he could not forget...so he jealously sought absolute power over the first object he came across.

Which happened to be the Earth.

And bit by bit he lost his own special power – the power to connect worlds. He became dependent on the life-forces of others, and fiercely jealous of those already in his sway. He tried to stop the inhabitants of Earth from growing – and tried to shut off their access to the stars.

'But there is a way out,' she concluded. 'One way that still leads to a different world. A means of open knowledge and connection. And that is the door the Ahu and Maddem both discovered, and apparently went through.'

'But *where* did they go?'

'To another dimension.'

'But surely,' interjected Tarfaxion, 'the 'secret stair' is just a metaphor for the gate to the hidden potential that resides in mankind? Do you mean to say that this stairway actually *exists*, in a physical sense?' He looked astonished.

'Yes, it exists,' said Prestal Clare with gravity. 'It is an actually existing portal, and Maddem discovered its whereabouts. It is the same path the Ahu followed. And now, it appears the Patagonians also suspect its existence, and may be searching for it even as we speak.

'Where?'

'We think it is on an island, somewhere in the ocean...but we don't know its location. I believe the Bloodleach is searching for it, also. He is desperate that his servants find the portal, and seal it off. Because if he doesn't block it off, then what he fears most could come true.'

'What does he fear most?'

'That those on earth could communicate, in dreams, with his great enemy, the Bird King. For the Bird King is the one the Starmaiden secretly longs and pines for...but whom she *cannot awaken*.'

'And he fears that *humans* could wake him?'

'Precisely. And the signs say that he is only sleeping fitfully, and may soon awake.'

'Signs?'

'A shadowy and horrifying figure has been seen in the hills at night, feeding on people's fear. This, we believe, is the Gardener of All Screams, the Bloodleach's avatar or servant. The Gardener could never manifest so blatantly if the Bird King's dreams had not grown troubled and confused. The Gardener, we believe, is here to oversee those who are carrying out the Bloodleach's designs...presumably he will be visiting Patagonia on his travels.'

Tarfaxion chimed in again: 'We believe there is something in man that is qualitative and irreducible. Call it soul, or whatever. The Patagonians are working to destroy this, and to make man a quantity, a cipher...a soulless being, doing the bidding of Bloodleach.'

'They are aiming for complete world domination, just as before, when they were named the Curia,' said Prestal Clare.

'Are you Scarlottians, then?'

'Our opinions on the late emperor are mixed, and it is not the right moment to discuss such things. Time is short. We know that a prominent member of the Dead Shadows cult has made direct contact with the Gardener, wrongly believing that he can control *it*, rather than the other way around. The Dead Shadows people are merely pawns in the Bloodleach's game, as are the Patagonians.'

'Dead Shadows are a bunch of harmless fools,' said Tarfaxion. 'Their leader is a man named Herb, a conceited buffoon who works in the Interior Ministry.'

'Herb! I know him...he was my host when I arrived here.' The shock was only superficial, though...deep down it seemed to fit. 'He was *warning* me about the Shadows cult.'

The abbess laughed. 'You see what Brother Tarfaxion means when he calls him conceited!'

But then I thought of the incident with his wife.

'Are you sure he isn't dangerous?'

'His plans will never come to fruition. In fact, we have reason to believe the Patagonians themselves are funding Dead Shadows, to sow fear in the population while they gather their threads together. A distraction more than anything.'

'I knew it!' shrieked Vonny, an odd look of ecstasy in his eyes.

'Furthermore,' continued the abbess, the goals of Dead Shadows are impossible to attain, because you could never destroy all life throughout the cosmos...even if you succeeded in wiping it out on Earth, it would only spring up in some other planet or dimension.'

I found myself nodding in agreement.

'All this we were going to explain to Pommas,' said Tarfaxion. 'That Dead Shadows are unimportant, a sideshow. But we never got the chance.' Now he informed the abbess of Pommas' murder, and she sighed deeply, tears forming in her eyes.

'So often it is the best who perish,' she said. 'But I had a feeling our next meeting would never take place. Pommas thought Dead Shadows were controlling the Patagonians. We were going to explain to him it was exactly the other way around. And the Patagonians think humanity should be enslaved, not abolished.'

'But what do *you* believe?' piped Molly suddenly. 'What do *you* want for humanity?'

'It's a complicated question,' said Prestal Clare, with another sigh. 'Let me tell you a bit more about our beliefs first. While the term Bird King is taken from the indigenous religion of the Mani, we ourselves are obviously European. It is not a matter of 'cultural appropriation', however...not least because the belief in Bird King actually *predates* that of the Mani. In fact, we believe they had it from a race called the Ahu, the same ones mentioned in the notebook you found.

'So although we ourselves believe in the existence of many gods and spirits, the Bird King is the one who, for us, keeps recurring again and again. He partakes of the inner essence of things, of existence and the universe itself. Some believe that the logos of things is Change, others that it is something *unchanging*, that Change itself is an illusion. But we believe in both.

'The world is constantly changing because it comes from the dreams of the Bird King...but there is something unchanging beneath it, and that is the Dreamer himself, the one the Mani call Bird King.'

'Are you saying,' said Molly with a frown, 'that the whole world is nothing but a dream?'

'Yes,' she laughed. 'But *what* a dream.'

'It seems pretty real to me,' said Molly, stomping her foot on the wooden floor.

'It seems 'real' because you are part of the dream yourself, and so am I. And so are the Patagonians, and if he knew it, yes, even the Bloodleach himself. And who knows, perhaps even the Bird King himself is part of his *own* dream. As to why there is a dream at all...who knows?' She laughed again; it was a beautiful crystalline sound.

'Does the Bird King know?'

'The Bird King is unconscious. And that is another of our key beliefs. It is up to *us* to illumine the Bird King's creation. Some do this through art, and my old friend Maddem was one of those people. But here we follow another path, that of meditation and training the mind. We must become the Bird King's consciousness. Does existence create consciousness, or the other way around? These things can't be answered in words. There is another language, the language of the birds. To speak it means to be as free as possible from the world of illusion. And they say it is only spoken in the Green Land...'

At this, a memory faintly stirred.

'The Green Land...where's that?' I asked.

'It is our lost homeland, the homeland that never existed, and which we must create. And that is what we attempt to do here, by directing our own dreams, and projecting their influence on the world, like a bird riding a thermal.'

'But what happens if this Bird King himself gains consciousness?' asked Molly , who seemed genuinely interested, in contrast to Vonny, who was yawning beside her. 'Wouldn't that mean your efforts are a waste of time?' The abbess and Brother Tarfaxion exchanged a significant glance, and as they did so, a faint tremor ran through the floor beneath us.

'An earth tremor,' said Prestal Clare. 'Very odd that it happened just as you said that. Some say that earthquakes and tremors *are* a sign the Bird King is trying to awaken, as the dream threatens to turn to nightmare.'

'Poor Bird King,' Molly murmured, in a strange, faraway voice, but the abbess smiled.

'It's okay,' she said. 'We don't know that he suffers.'

'But if he *did* awake, would it be a good or a bad thing?' Again the abbess and Tarfaxion looked at one another.

'Well, there you have cut to the heart of our problem,' said Prestal Clare with a frown. She was silent for a while, then slowly spoke.

'Some say that if he ever fully awakened, the world would immediately end.'

Brother Tarfaxion burst out: 'But it is his very *sleep* that allows the Bloodleach to carry out his plans.'

'No,' she shook her head. 'That is irrelevant, because we are the Bird King's agents...and *we* are not asleep.'

Tarfaxion looked doubtful, but said nothing.

'Of late, you see,' she turned to me, 'this compound has been split into two factions. Not bitter enemies, of course, but factions nonetheless. I myself refuse to take sides, but the problem is a real one.

'The first faction believes that we must do whatever it takes to *stop* the Bird King from awakening. The other believes that if he *did* awake, everything would turn to good...and even if the world ends as a result, just as the tears of the phoenix bring healing, so a new and infinitely better world will be created. The logical conclusion is that it is our *duty* to awaken him.'

'That is what I believe,' said Tarfaxion proudly.

'You would never see that brave new world, of course.'

'No, but I rejoice in merely knowing it would exist, and that others may experience it.'

'So, you see,' sighed the abbess, 'we have our problems. But enough about those. Tell us more about your own situation, now. You can speak freely, for we're all friends here. I sense the good in you,' she smiled. 'You have some powerful gift for the Bird King inside you, I can feel it.' She was looking at *me* as she said it.

Falteringly, I told her how I had come to Mantuaroa, and all that had occurred since my arrival. When I had finished she looked at me thoughtfully.

'Maddem, as I mentioned, was a friend of mine. And before he disappeared, he told me some people would later follow him. Maybe he wasn't completely sure, but he had dreamt of them, those who would bring back a powerful weapon to use against the enemy. The Patagonians, or Curia, as they were known until recently, had given orders for Maddem to be quietly killed off for his subversive epic poem. It hadn't been published, and still hasn't...the manuscript has disappeared...I suspect he may have taken it with him for safekeeping...but they came to know of it, and wished to suppress if before it reached the public. Maddem only escaped in the nick of time. He had acquired the password to go through the portal...he didn't say how. But he left behind clues for those who would follow.'

'That makes it imperative that, if these people *are* the ones Maddem foresaw, they follow him as soon as possible,' said Tarfaxion, 'before the Patagonians seal off access to the portal.'

Prestal Clare nodded and gave us a searching glance. 'And *are* you the ones? *Are* you up to the task? Are you ready to bring back a weapon from another world?'

'I am,' I said, suddenly feeling that I was.

'But I want to find out what happened to my friend Scuzzy,' said Molly. 'He's disappeared.'

'You're a friend of Scuzzy? You needn't worry. I have it on good authority that he is hiding in a native village, one whose villagers hate the government and will never give him up.' Molly looked greatly relieved.

Then the abbess turned to Vonny – but it appeared he had fallen asleep.

She laughed. 'Very well,' she said. 'To get through the portal you need a password, and I have no idea what it is. Maddem didn't tell me, nor did I ask.'

'But where did he learn it?'

'I don't know how or from who, but I believe he learnt it on the island of Cavendish.'

12

NULLY'S WHARF

We had to go. And time was running out. Scuzzy was in hiding, Pommas dead. No one but the abbess could help us.

'So how do we get there?'

'You have to go to the embassy,' she said. 'They have enacted strict new quarantine laws in light of the Grey Death, so it will be difficult to leave Mantuaroa. But the Cavendish Embassy will give you protection until they can think of a way to get you off the island.'

'What if they refuse to help us?'

'I will give you a letter of introduction,' she said. 'I am on good terms with some of the smaller island nations...and they are no friends of the Mantuaroan government, believe me.'

Vonny, when awoken, knew where the embassy was, and said he would drive us there. He had nothing to lose, he said, and perhaps he was right. After a solemn farewell from the abbess and Tarfaxion, we puttered off, missive in hand.

We filled Vonny in on what he had missed after falling asleep. He was starting to get a grasp on the situation, though he looked highly sceptical when discussing metaphysical entities such as the Bird King. He already knew, of course, that Cavendish was a cold and distant island a long way to the south, with very little infrastructure. And of course there was supposed to be a war brewing there – he had told us that himself.

The Cavendish Embassy was in an obscure street between Downtown and the south docks. Mantuaroa treated its Pacific neighbours with contempt (except for the larger and more powerful like Fiji), and the embassies

390

of the smaller countries were relegated to this one small street. Most doubled as shops, to offset the ludicrous rental costs the Mantuaroans imposed on the embassies of all non-Curia-aligned countries. The despised micronations maintained embassies here regardless, however, for Mantuaroa was the economic powerhouse of the Pacific, and they couldn't afford not to.

The sky was completely overcast now, and it felt like a storm might be brewing. We parked the car and entered the strange and gloomy street of embassies, a seedy, run-down lane whose tottering wooden buildings all seemed to have large and shadowy doorways.

'There'll be a plaque above each door saying which country it belongs to,' said Vonny.

Some of the embassies were grubbier than others; some were open shopfronts, where goods were on display– souvenirs, comestibles, or fireworks. Vonny was right about the plaques, and one said: *Cavendish*. The door was shut, and Vonny knocked loudly.

Before anyone could answer, an old woman stuck her head out from a window in the opposite building. The plaque over *its* door read: *St. Vigeans*.

'Cavendish scum!' the woman yelled, and threw something, before quickly slamming the window shut again. An egg had just missed Vonny's head before splattering on the side of the building. There were many stained and discoloured patches on the shopfront, suggesting previous missiles of a similar nature. Something about the woman had seemed familiar, however...I remembered the old crone from the Downtown café, and wondered if they were one and the same, before dismissing the idea as absurd. Surely not?

'I hope she doesn't alert the authorities,' muttered Vonny. 'An embassy should be sacrosanct, but...' He left the sentence unfinished...then the door opened and a woman stood blinking out at us. Her hair was grey and long, so long that it spilled across her shoulders, giving her a stately, aristocratic look. Doubtless she had been beautiful once, and even now there was a regal air about her. She wore a shawl, and small beads and feathers were woven through her hair...tastefully, though, and not in the manner of some extrovert neo-hippie. She looked at us questioningly.

'Are you the ambassador?' ventured Vonny nervously. She shook her head and smiled faintly.

'I am the Undersecretary,' she said. 'The Ambassador is in a meeting. Come in and wait, if you like. He shouldn't be long. Is it urgent?'

'Well, yes,' said Vonny, as we stepped across the threshold. She led us to an antechamber, a bare room with ricketty chairs, and bade us sit.

'You're Molly, aren't you dear? I was at the theatre the night you were abducted. You caused a right to-do. And these gentlemen are your abductors, are they?'

'No. I wasn't abducted, I ran away. What happened at the theatre after I left?'

'They had to completely improvise the second half, and it was awful. Passaro was *furious*. Didn't you have an understudy?'

'No. It wasn't thought necessary for a once-off performance.'

'I see. Now, would anyone care for a cup of tea?' Without waiting for an answer she left the room and came back with a tray of cups and a laser kettle, which she filled from an old tin flask.

'We don't use the tap water here,' she explained. 'We bring our own in from Cavendish when the supply boat comes. It's due soon, as a matter of fact.'

'And is it going back to Cavendish soon?'

'Oh yes, it always does.'

Then the sound of raised voices came from a nearby room. The gist of what was being said escaped us, but certain words and phrases were very clear. *Scurrilous lunk-eared mongrel* was one. *Brazen, bootlicking screech-monkey* was another.

'That's the Ambassador,' said the Undersecretary, sounding apologetic. 'He's a trifle...undiplomatic, I'm afraid. *I* was offered the post, you know, but I declined for lack of people skills. Perhaps I should have accepted,' she sighed, as a fresh burst of obscenities came through the wall.

She and the Ambassador were the only staff here, she explained – and in fact this was the only overseas embassy Cavendish actually maintained.

'We simply don't have the population to support a diplomatic corps. Those with any skills are in the military, as we're under constant threat of war from St. Vigeans now. And this embassy, too, may have to shut down, because if they quarantine our supply boat...'

'That's what we'd like to...er...' began Vonny. But a door slammed, derailing his train of thought. Someone stamped down the hall, and clattered loudly out the front door. Then another man came clomping down the hall and glared into the room at us. His red, haughty face and bulging eyes unnerved me somewhat.

'These people want to see you on a very important matter,' said the Undersecretary.

'Well?' he demanded, entering the room and staring down at Vonny, hands on hips. Vonny seemed to wither in that unrelenting glare. He stuttered and stammered. It was left to *me* to tell our story, while the Ambassador listened angrily, rubbing his chin in thought.

'We can get you out to Cavendish,' he said curtly when I had finished, and he had read the letter from Prestal Clare. 'The fast boat leaves today. You're in luck. I don't know anything about a magical portal, but it's clear that you should meet with our P-R.'

'The supply boat comes once a fortnight,' explained the Undersecretary, 'with supplies, trade goods, and coded messages. We don't trust telecommunications when they're all in the hands of the Curia, or whatever they call themselves these days.'

'There may be other ways to get you out,' snapped the Ambassador, 'but the fast boat is the surest. And so far it has been exempted from the general quarantine...so far. There's no Grey Death in *our* neck of the woods. But if they do quarantine us, we'll have to...'

'Shut down the embassy ,' finished Molly. The Ambassador glared at her.

'No bottled water, no embassy,' said the Undersecretary, with a sad smile. 'You'll be safe on

Cavendish, dear. And our P-R will be interested in that notebook.'

'P-R?'

'Prince-Regent. He's our head of state, and takes a keen interest in world affairs.'

'Do you have royalty, then?'

'We have aristocracy, and I am one of them. But it doesn't mean much anymore. There aren't any real differences between us and the commoners now. We're all in the same boat. The population's dwindling, and our lives become more impoverished and Spartan. Many youngsters leave and don't return. And those who stay don't seem to have their hearts in it. Despair is sniffing everywhere, like a pig in the night. Not even the newcomers are able to stave it off.'

'The newcomers?'

'I dare say you'll meet them on the island.'

*　　*　　*

An hour later we headed down to Nully's Wharf where the fast boat docked, to see if it had come in.

But as we did so, my artificial limbs suddenly went berserk, wrenching out of my phantom-grasp, and attempting to walk the other way.

Actually, 'walk' is perhaps not the best description – it was more of a psychotic frogmarch. I crashed several times into the side of a parked car, before jumping on the bonnet and attempting to march over its roof.

The Ambassador and Vonny hauled me down and grabbed my shoulders, one each side, but they couldn't stop or slow me, such was the newfound strength in 'my' legs. I was stretched out almost horizontal, feet dragging relentlessly on. If I could have viewed myself from outside, doubtless it would have been hilarious – but as circumstances were, I wasn't laughing.

Then I remembered the 'control circuits' – or so I thought of them. These were panels in the calves, whose contents I wasn't exactly sure of. But if I could get them open, perhaps I could shut the legs down.

'Have you got your army knife?' I hissed to Vonny. He pulled it from his pocket. 'Okay. Now hand me it and let go.'

'Are you sure?'

'Yes.'

'You're not going to try and hack your own legs off or something?'

'Just let go!'

'I smell a conspiracy here...' But he let go, just the same.

I pulled my trousers up above the knees. There were no screws in the panels, so I began to prise them open with the main blade. It was hard doing it while the legs were moving. The others, who now guessed what I intended, yelled encouragement as they ran along behind me. I rounded the corner into a shopping street and people stared as I goose-stepped past, hacking at my legs with a knife. They seemed to think it some outlandish piece of performance art: Schwarzkogler meets John Cleese.

Eventually I got the first panel off, and ripped the circuits out. The leg stopped working immediately, but the right one kept plummeting along, causing the left to buckle, and I landed in a heap. After that it was easy to get the remaining panel off. I put the circuits in my pocket in case they could be re-wired, but I was now completely crippled.

*　　*　　*

The others hauled me up and dragged me back to the wharf, now almost a kilometre away.

'We have to hurry or you'll miss the boat,' snarled the Ambassador. 'If you've quite finished playing the clown, that is.'

'I couldn't...'

'SHUT IT,' he roared, ever the diplomat.

'It was some kind of electronic attack,' panted Vonny. 'Someone must be hard on our tail...but who?'

People applauded as I was dragged past, thinking me exhausted after a particularly good performance. But now something else was happening. A weird, queasy, sickening feeling spread slowly through my chest and abdomen. Then I felt a sharp pain in my lower back, around the level of the kidneys.

'My organs,' I rasped. 'Did they put that stuff in my innards as well? That grey plastic? I think they're trying to shut my organs down.'

'Who are *they?*' hissed Vonny. But I couldn't answer.

'Is there a medic on the ship?' he panted.

'Yes,' said the Undersecretary. 'The captain is a trained

paramedic, and there are facilities on board.'

I ground my teeth in pain. It felt like there was crushed glass in my blood. My vision faintly blurred, and memories flooded back...of hospital, and an eagle.

After what seemed like hours, we arrived at Nully's Wharf. The boat was moored at one end, a jet-powered craft.

But as the Captain stepped on the wharf to greet us, a harsh, sardonic voice rang out behind us.

'Mr. Vonny Moss?'

We turned to see three men standing there.

'You're a fool, Moss. A real moron,' said the one in the middle, who looked like the leader, being slightly better dressed. He had a sullen, arrogant face and wore an old-style hat and coat, despite the tropical warmth.

Molly trembled. 'It's Ward Lardle, my agent,' she whispered to me. 'And the one on the right is his hit man, Muzza Gunt.'

'Did you really think you could bamboozle us with the tracking device, Moss? We tracked you down through this clown's legs, you dope. And we know all about you, too, Moss. Or should I call you *Plugg?*' As he said this, he held up a small electronic implement – I guessed it must be some kind of jamming device that they had used to override my legs, though where they had obtained it I couldn't imagine.

The other two gangsters now pulled guns from their pockets.

'The Molly creature is mine,' he chuckled coarsely. 'Now kindly hand her over, so I can liquidate the bitch. If you hand her over nice and easy like, I *might* let the rest of you go free.'

'*Fuck you*,' screamed Molly, from the bottom of her lungs. Then something unexpected happened. Three *more* men stepped from around the corner, pointing guns at the first three.

'I think not,' said their leader, in a cut-glass accent. His companions wore masks, but there was no mistaking *his* what-ho visage.

'Herb,' I cried.

'Yes, Herb,' he sneered. 'Did you really think you could escape the clutches of Dead Shadows? Your legs make you...valuable...to us. Would you like to see what we did to the man who created them?'

'Created them?' I stammered weakly.

'Yes. Don't you know they were designed by Nemet Breisler himself? You may recall from the newz that Breisler is 'missing'. Just have a look at what we did to him, ha ha.' He pulled out a phone with a projector, and beamed the footage onto the wharf in front of us (which considering the wooden surface, came out very well).

'*We mark now the opening of the real, inner Festival*,' intoned a voice on the recording. Four were present, wearing masks. The room was decked in red, and red curtains lined the walls.

I remembered reading that red was a sacred colour throughout the Pacific, due to its rarity in a world of mostly blues and greens. But I suspected it was used here not to further any sacred tradition, but rather to mock it. It was a dirty kind of red – not the hot colour of blood, but a rusty, bilious maroon.

A covered box had been placed on the red-draped platform in the middle of the room. One of the men, obviously the leader (Herb?), stepped forward and took the cover away, revealing a cage, and the four contemplated the sight. A severed head, presumably that of Breisler, lay with dark wells of congealed blood where its eyes had once been. Also present were two white doves – one dead, a bloody mess on the floor; the other still alive, but covered in hideous wounds. I contemplated

the scene in horror before realising what it meant –
doves, though associated with peace, will fight to the
bloody death if confined in close quarters. One of them
had killed the other, before pecking out the eyes of the
legendary computer scientist.

'*Behold, the secret, inner meaning of existence,*' said the
recorded Herb, in a drearily pompous voice.

'All *life is incurably corrupt,*' spoke the second.

'*But we are those who will make an end of it,*' thundered the
third.

And finally the fourth spoke; a woman's voice, but
tired, mechanical.

'*Let the Festival begin,*' it said.

And the four turned and left the room, then playback
ceased.

'And what is the point of that?' yelled the
Ambassador. 'Why kill this Breisler?'

'Most people simply can't *think,*' said Herb, with a
pleasant smile. 'They think enough to live from day to
day, sure, but not enough to see right down to the bottom
of things.'

'Breisler was a genius,' I croaked. 'Of *course* he could
think.'

'I am referring to 'people' in the general sense, young
Nicholas. Maybe you should think a bit yourself before
opening your mouth, and let me finish, eh?

'It's obvious that people *don't* think. Because if they
did, they would have to agree with Goethe's
Mephistopheles, that it would be better, far better, if
nothing ever was...if nothing had ever existed to begin
with.' He tore his mask off, and there was a excited,
almost sexual grin on his face. 'That's the terrible truth
behind the universe, my friend. For the suffering of the
world is beyond all comprehension, so that I shudder as
I attempt to imagine it. I shudder at the word *suffering*
itself. I even shudder at the word *shudder.*'

'You're a blathering nitwit,' roared the Ambassador,
clearly unable to restrain himself. 'You should be drawn
and quartered. Your moustache alone is a crime against
breeding and taste.'

'Does someone want to cap this waffle, and get down
to the nitty gritty,' said Lardle, who had been forgotten

in the heat of the philosophical discussion. 'How much do you want for the girl?'

Herb smiled, and pulled something from his pocket.

'This, my friend, is Raskar Pela. I got it from a contact in Chile. I pondered for some time how to get it to the maximum possible number of people. The water supply, as you know, is untenable, as not everyone has the iron gut necessary to drink it. I only ever touch bottled water myself...Perrier is my favourite.

'But then I hit on the solution: to distribute it by *air*.' Herb then explained at tedious length what Raskar Pela actually was. He rambled on for so long about its chemical structure that I expected the police to come, but the wharf and surrounds remained deserted, no doubt due to the quarantine that only the southern fast boat appeared to be exempt from.

Raskar Pela was apparently a juice made from the seed pod of a rare desert plant that only grew in remote corners of the Atacama. It was used (in very small amounts) by some members of the Wolves of Joy cult to engender a sense of despair, which the initiate would then have to overcome by sheer strength of will. This was regarded as a test of spiritual prowess, but not everyone succeeded – occasionally a user suicided, the despair being too much to handle.

But recently, a matter of weeks ago, a scientist affiliated with Dead Shadows had managed to isolate the part of the plant which caused this sense of utter worthlessness. He had then succeeded in synthesising it and producing it in saleable amounts. A normal scientist, hungry for money, would have sold it to an army for use in biological warfare...but not *this* scientist. He was pure, 'one of us', as Herb put it.

'And so we have hired a cloud-seeding plane,' Herb explained, revealing his plans like the cartoon villain he increasingly resembled. 'We have consulted with the *weather* bureau,' (he sounded so incredibly pompous as he said this), 'and they are almost certain that a huge storm is due, right around the climax of Festival. It's perfect! We now have enough Raskar Pela to precipitate across the whole of Mantuaroa, if the storm front is as wide as predicted. And the dose is so intense that the populace will kill themselves *en masse.*'

'And you?'

'I will be quite safe on another island, watching the experiment with the greatest of interest.' His attempt at detached objectivity didn't really come off. 'And from there, we can take it to *other* storms. We must take out as much of the world's population as we can. We may never get them all, but we'll make a noble attempt. And the best is – they will come to know the *truth* before they die.

'My wife, alas, will not be coming with us. She is having what the ignorant call 'pangs of conscience', and what *I* call 'wilful blindness'. Having seen the truth, she turns her back on it. Oh well, it can't be helped. We are all puppets of the mindless, empty cosmos. The revolting, sickening, hideous, empty, cosmos. The weak shall lead where the lesser fall...' Here he paused, and rubbed his pointy chin, eyes aglow.

'You know, I once heard a legend from another island...something about 'roads to the sea,' some ancient paths...but that is just a myth. In the end there is no escape.'

'But if anyone at all is left alive, you'll have failed as much as if no one had been killed at all. And how do you know there isn't sentient life elsewhere in the universe?'

'I...' snapped Herb, but he never finished his response, because I pointed and screamed.

'Who is that figure? The one whose innards fold in to eternity, to black frozen torture in endless cold? That hollow point, sucking all that lives?' Herb hesitated, unnerved, then flicked his head briefly around.

Then the shadow encompassed him, along with his henchmen, and that was the last anyone saw of him...his gun clattered to the ground and the light returned.

Ward Lardle looked utterly incredulous...but at least he had the foresight to dive for the gun. Unfortunately for him, though, Vonny was quicker. He fired, just as the mob boss was diving to wrestle the weapon from him, and Lardle dropped down dead.

Then Muzza Gunt pulled his own weapon and fired at Vonny...but managed to hit his colleague instead, leaving Gunt the sole member of the gangster trio still standing.

It was a standoff between him and Vonny.

'Everyone on the ship,' the latter yelled. 'Diplomats, too. If the mob tracked us then whoever else is looking for us will find the embassy as well. You'll just have to abandon the island...'

'Oh, my cookbooks and feathers,' sobbed the Undersecretary. The Ambassador tried to drag me onto the ship, but I was loathe to leave Vonny.

Then there was another startling 'pop' of gunshot, and both men toppled from the wharf into the water. They had fired simultaneously, a near impossible event — but I saw the clouds of blood billowing from Vonny's punctured body as it bobbed in the water, and I can assure you that this time his death *wasn't faked*.

No matter what his past transgressions, he died a hero in my view.

There is little else I remember of the journey after that. I think Molly stayed by my side most of the time. The captain-medic asked a lot of questions about my legs, which I answered to the best of my ability. He nodded slowly as he pondered on the extended mind and its limits.

'The device that was overriding his organs must have a physical limit in space. We will outrun it with distance, if it didn't already cease overriding them when the gangster was killed. And he will start to recover.'

But as my body grew stronger, a shadow passed over my soul. The same shadow I had seen on the wharf: the Gardener of All Screams.

I knew I would never be the same again.

PART TWO

13

CAVENDISH

It is some time since I last picked up pen.

We managed to get my legs working, and they have not been hijacked since. Furthermore, no lasting harm was done to my organs, although we still haven't figured out precisely what went wrong.

It is rare that I get any time away from Holly, the gloomy young female scientist who helped me fix them, and who has been stalking me since I arrived here. Lest you think that romance is in the air, however, it isn't...she merely wishes to study my legs, and innards. An odd character, she is almost as strange as this island itself.

Holly emigrated from England, just before the Southern Wolves set up camp here (more on them later), and so is not an Original (i.e. one descended from the first British settlers). When I first saw her she was sitting on the grey rocks, staring out over grey water, where the grass plain sloped straight to the shore. She looked me over, and said: 'You will make an interesting case study.'

But if she had truly spoken her mind at that point, she would have said: 'I have been restless for days, ever since I heard of the impending arrival of the Strangers, and can trace a more subtle sense of disquiet back for months. This disquiet confirms me in my belief – that this island can offer me no refuge. Outsider to the last, though I so badly want to be seen as 'respectable'...and while I don't know what it is I actually fear, *something* is out there, that's for sure.' I have learnt all this through a subtle study of her character; for she is not the only one to be engaging in research...

After telling me I would be an interesting study, she dipped her bare feet in the water, washing mud and grass away. Two birds flew overhead, petrels maybe, too high to tell. We watched as they winged into the distance.

'I was half hoping they would land here, and prove the legend wrong,' she said.

'What is the legend?'

'The legend says Cavendish is cursed, and that is why no birds ever land here. But there must be a scientific explanation, and I am determined to find it.'

'Magnetic fields, something like that?'

'Something like that.'

'Is it true that the island's original inhabitants, the Ahu, mysteriously disappeared?'

She said, predictably: 'I doubt there are any mysteries that can't be explained rationally. But yes, they disappeared.'

She is only twenty-four – so why does she talk like such an old fogey? And how can a place as beautiful as this be cursed? The earth itself seems strong here – a hard, calcite strength, which even now I feel pulsing through the soft plain behind me.

But there is something frightening, too, about the silent daytime emptiness. And at night, the way the wind blows. And beyond, to the south, nothing but ice...eventually. Does Holly feel any of this?

She says she misses the northern stars.

Once, when two of the island's wild horses began sporting on top of the hill, cantering in circles before bounding out of sight, she gave a faint smile, so that I was tempted to ask if her face hurt as a result, but wisely held my tongue.

The P-R has given her a tiny hut outside the camp, free to stay until she works out her allegiances, which of course she still hasn't done. She claims to be puzzled by the P-R, who is gruff, yet can be deeply moved by art; arrogant at times, yet also kind (he dotes, for instance, on a scruffy abandoned dog he has adopted). But while she hasn't 'figured him out', it is clear she feels the urge to impress him, and is worried what he thinks of her, although she tries to hide it.

Holly is not the island's only recent arrival, however.

That branch of the Wolves of Joy known as the 'Southern Wolves', previously scattered throughout Australia and New Zealand, have also made their home here. More exactly, they have set up an armed camp. To be gathered in one permanent settlement – most un-wolflike. But the times are a-changing. We have moved out of the Scarlottian era, and stand on the brink of a completely new age. In attempting to found a new society of like-minded people, however, albeit on this remote island, the Southern Wolves seem to have gone full circle, and are no longer wolves, but domestic dogs.

The camp is large and tethered into areas, home to different groups by age and sex. On arriving here they soon learned they were not the only ones on the island to train in arcane weaponry – for even the oldest Cavendish farmer can still wield a halberd, as the island has been threatened with invasion by its tiny neighbours numerous times, including, of course, the current threat from St. Vigeans. But what chance do halberds have against today's amazing weaponry? They are a symbol, and that is why the Wolves have also taken them up, because they understand the language of symbol...the farmers are merely pragmatic.

Some of the younger Wolves are becoming cynical about their mission, and that is a greater danger than physical extinction. These juvenile pack members seem rather sullen, so that I wonder why they have come all the way to Cavendish in the first place – or have they only become so since arriving? Is communal life inimical to the Wolves, as I suspect? It certainly seemed so on the morning I passed the wooden barracks after meeting Holly, crossing the training course and taking the long flying-fox ride back to Popinjay, the island's only town.

This was the day I was summoned to go horse-riding with the island's sovereign, the Prince-Regent, who is directly descended from a governor of the Napoleonic era, one who stayed and created a personal fiefdom after the British government abandoned the island (which then as now had little strategic value, given its uncouth locale). Cavendish survived off the radar for two and a half centuries.

I was helped into the saddle of a horse. The Prince-Regent, a bluff, towering monocle of a man, told us how important it is for guests to ride upon arrival, but Molly refused – she was terrified of large animals. I, despite my recovery, was still weak and had to be helped into the saddle. But clean exercise helps to expunge the memory of the Gardener, and also, in my own small way, I wished to imitate poor Vonny's final bravery, that such boldness might not perish from the earth. I will start with small things like riding a horse, though I quake with the pain and stress of it.

The Prince-Regent adjusted his monocle and glanced with approval. 'There's fight in the little bugger', he may have thought...or possibly it was just the horse he was admiring. I had never ridden previously, but he told me not to worry – the horse knew exactly what to do, and would follow his lead.

We left town by a well-worn trail, and in minutes were cantering on the downlands. The P-R must have noticed my breathtaken expression as the green-black, beautiful grassy plains unfurled.

'Bit bloody different to Mantuaroa, what?'

'Yes,' I murmured dreamily. Different...more solitary, colder...yet somehow more fertile in its coldness than the lush jungles...as if something fought for here would be *worth* more.

The P-R asked about my travels, and let me speak at will. The Ambassador had mentioned a notebook, but that could wait for tomorrow, he said. For now, just blather away. He, with his stiff upper lip, would seldom interrupt.

The horses carried us onwards, until rounding the top of a rise we saw waves of gold-green meadows skimming down to an iron-grey sea. Yes, this was Cavendish. The island, though in its dying days in many regards, is never forgotten once seen, and shall never perish from my heart.

The grass-swept hills, cold plains of the mind.

Few are aware the island exists, and economically, the place is sinking fast, a backwater. The arrival of the Wolves will scarcely change that. Only the stiff upper lip keeps the islanders going, and food is often scarce. Some youngsters leave due to the bland diet, while others move to Mantuaroa

City to the taste the fast life. Traditions are eroding. Perhaps they have been for ages, however, and only now is it becoming clearly visible.

The P-R told me he thought the decline could be traced to the day when the seat of government was moved from the Red Fort to the current capital of Popinjay.

But the horses; the horses haven't faltered. Two ran wild to the east, along the shore. Grey and stony as a Cavendish dawn their sheens were as they ran.

These horses were on the island before the Europeans came. The Ahu must have brought them from wherever *they* came from, or traded them perhaps, and they are still here, wild mostly, not used for transport, just a few kept for equestrian purposes, running in contests or ceremonial rides like the present one. And the P-R doubtless runs in his dreams across the hills with them, fearless and ragged and free.

My own dream last night, as I bunked in a wooden hut on the outskirts of Popinjay, was powerful beyond words.

I was stationed on a submarine in wartime. The claustrophobic space was filled with an eerie light − and rocked by occasional explosions. I went to look through the periscope to see what was going on, but it was blocked, as if someone had stuck their hand over it. So I thought I might try looking through one of the torpedo tubes instead. I stuck my head in − but someone was there. A pale face stared through the dark at me, and I noticed the glitter of cruel teeth. I had no doubt − it was the Vampire Girl, come to hunt beneath the waves. My heart sank. Would this piteous ghost *eternally* follow me?

I pulled my head from the tube, but could sense she was still there. Soon she would come crawling down, and corner me, in that cold metal tomb. With no mercy.

But then I remembered the shadow, the shape on Nully's Wharf. And the dream merged suddenly with my outer life. A snarl rose up within me, and I *stuck my head back into the tube.* The pale shape stared back hungrily, but I filled my lungs with air, and *roared* at it. The world turned on its side, and I went sliding up (or was it down?) the tube, and burst into blue and shining water.

The sun pierced through dampness, and the Vampire Girl was gone.

She was nowhere, had vanished into atoms...

14

PUPPET SHOW

I woke to the smell of wood-smoke, and a draught on my face. I groggily took control of my legs, and with a grunt of will pushed my too-shaky body out of bed. The pain in my torso had gone, but the memory of internal assault remained. My body is no longer my own private domain. It is far too vulnerable to be complacent in. But self-pity is out, especially in this unfamiliar landscape.

Someone knocked at the frame of my doorless hut, leaning his head in to tell me where the washrooms are. After splashing my face with icy cold water I stepped outside, shivering, to see many Wolves on the move. The flying-fox was in use, the island's equivalent of a commuter train line.

Someone tapped me on the shoulder, and it was Molly. Breakfast had been laid out for us in another wooden hut, and we ate stale buttered bread in silence, listening to the peppery morning yells around us. Molly seemed far from happy.

'This place sucks,' she complained. 'My mattress is hard as a rock, and it's damp and it's cold. I want to go home, but I keep on forgetting, I don't have one.'

But she didn't sound completely unhappy, and I was glad of that. We took a stroll, and ended up near the Wolves' camp by a more circuitous route than the fox express – a narrow muddy trail that that wound along a ridge above a meadow and a wood.

We stood watching the morning training session. Some were playing a strange game that looked like rugby in reverse – where the person with the ball has to get rid of it. But to do so he must run a line of hard defensive tacklers, then hit another player with the ball (who then becomes the bearer). If it fails to hit they have to start from scratch. There is no goal, the sport being a form of endurance training rather than 'play' as such. These new Wolves seem grimmer than the ones I had read about in the past, and which I only half believed in.

Then someone walked up behind us – it was Holly. 'I've been asked to take you to the Prince-Regent,' she said matter-of-factly. 'He wants to speak with both of you.'

I noticed something hanging around her neck on a cord, a small electronic device, and asked what it was.

'This? It's a kind of prototype camera that picks up different fields, making weird, ghostly images.'

'You mean like a Kirlian camera?'

'Not exactly. Those pick up coronal discharges, this one...' she launched into a long technical monologue which I won't pretend to remember enough of to render, at least three quarters of the words being unfamiliar to me. But she admitted the camera had been designed by Gallinule, the controversial scientist who had worked under Scarlotti.

'So it's *pseudo-science*, then?' I asked innocently.

She blushed, looking angry. 'It works,' she snapped. 'I tried it in England, and I'm about to try it here. And please don't ever use that horrible word again. 'Experimental' is better.'

'Where are you going to try it?'

'In a kind of spooky fortress called the Red Fort. We're not supposed to go there because it's old and falling down, but I thought it would make the perfect place to try out the camera. It's supposed to be haunted, if you believe in such things.'

'Can we come?' asked Molly.

'Well, I suppose so, after you've seen the Prince-Regent. I'll wait for you. I'll be spending the night there, so bring your bedding.'

She told us how she had once used it in an old house in England that was also supposed to be haunted. The camera's viewfinder had picked up the most beautiful interference patterns, which seemed to suggest complex emotional states. But whenever she had tried to capture the images, they only came out as a drab blur.

By this time we were at the P-R's executive building (he was head of government as well as head of state), which was the size of an ordinary house. She showed us into an antechamber, where a secretary bade us be seated. A few minutes later she returned to usher us into the P-R's office, and Holly entered as well.

The P-R was standing next to a huge antique desk, on which stood an equally antique globe. Something seemed odd about it, and then I realised it was upside down. I wanted to ask why, but thought it would be inappropriate in the presence of a man of such high bearing. For gone was the gruff-but-kindly, somewhat avuncular P-R who had taken me riding yesterday. In his place was a man who was abrupt, haughty, militaristic.

The Ambassador and Undersecretary were also present (along with a small scruffy dog), and if the P-R was grim, the Ambassador was positively fuming. While the former looked out the window in aloof silence, the latter raged and yelled. The Undersecretary sat calmly in the corner, knitting. As the Ambassador ranted, the dog yapped in unison, wagging its scruffy, manged and tattered tail. It seemed to think the Ambassador's yells were cries of happiness.

'Things are *worse* than when I left! I don't know what's worse...the pathetic boredom of the young, or the sordid corruption of the old. And these Wolves haven't changed a damn thing. They're only concerned with their own subjective realities. They would rather commune with the dead than face the living. And as for council and court, it's being eaten from within. Self-servers everywhere. Justice, the military...even the very wording of our proclamations. You can't fight against it because there's nowhere you can strike. It's a circle without a centre. They get inside my dreams, these weaklings, turn them sour and flat.' The dog then left off yapping and began to scratch its fleas. The P-R stooped and picked the mongrel up.

'It's inevitable,' he said. 'They're just instruments, however willing, of a great unstoppable force. And after all, what would our times have been without an ending?' He repeated the words *unstoppable force* several times under his breath.

I asked what all this was about, and he told me. He believed a coup was in the offing, and that he would soon be dead or deposed. Many of his greatest loyalists had died in the skirmishes with St. Vigeans.

But this was not all – the P-R also had some news for us, which filled us with dread. *He had received a message that morning from the government of Mantuaroa, demanding immediate handover of what they called the 'absconded criminals'.* The P-R was stalling them, and hadn't yet replied.

'So, you have *decisions* to make, damn it,' roared the Ambassador, bringing his fist down on the table with a mighty thud. Molly flinched, her eyes damp with tears.

'Ahem,' said the P-R in a milder voice. 'I've had my puppeteer prepare a show for you...to help you get a better grasp on the situation. If you would step into the other room to watch, I think it might be of help.' He led us into a room draped with thick black velvet curtains. A red glow pervaded, emanating from lanterns strung around the edge of the ceiling. On one side of the room was a large wooden booth, with red-gold velvet drapes across the front. We sat in the plush antique chairs that were set out for us, and all was silent, for the show was about to begin.

The curtains parted.

From a gleam beneath the stage, a group of crazy puppets could be seen, milling around and nodding at each other. Occasionally one would fight another, or occasionally make peace, hugging and shaking their puppet paws in rapture. This went on for some time, but all the while a strange, shadowy figure in the background wove unseen around the rest. Sometimes he would push forward into view, but before the other puppets noticed him he would dart back into the shadows. He had odd lips, thin yet rubbery, bloodless and sensuous at the same time. He had thin, stringy hair and a craggen face. He looked both more human than the other puppets, yet at the same time, less so.

But then it became apparent that this figure's subtle weaving was not merely for show. The other puppets had been bound, it seemed, in a subtle web – a thin black snaring rope, which was bunched up all around them. Then the craggen puppet pulled it tight...

What you are seeing, said a voice behind the stage, *is a subtle manoeuvrous empire. The Patagonians sow unrest all around the world. But now the seeds they have planted are sprouting up to haunt them, for rebellions are brewing, both against their local ensnared representatives, and even against the puppet-masters themselves. New political forms are taking shape. Some talk of a new World War brewing, or darker things. Whatever happens, it's clearly not going to be pretty...*

Then the scene shifted. The curtain rolled across, and almost as swiftly drew back again. Puppet horses danced around the edges, as the history of Cavendish played out before us.

In the beginning was a tribe called the Ahu, said the voice. *But Muslim slave raiders and Christian missionaries (sometimes, incredibly, working in cahoots) enslaved the Ahu leaders.*

The Ahu puppets were fair-haired and fair-skinned. A tribe of white people? Interesting...

The remaining Ahu gathered round and said: 'You have stolen our leaders, and you yourselves will not replace them, nor can you...nor lead us in the way we are accustomed to...so WE must lead ourselves.' And they did so, taking the roads into the sea. They simply disappeared from the island. The missionaries withdrew in shock and grief. And the slavers moved on somewhere else.

Puppet bones came sliding from above. They looked like chicken bones.

Bones in jars remained. This was the native form of burial. Among their many gods, the Ahu had honoured one in particular, known as 'Dreamking'. They wouldn't tell their own native word for him. But his worship spread through the Pacific under different names. Little else is known of their beliefs.

Now puppet soldiers marched on through.

Afterwards, military possessors arrived from Britain. Cavendish was an accursed, empty place, but the Napoleonic Wars were raging at the time, and also penetrated the southern hemisphere. The British soldiers stationed on Cavendish were inspired by its haunted atmosphere, and became an elite and self-reliant group. When Britain ordered the troops back home for lack of money, the officer in charge...

'My ancestor,' said the P-R proudly.

...refused, and chose to secede from the Empire. Britain was too engaged in other matters to worry about the loss of one small island. But farmers later drifted out from Europe to try their luck in the

southern temperate zone. At about this time it was noticed that all the birds had left. One sees them flying high above, but no bird has landed on the island since.

'Strange, but true,' the P-R interjected.

Falconry continued to be practiced for a time, but the birds were kept on a lengthy string in case they flew away. This, too, was abolished at some point, for the falcons were deeply unhappy.

Now the curtains closed again, and opened in a vigorous flash. Time had clearly moved on in the puppet world.

The nation of St. Vigeans, both populous and prosperous. A covert war was going on for control of an outlying isle. St. Vigeans hit strategic naval points to draw the troops away. Ouwai was the islet's name.

Two miniature navies clashed around the sides of the wooden stage. Despite the past tense, the narrator obviously referred to the present.

But certain puppets didn't yet wish to be seen wielding open sway on an elected government...

The craggen puppet raised its head again behind the scenes.

They promised St. Vigeans big things if they could win this one small islet, which they couldn't yet take openly for themselves. The situation was tense. But with the Mantuaroan government pressing us to return the alleged criminals or risk war, the existing conflict will escalate intensely...

Oh, this not so subtle hint. The switch between past and present tense was pathetic and cowardly, I thought. I rose to my plastic feet.

'Don't worry, we won't be staying,' I growled. I stood over the seated P-R with squared shoulders, staring him right in the eyes. 'Just show us the way, and we'll be off.'

I spoke in a cold, hard voice I had never used before. The Ambassador moved forward, as did servants from the shadows. They looked ready to clobber me for talking to their head of state that way, but the P-R waved them aside.

'No one is asking you to leave, Nicholas,' he said in a tired but authoritative voice. 'We simply need to assess the situation. As you can appreciate, things are looking grim. Now, the Ambassador here tells me you have a note, which might contain a clue...'

I pulled the now-grubby notebook from my pocket. It was a talisman, a thread connecting me with the dead man who had plunged me into the mystery...and perhaps with another little man, from an eternity ago. I thrust it into the P-R's hand rather sullenly. The P-R read in silence, and his brow creased gravely as he scanned the scribbled contents. Then he handed it back without a word, and placed his hands in the pockets of his ceremonial coat. His face looked startled and sad.

'Well?' I blurted, after a long, uncanny silence.

'Hmm?'

'Did you know Maddem, the Last Poet? And do you know where the 'secret stair' is?

'No, I'm sorry. I don't know what it means. We'll meet again in two days time to work out what to do. My spies will have given me more information by then, and the council will be summoned. Holly will keep you entertained in the meantime.'

He turned and left the room without another word. We were dismissed, stalks without a harvester.

15

DREAMS

Last night I had several significant dreams. In the first I entered an old stone castle, walking through a room of stuffed birds. They were faded, but one was still colourful and vivid.

I pointed, tugging at the sleeve of my companion (identity unknown), and saying 'Look, a good old Aussie parrot...' But my calling attention to it meant the other birds noticed it too, and came to life, flying down with frightening speed. They clearly meant to peck the coloured bird to death.

I rushed at them, waving my hands til they dispersed. The parrot settled near the door, unruffled. I opened it a crack to let the bird out. It went, but others were quicker. A dozen or more flew out in pursuit before I managed to get the door shut. There was nothing I could do.

The birds who didn't make it perched around, looking innocent. And that was the worst of all...

*　　*　　*

In another dream, Vonny, apparently having come back to life, was being called to account for himself. He was strapped to a chair in a darkened room, while a swirling blue light alternated with a painfully blinding white pulse in random, unpredictable bursts.

Wires had been attached to his head, and I realised someone (me?) was trying to read his thoughts. But, apparently sensing what was happening, he attempted to fill his mind with blankness and confusion.

Then, suddenly, he looked directly up at me...and I realised it wasn't an act.

His mind really was blank and confused.

*   *   *

A third dream was of Mantuaroa. In the yellow sprawl of the city, a funeral was taking place. A highly colourful, winged, carved and painted wooden coffin was hoisted on the shoulders of six Mani tribesmen, fullbloods by the look of them. Somehow I knew that they belonged to different, opposing tribes, yet for the time being they were united under the leadership of the Panganuans, the band who had originally settled the land where Mantuaroa City now stood. The coffin was that of a Panganuan known as the *Paramount Chief.*

Slowly the coffin floated, with its chestnut feathers, white wing tips, and fire-roasted plume. Red, the sacred tint of the Pacific, on Mantuaroa was also the colour of the native aristocracy. The great bird carried the chief to his final resting place, itself borne by six servants, mortals in the service of immortal death. The crowd parted to allow its passage.

A company of soldiers were watching...half-breeds in the service of the national government, nervously fingering their sub-machine guns. They were posted there in case of trouble. The sudden unexpected death of the Paramount Chief had created a power vacuum, and this, coupled with rumours of a organised rebellion, had put the authorities on their guard. Funerals held during Festival were normally joyous occasions, for it was considered fortuitous to die at this time. But in the case of royalty, things were different. Solemnities must be observed. And no one knew who would now assume leadership of the tribe, and thus of all the tribes, because he had left no successor of the blood, and many were waiting in the shadows.

Also watching the procession from the periphery of the crowd was an arrogant-looking half-breed, and a quadroonish girl, who stared at the former with shameless devotion in her eyes.

'The Bird King people,' she was asking. 'Can we trust them?'

'You mean the *cultists*,' he sniffed. 'They're white devils. We can't trust them at all. And they must pay for appropriating one of *our* gods.' He had forgotten, or was ignorant, that the god came originally from the Ahu.

'It is true,' said the girl. 'These devils disable us.' And *she* had evidently forgotten she was three quarters white. 'But what of the true tribes?'

'The Panganuans won't fight,' he snarled. 'Only among themselves. They need a leader to unite them.' It was clear who he thought that leader should be, although as a half-blood he was ineligible.

'What is needed,' he said, 'is a unity of *all* the tribes and factions. Just temporary unity...but enough to fill the white man's heart with fear.' He smiled through glittering teeth. 'And that will come about. I have worked on it and willed it. Behind the scenes, sister. My threads will soon be pulled together.' He looked out over the crowd, then spoke again.

'We can't rely on City Hall. It is weak, and easily countered by the national government. Those ditherers in City Hall hate me, but I have done what they could never do.'

'What?' she asked, eyes shining wide. 'Can you trust me?'

'Ha, I don't even trust myself,' he laughed. 'But I'll tell you this. Some of those you think of as enemies are really on our side, and some you think are friends, are not. Just as an example, there are factions in the military...'

But his words were cut sharply short by machine gun fire. The soldiers were getting nervous as the tension built, and had fired above the heads of the swarming crowd. Some in the crowd then panicked, starting a small stampede, which further increased the tension.

The man continued: 'Some from the hardline nationalist faction, seeing what *we* are about, will choose our uprising as their most convenient moment to rebel, thus decreasing the power of the military. So factions who are otherwise *opposed* can work together without even meaning to. It's a matter of playing them off in balance, like music,' he laughed. 'A delicate task. But if the notes entwine in harmony...'

Again the guns burst out, and this time the man and the woman made moves to leave.

'We'll meet tomorrow night,' said the man. 'I'll tell you further then.' He melted away as the crowd surged and heaved.

But as he hurried away, it was the image of his strange *backer* that he had in his mind, and that backer was...

I awoke, clutching a gone image.

16

FORTRESS

Holly told the P-R she was taking us on an overnight camp on the other side of the island, not mentioning the fort. She rounded up some packs and provisions from the storehouse, and we set off just after breakfast. Despite the uncertainty of the future, I felt happy – I was getting the hang of using my legs again. Holly's mood, too, seemed to have brightened. Only Molly seemed despondent, and I heard her muttering something about 'castaways.'

Our pace was slow, thanks to me, and Holly seemed frustrated but resigned to it. The path opened up, losing its white form in silent and trackless meadows. Soon we were tramping over frosty, pale-green hills. The sea would blink and flicker to our right – there was no danger of getting lost – but the wind, though light, bit at us with cold antarctic teeth.

It was nearly midday when Holly told us she wished to take a short detour, as there was something she thought we should see.

The sea's tumbling hiss grew louder as we filed down a grey stony track towards the shore. There we walked down the rocky beach for a while before encountering something strange, the thing Holly had mentioned. A section of smooth, flat, weathered rock divided into squares like ancient cobblestones. I asked if it was some kind of geological formation, but Holly said it wasn't.

'It's one of the roads to the sea,' she stated simply, pronouncing 'roads to the sea' in a slow, deliberate way, which on this stony shore made the phrase slightly sinister.

She put her pack on the ground and pulled from it a mask and snorkel.

'Bit cold for a swim,' I observed, my teeth chattering from standing still.

'We're just going to look, not to swim. And it isn't *that* cold...don't be a wimp.'

I glared at her, offended.

'I served my country, sacrificed my legs...' I started to say, but my teeth were chattering so much it wouldn't come out, and in any case she ignored me, removed her shoes and rolled her trousers up, before walking to a large flat rock some way out in the water. Molly and I followed reluctantly. It was thigh-deep before we clambered onto the rock.

She knelt on the edge, motioning for us to do likewise. Then she handed the mask to Molly, who hesitantly put it on.

'Stick your head in and have a look,' Holly said. Molly did as instructed, keeping her head in the water for a long time. I looked questioningly at Holly, but she sat motionless and stony-faced. We listened to the rhythmic hiss of Molly's breath through the snorkel. Eventually she pulled back up, and slowly took the mask off. A frown was visible through her dripping hair.

'Where does it go?' she asked, but Holly shrugged.

Curiosity aflame, I put the mask on, lowering onto my stomach as Molly had. The coldness of the water shocked my nerves – this was the first time it had touched my actual, non-plastic flesh. Once I was used to it, though, I focussed my attention, and saw through the blue, filmy water what was unmistakably an ancient, manmade road. Under the water the cobblestones looked green. They trailed into the distance, until the water finally blurred. Even more unusual were the two small statues, worn with time, which stood on either side of the road, like miniature guardians. I stared for a while, almost hypnotised, before slowly pulling my head back up.

As I shook the water out of my ears I could hear Holly telling Molly that there were other roads like this around the island, roads leading straight down into the sea. I thought of a song called 'Full Fathom Five' I had heard as a child...I thought of darkness, compression, rats. But where did these roads lead, and who had used them?

*   *   *

We arrived at the fort in mid-afternoon. The day had turned from overcast to stormy, and a peel of thunder rolled around the huge edge of the sky as we approached the high shadow of the rocks. We stood a few minutes at the head of the rolling plain, gazing up at the dark grey rise. Lightning flickered round the horizon, but far away and powerless, for no more thunder came, just the low moan of the wind and the hissing of the sea.

The fortress protruded like a dull red crown from the grey and granite-jagged crags around it. This was both the end of the island and its highest point. On the other side of the fort were nothing but crumbling cliffs. The red rock, which Holly had said was called *molon* (and unique to the island), formed a band across the centre of the headland, and from it had been laboriously carved the fort, which had housed a British military outpost long ago. Now it was crumbling, and most of what remained were the underground parts. Some visitors had reported a rattling sound, giving rise to the rumour it was haunted. The soft rattling would follow you at a distance, so they said.

A rocky track led up to the base of the fort. It was eerie watching the lightning playing sporadically at the edges of the world, when there was no rain, nor, after the initial peel, further thunder. It was one of the strangest things I ever witnessed. It felt like we were hemmed inside a vast and barren circle, a world of silence ringed by flickering chaos. As if we had stepped outside of everything, and were waiting for life to begin again.

Then we entered the ruins of the fort. As soon as we entered the first roofed section, the air became muffled and heavy with the dust of crumbling *molon*. Our shadows fell long against the rough-hewn walls, as Holly led us down a long, low, echoey tunnel. There were dark entrances on either side, but neither Molly nor I cared to look inside those sad and gloomy portals.

The passage soon began to slope downwards.

'Do you know where you're going?' I asked.

'No. Do you?'

'I'm not the one who's leading.'

'Well, be quiet then.'

In the face of such circular logic I ground my teeth and kept walking, heading deeper and deeper underground.

* * *

We came to a large gloomy chamber with a high ceiling and several dark alcoves set in its walls. There was a fireplace on one side and, amazingly, a pile of wood. There were few trees on this side of the island, and I guessed the soldiers must have traded or received wood from elsewhere...but surely this wood couldn't be from *those* times? Someone must have used the place more recently. There were ashes in the fireplace, but how old I couldn't tell.

Holly had brought along a small spirit stove, and we each had tins of food inside our packs, so we set about making a hot meal, sitting on the stone bench that lined one of the walls.

'A good place to stay the night,' she pronounced. It seemed there were only two ways in, apart from the chimney: the one we had come in by, and another that turned a corner before ending in a stairway that led (we ascertained) to a lookout post at the top of the fort.

'It's draughty,' said Molly. No one replied, and we continued preparing the food, and ate in silence. The red began to fade from the walls as the light drained slowly from the room.

* * *

Those same walls now trembled in the fire-flicker. Holly was telling us all about the magical camera. The patterns she had seen through the viewfinder in the English haunted house were vivid, colourful, overwhelming. But whenever she tried to capture them or print them out they became a blur of silly shadow, with only the merest hint at their former substantiality.

'What's England like?' asked Molly.

'Dying...just a sick little dying country at the end of the world,' she sighed. 'But it was once great. There is more of the *old* English spirit here on Cavendish, in its own way.' Her mood seemed to lighten, and we spoke of the island and its quirky population. She admitted it wasn't fair of the P-R to 'inform' us via the puppet show. But she defended him regardless...a good man, she believed. And then I asked her something that was weighing on my mind.

'Why haven't you been to the fort before? Were you afraid to go by yourself?'

She glared at me, then her face suddenly softened. 'I don't know. Maybe I *am* afraid. The shapes we saw in England, the patterns were really beautiful, you know, but they were *strange*. There was something weird about them. They didn't seem like they could be the ghosts of people. Maybe it's *parts* of people, left behind when they die. Or maybe they're not really ghosts at all, in the way *we* think of them. There's something scary about them, and the way they move. Something not quite right.' Molly shivered in spite of the fire, and moved a bit closer to me, as Holly launched into an account of her experiences at a country estate called Cranfield House.

How the colours had danced for her in that drab, grey abode! All sorts of flimmering, flickering patterns in the viewfinder, weaving in and out of one another with abandon. If they really were disembodied emotions, it might explain why they seemed so inhuman...because a person had *layers* of different moods. It was like taking a complex musical passage and only playing a single note of it...you simply wouldn't recognise it.

But there was a certain room in the house, a bedroom, whose occupant had died there, allegedly of a broken heart. The room had been preserved as he had lived in it, many decades ago. Dusty, leatherbound books filled a shelf above an ornate table covered with small but beautiful antiques. Linen drapes hung behind the bed, and folded sheathes of cloth in faded colours were stacked up neatly all around. On the other side of the bed was an oak writing desk, and it was here that Holly focussed her camera unsteadily.

There was an abstract figure, standing behind the desk, its colours dancing and swimming across one another. But then she realised with a sudden chill that *it had a face*. Furthermore, it was staring at her, mouth agape. She screamed, and almost dropped the camera. Only just in time did she remember to press the shutter, and the figure vanished from the lens.

On developing it, all she could make out of the shape she had so vividly seen were two dark, opaque patches. Were they the staring eyes of the dead man? An echo of some vital essence left behind? Or something else entirely? In any case, they were of such an abstract quality that she could never publicly exhibit them, for they would convince nobody.

'Will you give it a try now?' I asked intently. 'In the haunted fort?' In reply, she took a torch from her pack, shrugged, and left the chamber. I quickly followed, and Molly scurried behind. Holly led us down the passage we had entered from. The glow from the dying fire faded rapidly, and the yellow torch beam was weak.

We turned into a larger passage, where an echoey draught crept thickly all around. Then Holly turned the torch off. All we could see now was the tiny gleam of her camera's digital set-up.

She tried to focus, but to no avail. It seemed there was nothing there, just blackness in the hall. Had none of the soldiers stationed there died lonely at their posts, to appear as a sad, pale frost, for instance? Was there nothing, not even a wisp?

But then we heard a strange rattling sound behind us. Molly caught my hand. Holly moved instinctively in the direction it came from, but Molly asked her not to in a shaky voice.

'I'm scared,' she said, and Holly turned reluctantly around. We headed back to the chamber, where the fire was still aglow. Molly dived into her blankets like a turtle into its shell, and I couldn't blame her.

I could hear her whimpering and snuffling as I drifted off to dreamland.

*　　*　　*

And now the Friendly Girl appeared to me after a long absence. But she was different – less real. She stood far off in the distance, looking out to sea. A lighthouse swept around her, its bright beam pulsing in the twilight. Everything else was a soft, deep, murky blue...except her hair, red hair, which shone through the vaporous haze.

But 'I' was not 'I' – even in the dream I realised that. It was a distant scene I couldn't interact with. The Friendly Girl was looking for something, I couldn't work out what. I had never known her to be like this, so mysterious, aloof. The air was damp with water droplets – even though I wasn't 'there' I could feel them on my skin – and I realised I was looking at someone closed to me, our ways having long since diverged.

This, I knew must be my final glimpse of her, for she had matured, and I, as yet, had not. I must carry on my quest, wherever it might lead me.

But would we meet again, in an infinitude of time...in a garden in the rain?

Already she was lost to view, and lonely anguish tore at me, dragging me back to the world of harsh stone landscapes.

*　　*　　*

An uncomfortable rapping prised me from my sleep. It was Holly, jabbing at my shoulder. She halted my unspoken questions with a finger and beckoned stealthily, calling me to walk into the cold and clammy labyrinth of shadow-haunted rock. Unwillingly I thrust

428

aside my blanket. The cold was sharp and deep, but I steeled myself to follow, grinding teeth and all.

She led me down a fault in the rock, which I hadn't noticed before, having thought it an alcove, to the upper ledge of a space, part cave part chamber, where moonlight fell through an aperture in the rock. She pointed down to the floor below.

Something was huddled there – something skeletal and white. At first I thought it was the bones of some animal that had perished there. I was about to open my mouth, however, when the bones gave a strange, scuttling movement. Holly turned around, mouthing: *see?* But then the thing was still again.

Heart in mouth, I gazed at it intently. Then it moved again – a weird, scuttling crawl that chilled my blood. It softly shivered sideways then froze up again, crouching in the corner motionless and silent. It was like some ancient fossil – a trilobite or something of the kind – except alive, and big as a man.

'I'm going down there,' whispered Holly, waving her camera. 'Are you coming?' I nodded mutely through my terror. My fear that she would think me a coward was greater than my fear of the creature itself, and that was all.

She led me back down the fissure, then along a manmade corridor that forked off halfway down. This ended in some stairs, which led to another passage, which led in turn to the chamber/cave itself. Holly had it sussed out – she must have been exploring while I slept, despite her admitted fear. But my stomach sank as I gazed into the moonlight up ahead.

For I beheld the haunting sight of the creature circling the walls, keeping its black and beady eyes on us, apparently scared out of its wits.

Holly put her hands up, to show she meant no harm, but the creature, desperate to escape, began to climb the walls of the cave.

The rock was too steep, however, and the thing fell straight to the ground and lay there on its back, apparently stunned. Holly advanced, camera in hand. She stood over the creature and took a photo, presumably on the 'normal light' setting, as it looked at her through those black and beady solid little eyes...eyes like marbles, set into a flat odd skull of bones. A composite skull. The limbs and ribs, too, looked not so much like an actual skeleton as a patched together pile of bones from various (human?) bodies.

Holly stepped back. The creature slowly rose, ribs shimmering in the manner that disturbed me so. It backed towards the wall, gazing warily at us both. Its seemed to have lost its fear, though, for we showed no sign of attacking.

And then, amazingly...it began to speak. With a hollow, twitching, muttering voice it slowly said in English:

'*Up soldier...rise and fall...*'

Holly and I looked quizzically at one another.

'*It's time to sound the call,*' rasped the creature in a faltering, scraping voice. Where did the voice come from, I wondered with a chill...when it didn't have any vocal cords?

'*Muskets ready,*' it twittered again.

'Uh, hullo,' stammered Holly. 'What's your name?'

But the creature merely repeated: '*It's time to sound the call.*'

'Come on,' I said, still scared, yet fascinated. 'We'd better go...'

But Holly tried again.

'Is this your home?' she asked. The creature stared back.

And then it said: '*I'm scared.*'

That sounded familiar. It was Molly's tone of voice, just as she had said it in the corridor that evening, when we had heard the rattling sound.

'It must just...repeat what people say,' I said, frowning. Holly nodded slowly.

'*Muskets ready,*' rasped the creature. And so we turned and left the cave. My last image, looking back over my shoulder, was of two black marbles set in cold white bone staring after us forlornly. If the creature had eyelids, it would surely have been blinking.

17

THE TRUTH

The fort looked very different in the clear light of day. It looked sad and forsaken rather than sinister, though still impressive in its heaven-climbing grandeur. It seemed engaged in a doomed fight with the sky, having come to this craggy bluff to launch its final assault. Its inhabitants had fled, yet it hadn't noticed, so proud, sad and solitary was its nature.

The fort reminded me of the P-R himself – and if the latter were deposed, would the fort, too, fall into the sea? And what would happen to its final occupant, the skeleton?

We told Molly about our encounter as we sat on a big, flat rock in the shelter of the fort, breakfasting in the bright but chilly sun. She thought at first we were joking...but on realising we were serious turned quiet and pale. She seemed a bit suspicious, as if Holly and I were somehow enchanted now as well.

*　　*　　*

Holly announced we would go a different way back to camp. She didn't say why, but I couldn't be bothered arguing. This time the trail led inland, and after half an hour of walking we saw signs of habitation. A couple of farms, and what looked like a tiny hamlet in the distance, where the smoke of morning curled aloft from cooking fires or washfires. And fields, bursting with crops.

'One of the more fertile parts of the island,' said Holly, stating the obvious. These exquisite vegetable and cereal crops were how Cavendish managed much of its trade. But I could see little in the way of modern farming equipment.

We passed a meadow full of round, pied cows, where an old man stood leaning on a fence, regarding us. Red cheeks and white hair, and a cunning look about him, he looked like one of the 'hobbits' in the *Lord of the Rings* books I enjoyed as a child. When he spoke, his accent was so thick I had trouble understanding it. He also used many unfamiliar words. Holly, who had little trouble understanding him, had presumably picked up some of the local speech during her time here.

'Good marnin. Been garn rumma?' said the man.

'Nah,' said Holly. 'Been out fort.'

'Ah! Webout you gwen?'

'Out yenna,' she pointed. 'Back to camp.'

'Dar-de-way!' he said, with a sly grin. Then he seemed to consider something, before speaking again, frowning. 'Deffy for a cuppa an some tayties?'

'Cuppa' was obvious. Holly looked at us, and we shrugged. 'Okay,' she said politely. 'We will, thanks.'

We walked along the fence until we reached the front gate. The man let us in, and we followed him into a low-roofed, turf-covered farmhouse. The floor inside was also turf, and the whole place was simply yet pleasingly furnished. A rotund woman stirred an enormous pot on the stove as three cats hovered hopefully round her feet.

'Forners here fer yer,' the farmer announced.

'I tullye!' his wife exclaimed in surprise. But in no time at all she had served us with mugs of strong, black tea, and a plate of steaming tayties. 'Taytie' means 'potato', but in this case it referred to a kind of round, flat cake that is unique to this part of the island, made from potatoes, meal and vegetables, and reputedly delicious. I myself thought them plain, but nevertheless edible, and certainly better than the stale food we had been given in the capital.

As we ate, the man asked Holly about the fort and why we had gone there. Then, for some reason, he turned to me, and fixed me with a strange gleam in his eye.

'Seen tullas, eh...all pilly-pilly?' I looked at Holly questioningly, and she translated: 'Have you seen the bones,
which are all stuck together?'
'The creature,' I murmured. 'Yes, we *have* seen it.'
'What *is* it?' asked Holly, leaning forward intently. 'Wha the tulla? Fuwa dar? Where did it come from?'

The farmer gave her a crafty look, and leant back in his chair, pulling an old clay pipe from his worn shirt pocket. He clearly meant not to reply until he had packed his pipe and lit it. We sat impatiently while he went through this time-honoured ritual. Eventually he coughed and settled back in a cloud of smoke, saying he would 'larn' us a 'stolley' about the first time he had come across the creature. He spoke slowly, with Holly translating the occasional word, though we followed his meaning for the most part. His wife sat nearby, interjecting an occasional 'I tullye!'

The farmer knew not where the creature came from, but believed it had something to do with the magic of the Ahu. It had not inhabited the fort until quite recently. There were rumours among the farming folk, since the early days of settlement, of a clattering shape that stalked the hills, only half believed in. It became a kind of folk devil, blamed when things went wrong – an illness in the district, or an injured cow.

But one night, some farmers had actually *caught* it, in a barn.

A farmer had gotten up to see why his cows were mooing, disturbed. Apprehending the skeletal shape he was naturally terrified, and bolted the barn door, trapping the thing inside. He roused his neighbours, and they debated what to do with it. They ended up digging a square pit in the ground, just big enough for the creature, and found a piece of heavy iron to cover it with. Then they went into the barn with sticks and a rope.

They snared the creature and dragged it flopping and thrashing into the pit, sealing it in with the iron plate.

The plate had some small round holes, and it became the sport of the district to come and stare through the airholes at the weird prisoner. 'Tulla', they called it, or

'Boney' (Bonaparte being long remembered here). Children would poke sticks at it for fun, although their mothers told them not to.

Our farmer friend told us how he looked at it himself one day and was struck with a sight he had never forgotten. Those black eyes were staring back at him, expressionless. It sat there, repeating the same phrases over and over. *It's time to sound the call*, it would say. *Rise and fall.*

The dumbness moved him more even than anguish would have done. He didn't know if the thing felt pain like a person or animal (it didn't eat or drink, but that meant little). He didn't know how its eyes 'worked', or where the voice came from. But he knew he had to free it, and did so.

He snuck back that night with a large tractor jack, raised the iron door and set the creature loose. He guessed that after that, the thing sought refuge in the fort. And no one ever knew who had freed it, save his wife.

'But wha dem hilly larpoots dunno wun hart em, eh?' he chortled.

But I wondered why he had chosen to divulge his story now, and to strange 'forners' at that. I didn't have long to find out, however.

He now told us of a prophecy, a legend handed down from the first days of settlement. The settlers in turn had it from an old drunken priest, one of the missionaries who had tried converting the Ahu before they had disappeared.

After the Ahu had vanished, this priest had questioned his calling, remained on the island, and eventually turned to drink, which he purchased with Ahu weapons and relics from the newly arriving soldiers. In his extreme old age, wild-haired and with round, unseeing eyes, he told a group of farmers of this prophecy – of the final statement of the Ahu.

They were going, they said, because the slavers had taken their leaders – and the priests couldn't fill their shoes. But sometime, when the end of the world was near, some 'forners' (that was how the farmer phrased it) would follow them...and one of them, he told me with a sly look, would have *nae tullas in his lanks.*

'No bones in his legs,' Holly rendered automatically.

Then it clicked, and we stared at one another. I looked down slowly at my trouser-clad limbs, and the farmer smiled his crafty smile.

But how had he known – *or had he?*

*　　*　　*

Holly printed the photo out as soon as we got back, plugging the camera into a run-down antique printer. All we could see were lines of bright blood-red on deepest-black; a definite pattern, emanating from a central point, but hazed and out of focus. The three of us stood staring at it. Then a figure loomed over our shoulders, and a soft voice gently coughed. The P-R stood looking down at the photo with us.

'That is the sign of the shivering sun. It means the end of the world is near at hand.' He didn't seem at all interested in the camera.

'We've been to the fort,' stammered Holly.

'Indeed?'

'That's where we took this.'

'You've perhaps met our modular friend?'

'You mean...'

'The tullas, eh, all pilly-pilly,' I whispered. The P-R laughed, but it was a sad laugh.

'Indeed,' he said. 'The magic of the Ahu lives on, even in these benighted times. I wish I'd known them, I really do.'

'But how did you...'

'I pay great heed to the tales of our local peasantry...haunted fortresses, clattering bones...had to see for myself. The farmers don't know its origin. But *I* do.'

'You do?'

'The leaders of the Ahu, their finest warriors and magicians...bought and sold by the rabble that once landed here. The Ahu practiced bone burial, as you

435

know, keeping the bones of their dead in large clay pots. Desperate for leadership, they took out the bones of some of their most revered ancestors, and chanted over them for three days and nights. And the bones heard the call, for they turned into a guardian of the island.

'But something went wrong...the old magic had failed.

The guardian had no power and no mind. Whether the Ahu realised this before their disappearance, I don't know.'

'How do *you* know all this?'

'I found it in the diary of one of my ancestors. He heard it from one of the churchmen, a drunken derelict who let on more to my ancestor than he had to the peasants.'

'Where did they go, then, the Ahu?' Holly asked. 'Is it true they took the roads into the sea?'

'*Into the sea* is a wrong translation. No one knows what the word translated by *sea* actually means.'

'Then where *did* they go? Into *what?*'

'If you haven't guessed already...Ouwai, our far-flung islet, holds the portal. The secret stair. That's what the Patagonians want. And it's what they must not get.'

'Are the Ahu still in there?'

The P-R looked at us each in turn, fiercely.

'There's another *world* down there,' he said. 'I and my direct line of forbears have known it from the start. My ancestor took a solemn vow to preserve the secret. *That* was why he seceded from the British Empire. No one else on Cavendish knows, even today. Except for you...for as you have seen the bones, I feel compelled to tell you, somehow. Surely no one would believe you, in any case...' He began to pace round the room.

'Prestal Clare already told us about the portal,' I said. 'And about Maddem's dream. But the farmer, even though he didn't know where the Ahu went, said that one day some foreigners would follow them.'

'I know a similar prophecy. Only 'foreigners' weren't exactly the ones described. One day, when the end of the world is not far off, the secret stair will be breached by *koha toa*. That translates as 'fierce fighters', but it could also mean 'bold rebels', even 'splendid traitors'...the Ahu tongue was full of ambiguities. But anyway...when the sign of the shivering sun approaches, that day is said to be not far off. The day of the end of the world...' He looked pointedly at the camera printout.

'We'll go,' I said suddenly. 'I'm a fierce fighter. I was in a war. And I have no tullas in my lanks!' Although deep down I didn't feel fierce at all, something was making me blurt like this, and grind my teeth.

The P-R turned a hard and piercing eye on me. Like a diamond eye, it was. But before he could speak, a servant entered and drew him aside. There were furtive whispers, and the two of them left the room.

'...reported yesterday, came into contact with...'

'Did they indeed?' Their voices trailed off softly.

'Another *world*,' said Holly, entranced.

'I've been waiting for this my whole life,' I said. 'And I don't really have a choice.' I turned to Molly. 'They'll track us down, you know, no matter what. There's no hope for us, except the other world.'

'It never ends,' whimpered Molly. 'It never ends.'

*　　*　　*

The red lamps on the wall turned the dark glare of the fire-pit to a richer shade of deep red-gold. Echoes flicked around the pit, and we felt like songbirds in a torrent – powerless and wing-soaked. Warlike voices yelled out in a tremble...but the Ambassador was louder than them all.

'Traitors,' he roared, banging his fist on the oak bench with a mighty crack. Some looked around, wide-eyed, while others merely sneered.

'And when was the last *you* helped us?' called Henry, the First Chief Quartermaster. 'Off in Mantuaroa, feeding your straggling ego, ha!' Several voices rose in jeering affirmation.

'Traitors!' repeated the Ambassador with another crash. The P-R sat dignified, composed. His stern eyes swept the room, but he looked more sad than angry. He listened as the others screeched their dictates.

'We *have* to cede the islet to St. Vigeans. As for why they want it, who cares? It's just a miserable pile of dirt and withered trees.' Thus spoke Henry, with a loud and reddened face.

'They're coming for it *anyway*,' said Lincoln, the Education Clerk, squinting nervously and wringing his hands. 'This stuff about Nicholas and Molly is merely an excuse. *Someone* desperately wants Ouwai. We don't know why, but there you go...'

'Traitors!' the Ambassador roared a third time. But the P-R was more diplomatic.

'We know the Patagonians are using St. Vigeans as a front. And I also know why, though I am not at liberty to say.'

The Ambassador exploded. 'Who cares *why* they want the bloody islet,' he thundered, eyes ablaze. 'The inconvenient fact is that it's OURS! Will we let *anyone* violate our sovereignty? To hell with them!' The room suddenly went quiet. Only the click of the Undersecretary's knitting needles could be heard. Lincoln blinked, staring at the floor.

Then, bit by bit, a murmur grew...a murmur of dissent. I knew now why the P-R couldn't shield us...he sensed his own authority was drawing to a close. Most of those on the council would never agree to fight, and I could hardly blame them. In the face of superior technology, they have no hope.

If they hand Molly and I over to the Mantuaroans, and the islet to St. Vigeans, however, all such conflict will be averted...or so said the radio message from Great Powers.

I have no clue why they are so desperate to get hold of me. But I know why they want Ouwai, and that must not be allowed to pass...not until I fulfil the ancient prophecy.

I must take the secret stair.

18

OUWAI

My dreams become rich. In one, I fly back to Mantuaroa, soaring above dark green rubbery foliage. There are frigatebirds around the coast, and pelicans strut along the shore, wading into the water, beating it with their wings to stir up fish, which they scoop with catch-all beaks.

In the jungle are night birds, whose cries are sometimes frightening, sometimes amusing. There is a parrot who curses the names of local politicians; there are azure kingfishers, and hummingbirds that feed from large blood-red flowers.

And there are the Great Birds – avatars in island mythology, some of which are also Terror Birds. They roost in the distance, but I cannot make out their forms in detail – what I *can* see makes me think of the Feathered Devil. Could the legends be true? Somehow, I know instinctively (in the dream) that they *are* true, and that the Feathered Devil, newly discovered, is not a species, as the scientists thought, but a single entity, an avatar.

And then I hear a voice, singing:
A brand new king of air
Spies at the crowded figures on the ground;
Methinks he stole his chair.
Just forty storeys keeps him falling down.
And in the distance I behold a great and gleaming tower of blue glass overlooking a beautiful harbour.

The Model Building: a masterpiece of craftsmanship by squalid technocrats. Touch a panel and a wall becomes transparent; call up a moving, colour-coded dot thereon, and it becomes an image, often a grotesque and humorous caricature (as I learn when calling up the receptionist). Visitors, by contrast, are a simple photo taken on entering.

It has other advanced features: it shows only those areas one has permission to enter, plotting a trajectory in simple dotted lines, which become solid as you progress on the path. The top suite is unviewable, but as you look, a Grand Dot emerges, heading for an obscure chamber. A shadow passes over it, making you shiver.

Some of the 'crats who designed this building still work there. They are like spoiled children, working only when they wish, and only then on their pet creations. Their genius is indispensable, but only until the Patagonians have the set-up they require. After that it will be run by drones, and the 'crats will end up like their old idol Nemet Breisler.

The building is deserted in the early hours when you steal in. You take a central lift, which is controlled by thought, but the rebel 'crat who showed you in has second thoughts halfway up. He tries to go down again, but you are having none of it, and your thoughts cancel out his. The glass lift is now stuck between floors.

Then, slowly, slowly, the neighbouring lift begins to descend. At first you can make out only a blurred black figure...but then you see *it* as it presses forward against the glass.

And you scream. And it moves to *harvest* the scream.

The glass side crumbles at its touch, as it prepares to jump across...and so begins a 'thought race,' both comical and terrifying. It ends at the top, where the Patagonian waits, calling 'his' dog off. But for how long does he control it?

He ushers you into his office. All of Mantuaroa City is spread out below you, but your eye is caught by a man in the corner of the room, seemingly paralysed, a tropical plant growing out of his mouth. You shudder at the horror. The smell of must and decay makes you retch. But the Patagonian gives a crocodilian grin, as if to say 'there's nowhere to go from here.'

It is then that you look up...

For you remember that Maddem knew a 'word of power' necessary to access the secret stair...and it seems he has written it in *tiny letters on the ceiling*, right here in the sanctum sanctorum.

Tiny, tiny, tiny letters, so small the Patagonian has failed to notice.

And they spell the word:

Click.

You grasp at the letters as you wake from your dream.

*   *   *

And so I awoke on this 'miserable pile of dirt and withered trees', finding with daylight that the description failed to do the islet justice. Ouwai is small and bleak, certainly, but has a haunting sublimity that reminds me of the Sixth Symphony of the old music-maker Sibelius. I heard it on the flight to Mantuaroa, and now I see where it might easily have originated, had the composer ever visited these latitudes (and perhaps he did?). I remember the announcer saying it was Sibelius' penultimate symphony, and so what is still ahead of me?

I glanced back, across the still-sleeping figures of Holly and Molly, to see the P-R prying into the box of tools we had brought with us. I was just about to tell him we would no longer need them, for I had the password...when footsteps sounded from the shore. Was it the waiting captain? No, the boat was in the other direction.

Instead, it was a man I had never before laid eyes on. From where did he emerge?

This drab-looking person had odd lips, thin yet rubbery, somehow managing to appear bloodless and sensuous at the same time. He stopped in his tracks, hands in pockets, and I suddenly realised who he reminded me of: the craggen puppet. Despite the cold, my neck felt wet with unease.

He reached into his pocket to bring forth an object the size and shape of a pistol, but with a digital display. The P-R now noticed him, too, and his mouth drooped.

'Here as well?'

'We're everywhere, it seems.'

'And *that* is?'

'New sound weapon. Experimental. Watch.' Craggen puppet pointed it at a nearby rock and pressed a button, upon which we heard no sound from the 'gun', just the hissing of the rock as it disintegrated into a pile of fine sand. It was extremely unnerving.

Nothing now felt safe. Molly trembled and I held her close as the puppet spoke again.

'Nemet Breisler.'

'He was naïve and amoral,' breathed the P-R. 'What of him?'

'He was a genius. But he thwarted us on one major point, so we chose him to be the experimental subject of his own invention.'

'Aryan man's creativity used to end all creativity. So that's what you think, eh?'

'What you call 'creativity' is injustice.'

'Yes, yes, we know. Since the Great War Against Scarlotti you have come to fear it as a threat to your dominance. That's why you're here on this obscure islet. You're going to shut off access...'

'Our Lord, via his Avatar, wishes to shut off access. I am but his humble servant. He doesn't want people communicating with his enemy, the so-called Dream King.'

'And what if they did?'

'Then they might become immune to the Ubiquitor.'

'The Ubiquitor...so it's true, then.'

'What's that?' whispered Molly.

'Something they are rumoured to have created in the new South America. It makes everyone's emotional resonances and perceptions as alike as possible, and for this reason tilts everyone towards the lowest common denominator. As a side effect, it robs people of their imaginations.'

'So *that's* the reason Maddem fled,' I hissed, suddenly understanding. *But wasn't this a form of cowardice? If so, am I, too, a coward? But I am no poet...I have no duty to remain behind and fight. Or do I?*

The puppet nodded at me. 'The grey plate in the pilot you inadvertently discovered was a test receptor for this glorious device. Designed by Breisler himself...on

Mantuaroa, not South America, although it is now safely on its way there for further testing.'

'Testing? Like the pilot? *And me?*'

'Only your legs are susceptible to our control, not your mind. But that was not our doing. The technology is freely available...it's just that we are the only ones who understand its true potential.'

'The bodies at the cemetery...was that you, or Dead Shadows?'

'Those were ours. The subjects' deaths were heroic, inasmuch as that word has meaning, for they helped to fine-tune the most benevolent technological innovation ever to grace planet Earth. And now we have even smaller and less conspicuous ways to carry out the implanting.'

'But why did Dead Shadows claim to have killed them, and Breisler as well? Herb showed us actual footage...'

'Dead Shadows are useful idiots, nothing more. They were given Breisler's head as a gift, to make them feel important, and also to deflect suspicion from us, and that was what you saw, no doubt. Herb himself managed to make contact with the Gardener somehow, the Lord knows how...but he was stupid enough to think the Gardener was a servant to do *his* bidding. He found out otherwise on Nully's Wharf, when the Gardener took him to the Field of Blessed Emptiness.'

'To the abyss,' said the P-R.

'Call it what you like.'

'Is that where he's from?'

'I don't know. He first appeared to us when the Ubiquitor became operational. He seemed to materialise out of the machine itself. Even *I* was a little scared, cynic that I am. But he looked at me, and I found I could direct him with my thoughts, at least to some degree. Now we keep him in a sealed chamber, except when we let him out on some errand.'

'And so you are going to kill us.'

'Not yet. You see, I need to know how to access the portal here. It's not enough to seal it off. There is supposed to be another world down there, and we must have access to it so we can improve *it* as well.'

'You may torture us if you like. We will never tell you,' said the P-R, and he meant it...at least for himself.

'Ah, but what of this sad creature you call a friend?' The puppet snapped his fingers and three figures emerged from behind a large boulder down the beach. Two were guards, but the middle figure, bedraggled, head hanging limp...was *Scuzzy*. A guard held him by each arm.

Molly cried out, and ran to him. He raised his head a fraction and gave a cracked grin. He looked a broken man.

'And you think you can use this...friend of Molly's...as leverage over us?' snapped the P-R.

'You must know how to access the portal, otherwise what are you dong here? And if you don't tell me how to open it, I will have the Gardener drag this wretch into the abyss, and do what he wills with him.'

'We *don't* know. But even if I did I would never tell you.' 'Then I must call the Gardener...'

'Ha!' snarled the P-R. 'You think you control this Gardener? You're as deluded as the Dead Shadows dupes.'

'I can assure you, we...' *Do control him*, he was probably about to say...but history actually repeated. For the shadow loomed up. *The one whose innards fold in to eternity, to black frozen torture in endless cold...that hollow point, sucking all that lives.*

Molly screamed, but it ignored her, and ignored Scuzzy.

Instead it turned to the puppet, and then...he was gone, imploded.

We stood there, stunned, and the Shadow looked around, as if deciding leisurely who its next harvest would be. The guards dropped Scuzzy and sprinted up the beach, but failed to attract its attention. Instead it turned to...*me*.

I believe I screamed; for this was the Gardener of All Screams.

But for his next cull he chose the P-R, who *didn't* scream, holding fast until the moment of his vanishment.

'Run,' rasped Scuzzy. 'I'll deal with the Shadow. Find the portal he was talking about. Get through it, *and fuck these scum.*' Somehow he found the strength to thrust Molly roughly towards me; Holly and I took a hand each as we sprinted desperately for the portal, dragging her along behind us.

Looking back briefly I saw Scuzzy leading the spirit in a whirlwind dance, round and round, until one melded into the other like a Taoist symbol, and I heard him scream the old adage: *It's better to burn out than fade away.*

So, he was the last Rock Star, and the greatest of them all. But we didn't have time to honour his memory, nor the P-R's.

We ran to where the P-R had told us the portal would be. To my surprise, it was a large triangular stone like the capstone of an ancient pyramid.

'That's funny,' puffed Holly. 'He told me it was circular.'

'How do we open it?' panted Molly. I stepped forward to carry out my oneirically appointed task. I pronounced, in a loud voice: 'Click'.

The capstone vanished.

I poked my head into the dark hole, and saw

*   *   *

...the Wobbels and Goggits whirling like a galaxy of stars.

My legs spoke, and I asked them questions, for the hitherto dumb brutes had now been transfigured, and told me that most today can only see the 'passive, elastic spirit' (did they mean matter?), not the active spirit that moulds it, and thus are largely blind, seeing the ripples in water only, and neither the stone nor the thrower. But to see that is not enough, either. The bird cultists wish to attain that, my legs said...but it won't do them any good. It is better to 'play' life like a violin...

Then I noticed that the Great Pyramid still existed there, as did the ancient kurgan from whence the Grey Death seeped out.

And I saw a remarkable series of seven paintings by an unnamed sage – they had been forgotten, and perhaps I am the only one other than the artist to have seen them. I saw unmarked graves of martyrs in Tasmania, where Nicola now lives, and where she was taken against her will. The grave of an infant, too, who along with the martyrs had passed on to another plane of being. And a woman I somehow know is called Maddy, and who died of grief, but who now dines with Scarlotti, her one-time enemy, a martyr himself after his dreadful sacrifice. He has made amends for the assassination of Maddy's lover, but as punishment has been demoted from emperor to just plain soldier. And he gazes at an oil painting of Tegg, who sits beside the Friendly Girl...

Then I saw Vonny Moss shedding his many faces, before standing naked at the dark gate.

And the Introspector, sobbing amongst the ashes of his Great Books (did Maddem burn them?). Also naked, he crumbles to nothing, his crumbling in the library having been a mere foreshadowing of this.

And the little man himself appears, beckoning me to the Green Land...but the gate remains closed.

Scuzzy appears at the threshold, mouthing silent words at me: *'I am the last Rock Star. There will never be another...'*

And I saw the Wolves of Joy – not good fathers or mothers, but serving another role. Playing life like a violin.

And then the gate opened ever-so-slightly, and I saw the *Dreamking*, both frozen and ever-changing, in danger of waking, extinguishing, from the solid and meaningless matrix being grafted from his dream.

He created the Bloodleach – but why?

And why did he choose *me* as his agent? I am a non-entity...not great like Scarlotti, or like Maddy's martyred love...

*   *   *

I pulled my head from the hole.

I turned to Holly and Molly...the three of us mismatched...even this is not as it should be...but we will shrug and step through together, holding hands...

Holly keeps watch for the Shadow, while I note these last ramblings in a journal I have little hope my daughter Nicola will ever read.

And now I must find the impenetrable thicket of thorns, in the unreachable depths of a chasm that howls. To get by in that search, I expect I shall have to learn the language of the birds. That is the underlying language used by people who appear to be saying something different, but are not. It is the universal language, but very few speak it.

The dark stairs lead down, though I have a feeling I will find they are actually leading up, as in a drawing by Escher. But that is the least of my worries.

Holly, I will need your camera to help me navigate; and Molly I will need your chaos.

Now I lay this journal aside forever.

The Spanish Steps aren't hot, but they are burning.

AFTERWORD

With this bizarre final statement, Grandfather Lune's journal breaks off. His baby daughter, scarcely mentioned in the text (the Nicola referred to near the end), grew up to be my mother. The pain of her being taken away from him by my grandmother was evidently too great for him to want to talk about. But whether his stint in the army helped him to forget the trauma and to start afresh, only the reader can judge.

The 'portal rock' still remained on the island of Ouwai when my mother's expedition visited, but now resembled a hexagon. When they demolished it, no passage was found underneath it, although Grandfather's journal was discovered beneath a nearby stone, undamaged by the elements. Not only that, but his legs were still there, right near the vanished portal (if there ever *was* a portal).

It is mentioned in his journal that he will come back with a weapon, presumably a spiritual one – but so far he has not returned, and I can only guess whether he ever found Maddem, 'in an impenetrable thicket of thorns.'

So I sit here now in Lune River, Tasmania.

To the north is the crumbling city of Hobart, where the Patagonians have a stronghold, working over the flaws in their Ubiquitor, but here to the south there is still Silence. The Wolves of Joy are dead now, but I heard rumours of another youthful rebellion, so I must keep walking, further south, until I reach the end of the world, which is ever nearer at hand.

For I saw a little man myself, and he was heading that way.